BUFFALO JAKE

and the Last Animal Crusade

By

Joe Trojan

ISBN: 0-7596-6017-4

This book is printed on acid free paper.

1stBooks -rev. 12/19/01

CHAPTER ONE

The Discovery of Paw Print Writing

This book was written by pandas. Except for this first chapter, which I wrote to explain how I discovered the panda writings. If you've already read the story in the newspapers of how I deciphered the panda paw print language, then you can skip to the next chapter. If not, you might consider this first chapter to contain important background information. But don't judge the whole book by it—the pandas are much better writers than I am.

I was twenty-four in 1989. I had just graduated from college after stretching a four year program into six. It was time to get a job. But my grades were so poor, the mere thought of applying anywhere seemed like a monumental waste of time. With a general degree in biology, I didn't have the slightest clue what I should do with my life. Some stranger at a party suggested that I should apply to graduate school. I did. I was rejected by every college that I applied to except one—Tulare State Community College in California. You might think that Tulare State was located in Tulare. A lot you know. Tulare State is located in the middle of unincorporated nowhere. Tulare happens to be the closest place to this particular nowhere, which is not saying much because Tulare pretty much defines nowhere to most people who whiz by it on Highway 99. Tulare State was willing to take me, but I would be on academic probation for the first year. That was fine. I had been on academic probation for so long that it gave me a warm familiar feeling.

Toward the end of my first year, we had a visiting professor from some big name school. I honestly can't remember from which one or why he was visiting our school. If I could remember details like that, then I probably would not have been on academic probation. Anyway, the guy gave a lecture on his panda research. His name was Professor Derns. Yes, I do remember his name. Or was it Kerns? Sherns? Sterns? Anyway, he gave a lecture mostly on the increasing loss of panda habitat in China. At the end of his talk, he mentioned that he needed volunteers to help with his next expedition. I don't think he was actually expecting anyone to sign up. Or more accurately, he was probably hoping none of us geniuses from Tulare State would want to sign up. I signed up.

The expedition was supposed to be for ten weeks exploring panda habitat in Xiangling and Qionglai Mountains in the Schuan Basin. But it ended up lasting a little longer. When we were at the airport to return to the States, I went to look for a bathroom and got lost from the group. Professor Derns had the tickets. He left without me. I have always wondered if it was intentional. I tended to annoy him. I would think of a different way of looking at something, and Kerns would wish he had thought of it first. He wouldn't say so, but you can tell. That can be very annoying to people such as Sterns. The jerk. Did I mention that I ended up staying in China for eleven years?

In the eleven years that I spent in China, mostly in the Lingshan mountains, my research uncovered discoveries that rival any made in the history of biology. That might sound egotistic, but it's true. I have attempted to have my research published in the scientific journals so that the scientific community could independently confirm my findings. Every single journal has rejected my paper on the grounds that my findings are laughable.

This brings us to the issue of how papers are accepted for publication in scientific journals. When a paper is submitted, the editors send the paper to several prominent researchers that are considered experts on the topic discussed in the paper. These researchers decide if your paper has merit. In my case, they could not disprove my findings or fault my methods, they simply could not believe my data. It was too disturbing to their understanding of reality.

I felt the same way at first. To use a fancy phrase popular in scientific circles, my research requires a paradigm shift, which basically means a major change in thinking. Mine was a radical paradigm shift. A colossal paradigm shift. Anything so big could not have been discovered by a C-student from Tulare State. Even for those with better credentials, gaining acceptance of a paradigm shift is very difficult because the scientific community is, by necessity, fairly conservative. In any event, since the scientific establishment has refused to go to the Panda forests to independently study my findings, I have no choice but to go directly to the public. The fate of my research is in your hands. For the sake of the animals and humans, I hope you will read it with an open mind.

When I went to China with Professor Sherns to study pandas, the primary focus was on their survival in a shrinking habitat. When I

2

continued studying pandas on my own after he left, I was far more interested in how pandas communicate, which is not often considering that they tend to be solitary creatures for most of the year. But I did notice that when they do meet each other, they did a little dance. At first, I thought this dance was a form of courtship. But this theory did not fit the fact that the dance steps never seemed to be the same. Also, two pandas of the same sex appeared to communicate in the same way.

In my second year in the forest, I noticed that pandas will sometimes dance alone. This made me seriously doubt whether the dance was a form of communication at all. I tried to determine if there were any differences between the dances that the pandas did when they met compared to the dances they did when they were alone. No pattern emerged.

It was not until the beginning of the third year of my research that a major breakthrough occurred when I noticed a panda stop in the same place that I had observed another panda do a dance a few days before. When the panda stopped, she looked down at the ground and did the same identical dance that the earlier panda had done. After she left, I went to the location and studied the ground. Sure enough, the paw prints of the earlier panda were visible in the soft soil. The paw prints of the female panda, which were slightly smaller, were neatly contained within the larger paw prints. It seemed too incredible. Were the pandas communicating by reading each other's paw print patterns in the soil? When I recalled all the dances that I had observed between pairs of pandas, I realized that they had always traded positions. Were they reading paw prints?

For the next several months, I tested my hypothesis. It soon became apparent that my basic observation was accurate. The pandas were dancing in each other's paw prints. But were they communicating? Was it a form of panda braille? To test this part of the theory, I started "rewriting" the messages by sometimes obliterating some of the paw prints and by carefully moving some of the paw prints. This caused a definite change in behavior. There were some patterns that always caused the pandas to travel in a particular direction. When I "re-wrote" the message, the pandas did not travel in the predicted direction.

Most of the time, my rewritten message had no discernible effect other than apparent confusion evidenced by the panda's repeated attempts to "read" the message. Most commonly, the messages appeared to pertain to locations of other pandas and directions for finding fresh growths of bamboo. Surprisingly, they did not appear to relate to territorial claims. Scent marking may so dominate this function that paw printing writing has little additional value. On occasion, the writings seemed capable of conveying emotions such as danger. For example, I have seen a mother panda started crying for her cubs after reading a message. She gathered the two of them together and left very quickly.

At this early stage of my discovery, I had no idea how sophisticated paw printing writing was. But I was convinced that I had indeed discovered at least a rudimentary form of written intraspecies communication. Once I became comfortable with this idea, I started to notice other behavior that I had ignored before. Namely, that these kinds of dances were done by other species besides pandas. Not only did such animals as bears and wolves communicate this way, they also seemed capable of reading the messages left by pandas. Pandas also seemed able to read messages left by other species. The possibility that interspecies communication could be occurring at such a sophisticated level seemed too incredible to believe. I knew I would have to collect enormous quantities of confirmatory data before the scientific community would seriously consider my findings.

My research was frustrated, however, by the migratory patterns of the pandas. Many of the pandas I was studying would travel into very inaccessible regions during the winter. During the sixth year of my research, I was able to track the pandas much farther than I had ever done before. Even so, I finally lost them. I was about to return to my base camp when I heard a strange noise. It sounded like a panda, but the sound seemed to echo. There was a long silence, then I heard it again. The second time I was able to get a better fix on the direction from which it came. I spent three hours searching a vast stand of bamboo and underbrush on the side of a hill. I was already cold and hungry when it started raining. I was about to give up in frustration when I stumbled upon a small crop of rocks. Among the rocks was a small opening large enough for a panda to get through. I cautiously looked inside with my kerosene lantern.

If I had looked in the same cave when I first came to China, I would not have thought anything of it. But to my trained eye, what I saw was absolutely astonishing. On the bottom of the cave floor, formed in the soft sandstone, were the paw prints of animals. I walked into the cave several hundred meters. The paw prints covered the floor as far back as I could see.

4

Some of the patterns I recognized instantly. I realized that I had been learning their language without even knowing it. Other patterns were more complicated than I had seen before.

The next day, I moved my base camp to an area near the cave. It took me four years to fully decipher the paw print language. I spent another three years translating the story written on the floor of the cave. This book is the translation of the story I found on the cave floor. There are other portions of the cave that I have not yet translated. There were some portions of the paw print story that were obliterated by apparent changes in the flow of water through the cave. But in general, the pandas seemed to have a method of maintaining the integrity of the paw prints. I have not yet determined the process they use for softening the sandstone to create the paw prints or the process by which they are able to maintain the prints from erosion.

At first, I thought the stories that the animals wrote were historically accurate. While it is now apparent to me that most of it is historical, at least some of the story appears to be animal legend. The stories are extremely enlightening with respect to how animals measure such concepts as time, distance, and size. I have translated time periods and measurements of size and distance as best as I can based upon what I have learned. The pandas themselves seemed to take a strong interest in my fascination with their paw print language. It was only after translating their story that I found out why.

The age of the panda paw print writings is uncertain. I believe them to be 80,000 years old. This is based upon carbon dating of a piece of a panda toenail I found embedded in one of the paw prints in the cave. This is consistent with the results of carbon dating I had done on fragments of bamboo with panda teeth marks on them that I found in the deepest parts of the cave.

I have no doubt that many will accuse me of scientific fraud or else dismiss my research as delusional after living so long alone in the panda forests by myself. But in the end, the truth will come out. It eventually always does in science. Others will confirm my findings and confirm the accuracy of the translation that you are about read. Once the truth is known, none of us will ever be able to think the same way about animals or ourselves again.

CHAPTER TWO

The World Council of Living Things

No one could remember when the World Council of Living Things was first established. But there was general agreement among most animals that the Council was started before the invention of paw print writing. This was never a very helpful reference because no animal knew when paw print writing first started. But that did not matter. It was common for an animal who didn't know how long ago something happened to say that it happened before there was paw print writing. This was the same as saying that it happened a long time ago and was generally considered to be a fair answer.

While no one was sure of *when* the World Council had formed, the story of *how* it was formed was well known. Even before the formation of the Council, most animals had a natural curiosity about the other types of creatures around them. But for the longest time, there had been very little interspecies communication. There was a vague collective memory of an earlier time when there had been communication between different species, but the skill was lost over the ages in the face of the day to day responsibilities of survival. That is until one day when something happened that gave them a reason to communicate again.

The day of the fire clouds had started out normal enough with a lazy breeze blowing across the prairie. It would have been a perfect day, except for a powerful sun that decided to take full advantage of a cloudless sky, and share more of its warmth with the earth than anyone desired. The breeze tried to fight back. But by midmorning, the breeze knew the battle was lost. It retreated to the shade of a few trees that dotted the side of the river, and contented itself with rustling a few leaves now and again. Having been abandoned by the breeze for the duration of the day, insects buzzed about in orgiastic delight in the invisible cloud of each buffalo's natural aroma. The buffalo swatted at the insects with their tails, but mostly tried to nap their way through the worst of the day.

In late afternoon, the breeze ventured back out onto the prairie. Little gusts of wind blew off the river to jostle the stagnant heat of the day. It felt good against the skin- a mingling of both warm and cool currents lacing themselves through each animal's fur. The buffalo, gazelles, antelope, and all the others shook the day's dust off and congregated down by the river for the late afternoon drink. The animals lingered a little bit longer than they knew was wise. The late afternoon was slipping into early twilight. It was a dangerous time to be down by the river. The nocturnal predators were beginning their patrols, and the first place they checked was at the river's edge for any stragglers. But the cool water felt good. It was hard to leave.

Most herd animals had escaped the grasp of a predator at some time in their lives and were confident that if need be, they could do it again. It was always some other animal that had obviously made some stupid mistake that ended up getting taken down. Yet, the animals that had survived the longest had learned early on that confidence and trust in one's own instincts was fine, just as long as one never underestimated the skills of the carnivores. The wisest also knew that there were other dangers in the world besides the predators.

At first, the sound was too distant to be a cause for alarm. Only a few animals bothered to raise their ears to listen more carefully. Those that did concluded that it was nothing more than the rumble of some far off thunderstorm. As the sun sank half below the horizon, the shadows of the buffalo lazily stretched themselves out across the prairie to rest for the evening. An owl announced her presence for the evening's hunt for field mice with three distinctive soft hoots. Even the most daring of the animals knew it was time to leave the river and return to the relative safety of the herds on the open prairie. The last deep purple streaks of twilight faded to blackness.

The sound of the distant thunderstorm grew closer. It was not unusual for storms to develop in the mountains and sweep down across the plains without much warning. But there was something very peculiar about this storm. The rumble of the thunder was not quite right. The lightening and thunder usually announced the storm's approach by cracking and crashing, then breaking into a deep rumbling sound that faded away in its own good time. But on this occasion, the thunder was one continuous sound that was rapidly growing louder and louder to the point that the animals could not ignore it any longer. They looked up and found that the sky was on fire! An enormous storm cloud was racing toward them, spitting a tail of flames behind it! The animals did not know what to do. Some stood still, frozen at the sight. Others ran in all directions trying to escape. But before any animal could move more than just a few steps, the fire cloud was over them. A part of it broke off and exploded in the sky. Pieces of flame rained down on the earth, setting off spot fires all over the prairie. Animals were running in every direction, leaping over each other, racing away from one patch of fire right into another. The air was filled with every imaginable warning scent that the animals could emit. Usually one knew to race away from the direction of a warning scent, but the scents were everywhere, creating mass confusion. Some of the leaders of the herds realized what was happening with the warning scents and tried to shout instructions to the herds, but it was no use. The shrieking roar of the fire cloud blasting across the sky was so deafening that it knocked some of the animals to the ground.

The roar faded as quickly as it came. The fire cloud continued on its path, getting lower and lower in the night sky. When the sound faded, many of the animals were able to calm themselves enough to stop to watch it racing away. The little fires that had started were not serious. The night breeze was not strong enough to fan the flames. They gently crackled and smoldered, but presented no immediate threat.

Not long after the fire cloud disappeared from view, every animal was knocked off its hooves. It did not feel like an earthquake at all. An earthquake shook violently or rolled gently, depending upon its mood. This was very different. The earth jumped up, knocking them up into the air in a single sudden motion. Not high in the air at all. Just enough to throw off their balance. The earth rumbled a bit afterward as it settled back down. It was a strange night indeed. Certainly one that no one would soon forget.

In the morning, the animals expected another hot day. It did not come. A gray sky blocked the sun. A light dust drizzled down throughout the day, which added to the mystery and speculation about the events of the previous night. Reports were beginning to pour in from other buffalo herds about the strange fire cloud. Some of the buffalo did not think it was a cloud at all. It looked more like a rock. But rocks did not fly and they did not burn. It was all very strange.

Word soon arrived that the thing had hit the earth and left a big hole that was glowing red. It took two days for the central buffalo herd to arrive at the big hole. The buffalo were not the only animals that had come to see what had happened. There were species of every imaginable kind. Besides the buffalo, there were pandas, elk, bears, cougars, leopards, elephants, rhinos, zebras, and far too many others to list them all. The big hole was more like a small valley. The animals called it Red Valley because it was glowing red and burning when the first animals had arrived. Now the glow had mostly faded, but the rocks strewn about the floor of the valley were still too hot for any animal to dare to venture in. The animals stood on the edge of the valley with no idea what to think. Nothing before had ever aroused their curiosity as much as this thing.

Desperate to understand what had happened to their world, different species began exchanging information about what they saw. Species that would normally never communicate with each other were now cooperating. At first, no one expected to be able to communicate with other species. Each species had its own language. But when they began talking to each other, they found that they understood what was being said even though it was not in their species language. In fact, it was not in any animal's language. It was a hybrid language. The animals had rediscovered the Universal Language, which was the common root of all species languages. It was likely that all animals had once spoken a common language before their individual languages had evolved. But now that they were communicating again, the Universal Language seemed to come back to them instinctively. Cougars were talking to buffalo and deer. Lions were debating possible explanations with zebras. Gorillas were exchanging theories with elephants. The pandas were talking to them all. It was the pandas who seemed to have the best grasp of the Universal Language and were wandering about helping other species who were having some trouble with it. The re-discovery of the Universal Language and the exchange of ideas among the animals was in some ways far more exciting than the instant creation of the Red Valley by a fire cloud. Everyone was swept into the spirited exchange except for one species, the chakeedas.

The leader of the chakeedas announced that the fire cloud marked the beginning of the end. That more fire clouds would rain down on the earth until all the animals were destroyed. The animals looked up. The sky was still gray and drizzling with little flecks of dust. It had been that way since the fire cloud hit the earth three days before. While it was unusual, it did not seem like fire clouds were about to rain down on anybody. The chakeeda leader continued with his diatribe, warning the other animals that the only way for them to save themselves was to do exactly as he instructed. First, the communication among the various species must end right away. It was unnatural for different animals to be talking to each other. If it did not stop, terrible things far worse than the fire cloud would happen. Second, in these uncertain times, the animals would need to trust the chakeedas without question. Only the chakeedas were capable of leading the animals through this dangerous period to avoid more fire clouds.

Most of the animals were more puzzled than impressed with the chakeeda's raving. Buffalo Jerid, the leader of the central herd of buffalo, asked the chakeeda leader how they were going to listen to the chakeedas if they were suppose to unlearn the Universal Language. Many animals chortled at the apparent contradiction. But the chakeeda leader had an answer, "You shall all learn Chakeeda." Buffalo Jerid responded immediately and firmly, "I don't think so." They stared at each other until the chakeeda looked away first.

There were a few species that were very frightened and overwhelmed by the fire cloud and were more willing to listen to any animal that would give them guidance. The rabbears were one of those species. The rabbears had the body of a rabbit and a head that resembled a bear. They were generally shy creatures that lived in burrows, and were usually only aggressive in defense of their young. The rest of the time, they played among themselves, ate roots and grains, and scurried back to their burrows at the slightest sign of trouble. The rabbears and a few other species of similar temperament wanted to accept the guidance of the chakeedas. A few of the rabbears approached Buffalo Jerid and asked if he thought they should follow the chakeedas. Jerid said that the buffalo had no intention of allowing the chakeedas to tell them what to do. Many of the other animals standing around agreed. But if the rabbears would feel better following the chakeedas until the supposed danger of more fire clouds passed, then no one could stop them. With that, the rabbears and a few other species assembled around the chakeeda leader to receive his guidance. The rest of the animals continued their conversations late into the day before drifting off to their home ranges.

After the fire cloud incident, animals from different species who had met each other at the Red Valley would cross each other's paths at the river or some other watering hole. Where before they would have politely ignored each other, now they enjoyed keeping up to date. These were not lengthy exchanges. The priorities of day to day survival would not permit it. But the important thing was that communication in the Universal Language was continuing. Contrary to the grim predictions of the chakeedas, continued interspecies communications did not cause more fire clouds to rain down upon the animals. Yet, the chakeedas continued to warn that interspecies communication was unnatural and that any further use of the Universal Language would cause a deluge of fire clouds that would turn the entire earth into nothing but flames. The other animals were amused that the warnings were always issued in the Universal Language.

The buffalo started issuing their own warnings that if any more warnings were issued in the Universal Language, then fire clouds would rain down just to put an end to the warnings. When a year had passed without any new fire clouds, the buffalo held a celebration in honor of the chakeedas to thank them for their successful efforts to save the animals from fire clouds. Buffalo Jerid declared that the danger was over and now anyone could use the Universal language without fear of causing the earth to burn up. The chakeedas strongly objected and insisted that still too many animals were not obeying their warnings. Buffalo Jerid said the chakeedas were being far too modest, and that the chakeedas should not underestimate their own success. The chakeedas continued their protest, but by that point, they were drowned out by the celebrations going on around them.

Buffalo Jerid overheard the chakeedas talking among themselves. They seemed very upset by the Universal Language. He could not hear all of what they said, but the chakeedas apparently saw the Universal Language as a threat. It did not make sense. Why should they care? There seemed to be more to the ravings of the chakeedas than he first thought. It made him uneasy. For the first time, he felt an instinctive fear rise within him. He tried to dismiss the feeling. How could such small, pathetic looking creatures be a threat to his herd? Still, the feeling of danger lingered.

* * * * *

11

As the years went by, the annual celebration in late fall lost its original meaning. It was no longer called the fire cloud celebration. It became a time for the animals to play games and exchange ideas before the fall migration. The event became so popular that leaders of each species began getting together a few days before to organize the event. They began calling themselves the World Council of Living Things. That is how the World Council was born.

The meeting place for the World Council of Living Things was in a massive cavern by the sea. It was considered the largest and most beautiful cave in the world. The ceiling was at least as high as the tallest sequoia tree. The front of the cave, or at least what the animals decided was the front, had a natural platform made out of granite. The platform was about as high as a zebra is tall and big enough for about six buffalo to stand on comfortably. On one side of the platform, some distance away was an entrance to the cavern that was big enough for an elephant to walk through. On the opposite side of the platform, there was a very large lagoon that was big enough for a few whales and other assorted sea animals to swim about in comfortably. The lagoon was connected to the ocean through a long tunnel that was big enough for whales to go through single file.

The floor of the cavern gradually sloped toward the back wall, which had several tunnels in it that were only big enough for a panda to fit through. But what was most astounding was the water fall. An underground river shot out of one of the tunnels in the back wall and crashed down to the floor, forming the purest crystal clear stream that flowed into the lagoon. The cool wetness caressed the tongue with its freshness. Attendance was always high at Council meetings because no one wanted to miss the chance to drink the water. There were several slivered crevices in the ceiling on the side of the cavern near the entrance, which allowed plenty of sun light to creep in for the animals to see. There were also bright green and white crystal formations embedded in the walls, which sparkled in late afternoon when the sunlight hit them just right. The light from the crystals sometimes reflected off of the rippling water in the lagoon, causing patterns of colored light to dance across the walls of the cavern.

The chakeedas disliked the World Council of Living Things almost as much as they hated the re-discovery of the Universal Language. The chakeedas were constantly railing that the whole thing was unnatural. When they realized that they could not prevent the meetings, they tried to control them. Finally, Buffalo Jerid confronted the chakeedas with the one question everyone had in their mind. Why did the chakeedas hate the Council and why did they hate the Universal Language? The chakeeda leader would not respond. He stormed out of the meeting. After that, the chakeedas disappeared. It would be a long time before anyone would see one of them again.

CHAPTER THREE

The Compromise

"Thank you for coming to the last World Council meeting for the season," Buffalo Jerid began. "We will first hear from the pandas concerning the goings on in preparation for the fall Celebrations and games and such."

The leader of the pandas filled in the details concerning the assigned locations for the different species. It had long ago been discovered that if everyone just showed up to the Celebration, the confusion was enormous. The pandas had learned that some animals laid down territorial scents that were completely incompatible with the scents of other animals. The hybrid scents wafting through the air had created much anxiety and disorientation. The pandas announced changes to correct for this problem.

Of course, the idea of keeping predator-prey species separated as much as possible had been obvious from the beginning. Even though there had been an agreement that no predatory activities would take place at the Celebration, there was no point in unnecessarily tempting the instincts of the predators. Even so, some animals had complained that predators were attacking prey who were on their way to the Celebration and that this should also be a violation of the rules. The predators vehemently denied this and pointed out that there was no way for them to know the intended destination of their prey. The representative of the pandas stated that they had worked out a solution to this problem. There would be designated approaches to the Celebrations that would be off limits to the predators. The predators protested that prey could simply stay in the designated approaches forever and the predators would starve to death. The panda representative reminded the predators that the protections were only for a few days. Certainly this was not too much of an imposition on the predators as their contribution to the success of the Celebrations. The predators grumbled because privately they really did not want to give up their pre-Celebration feasts so easily. But after additional discussion, they conceded the point.

Toward the end of the meeting, there were some complaints about the assigned locations being insensitive to the planned migratory patterns that some of the animals had laid out for themselves for their journeys after the Celebration. The pandas said they would meet privately with those species that were having a problem and check into what could be done to reassign them to a location that would be more consistent with their migratory plans. Just as the meeting was about to break up, a small voice was heard trying to get everyone's attention. It was the representative from the rabbears. Her name was Kristin.

It was unusual for a rabbear to speak up at any meeting. In fact, no one could quite remember if a rabbear had actually attended a World Council meeting before. If they had, probably no one had noticed because they were simply that kind of animal. Of course, that is not to say that they were taken for granted. The herd animals were particularly grateful for the rabbears because of the rabbear's love of chicory. Chicory could take over an entire prairie if it was left unchecked by the rabbears. The herd animals had a very hard time digesting the stuff themselves, not to mention that it did not taste very good to them. For this reason, the role of the chicory-loving rabbears in maintaining the proper balance of chicory to prairie grasses was most appreciated.

A hush fell over the cave as everyone strained to listen to Kristin's small voice. Standing behind her were two rabbears, who nudged her forward. She began slowly in her soft voice, "We have been having a problem. We hoped you might be able to help us." She stopped, clearly uncomfortable with the attention of all the eyes upon her.

Jerid was anxious to make Kristin feel more comfortable and said, "If we can be of help, we certainly will. What can we do for you?"

"It is difficult to explain... Or maybe it's not... How should I say... well... ummm... the chakeedas... well... they've been rounding us up... lots of us... as many of us as they can," she said softly, "and killing us."

Kristin did not seem outwardly upset by what she was reporting. Her eyes were glazed over and she spoke as though she were explaining some strange dream she had a long time ago. The animals seemed puzzled. From the way she spoke, they were not sure if she wasn't just reporting a bad dream. They waited for her to continue, but she did not. Her gaze became fixed upon a rock on the cave floor, lost in her own thoughts and memories.

One of the other rabbears stepped forward. "It's true. They kill us every time they see any of us. They've all gone crazy. It's as if they were all mad. We need your help desperately."

Even the predator species present found the story to be very strange. Any good predator knew instinctively that it was essential to maintain a stable population of prey. To kill everyone made no sense.

Jerid responded, "It sounds very strange. Do you have any idea why they're doing this?"

"I wish I knew. We've tried to talk to them, but they just keep saying we're on their land," said the second rabbear.

"That's usually what they say right before they kill one of us," said the third rabbear.

"Their land?" asked Buffalo Jerid. "You mean their home range? Even if you were in their home range, why would it matter? Lots of animals share the same home ranges."

"That's what I thought at first, too. But their claim to the land is more than that. It's hard to explain. I'm not really sure that I understand it myself. But they say they own the land and everything on it. The trees, the lakes, the rivers. They even own us if we happen to be on their land," said the rabbear.

The animals snorted and chortled in amusement. The idea seemed ridiculous.

"That's just crazy. If I wander into their home range—I mean onto their land—then suddenly they own me? That's bizarre," said Jerid.

Some of the animals started joking with each other. The representative from the llamas said to the zebra representative, "You're standing on my land. I own you. Go get me some food."

The zebra representative turned to a gazelle next to him and said, "You're standing on *my* land. I own you. Go get the llama some food for me." The whole concept was just too silly for the animals to believe the chakeedas could be serious.

The joking, snorting, and chortling continued until Kristin broke from her gaze and said, "Because they own you, they believe they have a right to kill you." The joking stopped and the animals fell silent.

Kristin continued, "They believe they have the right to kill every living thing on their land because they own it. They believe they can strip the

BUFFALO JAKE
and the Last Animal Crusade

forests and prairies of all our food. And kill any or all of us if we exist on their land."

"So where are we suppose to live?" ask Jerid.

"That's just it. They say they have divided up the entire world among the chakeedas. No matter where we go, we'll be standing on land owned by some chakeeda somewhere," said Kristin.

"There are not enough chakeedas in existence to own everything," said Jerid.

"Maybe not yet," said the second rabbear. "But there are more and more of them every day. Someday soon there will be enough of them."

The atmosphere of the meeting had become more somber. Other animal representatives began telling their own stories of problems they were having with the chakeedas. As the afternoon slipped toward the end of the day, a very unsettling picture began to emerge from the bits and pieces of information that each species provided. The chakeedas no longer seemed constrained by the innate rules governing the natural balance of things. It was as if their instincts had somehow become wildly distorted. They had lost their place in the natural order, and now the chakeedas were scorching the landscape, destroying and killing everything in their path. It was a struggle for the animals to fully comprehend, but Buffalo Jerid knew that he did not need to fully understand it all to know it was terribly wrong. Even as his comprehension of how all the different stories fit together slipped from his mental grasp, the queazy feeling inside of him remained. His instincts told him that if something was not done soon, something terrible would happen to all of them. But it was not at all obvious what should be done. The animals gave it much thought, but no one seemed to have a clue as to what to do. Lacking any better idea, the animals decided that they should try to talk to the chakeedas. The rabbears protested that they had already tried that approach with no success, but Jerid stated that maybe if everyone went together, it might have more of an impact.

Considering that most of the animals would begin their fall migration right after the Celebration and games, it was agreed that contact should be made with the chakeedas as soon as possible. Otherwise, the animals would probably have to wait another season, which would not be good. The meeting was about to conclude and everyone was getting ready to leave when the panda representative climbed up onto the platform and approached Buffalo Jerid. Jerid leaned his head down and the panda pulled on his horn to draw him closer to whisper something in his ear. Jerid shook his head in agreement and the panda climbed down from the platform.

Buffalo Jerid turned to address the animal representatives again, "Before we leave today, we have to take care of a matter that I have been putting off for a while now. I know that you are all probably getting tired, but if everyone could stay just a little longer it would be much appreciated." There was general grumbling, but all the animals settled down again as requested.

Buffalo Jerid continued, "As many of you may be aware, there is only one species of Tamarin currently recognized by the World Council. There is now a group of Tamarins that feel that they should be recognized as having evolved into their own species. If we recognize the new species, they will be able to have their own representative before the World Council. So if the current representative from the Tamarins and the Tamarin from the proposed new species would please step forward, we can get started."

The two Tamarins climbed up onto the rock platform.

Buffalo Jerid looked to the Tamarin for the proposed new species and said, "Please explain why you feel you are entitled to separate species status."

"First, on behalf of my new species, I would like to thank..."

"It's not recognized as a new species yet!" interrupted the Tamarin species representative. "He can't say that!"

"We know that's why we're here. Please let him finish and you can have your turn. I promise," said Buffalo Jerid.

"Fine."

The Tamarin from the proposed new species gave his speech describing with great pride the detailed differences between his group and the old Tamarins. His species had developed a full mane around the neck and face and had beautiful golden hair. Their tails had evolved longer, and their legs were stronger so that they could leap much farther through the trees. They ate different foods and they raised their children differently. When the Tamarin for the proposed new species was finished, the official Tamarin representative was given his opportunity to respond. He gave just as long a list of similarities between the two groups and pleaded for the Council not to drive the two groups farther apart by declaring them separate species. Following the speeches, the animals began asking questions.

The lion representative asked, "When was the last time that anyone from the two groups mated together?"

Both Tamarins seemed somewhat put off and reluctant to answer because they both considered the question of their mating habits to be a personal matter and none of the business of the World Council. But when pressed, the representative for the Tamarins had to concede that he knew of no couples having a Tamarin from each group.

"When was the last time that such a couple existed?" asked the Zebra representative.

Neither Tamarin could recall, but the official Tamarin representative insisted that the lack of mixed couples was more the result of the distance between the preferred ranges of the two groups rather than any lack of attraction. The other Tamarin did not agree, but did not press the point too much because he was clearly uncomfortable injecting such personal matters into the debate and protested the relevancy of the line of questioning.

The lion representative responded, "But you would not pick a partner from another species, would you?"

"No, but..."

The lion representative interrupted, "Of course you wouldn't because you couldn't have children with a different species. But if you picked a partner from the other Tamarin group, your children would still be Tamarins, wouldn't they?"

"Well, yes... but..."

"That settles it for me... you're still the same species," concluded the lion representative.

Other animals were not so convinced that the lion had applied the correct test. But the problem was that no one could reach agreement on exactly what the test should be.

The representative from the antelope proposed that there could be species distinctions based solely on behavioral differences. The lion representative lead the opposition to such an interpretation, viewing it as a corruption of the entire species concept.

The lion declared, "If purely behavioral differences were sufficient, then any group could conspire to behave differently to gain independent species status. Where would it end?"

"Instinctive behaviors are not so easily manipulable," retorted the Antelope.

Buffalo Jerid tried to direct the debate as best he could, but with so many stubborn headed animals, it was very difficult to do. The debate dragged on, shifting in one direction, then another, never seeming to narrow toward a single conclusion. Unfortunately, this was typical of meetings of the World Council. The animals never seemed to be able to reach agreement even over the simplest things. It was not unusual for the meetings to become so quarrelsome that nothing was accomplished at all. It was truly amazing that the plans for the Celebration always ran as smoothly as they did. But the inability to reach agreement on anything else really worried Buffalo Jerid. If they were to persuade the chakeedas to stop their attacks, they would have to present a united front. As he listened to the animals fight over the definition of a single word such as species, the prospect of maintaining a united front for very long did not seem at all promising. Yet, Buffalo Jerid had no idea how to solve the problem. If nothing else, the present discussion needed to come to an end.

"Why do you want to be your own species?" ask Buffalo Jerid.

"Well, for one reason, we want to be sure that our interests are properly represented before the World Council," said the Tamarin for the proposed species.

"Has the current Tamarin representative ever done anything at the World Council that hurt you?" ask Buffalo Jerid.

"I guess not. But it might happen."

"But it hasn't happened yet," said Buffalo Jerid.

"I guess not."

"Then for now, I want you to attend the meetings with the Tamarin representative. The two of you can see for yourselves whether or not it is necessary for you to have separate representation. If you cannot reach a consensus together, then you can come back to the Council for us to try to help you," said Buffalo Jerid.

All the animals seemed to accept this proposal. Since it left the question of the definition of species unanswered, everyone could leave believing their own definition to be the correct one.

Buffalo Jerid tried to refocus everyone's attention back to what was most important by reminding them of the critical meeting with the chakeedas. He announced the location of an assembly point at which everyone was to meet at in the morning. It would only take a couple of days walking to reach the chakeeda leadership. As the animals filtered out of the chamber, Buffalo Jerid privately wondered if their agreement over what to say to the chakeedas would survive the two day walk. But there was no point in worrying about it now. Jerid returned to his herd in the hope of a good night's sleep.

* * * * *

As Buffalo Jerid had feared, the two day journey to meet the chakeeda leadership was marred by constant fighting among species. Each representative had his or her own entourage that came along. By the time they reached the outskirts of the main chakeeda nesting area, many species were not speaking to each other, and many of the entourages were developing their own strategy for independently meeting with the chakeedas. This was not good. Buffalo Jerid knew that he would have to do something. Drawing upon all the emotional energy he could muster, he began to give a speech for unity among all animals. But the words did not come in the right order and completely failed to match his feelings inside. He struggled to try to find the right words, but as he spoke them, they evaporated into the air without any impact. The crowd was losing interest, which only made Jerid more nervous and unable to form any coherent thought.

Just as Buffalo Jerid was about to give up, he noticed that the animals started taking a renewed interest. They started moving closer together, and animals that had refused to talk to each other were suddenly whispering back and forth. Buffalo Jerid was beginning to feel better about his leadership abilities when one of his lieutenants nudged his side and told him to look behind him. A contingent of chakeedas were emerging from their nesting area. The chakeedas spread out in a line and hunched down as they slowly approached. Even from this distance, their faces seemed filled with suspicion and distrust. Buffalo Jerid whispered to his lieutenants for the word to be spread for all the animals to stay still. Jerid wanted to allow the chakeedas to come out to meet them because it might be too dangerous to get too close to their nesting area. The chakeedas stopped when they were about three buffalo lengths from the animals.

The apparent leader stepped forward and said angrily, "What are you doing here? You're on our land. Get out of here."

"Greetings. I am Buffalo Jerid."

The chakeeda leader ignored the salutation. Jerid repeated his introduction more loudly as if the chakeeda had not heard him the first time.

"We really don't care who you are. You're on our land. Now get out of here! Now!" shouted the chakeeda leader.

"We really don't want to do that. We'd like to talk to you about some things," replied Jerid.

"But *we* don't want to talk to *you*. Now for the last time, turn yourself around and go back to wherever you came from," demanded the chakeeda.

During the course of this unpleasant exchange, Buffalo Jerid's lieutenants had wisely moved animals onto each of the flanks. The chakeedas were now surrounded on three sides with their rear as their only avenue of escape. The animals flanking the chakeedas began to move closer until Buffalo Jerid motioned with his head for them to stop. The chakeedas saw that they were temporarily at a disadvantage that they had not counted on.

The eyes of the chakeedas began darting about at the encroaching animals. The chakeeda leader's demeanor began to soften, "I've had a bad day. Maybe I was a bit impolite. What do you want to talk about?"

Buffalo Jerid decided that he needed to put the chakeedas at ease if there was going to be any productive discussions. Coming out and accusing them of plundering the planet was probably not going to be productive. A different approach was clearly in order.

Buffalo Jerid began, "We're concerned about you. The chakeedas have been acting... well... strangely."

Buffalo Jerid realized that accusing someone of being strange was not necessarily the best way to start a discussion either.

"Maybe strange isn't the right word... you haven't been yourselves and we wanted to find out if there is anything we could do?"

"Thank you for your concern," responded the chakeeda leader brusquely. "But there is nothing wrong with us. The only thing bothering us at all is your presence here. So if you and your friends will leave, then everything will be fine."

"Why do you want us to leave so badly?" ask Buffalo Jerid.

"Because you're on our land and you don't belong here!" shouted the chakeeda. "Why is that so difficult for you to understand?"

Buffalo Jerid could feel his patience with this chakeeda slipping away.

"Because it makes no sense. How can you suddenly claim for yourself alone what all the animals have shared forever and ever? We have a little problem with that," said Buffalo Jerid.

The chakeeda shrugged his shoulders and smirked as if it wasn't his concern.

Buffalo Jerid was not used to being ignored. He stepped forward so that he was now looking down into the chakeeda's face. His big nostrils flaring wider with each breath. "Let me explain for you better. We have a big problem with that and we came here to resolve it. We *are* going to solve the problem, aren't we?"

With his chin, Jerid nudged the forehead of the chakeeda. It was enough to make the chakeeda fall two steps back into his own entourage. The chakeeda had known that the animals were stronger, even much stronger, than the chakeedas. But the chakeeda now realized that he had no chance of winning a fight if this single buffalo were to charge him.

"Maybe I can discuss your concerns with the chakeeda leadership. I really can't make any decisions on my own," said the chakeeda. "What demands would you like for me to take back?"

Buffalo Jerid was surprised by this sudden change in tone. But he was also not at all sure how to respond. The animals really had not come to make "demands". They had come with the genuine intention of solving a problem with the chakeedas. Maybe finding some kind of mutual understanding. By now the animals had come around to the rear of the chakeedas contingent as they tried to crowd in closer to hear what Buffalo Jerid was going to say. The chakeedas did not understand what the animals were doing and were becoming more and more afraid. They began whispering among themselves, their eyes darting about for any weakness that they might exploit to fight their way out. The animals thought the chakeedas acted weird anyway, so they did not really notice their agitation.

"Look, just tell us what you want. I'm sure that we can agree to your demands," the chakeeda said nervously. "Just let us go back to our leaders and we will have an answer for you as soon as possible."

"I think we basically are asking for you to stop wiping out entire species. We really don't think that's unreasonable. Another thing, this is not your land. We have all lived together here forever and ever. That is the way it has always been and the way it should always be," said Buffalo Jerid.

"I understand. Sounds reasonable. Let me go back right now and I'll tell the leaders," said the chakeeda.

"When can we expect you back?" asked Buffalo Jerid.

"As soon as possible," said the chakeeda.

"In the morning?" ask Buffalo Jerid.

"I promise. Can we go?"

"Sure. No one's stopping you."

The animals parted to allow the chakeedas to leave. They ran back to the chakeeda nesting area as fast as their scrawny legs could carry them.

* * * * *

As the chakeedas came running back into the nesting area, they stumbled forward through the crowd of chakeedas and fell to the ground gasping for air, panting terribly for each breath. Beads of sweat dripped down their faces, their eyes wide with terror as they reached out for someone to carry them the rest of the way. The waiting chakeedas lifted them up and took them to the chakeeda leadership.

* * * * *

No one ever knew what the chakeedas reported to their leadership. But the next day, the highest leader of all of the chakeedas came out to meet with Buffalo Jerid. His name was Futo. His pinkish skin had ugly red veins running throughout his face.

Buffalo Jerid stepped forward to great him, but Futo ignored the welcome.

"I don't like you. Let me make that clear," said Futo.

"I understand," said Jerid.

"I've come here to negotiate. After we're done, I don't ever want to see you again," said Futo.

"That's fine," said Jerid.

"Let's begin," said Futo.

The negotiation lasted for the remainder of the season. When winter came, the negotiations broke off, but resumed again the following season when the first flowers blossomed. When the leaves on the trees started turning to red again and no solution had been reached, Buffalo Jerid was beginning to wonder if it would ever be possible to repair the relationship with the chakeedas. Futo refused to acknowledge that the chakeedas were causing any harm at all. The chakeedas believed that they were not destroying anything, but rather only making improvements to the land. The fact that the modified land was only suitable for chakeedas was of no interest to Futo. This problem and others all seemed to stem from the odd chakeeda concept that they could actually own the earth. Futo would never discuss the fundamental flaw in such thinking. It was not negotiable.

At one point Buffalo Jerid angrily asked, "Do you own the air, too? How far does this go? Should we stop breathing your air? Do we need your permission for that too?"

When Futo seemed to be taking the question seriously, Buffalo Jerid abandoned any hope of fixing the relationship with the chakeedas. There seemed to be only one solution, which came to be known as the Compromise. Under the Compromise, it was proposed that the chakeedas would be given free reign to do as they pleased with the Great Valley so long as they did not try to "improve" any other areas. Some animals were critical of the Compromise because they felt it gave the chakeedas too much. The Great Valley was certainly the most beautiful and diverse place on the planet. It extended from the ocean where the sun rose each morning, across the prairies, and wetlands to the farthest inland mountains where the sun set each night. One side of the Great Valley sloped upward to the great plains and the other side rose up and disappeared into a rain forest. To most animals, giving all of this to just one species seemed terribly unfair. But as things were, the chakeedas were out of control with their "improvements" and something had to be done. No one had a better idea, so the Compromise was reluctantly accepted.

Buffalo Jerid hated the Compromise. There was an instinctive feeling of danger that kept gnawing at him. The chakeedas were too easily accepting of the plan. But the one thing that comforted Buffalo Jerid was a dream he kept having. The dream was of a great buffalo who would be born one day who would be able to make the Compromise work. Buffalo Jerid came to believe in his dream and so did the other animals of the World Council of Living Things. The secret belief in the dream left the animals with the feeling that the Compromise was a temporary solution to control the situation until the Great Buffalo was born. In Buffalo Jerid's dream, the great buffalo would have visions that would help him solve the chakeeda problem. The animals would be able to recognize the great buffalo by one of his horns. It would be crooked and bent to one side. That is how the legend and prophesy of a future visionary Buffalo leader came to be passed down through the generations.

CHAPTER FOUR

The Stampede

Many, many seasons passed with the chakeedas living in the Great Valley. Buffalo Jerid had died at a very old age, and the buffalo herds had prospered for many generations due in no small part to the fact that the Compromise had worked for such a long time. But eventually the chakeedas began to venture out of the Great Valley with increasing frequency. Their attacks on the buffalo herds were becoming a regular event again. It was late in the birthing season when one of the attacks began.

A buffalo had just given birth. The new mother barely began to clean her calf off before she heard a familiar rumbling sound. The sound told her that a stampede had started at the head of the herd in response to the chakeeda attack. She knew when it spread back through the herd, she would be swept up by its singular momentum whether she wanted to be or not. There wasn't much time. She tried her best to help her new calf to his feet by gently nudging him with her broad forehead. Her voice quivered as she urged him to test his new legs. Within a few more painfully long moments, the calf made it to his feet. But his front legs were spread out too wide for walking let alone running. He struggled to straighten himself up.

The rumbling sound was getting closer. His mother's voice took on new urgency as she pleaded with her newborn to take his first step. The calf took a few tentative steps, but soon found himself sprawled out on the ground again. The sound grew louder and the earth began to vibrate from the pounding hooves of thousands of buffalo. The new mother became hysterical, screaming at him to get up.

The other buffalo around the little creature normally would have already begun to move in response to the vibration of the earth. But they waited trying to give the new mother as much time as they could to get her new calf to his feet. But within a few more moments, they all knew that the stampede would spread past them and to the rear of the herd. They would be swept up into the charging mass of buffalo whether they wanted to be or not. The calf tried his best to get to his feet, but the earth was vibrating so badly now that the simple task was impossible.

It was too late. The calf found himself surrounded by a blur of buffalo flying passed him. For a brief moment he saw his mother looking back at him. But soon even his mother disappeared into the dust of the stampeding herd. He had no idea what to do. He had no time to think about it before he felt something kick him from behind, then a massive beast came crashing down in front of him and disappeared into the dust. The calf tucked his legs underneath himself and hoped for the best. He had no way of knowing that he was making a potentially fatal mistake.

He soon felt a sharp wind on his back. When he looked up, his view of the sky was completely blocked by another massive buffalo leaping over his body. The tremendous beast ripped up the earth when its mighty frame landed in front of him, sending dirt clods sailing into the calf's face. He closed his eyes hoping it would be over soon. But the buffalo kept coming. Most were able to dodge past the calf or leap over him. But the dust soon became so thick that his small body was completely obscured. His tan fur blended perfectly with the dust settling on him. A stampeding bull charged directly into the newborn, sending him sailing through the air. When he crashed back to the earth, he was too dazed to move. He sensed that something was terribly wrong—his head was hurting badly. He felt something warm trickling down the side of his face. Not knowing what he should do, he remained sitting in the path of danger, crying for his mother. He heard a deep voice yelling at him. It was the buffalo that had run into him. When the calf opened his eyes, he saw the beast with his head lowered about to run him through with his horns. The calf closed his eyes as tightly as he could waiting for the impact. The solid horns were no match for the young body. He screamed as loud as he could. He felt himself rising up in the air, but there was no pain. When he opened his eyes, he found himself standing. The buffalo had simply picked him up and was yelling at him above the tremendous rumble of the stampede. "Just don't stand there! Run, little one! Run! Run as fast as you can!"

The calf ran. At first, he found himself dodging other buffalo trying his best not to be run over again. But within a short time, he discovered that the stampede had a natural rhythm. It flowed with the contours of the earth. Each animal moved in unison with every other animal. The various herds had joined together and had become a single creature of one mind and one purpose. Instinctively, his body became synchronized with the movements of the buffalo around him. As the stampede charged over the gently rolling hills, he found comfort in becoming a part of this larger creature. This is what he was made for, he thought.

The stampede thundered out of rolling hills of the grasslands and across the open prairie. It was heading for the central river that was the half way mark on the migration to the summer grazing grounds in the north. When the mighty herd came within smelling range of the river, the scent of fresh water charged its muscles with renewed energy. The exhilarating feeling of singular purpose and unyielding determination coursed through the herd and through the young calf.

When the great herd reached the river, it began to lose its singular identity again as the buffalo fanned out along its banks and plunged, panting and snorting, into the cool water. The river flowed down from the melting ice packs in the white cap mountains to the west. Its cool, fresh taste brought great joy to the thirsty herd as the buffalo splashed about in the cool, blue water. The calf drank from the river. It was the first drink of his life. Its pure, fresh taste was satisfying. After having his fill, he found a place to rest on the bank and stared at the river. The gently flowing current had a relaxing and tranquil effect. As he lay there resting, he began to wonder where all the water came from. He turned to an older buffalo that was lazily watching the water and asked, "Do you know where the water comes from?"

Without looking at the calf, the older buffalo simply pointed his head in the direction of the mountains and said, "It comes from that direction."

The calf thought about the answer for a moment, then asked, "Are the mountains filled with water?"

The older buffalo raised one eyebrow and turned to look at the calf for the first time. He stared at the newborn, trying to determine if the little creature was serious. He also was privately amazed that such a young creature was capable of asking such questions. The older buffalo had never seen such a thing before. It was very, very unusual. After a few moments, the older buffalo repeated the calf's question, "Are the mountains filled with water?"

"Are they?" asked the calf again.

The older buffalo had never been to the mountains and had no idea if the mountains were filled with water. He looked at the mountains, then at the river, then back at the mountains again. He then announced, "Yes, the mountains are filled with water."

The older buffalo thought his answer had ended the discussion, but after a few moments of careful thought, the calf asked, "So how long will it be before the mountains are empty?"

The older buffalo frowned and with a hint of irritation in his voice said, "What do you mean, how long before they are empty? They're never empty."

"But how can that be?" asked the calf. "At some point, wouldn't the river use up all the water?"

The older buffalo stared with a mean expression at the young creature, trying to intimidate him into silence. But the calf, not knowing any better, waited patiently for an answer. There were several other buffalo that had become interested in the conversation and were also now waiting to hear the answer.

Finally, the calf said, "If you don't know, just say so." The other buffalo chuckled and snorted.

The older buffalo exploded angrily, "Of course I know the answer! The answer is that the mountains are so large that they never run out of water."

The calf started to object to this answer, but the older buffalo cut him off saying, "The river has always flowed and always will flow. And there isn't anything in the world that can keep the river from flowing. That's all that is important and that's all you need to know."

The calf looked at the river and at the mountains and hoped that the older buffalo was right. It was a beautiful river. The sun glinted off the small white caps that the breezes churned up on its surface. He watched as more buffalo arrived and swam across. He looked down river for the first time to where the river divided. The main portion of the river turned to the southeast. But a shallow, slower moving branch broke off to the northeast. This branch was connected to thousands of small streams that fed the great wetlands. The buffalo avoided the wetlands by always crossing the river before the fork.

Even though the buffalo never ventured into the wetlands, they still held a certain fascination for them because of the great flocks of geese, heron, mallards, and other water fowl that darkened the sky on their way to their summer homes. As the calf looked down river, he saw the shadows of more flocks on their final approach to the wetlands. When he looked up at the sky, he couldn't believe what he saw. There were formations of birds of every kind, color, and size as far as he could see. The sky was so crowded that the formations were stacked on top of each other waiting for their turn to descend.

The older buffalo looked at the calf staring intently at the sky and knew he was preparing to ask another question. So before the calf could ask anything about the birds, the older buffalo asked, "Who are you anyway? What is your name? And where is your mother?"

The calf didn't know the answer to any of these questions.

"Well, you better find your mother soon, little one, rather than worry about the river or the birds." With that, the older buffalo got up and walked away before the calf could ask any more difficult questions.

$$* * * * *$$

The calf had been so amazed by everything he saw, he had not noticed how hungry he was. Instinctively, he knew he had to find his mother if he was going to eat. He started his search by wandering about among the buffalo calling for her. When this failed, he started looking for any buffalo he might recognize. But the buffalo that he had been around when he was born and the buffalo that he had run with to the river were no where to be found. The buffalo he did talk to, told him not to worry, that he would find his mother. But the expressions on their faces told a different story. They all knew that once a calf lost his mother in the vast herd, it was almost impossible for the two to find each other again. The calf was usually dead within a few days.

It was late in the day before the calf began to realize just how large the herd really was. He was very hungry and seemed no closer to finding his mother. He closed his eyes and tried to remember her scent and what she looked like. In his mind, he could see her standing on the side of a hill with no other buffalo around calling for him. The sun was almost touching the horizon. The calf could see his mother taking one last look back at the foothills, casting their first shadows of the evening over the golden grasses, before reluctantly returning to the safety of the herd. The image in his mind seemed so real. He opened his eyes and looked in the direction of the foothills. The calf weaved his way to the edge of the herd and began trotting in the direction where he had seen her.

The sun was quickly disappearing. It was getting difficult to distinguish one hill from another in the darkness. The calf thought this was strange. He did not remember it being so dark the last time he was here during the stampede. He looked back at the herd and realized it was getting darker everywhere. He wondered if he should wait for the light to return. The problem was he was not sure when it would return, if ever, and he was very hungry. He decided to continue on his path because he was pretty sure his mother was just over the next hill if his vision had been correct.

When he reached the top of the hill, he looked down and saw a lone buffalo. Her head hanging down, but still crying out for her calf. The calf returned the call. When she reached him, she licked the dried blood from the side of his head where he had been kicked, and checked to make sure he was alright. The calf wanted to begin nursing. But his mother would not allow it. She said they had to return to the herd immediately. It was not safe. She could already smell the scent of chakeedas in the air. They had to hurry. The scent was growing stronger.

Mother and calf increased their pace as they ran through the evening shadows of the foothills. The smell of chakeeda was too close now. She looked to her side and saw several chakeedas coming toward them. She looked down at her little one and knew he could not out run them. When she glanced back in the direction of the chakeedas, she saw they had all stopped. It was hard to see in the dimming twilight, but she was almost certain she saw an arctic wolf standing in their path. It was hard to believe because no arctic wolves lived anywhere near here as far as she knew. There was no time to figure it out. She hurried her calf along. As they approached the river, several buffalo bulls came out to meet them. The scent of chakeeda faded when their escort arrived. With the approach of darkness, the herd formation had become much tighter as a standard safety measure. An opening was made for mother and calf to reach the protection of the interior of the herd. For the first time, the calf was able to nurse.

The next morning, the story of how the calf had found his mother had spread throughout the herd. The leader of the buffalos was a large buffalo named Buffalo Lee. He was not the imposing figure he had once been.

Age had diminished his muscular bulk and his face had acquired several scars from a lifetime of battles with other buffalo bulls for supremacy over the lead herd. Buffalo Lee had maintained his position mostly by shear strength. He knew he was no great thinker. It was important to know one's own limitations. When Buffalo Lee heard about the newborn buffalo with the vision, he at least knew enough to know that it might be important. He sent a message for the young beast to be brought to him. When the calf arrived, Lee snorted in amusement.

"Aren't you the same calf that asked me where the river water came from?" asked Buffalo Lee. The calf acknowledged he had.

"I thought you seemed different," said Buffalo Lee. "I heard you found your mother through a vision. Is this true?"

"I'm not sure I know what a vision is. I closed my eyes and I saw where my mother was, so I went there," said the calf. "Is that strange?"

No one answered.

"Explain what you saw," requested Buffalo Lee.

The calf told the whole story to Buffalo Lee and his assembled lieutenants. They all stared intently at the calf, not wanting to miss a single word. When the calf was done, Buffalo Lee walked a little distance away and trained his gaze on the white cap mountains while he resumed chewing on his cud. While everyone waited for Buffalo Lee to finish thinking, Buffalo Lee's lieutenants murmured among themselves about the possible significance of the calf's vision. After a long while, Buffalo Lee returned to where the calf and his mother were standing. He looked at the fresh wound on top of the calf's head.

"How did that happen?" asked Buffalo Lee.

"I was kicked in the head during the stampede," said the calf.

Buffalo Lee leaned down so that he could examine the wound more closely. It was right where the calf would one day grow one of his horns. Buffalo Lee shook his head slowing up and down and snorted again.

"What do you want to name him?" Buffalo Lee asked the calf's mother.

"I think I should call him Jake," answered the mother.

"Then Jake it is. You will be known as Buffalo Jake," announced Lee. "And from now on, you and your mother will be members of the lead herd. Do not stray off."

"Why?" asked the calf.

"You ask too many questions," said Buffalo Lee.

Buffalo Lee assigned four of his most trusted lieutenants to watch over Jake and his mother. He did not have to explain the importance of the assignment. Everyone understood. Except, of course, Jake who had no idea why the leader of all the buffalo had taken such an interest in him. He sensed that whatever the reason was, it was an important one. But for now, he was content to enjoy all the attention he was getting.

* * * * *

Every day at dusk, Buffalo Lee had a meeting with his lieutenants to plan the next day's grazing and watering patterns for the herds. It was a ritual that had been started long before the invention of paw print writing. Today the daily planning meeting was held on a rise on the opposite side of the river from the foothills where Jake had found his mother. When Buffalo Lee arrived, his lieutenants were already assembled. After the meeting with Jake and his mother earlier in the day, no one had thought of much else other than what the young calf's vision might mean, and that is what the lieutenants were discussing when Buffalo Lee arrived. Buffalo Lee had chosen to graze by himself after the meeting with Jake and his mother to collect his thoughts and had not really spoken with any of the other buffalo all day. So when he heard his lieutenants talking so opening about little Jake, he was quiet upset.

"What do you think your doing?!" yelled Buffalo Lee. "I never want to hear another word about this outside of our meetings. If anyone in the herd asks, I want you to say you don't know anything. If the news of this calf spreads, the chakeedas might find out and they certainly would try to kill him."

Buffalo Lee's lieutenants all began chomping on their cuds with greater vigor as an acknowledgement of the truth of what Buffalo Lee had said.

"Anyway," continued Buffalo Lee, "there is no reason for us to think Jake is the buffalo of legend. We will have to wait to see."

One of the lieutenants said, "But the story is the same and the blood where his horn is, well, its not exactly the same, but..."

Buffalo Lee interrupted, "I know it might be him. If he is, he will come to lead the herd through his own strength. We can't do it for him. If we try to help him too much, he might become leader of the herd because of us, not because of himself. And if that happens, what if he isn't the buffalo in the prophesy? And what if he is not fit to lead? We must allow it to happen naturally. It will be difficult not to help him, but it's the only way we can be sure."

Buffalo Lee's lieutenants acknowledged that they understood.

"The only thing that we should make sure of is that the chakeedas do not kill him. I think that really is not interfering too much with the prophesy."

The other buffalo agreed. As they settled down for the evening, there was not a single one of them that did not feel the excitement in their hearts. They all secretly believed that Buffalo Jake was the great buffalo of the legend. It would be many seasons before they would find out if they were right.

CHAPTER FIVE

In Search of the Buffalo of Legend

Growing up within the central herd was not fun for Jake. Buffalo Lee's lieutenants were obsessive about protecting him from any potential harm. Buffalo Lee had given specific instructions to them that Jake was not to be treated any differently. But as a practical matter, it was impossible to protect him and treat him as an average calf. The lieutenants not only had orders to protect Jake, they also had to conceal the fact that he even existed from the chakeedas. Lee feared that the chakeedas might be able to tell that young Jake was the leader foretold by buffalo prophesy just by looking at him. The buffalo were not sure how the chakeedas might do this, but it was better not to take the chance.

As the seasons passed, the buffalo leadership became more and more convinced that Jake was the Great Buffalo predicted by Buffalo Jerid's dream. Jake had begun to have dreams of things that later came true. He would dream of a chakeeda attack on the herd. Several days later the attack would occur right where Jake had dreamed it would happen. He would dream of a grass fire in a particular area and that too would happen several days later where he saw it in his dream. When the buffalo leadership traced his lineage, it was discovered that he was the grandson of Buffalo Jerid.[1] This added to their sense of hope that Jake was the chosen one. But as Jake grew older, his dreams became less frequent and eventually stopped altogether. This naturally cast doubt on his status. What if Buffalo Jake was not the great buffalo? What if the real leader had been born while they were directing all their attention to Buffalo Jake? What if the real calf had been attacked and killed? But what concerned them more was the possibility that they had done something wrong in raising Jake. What if they had accidentally destroyed that part of Jake that would give him the special ability to find the solution to the chakeeda

---

1. Research note: It appears that the paw print language does not distinguish between grandfathers, great grandfathers, great, great grandfathers, etc. All previous males from whom an animal is the direct descendant are referred to by one word, which loosely translates as grandfather. As a consequence, there appears to be no way to determine how many generations before Buffalo Jake that Buffalo Jerid lived.

problem? What if that was the real reason he had lost his ability to have visions?

The buffalo leadership still waited for one sign. The crooked horn. Jake had still not grown his horns. Many thought that he should have by now. Others said he was still young. As time went on, Jake grew more and more restless. He felt he was trapped within his own herd. Jake had still not been told who he was and why he was treated differently.

While the leadership debated when they should tell him, a small group of buffalo from the fringe herds had their own plans for Jake. Life in the fringe herds was not easy. These were the herds that were most vulnerable to attack from packs of wolves and hungry mountain lions. As a result of the greater stresses on the fringe herds, they tended to breed stronger and more aggressive buffalo. After several generations, the fringe buffalo would challenge the central herd for dominance and usually win. The central herd would become a fringe herd and the cycle would begin again. Sometimes the fringe herd would breed more than just stronger and more aggressive animals. Sometimes it would also create particularly intelligent and cunning creatures.

Nick, Anthony and Glade were three particularly wild and unruly buffalo that were about the same age as Jake. They belonged to no particular fringe herd. They wandered among them all. Nick was the leader of the trio who kept them on the move. Their reputation for aggressiveness bordered on foolishness. The three young buffalo were at the size that predators liked best. Still small enough for them to take down, though it might be more of a fight, but big enough to make it worth the effort to feed the whole wolf pack. When a pack of wolves set their eyes on a fringe herd in which the three young buffalo were travelling, the trio would not wait for the attack. They would charge the wolves and chase after them. Many other buffalo thought this was just stupid. The wolves frequently would just watch the buffalo and an attack might not occur for days. The trio did not care. Even after chasing the wolves off, they sometimes continued to pursue them to provoke a fight. On more than one occasion, the wolves were able to encircle the three buffalo and retaliate. The wolves inflicted serious bites and rips in these fights, but the buffalo inflicted enough injuries to the pack that the wolves would retreat.

As a result of these battles, the reputation of the three buffalo spread through the wolf packs and even among the mountain lions, some of whom had occasion to witness the trio's bizarre behavior. Their reputation was heightened by Nick's propensity for telling the stories of their exploits over and over again to anyone who would listen. No one minded much since he was an excellent story teller. After a while, they became known as the wild three, and were able to roam anywhere they wished without being molested by predators.

Having suppressed the threat to themselves presented by the wolves and mountain lions, the three began looking around for a new challenge. Their attention turned to the central herd. The obvious question was why was the central herd the central herd? What was so special about the central herd that it should direct the movements of the other herds? Why should there be a central herd at all? The three decided to foment a rebellion against the central herd. They began to spread rumors that the central herd was short changing the fringe herds and was keeping the best grazing areas for itself. The wild three made every attempt to incite the fringe buffalo, appealing to their sense of pride and self-respect, demanding that they deserved better and should strike out on their own.

The trio's attempt to lead a rebellion quickly turned into a non-event. There was a big difference between winning a fight with a pack of wolves and restructuring the relationships among all the buffalo herds. The instinctual wisdom of countless generations of buffalo had taught the creatures the advantages of their herd structure. Three young, rogue buffalo were not about to undo the entire social evolution of the species.

One morning, when the three were puzzling over their failure, an older buffalo approached them to find out why they were so insistent upon trying to rip apart the structure of the herds. It became apparent from listening to the three that they had missed out on an important part of their education as young buffalo, no doubt the result of their endless roaming from one herd to another. The older buffalo explained how things worked and that much of it could not change because it was probably instinctual. How much of their behavior was instinctual was a favorite topic of debate among the buffalo. In fact, all species found pleasure in debating the issue, even though it was usually agreed that there was no way to come to any conclusions. Those were considered the best kinds of debates. But regardless of where the dividing line might be between learned and instinctual behavior, all buffalo knew that the herd structure itself was solidly within the realm of instinctual control.

At this point in the older buffalo's explanation, Nick asked, "Why is it that my friends and I do not seek to become a part of the herd structure? If it were instinctual as you say, wouldn't we feel compelled to do so?"

The older buffalo answered, "Many instincts can lay dormant like a tree waiting for spring before growing its leaves. The tree's ability to grow the leaves is always there. But the leaves will not grow until the tree feels the warmth of the sun in spring. By roaming about without belonging to any herd, you have not received the same message that the tree receives from the sun. If you had been a part of a herd, then your experience would have awakened your instinctual response to the herd structure and you would not be trying to change it now."

Nick would have to think about this. He decided it was best not to press the issue right now. The older buffalo went on to explain how buffalo from fringe herds had a right to challenge any buffalo in the central herd at any time. If any one of them could win in a fight, they could become a part of the central herd and even seek to fight for the leadership of the central herd. In this way, fringe herds could become the central herd. The three thanked the older buffalo for his knowledge and continued on their way.

"What should we do next?" asked Anthony.

"Isn't it obvious?" answered Nick. "Our new quest will be to take over the central herd."

None of the three had ever actually been near the central herd. They had occasionally seen it in the distance, but had never come in close contact with any of its members. At the moment, none of them was actually sure of where they might find the central herd. The obvious choice was to go to the center of where all the other herds were. But from where they were, it was not at all obvious in which direction the center might be. At the moment, there were buffalo in all directions. There was obviously more to this business of organizing the herds than they had ever expected.

It was late in the afternoon when the three finally were able to locate the center. Just as one would expect, there was indeed a buffalo herd that seemed to stand out from all the rest. None of them was sure why it stood out, but there was something about it that was different. The trio surveyed the situation, trying to think of an appropriate plan of action. Nick decided that a direct assault would be best. The central herd would never expect it. A sudden charge would be such a surprise that the herd would scatter. This would give Nick, Anthony and Glade the opportunity to size up any weaknesses among its members and how they were organized. Depending upon what they found out, they could decide what to do next. They were ready.

They charged the central herd at full speed. Just as they were about to blast through their ranks, they found themselves veering sharply off their target. Not a single member of the central herd had even budged. A couple of buffalo turned to confront the three. For the first time, Nick felt he was in danger. The fights with the wolves had seemed like a fair fight to Nick. This was clearly not. These buffalo were enormous! He had never imagined that they were so large. They had certainly never looked that big before when he had seen the central herd from far away.

"What do you want?" asked one of the two buffalo that came out to confront Nick and his gang.

"Nothing. Absolutely Nothing. We'll be on our way," answered Anthony.

"Not so fast," said Nick, suddenly regaining his courage. Nick tried to look beyond the buffalo in front of him to see more toward the interior of the herd. He had never seen such a dense herd before. You could only see maybe two animals beyond the edge. This aroused Nick's curiosity.

"What are you hiding in there?" asked Nick. Nick had heard rumors of something very secret being hidden within the central herd, but he had never thought anything of it until now.

The large buffalo charged at Nick, which was more than enough for Nick to decide he did not need an answer to his question immediately. When they reached the edge of the fringe herds again, Nick complained loudly to anyone that would listen that it was not right for the central herd to be concealing things from them. If it affected all buffalo, then they all had a right to know. Once again, the fringe buffalo were not impressed. The central herd did not have to make an announcement for the other buffalo to surmise what was being hidden. Enough information had filtered its way through the herds for them to know with reasonable certainty what was going on. Everyone also understood the importance of not talking about it. Everyone except for Nick. He saw it as his destiny to disrupt whatever he did not understand, and whatever secret plan the central herd had devised fell into that category.

The trio set out to quietly learn all they could about herd structure. They had never known how complicated the relationships were. It was fascinating stuff to them. They were particularly interested in the intricacies of the communications structure between the herds, especially the various types of signals given by the central herd to control the movements of all the other herds. It was within this communications network that Nick found the weakness for which he had been searching.

After hashing over the details with his cohorts, they agreed to put his new plan into action as soon as possible. First, they would have to precipitate a stampede. To do this, they began spreading rumors that the chakeedas were grouping for a major attack on the herd. Even though there were no signs that the chakeedas were planning any such attack, the mere spreading of the rumor made the animals very nervous. It soon became common knowledge that the time of the attack was getting closer and closer. Nick's first step of circulating disinformation was his first test of the accuracy of his newly acquired knowledge of the communications structures within the herds. After several days, the central herd felt compelled to do something to relieve the growing tension and uneasiness. As Nick had predicted, the central herd ordered a stampede to let the buffalo run off their nervousness and to move the herds away from the perceived danger area.

As soon as the stampede started, the three began the second phase of their plan, which exploited the most serious weakness Nick had found in the central herd's signaling system. The three split up and maneuvered themselves to key positions around the central herd. Once they were at their assigned location, they began disrupting the signals going out to the fringe herds concerning the direction the stampede was suppose to take. The stampede began losing its usual cohesion, and the herds soon began breaking off in different directions. But that was not Nick's primary objective. Nick disrupted the final signal that was at the heart of the weakness he had found. Just as he predicted the central herd itself divided in half and went in different directions. The center was now sliced in half and fully exposed. Nick scanned the interior for anything unusual. It did not take long for him to spot what was out of place.

There was one younger buffalo that was about the same age and size as himself. It clearly did not fit in with the enormously large buffalo around it. The fully mature buffalo seemed to be running so close to him that he would be run over at any moment. The sudden division of the central herd caused immediately confusion among the leadership. They did not understand at all what was going on and were frantically shouting orders and sending signals in an attempt to bring order back to the herd. Nick knew they did not have much time before the leadership would be able to begin correcting the situation. The trio moved in on the young buffalo and were able to break him away from the stampede. Nick, Anthony, and Glade were soon racing away from the central herd with their prize. Nick and Anthony were on each side of the young buffalo and Glade was taking up the rear so that he could not escape.

When the stampede was over and Buffalo Lee heard the news of what had happened to Jake, he was too sickened by the loss to be able to say anything at all. Lee began receiving reports as to the identity of the rogue buffalo. He was not angry at Nick for what he had done. Lee felt that Nick and his friends would not have taken Jake if they had known who he was. There was no way that Nick could have known that he was placing all buffalo, in fact all species, at risk of extinction at the hands of the chakeedas by taking Jake. Lee was more mad at himself for not being prepared for what had happened. Ultimately, he would have to bear the responsibility for the loss of Buffalo Jake. His only hope was to find Jake as soon as possible before something happened to him.

For the first time ever, Lee ordered that the herds divide up. By splitting up, the herds were able to roam over an area within a few days that would have taken the whole summer if the herds had stayed together. But the reports that came back to Lee were all the same. There was no sign of Buffalo Jake anywhere.

* * * * *

During their time as young buffalo roaming away from the herd, the wild three had explored every twist and turn of every gulch and gully in the buffalo range. So every time one of the buffalo herds came close to them, they knew where to find the closest place to hide themselves and Jake. Their first few days together were spent running and hiding and backtracking. Planning their every movement to avoid detection consumed all of their energy. There was no time to discuss much of anything else. Other than a basic exchange of each other's names, Jake knew nothing about these buffalo and they knew nothing about him. Even so, Jake was more than willing to cooperate. He did not perceive that the trio had any intention of hurting him and being able to run free was a welcome change from the life he had led concealed within the central herd. He was not ready to go back to that life just yet, if ever.

After awhile, the herds moved farther north to continue their search. For the first time, it gave Nick and Jake time to talk. Nick immediately launched into his favorite stories of his triumphs over the wolves and mountain lions. As he told each story, Nick seemed to literally reexperience the battle all over again. He charged at imaginary wolves and slammed them with body blows that sent them flying through the air. He raised up on his hind legs and crashed down on snarling attackers. He cringed in pain as fangs pierced different parts of his body. He made it seem all so real that Jake was sure he would soon have to join the imaginary battle to avoid being killed himself before Nick reached the end of the story. After Nick felt assured that Jake knew just how impressive a buffalo he was, Nick had a few questions for Jake.

"So why are you such a secret?" asked Nick. Jake looked puzzled.

"What do you mean?" asked Jake.

"Why are you kept confined within the central herd? There must be some reason," answered Nick.

"I did not know I was confined. I have always been treated very well by the other buffalo," said Jake.

"They never told you anything? They never told you why you had so many large buffalo surrounding you?" asked Nick.

"No one ever said anything about it. If that's all you've known, you really don't question it," said Jake.

"They must have said something to you," said Nick.

"They said lots of things. They were always teaching me things," said Jake.

"Like what things?" asked Nick.

"Lots of things. They said that I might need to know many things someday. They did not say why. They just thought I should know everything," said Jake.

Nick had hoped that Jake would disclose the secrets of the central herd. Instead, he had only added to the mystery. But for now, they would have to leave it that way. What impressed Nick the most was the response of the buffalo herds to the loss of Buffalo Jake. Nick had never seen such a massive search for a lost member of the herd before. Jake was clearly far more important to the herd than the trio had ever imagined. Nick knew there were many things that he still did not understand about herd structure. He started to worry that the herd might really need Jake for some critical task. Nick did not want to hurt his fellow buffalo, he only wanted to know the secrets. He began to think that maybe they had messed with something that they should have left alone. Maybe it would be best to return Jake to the herds. When Nick told Anthony what he was thinking, Anthony was strongly opposed to returning. Anthony was sure that their lives would be very short if they tried to go back now and insisted it would be better to wait awhile. Nick accepted his brother's assessment of the situation. He might not have done so if Nick had known that they would not see the buffalo herds again for many seasons.

* * * * *

Nick decided that they could not stay on the prairie if they wanted to avoid the herds. They had heard about a place that was perfect for almost any species. It was so large that it had prairies, forests, wetlands, and all kinds of other places for all sorts of animals to live. This perfect place was contained in one immensely large valley. It was called the Great Valley and seemed like the perfect place for the three to spend their time until they decided to return to the herds.

After many days of travelling, all three were growing weary of their quest to find the Great Valley. The farther from their home range that they travelled, the less and less there seemed to be for buffalo's to eat. Not all types of grasses made an equally good cud. Nick suggested that they would travel as far as they could for the day and if they did not find the Great Valley by dusk, they would turn back. But late in the day, they saw what appeared to be the rim of a valley in the distance. It was agreed that it would not make sense not to at least find out what was there. As evening arrived, the buffalo pressed on in the darkness. It was very late when they descended into the valley and decided to rest for the night when they reached the valley floor.

In the morning, they were very disappointed to find that they still had not reached the Great Valley. The grasses were sparser here than they had been anywhere else. They found a small stream for a morning drink. Even the water tasted terrible here. It was agreed that it was time to go back.

As they were getting ready to leave, two rabbears poked their heads out of their burrow. Their names were Tom and Joe.

"What are you doing here?" asked Joe.

"We're in search of the Great Valley. Do you know where it is?" asked Nick.

Tom and Joe exchanged comments in their species' language to confirm that they both had heard the same question.

"We're not sure we understand your question. You *are* in the Great Valley," said Joe.

"You have to be joking," said Nick.

"No. This is it," said Joe.

The buffalo looked around again at the desolation. It did not seem possible.

"We were told the Great Valley was a fantastic place," said Anthony.

"Well, it was. It used to be teaming with all kinds of creatures. It *was* fantastic. But after the chakeedas moved in, things changed. I don't think there was a single part of the Great Valley where they didn't find something they wanted. They went in and took what they wanted and didn't care if they destroyed everything else in the process. They used up everything. The forests. The prairies. The wetlands. That's why everything is so barren now," said Joe. Jake was surprised at just how chatty these two rabbears were. It was uncharacteristic of their species.

"Have you talked to them?" asked Jake.

"The chakeedas?" asked Joe.

"Yes."

"You can't be serious. They try to kill us on sight. They say we're the problem. Digging up *their* prairie," said Joe.

"I spoke to one of them once," said Tom. "I tried to ask them why they were doing this. They did not understand what I was talking about. They have no memory of what the Great Valley looked like before. When I explained it to them, they thought it was sad. They said they would try to be more careful. But nothing changed."

"Something has to change," said Nick. "If they keep this up, they won't even have anything left for themselves."

"I'm not so sure," said Joe. "Look over there." Joe pointed with his head toward the opposite side of the valley. Through the haze, they could see a steady stream of movement flowing into the valley. It looked like a line of ants. When one looked closer, there were actually several streaming lines. But they were not ants. They were chakeedas returning with food and materials they had taken from other areas.

"Is it always like that?" asked Anthony.

"No. Sometimes we don't see them for many days, then they'll start again," said Tom.

Tom stared off in the direction of the stream of chakeedas and added, "Every night, they return. They seem to be afraid of being away at night."

"If the buffalo on the World Council had not agreed to let the chakeedas have the Great Valley, we wouldn't be in this mess now," continued Joe.

"You're blaming the buffalo for the chakeedas?! You can't be serious!" shouted Nick.

Joe and Nick proceeded to get into a heated argument over whether the deal struck with the chakeedas had been an intelligent decision. The rabbears did not have a better solution, but they still found the agreement with the chakeedas to be a mistake. Nick fiercely defended the decision. The compromise had been agreed to by the entire leadership of the World Council; not just the buffalo on the Council. Tom responded by reminding Nick that it had been the central herd buffalo that had negotiated the deal and the other animals had little choice but to accept what was negotiated. Nick strongly disagreed. The other animals could have proposed any solution they wanted. Nick vehemently defended the negotiation strategies adopted by the central herd as the best one could hope for at the time. Anthony joined the verbal assault. Even though the brothers had tried to remove the central herd from power only days before, they viewed their dispute with the central herd as a buffalo to buffalo issue. When it came to rabbears attacking the leadership of the central herd, that was a different matter altogether and the argument raged on.

Jake was not interested in listening to the fight and started climbing back up the side of the valley to get a better view. When he looked back, he could still see patches of forest and other small areas that had not yet been decimated by the chakeedas. He looked across the emptiness to the other side of the valley. Jake squinted as best he could, trying to bring the stream of chakeedas into focus. As his eyes adjusted, he was able to make out other lines of chakeedas that he had not seen before. The lines ran down into the valley and toward the sea where the chakeeda nesting area was located. Jake could not actually see the nesting area. The valley was very long and it was too far to see from where he was. But he knew it was there and what it looked like. It was a strange feeling. He did not remember anyone ever telling him about it and he certainly had never been there. But all the same, he was certain that he would recognize it if he saw it.

As Jake stared out across the ruins of the valley, he began to feel dizzy. He spread his front legs just a bit to keep his balance. He was certain that he had stood in this place and looked out across the valley before. But this time, something was wrong. Something was very different. He looked back at the lines of chakeedas streaming into the valley. It was not right. Jake knew he had not caused this problem, but he had a weird feeling that he was somehow connected to it.

Jake had never seen a chakeeda before, yet his mind searched for some piece of information that he was certain he knew about them. He tried hard to think of what it was, but the thought lingered in the shadows of his mind unwilling to be remembered just yet. Every time he tried to approached it, the thought retreated further into the darkness. He would stop the chase and it would come back and stand just outside the range of his vision. The thought would sneak a little closer to him, teasing him. Jake would begin to see the blurry outline of the thought before it would once again dart into the shadows. He began to realize that he was not stalking the thought. The thought was stalking him. He had an unsettling feeling that one day it would slither up his leg and wrap itself around his throat without him knowing. When he finally felt it tighten its grip, he would shake his head violently, but there would be nothing he could do.

* * * * *

When Jake returned, Nick, Anthony, Joe, and Tom were still arguing. Jake snorted in disgust.

"It's time for us to go," announced Jake.

Nick and Anthony looked at Jake with some degree of defiance, not sure if they liked him telling them what to do. Nick stared back without emotion.

"We will be back," said Jake to the rabbears. "We're going to see what's beyond the valley on the other side." Jake, Nick, and Anthony set out across the valley floor. Glade had developed a sore front hoof, and it was agreed that he would stay behind until it healed.

As they continued on their journey, which seemed to be increasingly led by Buffalo Jake rather than Nick, they heard and saw the same story. The chakeedas were stripping the land bare and taking what they could back to their nesting area in the Great Valley. The animals that were not killed, were left to starve to death on what little food remained. The three buffalos wandered from one region to another, but the mark of the chakeeda was always ahead of them. The sight of stripped and ravaged lands told the story. They ate what suitable grasses they could find, but had to return to the prairie several times to feed properly to maintain their strength. Each time they returned, there were no other buffalo in sight. At first, they thought this was a good thing because they did not have to hide, but after awhile it seemed very odd that they were the only buffalo around. None of them could explain the absence of hundreds of thousands of buffalo. They engaged in a conspiracy of silence to ignore the unsettling observation.

As each region they travelled to seemed to tell the same story, Nick and Anthony were getting more and more depressed over the apparent hopelessness of the situation. But Jake was different. He seemed to be quietly taking it all in. They often saw him staring calmly at the destruction. The steady expression on his face told them that he was obviously giving it great thought. But when they asked what he was thinking, he acted as if he had not even heard the question. It would be a long time before they would see another buffalo. Even though they searched, they never did find Glade again.

As the seasons passed, Jake seemed to acquire a quiet confidence about himself. It was as if he were uncovering some purpose to his life. Some reason for his existence was slowly coming into focus for him. He still was not sure what it was, but he sensed he was on the right path to finding out.

They were now in the spring of the third season since they had left the buffalo herds. They were much bigger now, and their horns were now of respectable size. They really did not notice the process of growing them because it happened gradually. But once they did have their horns, there was one thing that was very noticeable. One of Jake's horns was definitely crooked. It should have sloped upward. But instead it was definitely bent in the wrong direction. Nick and Anthony had strayed from the influence of the herds at such an early age that they did not know much about buffalo culture, but one thing they did know about was the legend of the great buffalo that would someday be born to save the buffalo from some terrible event. They also were beginning to remember something about the buffalo of legend having some kind of crooked horn.

Late in the day when the three went to the nearest watering hole, Nick asked Jake, "Do you know who you are?"

Jake stared at Nick with an expression of mild amusement.

"No, I don't. Why don't you surprise me," said Jake.

"I'm serious. You're the buffalo that will save all buffalo. In fact, all animals, I think," said Nick.

Jake took a drink, then asked, "Do I have to do this before the sun sets today or can it wait until morning?"

"Fine. If you don't believe me, look at your reflection in the water," said Nick. Jake looked into the water.

"Now what?" asked Jake.

"Don't you see it? One of your horns is crooked," said Nick.

"My crooked horn is going to save all buffalo?" asked Jake.

"Exactly. Well, not exactly. Didn't they ever tell you about the legend of the great buffalo that would be born with a crooked horn?" asked Nick.

"Are you making this up?" asked Jake.

"No, I'm not making this up," retorted Nick. Anthony and Nick together were able to convince Jake that they were being serious.

"I'm just very surprised. The central herd was always telling me all sorts of things. I would think that they would have told me the story of such an important buffalo," said Jake.

"Not if you were it," said Nick. "It all makes sense now. They must have known somehow."

"But why wouldn't they tell me?" asked Jake.

"Maybe they weren't sure. If you were the buffalo of legend, then they wouldn't need to tell you. It would just happen," offered Anthony.

"So what do we do now?" asked Jake.

"You're suppose to tell us, oh great one," said Anthony.

"Knock it off," said Jake.

"What do your instincts tell you?" asked Nick.

"My instincts tell me that what we've been doing is the right thing to do," said Jake.

"O.K., then we'll continue doing what we've been doing," said Nick.

* * * * *

The legend of the great buffalo was more than just a buffalo legend. It was a promise that had been spread among all the animals through the World Council of Living Things. With the full emergence of Jake's crooked horn, it did not take long before other animals began to notice. Word began to spread. This was not good.

Only a few days after Nick saw his crooked horn for the first time at the watering hole, a pair of falcons swept out of the sky and landed on a tree branch ahead of the trio. The nesting pair were named Karen and Trevor. They began frantically screeching about some terrible danger. From what Jake and Nick could decipher, there was a large group of chakeedas approaching. They were moving very fast for chakeedas. They were asking about stories they had heard of a buffalo with a crooked horn. Jake needed to get out of the area immediately. Jake and Nick thanked Trevor and Karen for the information and began heading in the opposite direction of the chakeedas. Trevor said that he and Karen would fly over them until they were a safe distance away just in case there were any other chakeedas in the area.

* * * * *

The trio found themselves instinctively heading back to their home range on the prairie. It was where they felt safest. On the second day of their journey back, Jake said, "I don't think that I'm ready to go back. I don't have a solution. Even if I am this buffalo of legend, I don't know what I'm going to say to Buffalo Lee."

Nick did not answer for a long time, then he said, "Don't think about it now. If you're the buffalo, then a time will come when there will be a choice to be made and no one will know what to do except you. You will know what must be done and you'll do it. I don't think anyone is expecting you to know the answer right now."

Jake shook his head in acknowledgement. It sounded good to him. He had never been a buffalo of legend before. It had only been a few days since he had found out. He was still trying to understand what it meant and what was expected of him. He would not have to wait much longer. The scent of the herd was growing strong. By mid-afternoon, the three climbed the last hill and looked down upon the buffalo herds. The sight was fantastic. Before them was a sea of buffalo peacefully grazing. They were home. The images of the past three seasons of devastation and destruction flooded back into Jake's mind. He looked out upon his buffalo and realized it could just as easily happen to them. A protective instinct rose within him. He would not, could not, let the same thing happen to his buffalo.

When word spread of Jake's return, Buffalo Lee and his lieutenants came out to greet him. The buffalo of the central herd who had once towered over Jake, found themselves looking slightly up to him. Jake had grown into the largest buffalo of them all. His size alone commanded respect. When Lee saw the crooked horn, he shook his head with approval.

"Welcome," said Buffalo Lee. "We've waited many generations for your arrival." The other buffalo from the central herd shook their heads and snorted in agreement. They had much to discuss, but one thing was certain. There was no question in anyone's mind, Buffalo Jake was the crooked horned buffalo of legend.

CHAPTER SIX

Buffalo Tag

It had been many seasons since Buffalo Jake had returned to the central herd. The desire for dominance had grown stronger within him with each passing season. He could feel the rawness and hot tension of it burning in his muscles, driving him to charge whomever was above him in the hierarchy. It was an instinct that focused his mind, easily inflamed his temper, and gave every moment of his life overwhelming purpose. The possibility that Jake might be the buffalo of legend had no impact on the battle for supremacy because the other buffalo were driven by the same uncontrollable desires for dominance. The limits of Jake's physical strength, intelligence, and instincts were forged in the same contest of wills that had created the hierarchy of the buffalo herds throughout the ages. It took many seasons of these heated battles, but Jake finally became the leader of the central herd. He was in his prime.

* * * * *

It was the first day of the Annual Celebration. It had started out perfectly. The sky was a bright, bright blue for as far as an eagle could see. Panda Kim Ha had arrived on the prairie and was waiting to meet up with Buffalo Jake. The mountains in the distance were so sharply defined against the blue sky that Kim Ha felt as if this was the first time she had really seen them. They were so crystal clear that she thought she could reach out and touch them. She found herself reaching toward them with her paw. She couldn't touch them, of course. Kim Ha knew that. But she was still a little disappointed. She looked around to make sure no one had seen her, and wondered how many animals had been caught off guard pondering such things and had ended up as some carnivore's meal. Kim Ha quickly looked behind herself and sniffed the air all around. No, she was safe. No carnivores in the vicinity. The fact that the rules of the Celebration prohibited predation did little to sooth her natural instinct to sniff for carnivores anyway.

A crisp, cool breeze swept across the prairie, gently ruffling Kim Ha's fur. It was perfect weather for pandas. It was a time of anticipation as the animals waited for their instincts to drive them on to their winter ranges. Or, it was a time of waiting before the irrepressible desire to go into their dens for winter hibernation took over. But most of all, it was a time to enjoy life.

There were several games played at the Celebrations. For several seasons, Kim Ha and Jake had been partners in a game called buffalo tag. The pandas, raccoons, and rabbears would climb on to the backs of the buffalo, then one buffalo with his or her rider would stay in the middle of the prairie while the others would go to one end of the prairie. The side boundaries of the playing field were marked off with scent glands before the game started. The buffalo in the middle of the field would rear up to signal that he or she was ready. Then all the buffalo with their riders would stampede for the other side of the field. It was the object of the buffalo in the middle to maneuver so that his or her rider could tag as many of the other riders as possible as they stampeded to the other end of the field. This was difficult because the marked off part of the prairie was large enough for a buffalo to easily maneuver around the tagger. But once another rider was tagged, then that buffalo and rider went to the center of the field to become one of the taggers. The stampeding back and forth across the field would continue until there was only one buffalo and rider that had not yet been tagged. They, of course, were the winners.

Kim Ha was very much in tune with Jake's moves because they had been a team for so long. One of the tricks that Jake and Kim Ha had pioneered was buffalo hopping. The problem that buffalo hopping was designed to solve was the difficulty that taggers had with just reaching out and tagging the other rider. If it was a raccoon, the raccoon might easily move out of reach by climbing along the buffalo's back or on top of the buffalo's head. To solve this problem, Kim Ha would hop onto the other buffalo's back and tag the other rider. As a result of this technique, a new rule was instituted that if the buffalo that you had hopped on to could get to the other end of the prairie before you could hop back onto your own buffalo, then you and your buffalo were out of the game.

After four days of Celebrations, it was time to begin the winter migration. Kim Ha and Jake did not win, but they had fun all the same. Buffalo Nick and Rabbear Joe were the winners—the same pair that had such a fierce argument when they first met in the Great Valley. But they had an unfair advantage because the lack of good bamboo this season had weakened Kim Ha. After the games were over, Buffalo Jake agreed to give Kim Ha a ride back to her forest to help her conserve energy.

They were having a nice time remembering the events of the Celebration when Buffalo Jake came to a sudden stop. He blinked and squinted trying to make out the details of what he could not believe he was seeing. Jake looked back at Panda Kim Ha with a troubled expression on his face. Kim Ha climbed on top of Jake's neck for a better view. It was a brutally ruthless sight. In the distance, there was a group of chakeedas chasing down rabbears and ripping their legs off and slashing their bodies open. The chakeedas were leaving the severely wounded rabbears bleeding on the ground to die as they chased after other rabbears to kill them for the sheer joy of killing. Even from this distance, one could hear the hideous laughter pouring from the chakeedas' smiling faces. It was as though they were infected with some insidious disease that robbed them of their animality.

Buffalo Jake charged ahead. When they arrived at the site of the attack, Jake reared up on his hind legs, raising his mighty body high in the air, and let out a deafening, pain-filled scream. The power of his anguished cry was so awesome that animals across the prairie could feel its vibration hit their bodies. It was hard to believe it was coming from a single beast. Kim Ha covered her ears with her paws to try to escape the deafening sound. It seemed to go on and on, echoing off the sky and bouncing back to earth.

When his cry subsided, it seemed the entire world had fallen silent. All Kim Ha could hear was the ringing in her ears. And soon even that faded to absolute silence. Not even the wind dared rustle a leaf for fear of Buffalo Jake's wrath. The buffalo lowered his head and did not move. He stood perfectly still. A long moment past, then another. No one moved. The chakeedas stood completely still, shocked into silence. Kim Ha felt the rise and fall of Buffalo Jake's breath and her own heart beating. Another long moment passed. The soft sound of the dying rabbears whimpering rose above the silence. She desperately wanted for Jake to do something to help them, but she said nothing. She was still too awestruck by his mighty power. He stared ahead with such intensity, Kim Ha thought he might kill the chakeedas by just the sheer force of his will. She did not know what he was waiting for, but she dared not move or speak for fear of disturbing his intense concentration.

In the distance, far beyond where the chakeedas stood, Kim Ha could see a massive cloud of dust building up along the entire horizon. It kept building until it cast an erie haze over the setting sun. Kim Ha looked to each side of her. The massive cloud was coming from all directions. Then the sound came. A deep, deafening rumble. As the dust clouds approached, Kim Ha could not believe it. There were buffalo and elk and other large herd animals that lived on the prairie coming from every direction. She had little time to absorb what was happening because Jake charged ahead toward the center of the rabbear slaughter.

The chakeedas panicked. They raced in one direction, then another. With perfect precision, Jake shifted his direction for a collision course with his moving target. With every adjustment Buffalo Jake made, so too did the hooves of the charging herds as if they had somehow shifted control over their muscles to Jake. The chakeedas ran about frantically in circles until they ran back to the rabbears and grabbed some of them for protection. As the animals all converged on the rabbear slaughter, the earth rumbled and shook with such violence that Kim Ha wondered if the earth itself might not give way under the pounding force of so many angry hooves. The front of the charging herds began to arrive and come to a stop. The sound of hooves faded into the distance until the last of the animals far in the rear came to a halt. All was silent again. Not even a whimper from the dying rabbears this time.

Kim Ha tapped Buffalo Jake on the shoulder. He lowered his front legs so that she could dismount. She found Rabbear Kristin at the center of the slaughter. Kim Ha lifted Kristin's body up, but her spirit was gone. The animals waited as she went from rabbear to rabbear. When she was done, Kim Ha's white fur was covered in blood. She looked over at Buffalo Jake and spoke with her eyes. All the rabbears were dead. A light drizzle was beginning to come down.

Every animal there knew that no carnivore killed its prey this way. Buffalo Jake felt numb. He asked the question that they all shared.

"Why?"

There was no answer.

"How could you do this? Why?" asked Jake again.

"It's blood sport. You have your games, we have our's," answered a chakeeda.

Jake rose up and kicked the chakeeda in the head. The other buffalo within hearing range surged forward. The group of chakeedas were crushed within moments.

CHAPTER SEVEN

Meeting by the Sea

After the rabbear massacre, the leader of the chakeedas sent a messenger to Buffalo Jake. When the chakeeda messenger arrived at the edge of the prairie, it created somewhat of a stir among the buffalo herd. The chakeeda might have described his arrival in more dramatic terms since he was almost crushed to death under the hooves of several young males that took an instant dislike to his presence. The chakeeda would have discovered just how unwelcome he really was if it had not been for a lone oak tree on the edge of the prairie that the greasy little creature quickly climbed.

It did not take long for the news of the arrival of a chakeeda at the edge of the herd to reach Buffalo Jake. Jake showed no interest in personally investigating the matter. He had confidence that whomever was responsible for defending that sector of the herd would handle the matter appropriately. But when he was told that the chakeeda had been chased up a tree and was now trapped by a group of determined bulls, Jake had to chuckle. This might be worth seeing purely for entertainment value, Jake thought as he followed Buffalos Nick and Anthony to the scene.

When Buffalo Jake arrived, he looked up into the branches and said, "Greetings, chakeeda, you seem to have a bit of a problem."

"Are you Buffalo Jake?" asked the chakeeda.

"Maybe. If I was Buffalo Jake, what would you want to say to me?"

"First, I would complain that this is no way to treat a messenger. We don't treat your messengers this way. How is there suppose to be communication between us if you kill the messenger?" said the chakeeda.

Jake sniffed the air and said, "I don't smell the special waters of the meeting place. Didn't you bathe in the special waters?"

The chakeeda shook his head no. But not willing to concede the point, the chakeeda added, "That shouldn't make a difference. I can't smell anything special about the so-called special waters. It should not effect my status as a messenger."

"Maybe. Maybe not. Did you at least tell these buffalo that you were a messenger?" asked Jake.

The chakeeda knew that he had not, but he lied and said, "I don't remember.

They should have known anyway."

"Really? Are we to assume that you believe that my friends here were born with such knowledge that on this particular day at this particular time, a chakeeda would climb a tree with a message for me?" asked Buffalo Jake rhetorically.

The chakeeda was visibly agitated. He couldn't believe that he was losing an argument to a stupid animal. This was ridiculous. As he tried to figure out how this had happened, his thoughts were interrupted by the sound of Buffalo Jake's gravelly voice.

"What?" asked the chakeeda.

"The message?" repeated Jake. "You said that you were a messenger. Are you a messenger with a message? Or are you a messenger in search of message? Because if you are in search of a message, I'm sure that we could make one up for you."

The crowd chortled and snorted.

The chakeeda did not appreciate being made fun of, yet he also could not help but be impressed by his adversary. He had always been told that grazing animals were stupid creatures that operated purely on instinct. Buffalo Jake hardly fit that stereotype. In fact, none of these animals fit that description. But he reminded himself not to read too much into their behavior. It was very easy to imagine that they had sophisticated chakeeda-like emotions and intelligence. But, of course, such perceptions were deceptive because they were purely the product of the active imagination of the superior chakeeda mind. He had been reminded many times that he must guard against the temptation to interpret and give meaning to animal behaviors. He reassured himself that the appearance of their intelligence was nothing more than an illusion created by his own mind.

After re-gaining his composure, the chakeeda said, "Of course I have a message. The Great Leader of the chakeedas, the most high chakeeda Real, requests your presence at a meeting to occur in five days at sunrise at the meeting place by the sea. The topic shall be the massacre."

There were murmurs among the crowd of buffalo. That the chakeedas wanted to discuss the rabbear massacre was certainly a surprise.

"Will you be there?" asked the chakeeda.

"Of course. Who shall we say sent us?" asked Buffalo Jake.

"My name is Ajar. Now will you call off these wild beasts so I can leave?" asked the chakeeda.

Buffalo Jake motioned with his head and a narrow path was cleared for the chakeeda's exit. The chakeeda left quickly without incident.

* * * * *

The meeting place by the sea was located at a point that connected the prairie to the Great Valley. It was in the southeastern corner of the prairie. The chakeeda messenger had found the buffalo herd grazing along the western edge of the prairie.

There were cliffs along the southern edge of the prairie that dropped off into the Great Valley. These cliffs formed the northern rim of the Great Valley and stretched almost all the way to the sea. Right before reaching the sea, the cliffs collapsed into a gentle slope that connected the prairie to the Great Valley. This was known by all as the meeting place by the sea. There was always a steady ocean breeze at the meeting place. The tall grasses there were different from those on the prairie. They offered no resistance to the will of the wind. The slender, green reeds swirled about and danced back and forth in any pattern that brought the wind pleasure. The tranquilizing beauty of it was not lost on the animals. But most chakeedas seemed too busy to notice.

After the chakeeda messenger left, Buffalo Jake gave the order for the herd to change direction to travel southeast to the meeting place by the sea. The herd's estimated time of arrival was in four days. It was more than enough time for Jake's lieutenants to engage in all sorts of wild speculation concerning the real purpose of the meeting. Jake seemed oddly silent on the issue and never gave any real indication of which theory, if any, he thought was correct.

On the third day of the journey, Buffalo Jake grew tired of the constant speculation and began butting heads with some of his lieutenants in a manner usually reserved for only serious challenges to authority as leader of the herd. After the head butting was completed, Jake lectured his lieutenants that whatever Real had in mind for the meeting was irrelevant. He would set the agenda; not Real. Furthermore, he was most disappointed in all of them. All he had heard for the entire trip was what the chakeedas might want. That was not the issue. The issue was what could be done to control the chakeedas. That was obviously a far more difficult problem, and one that every one of his lieutenants should be thinking about if they wanted to actually do something useful rather than speculate about the whims and desires of the ugliest, smelliest little species on the planet.

After Buffalo Jake was finished with his tirade, he looked about at the faces of his lieutenants. They seemed both humbled and dumbfounded. They felt they had done nothing to provoke Buffalo Jake. Yet their expressions also indicated that they truly felt bad that they had disappointed him. Seeing this, Buffalo Jake realized that none of them had really done anything to deserve such an attack and that he was punishing them for his own sense of deep frustration at not being able to solve the chakeeda problem. He made a mental note to himself to be a better buffalo than that in the future.

"What we need is a good stampede," said Buffalo Jake to his lieutenants. All agreed. "Let's do it."

The herd was soon thundering across the prairie, giving Buffalo Jake a chance to clear his head.

* * * * *

On the morning of the meeting, the fog was extremely thick. The front line of the buffalo herd advanced toward the meeting place cautiously. As they drew closer, the buffalo could hear the chakeedas huffing, panting, and grunting their way up the gentle slope before they could see them in the heavy ocean fog. When they came into view, Buffalo Jake waited for them to catch their breath. But before Jake could say anything, the leader of the chakeedas launched into a verbal attack on Jake.

"I want the names of every single one of the buffalos that participated in the massacre!" screamed Real as best he could between breaths. "I cannot and will not stand by while wild animals senselessly slaughter innocent chakeedas! We demand that you turn these crazed beasts over to us immediately!" Real desperately gasped for air, completely red faced.

Buffalo Jake was stunned. His lieutenants were stunned. Every animal within ear shot was stunned. There was a long silence while Buffalo Jake tried to comprehend what Real was saying.

After catching his breath, Real continued, "What's the matter, oh great Buffalo Jake, you've had several days to think of an excuse for this outrageous conduct. Can't think of one? I'm not surprised. There is no justification for it. It's a disgrace to your species."

Jake began to understand what Real was doing, and the more he understood, the angrier he got. Jake's eyes narrowed and through clenched teeth he said, "I should have known that you would stoop to something like this, Real. Buffalo Lee warned me about you. He always said that you were the ultimate master at distorting reality. But not this time. You're not going to get away with it. I was there. I saw what happened! You disgusting little..."

Real began to interrupt Jake in an attempt to regain the momentum. But Jake reared up in the air and slammed his hooves right down in front of Real and screamed in Real's face, "You'll shut up and listen!"

Jake was right in Real's face now. His hot breath turning the cool morning air into a blast of steam that Real could not escape. Real's body guards took a step forward towards Jake. The herd responded instantaneously by moving forward toward the chakeedas, many lowering their heads to expose their deadly horns. This caused the body guards to stop their advance on Jake. Some sort of strange greyish-black sticks were given to the body guards from the chakeedas in the rear. The body guards whispered to themselves. There seemed to be an argument about something, but finally the body guards stepped back pulling Real with them.

Jake continued, "I was there. I saw the slaughter of the rabbears. Your chakeedas did not kill them to eat them. They did not kill them because they needed them to survive. They killed them for the pure fun of it. They killed whole families just for the sake of killing and then they laughed about it! The whole thing was sick! There was no way that I was going to stand around and watch such a massacre."

"You understand so little," said Real. "What my chakeedas did was for the good of the rabbears. We had to kill a few of them for the greater good of their species. Their habitat has been shrinking. There is less food to support the little creatures. If we did not reduce their numbers, then there would not be enough food in their home range to support them all. They would all starve to death if we did not kill some of them. So you see, what we are doing is for the greater good of their species."

"So that explains why your chakeedas were laughing so hysterically while they were massacring the rabbears? They were actually rejoicing because they were doing so much good for the rabbears, is that it?" asked Buffalo Jake.

"Well, some among us view it as a sport. They may enjoy their sport. But that doesn't change the legitimate purpose of thinning the rabbear population," said Real.

"Thinning the population?! You haven't thinned the population, you've driven the rabbears into extinction!" shouted Buffalo Jake.

"We haven't done that. Their loss of habitat was the real reason for that," said Real.

"But you caused the loss of habitat. Is their loss any less tragic just because you stole their homes and their food instead of killing them eye to eye?" asked Buffalo Jake.

"We have a right to survive, too. We need the space. Our numbers are growing rapidly," retorted Real.

"Then maybe someone should thin the chakeeda population," said Jake. This comment brought an enthusiastic response from the herd.

"It's not the same," said Real.

"Why not? It certainly would be for the greater good," said Jake.

"We are chakeedas. Don't you understand what that means?" asked Real.

"No," said Buffalo Jake.

"Well... we know what's best. We know how these things should be handled. You should trust us to manage things properly. We really do care about you," said Real grinning.

"Why do we need you to manage things? Why is it that the rules of natural balance were working just fine until you came along. Now suddenly you have to begin killing the rest of us off for our own good. Do you really expect us to accept that kind of twisted logic? Would you accept the same bizarre fate for your own species?" asked Jake.

"I don't expect you to understand, Buffalo Jake. You are not your grandfather. He would have understood. You should follow in his hoof prints," said Real.

"What nonsense. My grandfather struck a deal with the chakeedas so that we could all live in peace. You were given the entire Great Valley to do with as you pleased. I have overlooked your occasional violations of the Great Valley agreement—even though each was offensive. But the violations are no longer occasional. Chakeedas are spreading out of the Great Valley as if no agreement existed at all. I came here today to tell you that this must stop. I demand that you honor the Compromise," said Jake.

"We never agreed to stay in the Great Valley forever," said Real.

"Yes you did. It is written in the Meeting Place of the World Council of Living Things," said Jake.

"That's very nice, Jake. But my species has special wants and needs. They must be met. We have outgrown the Great Valley. We have outgrown the World Council of Living Things. We will do as we please and there is not a thing you can do about it," said Real.

Jake's lieutenants looked to Jake, waiting for him to put Real in his place. If this had been a challenge by another buffalo, Jake would have simply engaged the challenger in a head butting contest. But this was different. Real was saying that the chakeedas no longer felt obligated to play by the rules that had kept the entire planet in balance. He did not have an answer.

"We are finished here," said Real. "This time we will let you off with a warning. But if I ever hear of another attack on any of my chakeedas, I will demand the identities of the perpetrators. We can't have wild animals attacking us."

"Even when they are defending their family and friends and homes?" asked Jake.

"You are far too sentimental. Things are going to be different. Why don't you just accept that? There's nothing you can do about it," said Real.

"Don't underestimate us," said Jake.

Real ignored the remark and turned to leave with his contingency of chakeedas. When Real was out of ear shot of the Buffalos, Real turned to Ajar, his most trusted lieutenant, and whispered, "Jake is becoming too dangerous. I want him killed."

"Any suggestions on how you want it done?" asked Ajar quietly.

"Wait for the right opportunity," said Real. "I don't want there to be any way to trace his death to us."

"I will probably need Blueth to help me," said Ajar.

"That's fine," said Real.

The fog had retreated enough now to see the shore line. Real looked down at the breaking surf without seeing it. His mind was self-absorbed trying to foresee the consequences of Buffalo Jake's death. One could expect a violent reaction from the animals at first. But the violence would be random and unorganized. Maybe a few hundred chakeedas would die, but nothing significant. Not a real threat. There were no animals with the interspecies charisma that could take Buffalo Jake's place. With Jake out of the way, Real could execute on his plan to take over the leadership of the World Council of Living Things from behind the scenes. He knew better than to ban it completely. Another Council might spring up in its place. He would allow the Council to continue to oppose the chakeedas to give the animals a meaningless outlet to voice their hostility at levels controlled by Real that would be mostly harmless.

Real repeated his warning to Ajar, "Remember that it is absolutely critical that none of the animals find out that we killed Jake. If they find out, I'll have no choice but to deny any knowledge of your activities... It is for the greater good of our species. You do understand, right?"

Ajar frowned, but acknowledged his understanding with a nod.

"When I hear from you that he's dead, I'll send our deepest condolences to his herd," continued Real. "And I'll go to the World Council and hail my long time friend as a great hero. That will be good."

"You might want to remind them that your grandfather knew Jake's grandfather, Buffalo Jerid," said Ajar helpfully.

"That's good... very good... I'll be the successor to our common legacy," said Real.

Real gazed past Ajar, trying to imagine the sight of Buffalo Jake's lifeless body. Real smiled.

"I was just wondering... can I tell my friends that I killed Buffalo Jake?" asked Ajar.

"Oh, no! At least not at first... but don't worry. After Jake's dead, you will be rewarded many times over. It'll be a great day for chakeedas, Ajar... a great day indeed. Once we have control, then we can tell the rest of the chakeedas. You'll be a great hero for slaying the evil beast."

Ajar waited to be excused from Real's most honorable presence, then went off in search of his long time co-conspirator in these matters, chakeeda Blueth. They would plan the details of Jake's violent death.

CHAPTER EIGHT

The Map of the Web of Life

After the meeting with Real, Jake gave instructions to Nick regarding grazing and watering patterns for the next few days. He had some thinking to do that he had to do alone, and he told them where he would meet up with them. When they asked where he was going, he did not say. They asked him to be careful, but showed little real concern for his safety. After all, Jake was the largest, most powerful member of the herd. It was hard to imagine a predator that would try to take him down.

Jake's secret destination was the Cave of The Map. Along the way, he became absorbed in trying to figure out what made Real the way he was. Jake wondered if Real actually believe the fiction that he regularly invented. If he believe his crazed stories, then that would indicate that he had some terrible illness of spirit and couldn't be blamed for his actions. But Jake did not sense that Real was crazy. If that were the case, then he would have begun foaming at the mouth a long time ago, and all that would be left of him now would be his dried bones.

Instead, Jake suspected that Real was fully aware that his version of reality was fabricated and distorted. What troubled him deeply was how an animal could live such a lie. Was it a characteristic of the chakeeda species? Were all chakeedas like Real? The more that Jake saw of the chakeedas, the more he feared that the answer was yes. There was simply no way that Real could be individually responsible for all of the outrageous and destructive acts of so many chakeedas. Something had gone terribly wrong with the species. He needed to know why. Or at least he needed to find some answer that would give him some insight into what he should do next. He hoped to find that answer at the Cave of The Map.

The Cave of The Map was only about a days walk north along the coastal plain from where Jake had met with Real. It was early autumn. The winds were once again beginning to whip off of the ocean. The wind's cool chill made Jake hungry as it should. His body instinctively knew that there were not many good grazing days left before the snows would come and bury the best food until spring. The winds took their forewarning of winter swiftly over the rocky shore cliffs, sinking across the coastal plain on their journey to find a soft resting place among the rolling hills beyond. The grasses were still tall this late in the year. There were three different kinds that grew in this part of the prairie. Buffalo Jake stopped in early afternoon to enjoy the flavorful selection. It was during this stop that Buffalo Jake began to get an uneasy feeling that something was out of place. He looked about him and listened. He saw nothing unusual and all he could hear was the sound of the wind and the grass. He tried to sniff the air, but all he could smell were the scents from the nearby ocean. Still, he had the feeling that something was out of place. He decided it would be best to move on. Yet, the feeling continued to follow him. Sometimes the feeling was strong. Other times it seemed to fade away. The instinct to stop and graze on the autumn grasses was strong, but Jake's feeling of uneasiness kept him moving.

Suddenly something rose up from the edge of the cliff into Buffalo Jake's peripheral vision. Before Jake could react, he felt the impact of several claws on his back and then the sensation of something digging into him! Jake yelled and rose up on his hind legs trying to shake off the attack! The attacker, or attackers, Jake was not sure of the number, rose up in the air and began squawking. Jake looked up and saw that it was only a group of sea gulls.

"Sorry we startled you," said one of the sea gulls.

Jake re-composed himself and said, "It's O.K.. Glad to have the company."

The gulls landed on Jake's back again and began pecking at insects.

"By the way," said Jake, "You didn't happen to see anything unusual around here, did you?"

"Unusual? Like what?" asked one of the gulls.

"I'm not sure. Just anything."

The gulls looked at each other and spoke in their own language.

"We don't think so," said the gull that had been doing the speaking.

Jake was going to ask the gulls to fly around to take a look. Maybe it was just loneliness. Maybe not. In any case, the feeling of uneasiness was gone now so he did not say anything further. He even felt comfortable enough to stop to graze. The gulls stayed with Buffalo Jake for most of the rest of his trip to the cave. When Jake had to turn inland toward the entrance to the cave, they said their good-byes and flew away. The entrance was only a few hills away.

Jake arrived at the Cave of The Map at sunset. He was about to enter when he thought he heard something behind him again. He turned and sniffed the air. Nothing. It must be his imagination, he thought or maybe hoped. As Jake entered the cave, he looked down at the well worn greeting on the entrance floor. It said, "Welcome to the Cave of the Map. No unauthorized scent marking permitted. THAT MEANS YOU!" Jake felt sorry for any animal that violated this rule. The normally peaceful pandas that ran the operations in the cave could become quite violent when the rule was broken.

The cave itself was an amazing place. Streaked throughout the walls of the cave were veins of an interesting rock that naturally fluoresced. The rocks illuminated the interior of the cave with green, white and pink light. The interior itself was almost as large as the Meeting Place of the World Council of Living Things. But the ceiling was not as high so it did not seem as spacious.

The Map was an on-going project of the World Council of Living Things that had been established by the original founders. Its objective was to map the interrelationship of all living things. Why the founders had considered it important to do so was not known. But no one ever questioned the importance of the project. The original intent was no longer important. The Map had become a symbol of the importance of all life. It gave the animals a sense of their place in the world and a sense of belonging to the community of all living things. This symbolic meaning was important to all animals regardless of whether they ever actually saw The Map during their lifetime. The knowledge that The Map existed, and that they were on it, was enough.

The pandas were responsible for maintaining The Map. They took their duty to constantly update and expand The Map very seriously. It was the hope of all pandas that at some time during their lives, they would be selected to work on The Map. It was customary that only the most intelligent pandas were selected because The Map was far more than a complex web of patterns of lines and paw prints. Much of its information was communicated through scent. That is why the message at the entrance to the cave strictly forbade indiscriminate scent marking. The random release of territorial scent markers could seriously confuse the complex pattern of scents and potentially destroy the affected parts of The Map. While pandas were normally considered passive, animals that broke the no scent rule quickly discovered the panda's capacity for snarling and ripping out clumps of fur. Needless to say, the rule was rarely broken. The only exception to the no scent rule had to do with the construction of The Map itself.

Periodically representatives of each species would arrive to remark their scent at places on The Map specifically designated by the pandas and no where else. With so much pressure to perform, some animals froze up and could not activate their scent glands. This was most distressing because the scent glands of most animals were usually free flowing. The stress of not performing added to their anxiety, making it even more difficult to perform. The pandas had become used to dealing with this problem. They had learned the hard way not to press the issue. The story of how the pandas had learned to deal with scent anxiety problems was one of the funnier stories in the long history of the construction of The Map.

Once a boar that was new to the experience was having difficulty performing. The panda that was directing the boar had insisted that the boar try harder. But the harder the boar tried, the more his scent glands dried up, which only made the panda more impatient. When the panda started squealing at the boar, the boar began to panic, which caused his scent glands to completely open up. When the panda smelled the excess discharge of pheromones, he started screaming for the boar to stop. But the boar couldn't, so the panda reached toward the boar to cover the boar's scent glands with his paws. Unfortunately, the boar thought he was being attacked and raced about the cave in a complete panic spewing boar pheromones everywhere. It was a complete disaster. The pandas were much more patient with poor performers after that and obtained much better results.

On this particular day, a raccoon and a platypus were patiently waiting just inside the cave for instructions on where to mark their scent. Their eyes grew wide when they saw Buffalo Jake come in. They looked at each other, not sure if it was really him. They had only met him once before at a meeting of the World Council of Living Things. After a moment, Jake noticed the two animals backed up against a wall to his side. At first they seemed frozen. Jake leaned down to check to see if they were breathing. When he did, he recognized both of them and greeted them both by name. They were so surprised and honored that Buffalo Jake had remembered their names that they were barely able to squeak out a reply.

They both had day dreamed about what they would tell Buffalo Jake if they ever had a private audience with him. But now that the moment had unexpectedly arrived, they could barely compose a complete thought in their species language, let alone in the universal language of animals. Jake sensed their dilemma and told them that it was a pleasure seeing them again, but he was on official business so he could not talk right now. But he would like to consult with them later if they had time. They gratefully agreed to a later discussion.

Jake stepped further into the interior of the cave and took a moment to allow his eyes to adjust to the strange colored florescent light. The pandas at work on The Map looked up to see who had entered. They motioned their greetings, but returned to their work. Everyone continued working except for Panda Jee Young, who came over to greet Buffalo Jake. Panda Jee Young had been in charge of all operations in the Cave of The Map for the past 16 seasons. How the pandas had come to dominate the management of The Map Project was a long story that no one could remember in any detail. This was surprising because the pandas were also in charge of recording the history of such things, but somehow they had overlooked their own role in the creation of The Map.

Panda Jee Young was well suited to her job. She was a no-nonsense panda that kept operations running efficiently and was far more high strung than most pandas. Considering the shear size of The Map Project and energy required to run it, such a trait was extremely valuable. Over the past 16 seasons, Panda Jee Young's name had become synonymous with the project. It was hard to imagine how the operation had ever worked before her arrival and how it could survive if she ever left.

In her typically efficient way, her greeting of Buffalo Jake was short and to the point. She asked if there was anything special that Buffalo Jake needed. Jake said no, he was just here to do some studying. Jee Young said that she would like to serve as Jake's escort, but she knew that he could find his way around the cave without her. And since she had other business to attend to, she would be getting back to her work if Jake did not mind. Jake did not mind at all. In fact, he insisted. Jake was most grateful that Jee Young ran the cave, but she was such a high strung creature, it made Jake nervous when he had to spend very much time with her.

Jake walked slowly back to the part of the cave that he had come to see. He had been there many times before. He was in no rush to get there. It was that part of The Map where the chakeedas had been placed by Buffalo Jerid a long time ago. This part of The Map was so highly sensitive that even Panda Jee Young was not authorized to make any changes. Even the slightest modification had to be approved by a two-thirds vote of the World Council of Living Things. Jake's grandfather had instituted this rule with the full knowledge that the World Council of Living Things had never approved anything by a two-thirds vote. Getting so many different species to agree on anything by even a simple majority was difficult enough—a two-thirds vote was virtually impossible. So as a practical matter, the chakeeda portion of The Map was the only portion that had never changed.

Jake had come to study this part of The Map many times in the past two seasons in the hope of finding some insight into the chakeeda problem. Jake kept hoping that Buffalo Jerid's wisdom from an earlier time would deliver him from his confusion. But it was not a simple kind of wisdom to understand. His grandfather had created the most intricate and complicated section of The Map in his effort to make a place for the chakeedas. Few animals were capable of understanding it. Jake thought he understood it at times, but then the feeling of comprehension would slip away into the maze of lines and symbols before him. It was a terribly frustrating process.

The pandas had moved a part of The Map near where Buffalo Jake was working so that Jake could have a portion of the cave floor to make his own calculations. He would study Buffalo Jerid's work for long periods of time, then erupt with a frenzy of hoof scratching of his own in the work area. When Jake needed a clean floor, he simply rolled back and forth on his back to clear his previous markings. This process would go on and on until he would finally, exhausted, drift into sleep. When he awoke, he would go outside for a drink of water and a few blades of grass, then return to his work to do it all over again.

After many days, this process had brought him to one undeniable conclusion. It was the one conclusion that he had feared the most and would have done anything to avoid. But there was no avoiding it. No matter how he approached the problem, all of his ecological calculations came out the same way. His grandfather had been wrong. Buffalo Jerid's calculations had been based on outrageously optimistic factual assumptions about the carrying capacity of the Great Valley, the World, and the needs of the chakeedas. Even in his grandfather's time, the assumptions had been so optimistic that he had to engage in the most elaborate of calculations to justify them. Other animals had attributed the complexity of the calculations to his grandfather's brilliance instead of realizing that they were a way of concealing potentially dangerous misconceptions. It was very difficult for Buffalo Jake to admit to himself that Buffalo Jerid was not the legendary leader that animal lore had made him out to be. Not only was he not a heroic leader, it was arguable that his grandfather had helped lay the foundation for the disaster that now faced the planet by striking a deal with the chakeedas based upon facts that were mostly fantasy.

Buffalo Jake had spent days trying to find some justification for what Buffalo Jerid had done. But even when Jake used the most optimistic assumptions that he dare, the conclusion was the same: the chakeedas had no place on The Map. Anywhere they were put on The Map destroyed the ecological balance of the web of life around them. When one calculated the long term effects, the destructive presence of the chakeedas spread out over the entire map at an ever accelerating rate with no natural barrier of any kind. The only limits seemed to be their own capacity to destroy themselves. But even then, it was too late for most species on the planet.

Buffalo Jake kept on making calculations. He was plagued by self-doubt that his skills at computation might not be good enough for the task. He checked and double checked everything he did. There was also another problem. No animal had ever been confronted with this kind of challenge before. His calculations were purely theoretical. The whole thing could be wrong. He had no practical way to test the accuracy of any of it in the real world. His worry and doubt could be seen in his broad, powerful face. Jee Young's assistant, Panda Soo Young, approached him.

"Excuse me, I know you're busy. But there is something that I need to talk to you about," said Soo Young. Jake raised his head. Soo Young continued.

"They're ripping holes in The Map. We've been trying to repair them, but we can't. I think we're going to reach a critical point soon, and the entire web is going to rip apart. I just don't know what to do anymore. I feel so bad about it. I just don't know what to do," said Soo Young, her voice trailing off.

"Don't worry. We're going to take care of it," said Buffalo Jake. Jake would have liked to have offered Soo Young more encouragement to reassure her. But it was sometimes better to convey strength through silence, especially when one's own shaky voice might betray one's own fear and doubt.

"There's work to be done," Jake said as firmly as he could. Soo Young accepted that and returned to her own project for the day feeling a little better.

There was no avoiding it. If the world was to be saved, the chakeedas would have to be removed from The Map. There was only one way that happened to any species. They would have to be driven into extinction. Jake had no idea how to do it, but it would have to be done. He instinctively knew that such a monumental task would require the cooperation of the entire World Council of Living Things. Yet, it would be impossible for all of the animals to understand his ecological calculations. He instinctively realized that he could not appeal to just their sense of reason. He would have to appeal to their passion. He would have to inspire them with a sense of outrage, injustice, and terrible danger. Jake thought that the chakeedas had already done most of his work for him.

Buffalo Jake looked over his grandfather's work one last time. There was no longer any question in his mind that Buffalo Jerid had been wrong. He inhaled deeply and exhaled slowly. He was relieved. The confusion that had paralyzed him was now gone.

As Buffalo Jake left The Cave, Panda Jee Young asked, "Are you finished?"

"Yes, I am," said Buffalo Jake.

"Did you find what you were looking forward?" asked Jee Young.

"No, not really," said Jake. "But I did find the truth."

"That's a very difficult thing to find," said Jee Young.

"Yes it is," said Jake "And a very difficult thing to know what to do with once you find it."

"Listen to your heart. Your heart will know what to do with it," said Jee Young.

Buffalo Jake was genuinely surprised by Jee Young's comment. He thought that he had understood her. But she was clearly more contemplative than he had believed.

"Thank you," said Jake. "I will listen to my heart. But my heart is sometimes angry."

"As it should be," said Jee Young.

Jake shook his massive head in agreement and stepped out of the cave into the night air. He had no idea what day it was or what time it was. It did not matter. He was at peace with himself.

The night was moonless. Jake sniffed the air. The ocean was close enough for the on shore breeze to whined itself through the foothills to the mouth of the cave. It smelled good. But not as good as the familiar smells of the prairie. The thought of home made Jake anxious to get back to his herd. He had not thought much about the herd over the past few days. But now it was time to return to consult with his lieutenants to make plans for an emergency meeting of the World Council of Living Things.

* * * * *

Ajar and Blueth were not stupid. They had been waiting far down wind of the cave for the last few days ever since they followed Jake there. Ajar had been napping when Blueth shook him awake in time to see Buffalo Jake exit the cave and bid his farewell. They smiled at each other in the darkness. It was a perfect night for an assassination.

Buffalo Jake had just disappeared from view of the cave when he heard someone call his name. He stopped to listen. He heard someone racing toward him, but he could not see any shapes. He heard his name again. It was a familiar voice this time. Then she came into view. It was panda Kim Ha.

"Hi, Jake," said Kim Ha. "I was wondering if you could give me a ride back to the base of my mountain?"

"Of course," said Jake. "I had no idea that you were working in The Cave now. I didn't see you in there. Why didn't you say hi?"

"You seemed so engrossed in what you were doing, I didn't want to disturb you. It looked important," said Kim Ha.

Jake sunk down to his knees so that Kim Ha could hop on his back.

"Are you ready?" asked Jake.

"Ready," said Kim Ha.

Together, they slipped off into the darkness. Ajar and Blueth cursed their luck, but did not bother to follow them. Their instructions were clear. There were to be no witnesses. If the panda managed to escape, it would be disastrous. Buffalo Jake's assassination would have to wait.

CHAPTER NINE

The Emergency Meeting of the World Council of Living Things

At the emergency meeting of the World Council, the animals were nervously waiting for Buffalo Jake to arrive. Never before had the animals shared such a feeling that something very serious was wrong. Something very dangerous was lurking close to them. It was hard for them to describe to each other. They tried to compare it to the sense of foreboding before a large, powerful storm, or the quick rush of fear when being chased by a predator, or the feeling of danger when one smelled smoke from an approaching forest fire. All of those situations described a part of the feeling and all were also inadequate. Maybe the real difference was that this fear was not going to go away. It stayed with them when they were resting in their nests and burrows. It remained with them throughout the day no matter where they went. It compelled them to look behind them even when they knew there was nothing there. It was a new kind of fear that drained the most basic joy from life because it never left and could not be fought. If the chakeedas did to their home ranges what they did to the Great Valley, there would be no place to stand, no food to eat, no water to drink, and no place to sleep. How could anyone fight that?

The more that the animals talked among themselves, the more uneasy they became. Would every jungle, forest, and prairie be turned into the hideous, poisoned wasteland that was now the Great Valley? When Buffalo Jake arrived, the whispered conversations exploded into a thousand shouted questions. The representatives for the elk, antelope, gazelles were the most panicked. The Great Valley was the only route to their winter grazing grounds. If they could not make it through the Great Valley, they would starve to death. The big cats had been trying to maintain their typical aloof attitude. But when the elk's representative explained the gravity of the situation, the big cats suddenly took an interest in the conversation. Not because the big cats were great friends of the migratory herds, but if all of them died of starvation, what would the big cats eat? With the realization that their favorite prey would not survive the winter, the leopards and lions became quite vocal with their growls and hisses insisting that something had to be done and soon.

Jake spoke up. The great buffalo said in his deep voice what was in the back of everyone's mind, "The chakeedas must be hunted before they drive us all into extinction." He said it calmly without emotion as though it were a simple, unavoidable fact. The entire meeting fell silent. During the silence, everyone's head turned toward the great carnivores. If the chakeedas were to be hunted, the responsibility would fall on the carnivores. Everyone waited for the carnivores to speak. The representative of the great leopard spoke first. She said, "It is not possible." She paused and scanned the meeting as though there was nothing more to be said. As though everyone should naturally understand why it was not possible. She then went back to grooming herself as though the issue were closed. Of course, she was right. Everyone did understand why it was not possible.

Whether it was instinctual knowledge or learned through generations of experience was not known. But everyone knew the rule of natural balance. The rule of natural balance stated that if an increase in the number of predators caused a decrease in the number of prey, then it was a natural rule that the number of births would increase among the prey in the next birthing season to compensate for the loss caused by the predators. If for some reason there was not an increase in births, maybe because of not enough food for the mothers to eat that season, then the rule stated that there would be a drop in the number of predators. If the number of lions increased and ate more zebras, then the zebras knew that there would be more baby zebras born in the spring if food was plentiful or else there would be fewer lions next year. The process was chaotic at times, but the rule of natural balance prevented any animal from being driven into extinction by any other animal under normal circumstances. Hence, it was obvious to all that it was not possible to hunt the chakeedas into extinction.

Then the panther spoke. "Who eats chakeedas, anyway?" The carnivores looked among themselves to see who was going to take responsibility. But it soon became apparent that no one was instinctively assigned to eat chakeedas. This was truly bizarre. The animals looked about at each other with puzzled expressions, tilting their heads from one side to the other. How could it be possible that the chakeedas could have no natural predators? It made no sense at all. Up until this point, many of the animals still had privately hoped that the chakeeda problem would resolve itself. That nature would take its course and the natural order of things would soon be restored. But if the chakeedas did not have a natural predator... Ever so slowly, the implications of this strange fact started to sink in. The chakeedas seemed to be able to find food everywhere. In the jungles, in the forests, on the prairies...If they could find food anywhere, then what was stopping them from living everywhere? With no natural predators and no limit to what they could eat, it seemed inevitable that they would simply take over jungle after jungle, forest after forest, savanna after savanna until they took over the entire planet! The whole planet would soon look like the Great Valley!

The representative from the badgers took the floor and began to speak in his impatient manner. "Are we just going to give up? Is that it?! Are we going to let these insane creatures ruin the entire planet! Well, poor, poor us. If we're not willing to put an end to this insanity, then maybe we all deserve to die! I for one do not intend to stand around licking my fur and grooming myself waiting for death. I vote for action! If all predators were to commit themselves to a steady diet of chakeedas, then certainly we could reduce their numbers."

"WE? WE!?", screamed the representative of the mountain lions. "Have you ever tasted chakeeda!? They're stringy, bitter, and very hard to digest. Furthermore, they have no understanding of the natural rules. Even after you've killed one of them and have one half eaten, the others still try to rescue the body. They're crazy. What do they want with a dead body? One time they chased me for half a day after I killed one. They are very strange creatures, very unpredictable. That's dangerous. So it's just not as simple as the predators agreeing to eat chakeeda because the chakeedas simply do not understand the natural rules."

The badger was not willing to give up so easily. "Well, what if the predators kill them and the scavengers eat them. I know that no chakeeda is going to take lunch away from any member of my species!" said the badger with obvious pride.

The mountain lion responded, "If they can take a kill away from me, then they could take it from you."

The badger relied heavily on his mean and stubborn reputation to discourage other animals from stealing his food. The badger could not let the mountain lion make such an insulting comment without taking action. He lunged at the mountain lion with claws out and teeth showing. The mountain lion counterattacked, sending the badger sailing into the side of the panther representative who tried to nonchalantly pretend that he did not feel it, even though the force of the impact had knocked the wind out of him. The badger charged again and crashed into the lion sending the two rolling across the ground, viciously growling and hissing the entire time.

The bears allowed the fight to continue until Jake indicated with a nod of his massive head for them to put an end to it. The two bears waded through the crowd of animals and simply picked up the two fighters and dropped them on the ground from a significant height. This put things in proper perspective for the badger and mountain lion as both looked up at the massive bears. Each was easily many times the size of the mountain lion. Together they made a formidable force. A ripple of amused noises came from the crowd.

Jake brought the delegation back to order and said, "If the badger and mountain lion are finished demonstrating their superior survival skills, would they mind if we returned to the chakeeda problem so that we can get out of here?" Everyone was certainly for that idea because the cave was getting hot and many of the delegates were already panting.

As the discussion continued, it became apparent that there were many fundamental practical problems with the carnivores trying to hunt the chakeedas out of existence. The representative from the armadillos estimated that the chakeeda population currently stood at about two million. The armadillos had a constant fascination with numbers. No one knew if the numbers recited by the armadillos were actually correct, but no one else had any better estimate even though two million seemed like a very high number.

"So", asked the armadillo, "how many zebras, elk, caribou, and other prey do the carnivores eat each year?"

Neither the carnivores or any of the herd animals knew the exact figure, but all agreed that the number was not anywhere near two million.

"Therefore", continued the armadillo, "it would take several years at the very least to hunt the chakeedas out of existence even if there was an increase in the carnivore population. And during that time, what would happen to the great migratory herds if their populations are not kept in check?"

Everyone agreed the armadillo's question was a very good one. The migratory herds naturally tended to have the largest populations among the mammals. So fluctuations in the sizes of the great herds tended to effect everyone. Different theories were discussed for controlling the herd populations. But all were rejected by the herd representatives as being unworkable. Because of the apparent resistance of the great herds to population control, the badger accused them of trying to benefit from the chakeeda crisis at the expense of the other animals.

The caribou representative took the floor to respond to the accusation, "Obviously, the chakeeda problem threatens the great herds more than anyone else right now. Even though the caribou do not use the Great Valley as a route to our winter grazing grounds, other herd animals here do. So you have no right to accuse us of trying to benefit from this great tragedy. Furthermore, we are all concerned about what will happen. There is only so much good grazing ground available. If our populations explode, then certainly the prairies and savannas will be grazed out by midsummer. Few of us would survive the fall migration south if our stomachs were empty before we even began. So I move that not all of the carnivores be assigned to chakeeda extinction. Some need to continue to control the size of the herds. For example, I think the timber and arctic wolves should be exempt."

This brought immediate and angry objections from the zebras and gazelles. The Zebra representative took the floor and said, "Obviously, the great representative from the caribou is trying to exempt the wolves because the wolves hunt caribou. But where does that leave population control for the migratory herds on the savanna? If the wolves are going to be exempt, then the big cats should also be exempt."

At this point, the meeting deteriorated into a shouting match with everyone growling and snarling over whose plan was the best. Jake looked down on the confusion from his platform. The scene was quite disappointing. The cave had gotten unbearably hot. There wasn't an animal in the place that was not panting, except of course for the marine mammals that had all taken to the water. Along with the heat, the confusion of animal scents was adding to the agitation of the crowd. The arguments had activated just about everyone's territorial and warning scent glands. This only made matters worse and caused a few skirmishes to break out among natural rivals. Clearly, it was going to take more than a few bears wading into the crowd to get things back under control.

With a nod of his head and a knowing look, Jake signaled to the gray and sperm whales in the lagoon to cool the meeting down. In perfect unison, both whales raised their massive tail fins high out of the water and brought them crashing down sending a wall of water over the crowd. Many tried to escape the miniature tidal wave, but there was nowhere in the cave that was out of range of the whales. The whales repeated the procedure several times until everyone was thoroughly soaked. When the whales were done, the cave had cooled considerably and the territorial scents had been washed away. Everyone was much calmer, even the badger seemed subdued by the experience. Jake waited until the dolphin and sea turtle representatives had rescued the small animals that had been washed into the lagoon before he resumed the meeting.

Everyone looked up at Jake and waited. He was looking back at them without really seeing them as though he were somewhere far away. He let out a heavy, painful sigh, hung his head and began to speak in a deep, but soft voice.

"You do not understand. You simply do not understand. Look around you. Haven't you noticed? Doesn't the meeting seem at little less crowded?"

The animals looked about. It was true. Not everyone was here. The representative from the snow leopards was not there. Indeed, there were several species that were not represented. The cave suddenly seemed very large without them.

Jake continued, "Haven't you wondered why there are some species missing? Well, it's not because they didn't want to come because I am sure that they would very much like to be here right now. They're not here because they couldn't come. Because they can't be here. Because they're dead! The chakeedas killed them all. They killed them for pleasure. They killed them for food. They killed them for their skins, and they killed them for their horns! They destroyed their homes and drove them away from their watering holes and sometimes the chakeedas simply took all the water and food for themselves leaving them to die from thirst and starvation."

81

What Jake was saying sounded just too strange and too scary to the animals to be true. How could the chakeedas do that and why would they do that? There were murmurs among the representatives that Jake must not be feeling well.

Panda Pei Woo politely interrupted Jake and said, "Well, maybe they couldn't make it to the meeting. Or maybe they're just late. You know that snow leopard, what's his name, he'll show up with some funny story about why he couldn't make it. Or maybe..."

"NO!", yelled Jake angrily. "He's not coming. Not now! Not tomorrow. Not ever again. He's dead. He is gone forever! All snow leopards are gone forever because they're all dead! Why can't you understand that? You, Pei Woo, of all animals should understand that. You saw the chakeedas slaughter the rabbears. You heard their hideous laughter. You saw the sick gleam in their eyes!"

Pei Woo stared down at the water lapping at the banks of the lagoon and wished she could just run far, far away. Jake turned his attention to the delegates.

"Most of you have seen what has happened to the Great Valley. Or have you also forgotten? Well let me refresh your memories," said Jake.

Jake motioned to three members of his herd that were standing at the opening to the cave to bring in the first witness. The first animal to be escorted in was a brown bear. The delegates gasped and many turned their heads when they realized who it was. Her name was Nicole. To many, she was known as the peace keeper. Her mere presence frequently had the effect of settling disputes over territory and resources. But what the delegates saw now was an animal close to death. Her once powerful body had withered to half its former size. Her face looked tired and her eyes seemed glazed over.

As she tried to lift herself onto the stage, she was able to raise her body half way, but then her strength would give out and she would fall back to the ground letting out a pained whimper when she hit. Before she would have been able to leap up on the stage without any effort at all. But now after her third try, she was forced to rest a minute to regain some strength. Jake surveyed the delegates and saw their pained expressions.

The delegate from the flying squirrels spoke up, "This is cruel, Jake. Is this really necessary?"

Jake said nothing. He had a point to make, and he knew Nicole understood.

But when it was apparent that Nicole was not going to make it on her fourth try, Jake motioned to Buffalo Nick to assist her. With his broad forehead, Nick was able to help lift Nicole onto the stage. She collapsed on the stage and rested a moment before trying to approach Jake.

Nicole could feel herself drifting off. She was no longer a part of her body. She floated above it and look down wondering to whom it belonged. But before she could drift away, Jake gently nuzzled her face.

Jake whispered to her softly, "Nicole, please don't fade on me now. You've come all this way to tell your story... please... it's important... The animals don't understand... you have to explain what happened."

Nicole was not responding. Jake continued, "I'm sorry, but you can't sleep... we need you now. Please, Nicole, wake up."

Jake gently nudged her head up. Nicole opened her eyes and looked out on all the animals. She knew Jake was right. She had to warn them. When she tried to hobble to the middle of the stage, all the animals could now clearly see that Nicole's had lost her right hind leg. The stub of her leg was a terrible mess. It was still raw and inflamed in places and caked with dried blood in others. How she could still be alive, no one knew.

Before beginning her story, Nicole tried to position herself to ease the throbbing pain in her stub, but no position seemed to help. Jake sat down behind her so that she could lean against him for support. This seemed to make the pain tolerable. Not so much because it eased the physical pain, it did not, but rather because the closeness of his body gave her warmth and her mind a warm sense of friendship and security that she desperately needed. Feeling Jake's strength, and seeing her many friends in front of her, she knew that she was finally home. Her nightmarish ordeal would soon be over.

Nicole began speaking, "I was foraging in the forest... at the bottom of the white cap mountains. Everything was fine... it was a very nice day for foraging... a very lazy day... I decided to start up the mountain... you know, it's a beautiful view up there."

Nicole turned to Jake and asked in a faded voice, "Have you been to the mountains, Jake? They're beautiful."

"No, I haven't. But I'm sure it's nice", Jake said patiently.

Nicole continued, "Sometimes I'd go up there and just sit and look out over the valley. It was so quiet there... It was especially nice late in the season when the leaves change."

Nicole closed her eyes and rested her head against Jake's body and let her mind drift off to her mountains. Jake was trying his best to stay calm, but this wasn't working. Nicole used to be so strong and powerful. The sun would be setting soon, which meant that the cave would be too dark to continue the meeting.

Jake let Nicole rest for a few moments, then said, "Nicole, please... try to concentrate... please try to remember... what did the chakeedas do to you?"

Nicole opened her eyes and looked at her throbbing, bloodied stub. She started quietly crying as she realized things would never be the same again... that she would die living this horrid nightmare. Her hate for the chakeedas gave her the strength to continue.

"I was foraging... and I started up the mountain... I picked up the scent of blueberries. When I followed the scent, I found a beautiful thicket of blueberries. I should have known that something was wrong because I picked up the scent of chakeedas when I got closer. I remember that I stopped and sniffed around, but the scent seemed so faint. And I remember thinking that I must be imagining it because I had never seen a chakeeda this far north. But when I got to the blue berries, the chakeeda scent was just too strong to ignore. So I sniffed the ground and sure enough, the chakeedas had been there. But not recently. The scent was at least three days old. So... I... I started eating the blueberries... and when I waded into the thicket... that's when it happened." Nicole looked down at her stub and covered her face with her paws trying to hide her tears.

Jake said, "Please, Nicole, tell us what happened."

Nicole continued, her voice barely a whimper, "Your not going to believe this- I still don't understand it myself- but when I stepped into the thicket, this thing... I still don't know how to describe it... this thing... this mouth with horrible teeth... it attacked me... it was made of something... like stone... but stronger... the pain... it was terrible... its mouth closed over my leg and wouldn't let go... it bit through my muscles to the bone... when I tried to struggle, it scraped my bone... I can't describe the pain it was so horrible... I kept crying for help... but no one could hear me..."

"Was it alive?" asked Jake.

84

"No," answered Nicole. "At first I thought it must be alive... it had the scent of chakeeda all over it... but it wasn't alive... Like I said, it was like stone, but sharper and stronger. And it was attached to a vine, not really a vine... but like a vine that was made out of the same stone-like stuff and the vine was wrapped around a tree. I tried and tried to bite it, but it was so sharp and strong that it broke my teeth and made my mouth bleed. But I kept trying anyway, but it just wouldn't break... I couldn't believe it... I even tried knocking down the tree.. but it was much too big...

"The pain was just too great and I blacked out. I don't know how long I was out, but when I woke up it was dark. When I looked at my leg, it had swelled up to three times its normal size... it had swelled up around the thing so that I could barely see it... I just kept looking at it thinking this had to be a nightmare... that this couldn't really be happening... I tried to sleep, but it hurt too much... my leg just kept throbbing and aching terribly... it felt like my skin was going to burst if my leg got any bigger... I think I finally fell asleep again... I'm not sure...

"But in the morning, I woke up and smelled a strong scent of chakeeda. I opened my eyes and standing just a body length in front of me were two chakeedas. They seemed to be speaking to each other... but they were just making noises... they weren't speaking words... from the way they were acting, I could tell that they were not sure whether I was dead or alive... I didn't think they saw me open my eyes so I closed them again... I could hear and smell them slowly approach me...

"I waited until I could smell them right in front of me, then I exploded at them! I grabbed one and knocked the other to the ground. I snapped the neck of the one in my grasp and reached for the other, ripping into its leg. But it scrambled out of my reach. When I jumped for the chakeeda, the stone teeth yanked me back. The pain in my leg was so great that I was sure lightening struck it. When I realized what it was, I attacked the stone vine again. That's when I heard the laughter... that unmistakably hideous sound of chakeeda laughter. I wanted to attack him, but I felt very tired and dizzy... and I was so very thirsty... my head felt as if it were burning... so I just growled at him and laid down facing it to rest. He stopped laughing and started examining his own leg. He was bleeding pretty badly. I don't remember what happened after that."

Nicole stopped to catch her breath, She was wheezing badly, but she wanted to finish her story.

She continued, "I must have blacked out after that because when I woke up, both chakeedas were gone. After that I don't remember things too well... I would wake up because of the pain and see my leg... it was so big... it wasn't even a part of me any more... then I would fall asleep... my head would get so hot and ache... and everything seemed so blurry... and I was just so thirsty... I remember dreaming about water... then waking up with my tongue feeling like it was so big that I would choke...

"I don't know how many days passed... but then I heard the sound of chakeedas again... but this time there were many more of them... I knew they were coming to get me...I had no choice... I really didn't have a choice, Jake... no choice at all... I had to do it... I had to bite off my own leg to escape." Nicole closed her eyes to rest.

One of the buffalo that had escorted Nicole in continued the story, "We found her on the bank of the river at the bottom of the white cap mountains. At first we thought she was dead. But then she started whimpering. With the help of a troop of orangutans, we were able to revive her enough for her to tell her story."

Another one of the buffalo that had escorted Nicole interrupted, "They were not orangutans, they were monkeys." The first buffalo insisted they were orangutans. This led to a small argument over the difference between orangutans and monkeys. When the two buffalo saw Jake's icy stare of disapproval, they quickly decided that the animals that had helped them must have been orangutans with tails, even though everyone knew that no such species existed. Jake simply shook his head.

"Anyway," said the first buffalo, "we took turns carrying her and got here as soon as we could. Some wolves went to find the thing that attacked her."

Nicole was visibly drained from telling her story so Pei Woo and Kim Ha helped her to a cool spot at the back of the stage to rest. Jake had the buffalo bring in the next witnesses. Each animal had a story to tell that was at least as horrifying as Nicole's. Some told of their homes being needlessly destroyed by the chakeedas. Others told of their children being beaten to death by the chakeedas, then their young bodies ruthlessly stripped of their fur. Those parents that tried to defend their children were slaughtered. Still others told of ground in the Great Valley burning their feet and the water burning their mouths.

86

By the time the last witness was finished, the delegates' compassion for Nicole had turned to seething anger at the chakeedas. The carnivores were hissing, growling, and snarling at the thought of sinking their teeth into the chakeedas. They bared their teeth and took swings at thin air imagining their claws striking chakeeda flesh. All the animals were in a frenzy, boasting of what they would do to the chakeedas. This is what Jake had wanted. The animals were finally understanding that the chakeedas were their only real enemy.

But Panda Kim Ha soon changed the mood when she said, "You may be mad now, I am too, but don't forget the Rule of Natural Balance. We can't fight natural rules. I don't see how we can fight the chakeedas. We must find another way."

The animals murmured among each other that what Kim Ha said was true. The situation seemed hopeless.

Jake had worked too hard to get the delegates to this point of understanding to let Kim Ha ruin his plan now. Jake charged to center stage, almost trampling Kim Ha under his hooves.

"Kim Ha is wrong! Don't you see?" yelled Jake, "The chakeedas have broken the Rule of Natural Balance. They have not only broken it, they have destroyed it. They've replaced it with a whole new set of rules and under the new rules, only the chakeedas survive. Oh, if you're lucky, maybe you won't be in their way today. But someday you will be, and when you are, they won't hesitate to wipe you out. Some of them may pay lip service to the Rule of Natural Balance, but in the end, you, your children, your homes, your food will be wiped out under the new rule.

"So don't you understand? If the chakeedas are not going to obey the Rule of Natural Balance, then we can't either. We must kill the chakeedas, not for food or for immediate personal safety, but rather we must kill them for the survival of us all. We must kill them all!"

The animals were silent. They were all trying to absorb what Jake was saying. It was a strange idea. The predators killed out of instinct. There were several instincts that would drive them to kill. But none had ever felt an instinct within them to exterminate an entire species for the sake of survival. Jake felt the momentum slipping away. His mind was racing to find the right words to fight the collective sense of hopelessness when a pack of seven grey wolves came charging into the cave and leaped onto the platform.

Three of the wolves dropped strange objects from their mouths. The objects made a eery sound when they hit the stone floor of the stage; a sound that none of the animals had ever heard before. The scent of these strange objects slowly drifted through the air of the cave. The scent was unmistakably chakeeda. But there was also another scent. A scent of blood. But not chakeeda blood. It was the scent of the blood of bear and wolf. The objects had strange teeth and on the teeth of two of the objects was the dried blood and fur of a bear. On the third, the blood and fur of a wolf. Certainly everyone had seen the signs of death before. Death was a part of the Natural Balance. But this was different. Every animal could smell the oppressive scent of evilness that rose from these foreign objects.

"This is how the chakeedas would have you die! And this is how the chakeedas would have you watch your children die!" Jake screamed.

The animals stared at the hideous objects of death at Jake's hooves. The animals looked about at each other. All were finally beginning to understand. The chakeedas were no longer animals. They were no longer one of them. What ever they were now, they would have to be killed if the animals were to survive.

"Then it's settled," Jake said, "The chakeedas will be destroyed."

All shook their heads in agreement. No one bothered to ask how Jake thought it would be done because everyone now understood that it must be done. They knew that when the time came, Jake would tell them what to do. The meeting was over.

As the delegates began to leave, Pei Woo came up and stood next to Jake.

"Jake...Nicole..," began Kim Ha.

"I know," said Jake. Elephant Jabari wrapped his trunk around Nicole's body and promised to find a proper resting place before her remains were returned to the cycle of life by the scavengers.

It was dusk when the animals filed out of the cave. The sun was just disappearing on the horizon. The clouds were a beautiful collage of purples, blues, reds, and oranges when the animals walked down to the river to drink. They all sat in silence and watched the clouds fade as the moon replaced the sun. No one dared moved for a long time. The sound of the chakeeda traps still echoed in their minds.

CHAPTER TEN

Jake's Dream

The day after the World Council's meeting at which Nicole had told her story, Buffalo Jake was quietly grazing with his herd, trying to sort through all the comments made by the other animals. He was so emotionally exhausted that all the ideas just mushed together into an indecipherable mess. He knew he needed to give it a rest. The grass was fresh and had a good flavor to it this time of year. It was tangy, and a little sweet, but not too juicy. Jake liked that best. It formed a good cud for ruminating. As he munched on his cud, his mind drifted back to the chakeeda problem off and on all afternoon. Occasionally, one of his herd would ask him if he was having any luck, but he would have to shake his head no. Sometimes birds would sit on his head and make suggestions. But none of their ideas seemed very well thought out to Jake. He concluded that a bird could just fly away if the plan fell apart. That's why their plans all seemed to him to be slightly shortsighted.

By dusk, Jake was becoming quite depressed. He started to wonder if it was even possible for him to conceive of a way of killing so many chakeedas. Jake thought that maybe the problem was the fact that he was a herbivore. Maybe if he was a carnivore, then he could figure out a way to kill chakeedas. This made him wonder whether herbivores and carnivores really thought that much differently. Jake tried to imagine what he would do if he was a carnivore. He supposed that he would want to eat them. But there just were not enough carnivores to do the job. Anyway, everyone knew that the carnivores were lousy hunters. Sure, they growled a lot and were certainly dangerous. But they were actually very inefficient. Usually, their efforts were wasted because their prey either out ran them or outsmarted them most of the time. Jake concluded that a massive attack by carnivores would never work.

It was dusk when Jake led his herd down to the river for the evening drink. It was after this ritual when Jake's lieutenants usually reported the day's activities to him. These reports included any changes in the hierarchy under him as a result of successful challenges by younger buffalo. His lieutenants also reported any defections to other herds as well as any births or deaths. But most importantly, Jake received recommendations on which direction the herd should be taken the next day for the best grazing. Normally, Jake was an attentive listener. But this evening his mind kept drifting off to think about the chakeeda situation. Or more accurately, Jake was frustrated by the total lack of thoughts he was having on the subject. He started to wonder if maybe he should resign from the leadership of the World Council of Living Things. Maybe he just wasn't good enough.

As Jake pondered the thought of resigning, he heard the voice of one of his lieutenants ask, "So which way shall we go tomorrow?"

Jake realized that he had not heard a word they had said. He looked about at their broad, powerful faces and decided to bluff it.

"We will take a zig-zag pattern going southeast first then zagging southwest in time to arrive down stream by dusk," said Jake.

Jake looked at their faces to see if this made sense in the context of their reports. It clearly did not. But because the herd, including Jake's lieutenants, had so much confidence in him, no one questioned his decision. They all assumed that Jake must have a very good reason beyond their ability to comprehend for wanting to cross over some of the same territory that the herd had grazed on just the day before. Except for Buffalo Nick who knew better, and gave Jake a look that told him as much.

After the reports, Jake went up to a bluff by the river. The bluff was high enough that Jake could see his entire herd stretched across the plain. The sun had set so the herd appeared only as dark shadows. But from the stillness of the shadows, Jake could tell that all was well. A cool breeze was blowing off the river, which was a welcome respite from the day's heat. Jake lay down and tried to enjoy the calm, cool breeze ruffling the thick hair of his mane. He watched the river gently meandering through the center of the plain with the light from a quarter moon glinting off the occasional ripples in its surface. The peaceful sound of the flowing water calmed his nerves. He scanned his herd one last time to reassure himself that all was well before trying to get some sleep.

After dozing off, Jake began to dream. It was morning. The sun was brighter than usual. For the sun to be so bright, he realized that he must have overslept. He opened his eyes and looked up at the sun blazing overhead. He was angry at himself for oversleeping, but he was also

90

curious why no one had awakened him. When he looked out over the plain, he did not see his herd. How strange, he thought. Why didn't someone wake me? He tried to remember the grazing plan for today. He could remember that it was going to be a zig-zag, but was it northeast or southeast first? He could not remember. He reassured himself that the plan would come to him after he was more awake and that there was surely a simple explanation for why the herd left without him.

He trotted down from the bluff to the plain. When he leaned down to gather grass for his morning cud, a weird feeling came over him that something was very wrong. It was a gut feeling that something more than just the herd was missing. He looked across the plain searching for what his instincts were trying to tell him was missing. He watched the warm breeze blowing the grass in waves, then it hit him. There was no buffalo scent in the air. Not even a residual scent. He began sniffing the air in all directions. Nothing. Maybe he was too close to the river, which was the direction from which the breeze was blowing. So he walked toward the center of the area where he had seen his herd resting the night before. He sniffed the air and the ground, but there was no scent of buffalo at all. He thought he must be in the wrong place. He looked down at the grass. If the herd had slept there last night, the grass would be flattened. It was not. He must have gotten mixed up, he thought. They must be on the other side of the bluff. He remembered that he had not looked on the other side of the bluff when he got up. He thought if he had just twisted his head in the opposite direction, he would have seen them all there.

As he climbed back up the bluff, he knew that he was just kidding himself. He knew that he had not gotten the direction wrong because he distinctly remembered looking to the north of the bluff and seeing his herd last night. But the situation was too scary. So he lied to himself that he could be wrong about the direction. He imagined he would see them all on the other side of the bluff in just a moment and that he would laugh at himself for thinking strange thoughts. He walked up the bluff slowly enjoying the feeling that everything would soon be alright. For a brief second, he wondered what he would do if they were not on the other side. He told himself that it would be O.K.—that certainly he would figure it all out before the day was over, and he would make sure that he never overslept again.

On the other side of the bluff, there wasn't any sign or scent that buffalo had ever been there. In fact, there wasn't any sign of life at all. As far as Jake could see, the ground was barren and black. At first Jake thought it looked like the day after a prairie fire. But there was no sign that grass or bushes had ever been there. There weren't any ashes blowing across the blackened plain. Nor did it smell like the results of a prairie fire. Sometimes the burnt smell would last for a whole season after a fire until the grass grew back. But this smelled much different. It was a strange smell that Jake had never encountered before. A hot wind hit Jake from behind and he turned around to see where it came from. He saw that the prairie with it lush grass from which he just came was now just as barren and black as the other side of the bluff. Jake looked under his hooves and in all directions. As far as he could see, the ground was just the same. Even the luscious evergreen forest to the northwest was gone. What added to the eeriness is that Jake couldn't hear anything. The entire earth seemed perfectly still and silent. The only movement Jake saw was the waves of heat coming off the smooth black ground. Jake looked up in the sky for some sign of birds, but there were none. The sky was an ugly yellowish, faded blue color and the sun seemed much larger than usual.

Jake thought to himself that this must all just be a bad dream. He shook himself awake and looked around. Nothing changed. He started running as fast as he could across the plain. He ran and ran, hoping to reach the edge of the blackened earth. But no matter which direction he ran in, the earth was the same. He finally stopped and looked around for some landmark, but there was none. He was out of breath and hot from running. His hooves ached from running on the hard surface. He bent down to smell the blackness. The ground looked like millions of black pebbles somehow stuck together. They smelled terrible. As Jake stood there panting, he thought that this must not be a dream. The pain in his legs and hooves felt very real. And the dryness in his mouth was very real too. He looked about him again and he started to wonder if the world he remembered was just a dream. Maybe this was the way it had always been. The great expanse of hot, hard ground before him looked as if it had always been there. Jake looked around again. He wondered how anyone could tell that rivers had flowed here and forests had grown over there. No one would ever know this plain had been teeming with life just yesterday.

In the distance, Jake thought he saw something. It wasn't much. But it looked like something poking through the surface. He went over to it and saw a crack in the blackness and sticking through the crack were a few blades of grass trying to grow. This made Jake smile. He was not alone. Then he heard a sound coming from the crack. It was so faint that he could barely hear it. But slowly it grew just loud enough for Jake to make it out. It was the sound of animals. It was the sound of thousands of animals in pain. Jake could hear the desperate cries of almost every animal represented in the World Council of Living Things. Then he heard the sound of his herd. They were calling for him to help them. Jake frantically dug at the crack with his front hooves. A few black, sticky pebbles came loose, but the heat had sapped his strength so much that his efforts were hopeless. In fact, the more Jake dug, the smaller the crack got until finally it disappeared altogether.

He shouted, "Is this what you wanted, chakeedas? Are you happy now? Are you better off now that the world looks this way? Are you better off now that you have the whole planet to yourself?! Do you eat better now? Do you sleep better now? Are your lives better now?! Well come and kill me. I'm the last one. Kill me and nothing will be left standing in the way of your progress. Go ahead and kill me! Kill me now!"

Jake was startled by a voice from behind him. The voice said, "No, they are sorry." Jake turned around and Kim Ha was standing there. Behind Kim Ha were hundreds of chakeedas.

Kim Ha continued, "They are sorry, but they had to do it for their own survival. They explained it all to me. They take care of me and they will take care of you now."

Jake screamed at Kim Ha, "Tell them I don't want to be taken care of!"

Kim Ha was unmoved, "You have no choice. They will take care of you now."

The chakeedas started moving in on Jake. They were talking, but the words made no sense.

Kim Ha said, "Do not struggle, Jake. They will kill you to save you if they have to. You are the last one."

Jake was in a total panic. He lowered his head and smashed through the line of chakeedas surrounding him. He could hear the screams of the chakeedas chasing him. Jake kept running even though his mouth was parched and his head seemed dizzy from the oppressive heat. He kept running until he felt the coolness of a shadow. He looked up and realized he was underneath something. Something very large. But what it was, he could not tell. He stopped panting just long enough to sniff one of its legs and it smelled like an elephant. He walked to the edge of the shadow and looked up. It was an elephant. It was taller than any tree he had ever seen. A rhino just as large was standing next to the oversized elephant.

Jake looked back at the chakeedas and noticed that they had not chased him under the elephant. But as more arrived, they began to surround it.

When Kim Ha arrived, Jake told her, "Tell them to go away or else my elephant and rhino friends here will crush them all!"

Kim Ha just smiled and the chakeedas started moving in. Jake threatened Kim Ha again, but the chakeedas came even closer. Then Kim Ha peeled off her fur and stepped out of it. Jake realized it was not Kim Ha at all, it was a chakeeda.

The chakeeda said, "Even Kim Ha is dead."

Jake screamed at the elephant and rhino, "Crush them! Crush them! Hurry up! We don't have much time!"

But neither would move. Desperately, Jake started ramming one of the elephant's front legs. Still the elephant would not move. He did the same to the enormous rhino, but it would not move.

The chakeeda that had been in Kim Ha's fur laughed and said, "Don't be stupid, Jake. There are no more elephants or rhinos. These two were the last left standing, but they are now dead."

As Jake felt the first chakeedas grasping at his body, he woke from his nightmare and jumped to his feet. He looked around prepared to gore as many chakeedas as he could. But the only thing that he felt on his body was the cool night air blowing from the river. He looked down from his bluff and saw his herd peacefully resting. He heard the sound of the crickets and bull frogs and the gentle ripples of the river. He looked up at the night sky and saw the stars and moon. He looked toward the evergreen forest and saw the majestic shadows of the ancient trees. It was all so beautiful.

But then he looked toward the Great Valley and saw an ugly yellow glow rising up from it. He was not worried this time because he now had the solution to the chakeeda problem. He would assemble the largest herd of elephants and rhinos ever, and direct a massive charge through the Great Valley crushing the chakeedas with wave after wave of elephants and rhinos. It was the only chance they had.

CHAPTER ELEVEN

The Struggle of Panda Pei Woo

After the emergency meeting of the World Council of Living Things, Pei Woo went into the mountains to forage for tender bamboo shoots and think about what had been said. Pei Woo was sure that the chakeedas could not be as bad as Jake made them out to be. And even if some of them were bad, that did not mean that all of them should be killed. Especially... well... Pei Woo knew at least two chakeedas that deserved to live.

Their names were Betty and John. She knew they were good because they had raised her and her sister, Kim Ha, when they found them in the forest when they were small cubs. They had been orphaned when their mother died when they were not yet weaned. If Betty and John had not found them, Pei Woo was sure they would have died. At the very least, Pei Woo felt that she should warn Betty and John. But if the other chakeedas found out, they would probably be ready for the attack. Pei Woo tried not to think about it. How did life get so complicated?

Pei Woo broke off some bamboo shoots and began to chew. She let out a disgusted whining sound and spat the leaves out. The best bamboo had been in the Great Valley, but no panda dared venture into the Great Valley out of fear of the chakeedas. There was also good bamboo at the base of the white cap mountains, but all of it had been eaten. As hard as it was for Pei Woo to accept, the only bamboo left was here at the very fringe of the bamboo range. The leaves were not as healthy and usually tasted bitter. Pei Woo could usually tolerate the bitter flavor, but this was too much. She broke off another branch and tried the leaves. She immediately spat it out. She looked around for another stand of bamboo, but none was in sight.

She was quite hungry at this point so she started looking about for some tasty insects. Some grass hoppers would be good, she thought. Or maybe a jumbo sized dragon fly. Her mouth watered at the thought. She listened for crickets, but it was too early in the day for them to be making any noise and she had not seen a dragon fly since midsummer. Pei Woo wandered aimlessly through the forest until she came to a small stream.

She found a log lying across the stream. She sat down on it and dangled her rear paws into the cool water. She began peeling off the bark next to her on the log. It wasn't like eucalyptus bark, which was very tasty. She looked about for a eucalyptus tree, but none were around. She peeled another piece of bark off the log and found three grub worms underneath. Her eyes became big at the sight of such a juicy meal. She quickly consumed them. As she continued to peel back the bark, she found nothing else of interest. The log was mostly infested with ants and reddish colored mushrooms. Nothing to make a real meal out of.

Pei Woo looked down at her reflection in the stream and finally admitted to herself what she had been worried about for sometime. She was substantially underweight for this time of year. She instinctively knew that if she was going to survive the winter, she would have to weigh much more than she did now. She had eaten all the food she could find, but that just wasn't good enough this year.

A cool breeze blew across her back, sweeping her fur upward and allowing the coolness to reach her skin. It reminded her of the lateness of the season. A sense of urgency swept over her. She had to find food soon. But where? Before Pei Woo could give the question much thought, she smelled something strange in the air. The smell made Pei Woo uneasy. Something told her it was a dangerous smell. But before she could figure it out, she heard a familiar voice say, "Hi, Pei Woo... How are you?"

Pei Woo quickly looked to the bank of the stream and saw Betty and John standing there. Behind them was another chakeeda that Pei Woo had never seen before. Pei Woo sniffed the air in the direction of the chakeeda. The smell made her fur instinctively stand on end. Pei Woo decided to stay on the log. John could tell that Pei Woo was disturbed by the presence of the other chakeeda, so John whispered something to the chakeeda. The chakeeda said something back and left.

Even though Pei Woo had heard what the chakeeda had said, she had not understood the words. Pei Woo thought it was very odd. Even when the other animals no longer were able to communicate with the chakeedas, Pei Woo had always been able understand them. But what bothered Pei Woo even more was the feeling that she was being deceived. Pei Woo could tell that the strange chakeeda had not really left. She knew that he had to be close by because the strange scent of danger was still heavy in the air. It never occurred to Pei Woo that the scent might be coming from Betty or John.

After the strange chakeeda disappeared, John said, "Well, are you going to greet us or just sit on that log all day?" Pei Woo didn't know what to do. She was just too hungry to think clearly. In frustration, she looked back down in at the water and let out a low sounding growl. This caused John to take a step back. Betty reacted differently. She said in a scolding motherly tone, "Pei Woo, what's the matter with you? Get over here this instant." Pei Woo leaned in her direction in blind obedience to her motherly voice. But then a strong breeze whipped through the branches above her. She took a deep breath and the heavy scent of danger alerted and focused her senses. She pulled back.

There was a time when the scent of danger would have sent Pei Woo scurrying to Betty's side, but something was different now. Something that Pei Woo could not quite figure out. Betty spoke again. Her soft, familiar voice was still reassuring. But Betty's voice did not command instant obedience as it had before Pei Woo had left Betty's care many seasons before. Pei Woo remained sitting on the log dangling her hind paws in the water hoping that maybe Betty and John would simply go away.

Betty tried a different approach, "Pei Woo, you look so thin for this time of year. Why haven't you been eating?"

"It hasn't been by choice. There just doesn't seem to be enough bamboo shoots to go around anymore," said Pei Woo.

"Well, we heard about that. They say that it's because all of the bamboo dies off all at once every few generations," said Betty.

Pei Woo knew about the die offs. But the pandas had always migrated from these forests to the Great Valley. The cycles were such that the bamboo in the Great Valley never died off at the same time as the bamboo elsewhere. Pei Woo wanted to tell Betty this, but she was not in a talkative mood and she really saw no point to it.

Betty continued, "Well, my little Pei Woo, we thought that you might be hungry, so we brought you some fresh bamboo." John had stepped back into the forest and returned with a bundle of bamboo. When Pei Woo saw the bundle, her mouth immediately began to water at the sight of such fresh, green shoots. She had not seen anything so tasty since the beginning of the season. Her hunger was greater than her fear. She found herself moving across the log toward the bamboo before she had a chance to think. She shoved a paw full of leaves into her mouth and savored the sweet, juicy taste. The flavor was delightful. Pei Woo's whole face smiled for the first time in a long time.

When Pei Woo reached for another shoot, she discovered that John had moved the bundle out of her reach. Betty handed Pei Woo another shoot and said, "So what have you been up to?"

"Not much," said Pei Woo with her mouth full. John whispered something to Betty and Betty nodded. When Pei Woo asked for another branch, Betty gave her only half a shoot.

Betty continued, "We haven't seen you in a long time. We missed you. It's so nice to see you again. Your coat looks beautiful."

"Thank you," said Pei Woo.

"We want to hear all about what you've been up to. Tell us everything," said Betty.

When Pei Woo had finished the half branch, Betty withheld giving her anymore.

"We brought plenty of bamboo, but you can't talk while you're eating," said Betty.

While Pei Woo wanted the food, she was still suspicious of the situation and needed more time to think before she told Betty and John about anything. So Pei Woo said cautiously, "There's not much to tell. What do you want to know?"

"Well, how are the other animals?"

"They're fine," said Pei Woo.

"We heard that you spend a lot of time with Buffalo Jake these days. How is he?"

"He's fine." Pei Woo stared at Betty and back at the bamboo behind her. She handed her a few leaves.

"What is Jake up to these days?" Betty asked.

At this comment, Pei Woo narrowed her eyes in a sign of disapproval. No animal called Buffalo Jake just "Jake" except for his most closest friends and advisors, and even then, only rarely. Pei Woo found Betty's implied suggestion that she was within Buffalo Jake's inner circle to be offensive and an insult to the great leader of the World Council of Living Things. It demonstrated a lack of respect for Buffalo Jake. The Betty that Pei Woo once knew would never have made such a mistake.

From Pei Woo's expression, Betty realized that her attempt at informality had backfired, "I'm sorry, what I meant to say was 'How is Buffalo Jake doing these days?' What is he up to?" Betty offered Pei Woo a bigger branch of bamboo.

"Leading the buffalo herds, I suppose," said Pei Woo sarcastically, still not willing to completely forgive Betty even as she stripped the fresh bark from the bamboo branch.

John was growing impatient. He motioned for Betty to step back among the trees with him. Pei Woo could hear their whispers. Even though she could not understand the strange words, she could tell that the conversation was quite heated. Pei Woo stared at Betty and John, then back at the bundle of bamboo. This might be her chance, she thought. If she could grab the bundle of bamboo and walk away while they weren't looking... It seemed like a good idea. She took as much as she could in her teeth and tried to pick up as much as she could with her front paws. In this position, she would have to walk upright. Walking upright was not an impossible task for pandas, but it was awkward and she knew it would slow her escape. She tried it anyway.

She did not get far down stream before she heard Betty's voice, "Pei Woo, where are you going? Don't you like us anymore?" At that moment, the wind shifted. She sniffed the air. The smell of danger was heavy again. She looked toward the woods to see if the other chakeeda had returned. She could not tell.

"No... I just thought that you were leaving... I was just moving down stream because... because... it's nicer over here," Pei Woo stuttered.

"Yes, it is nicer here. More sun. Let us help you with that," said Betty. At which point, Betty and John took the bamboo away from Pei Woo. Her heart sank. She looked at her body hoping that she might have gained enough weight on the few branches she had eaten so that she would not need anymore of Betty's bamboo. When she looked down at her stomach, the sight of her thin body made her want to cry.

"Pei Woo, we need to talk to you about something important. John wants me to tell you that we know about the secret meeting that Buffalo Jake held. We know about his plan," Betty said. She was bluffing. The chakeedas were only guessing that there had been a secret meeting, and they certainly had no idea whether Buffalo Jake had any kind of plan.

Betty continued, "You have to help us. We only want to prevent the senseless slaughter of animals. There is no way they can win now."

Pei Woo knew that the plan depended upon complete surprise. If the chakeedas knew, the chakeedas probably would slaughter them. She tried to focus her thoughts, but her hunger was so great that clouds of dots kept dancing in front of her eyes.

"When is the plan set to begin?" asked Betty.

"At the next full moon, I think," said Pei Woo.

John and Betty stepped back and started arguing in whispers. The bits and pieces that Pei Woo could hear were in that strange language that she could not understand.

Betty returned and asked, "So they're going to try to kill Chakeeda Real at the next full moon? That won't stop the rest of the chakeedas."

Pei Woo froze. A feeling of shame and fear swept over her. If the chakeedas had a spy, they would have at least known that the plan involved far more than killing just Chakeeda Real. Pei Woo did not know the details of Jake's plan, or if he had even fully developed it yet, but she knew it would involve far more than attacking Real from the way Jake had been talking. Even in Pei Woo's starved condition, her mind realized the chakeedas had known nothing until this moment.

"Betty, you can't tell anyone," pleaded Pei Woo, "Please promise me you won't tell anyone!" Pei Woo was getting hysterical, making all sorts of panda distress sounds.

"Pei Woo, just calm down, you did the right thing. I just need to ask you a couple of more questions. Which animals are involved in the attack?"

Pei Woo's mind was racing. How could this have happened. She looked at the bamboo and hated herself for being so hungry. She had to warn Buffalo Jake. She started heading for the log to cross the stream.

"Where do you think you're going? Do you want to starve to death? We have bamboo. Where else are you going to find bamboo like this? We can take care of you. The world is changing. You can't survive on your own anymore."

Pei Woo wasn't listening. She was consumed by the thought of finding Buffalo Jake. As she reached the log, she felt John's hands grabbing her shoulder. She looked back at him. This was the first time she had been so close. He did not look like the John she knew. Pei Woo cried out and slammed her front leg into John's chest, easily throwing him back. She started across the log again, but felt a swarm of slimy chakeeda hands yanking her back. Pei Woo fell on her back. She tried to fight back, but her body would not respond to her commands. She felt so sluggish. She could not move. She wondered how her body could go to sleep at a time like this.

As Pei Woo's eyes closed, she heard Betty say, "It's better this way, Pei Woo. We'll take care of you. You're different from those dangerous wild animals. We can still help you."

Those were the last words that Pei Woo heard before she fell into a deep sleep that would last for days.

CHAPTER TWELVE

The Misty Forest

During Jake's morning briefing with his lieutenants, he told them that he had a solution for the chakeeda problem. Jake ordered that a message be sent to the representatives from the elephants, rhinoceros, panthers, and leopards instructing them to meet him in the Misty Forest in fifteen days, which was the soonest that Jake thought they would be able to get there. The timber wolves would meet each representative on the edge of the Misty Forest and act as their escort to a secret location. If Jake's plan was to work, the chakeedas must not find out about it. The element of surprise would be crucial. Therefore, the Misty Forest would be the best location for the meeting because the chakeedas did not like to go there because it was too scary to them.

Instructions were given to have the condors fly to the savanna to inform the elephants and rhinos. This would take at least two days. First, it would take about two days for one of Jake's lieutenants to travel to the base of the rock ridge mountains to find the representative from the dall sheep, a species of bighorn sheep. It would take another day for the dall sheep to climb the rugged heights of the rock ridge mountains to the ledge where the representative of the ocean condors nested. The ocean condor would fly to the savanna to inform the appropriate representatives. Jake estimated that it would take the species representatives about ten days to reach the Misty Forest.

Jake's one fear was that one of the messengers would be injured by a rock slide or flood or some such thing. He was not worried about his messengers being attacked by predators because they all would carry the scent of the special water found only in the meeting cavern of the World Council of Living Things. Jake's lieutenant would bathe in the special water before he left. Each messenger along the way would rub against each other to transfer the scent. It was understood by all living things that any animal carrying the scent was on a special mission from the World Council. All predators respected this scent. Of course, the scent would not protect the messengers from the chakeeda's indiscriminate traps. Therefore, the condor was given instructions to fly to the prairie where

Jake's herd was grazing after completing her mission so Jake could know if anything had gone wrong. All the messengers were told not to speak to any other animal about their mission and to be sure they were not seen by chakeedas. The future depended upon the secrecy of the mission.

The Misty Forest was called that because the trees were so tall that they blocked out almost all the sun light from reaching the floor of the forest. The limited plant life included a few small ferns and various species of mushrooms and molds that lived off an occasional fallen tree. But the most dominate feature of the Misty Forest were the barren, black trunks of the trees that soared high into the canopy of the forest. The problem was that all the trees tended to look alike, which made it very easy for outsiders to get lost if one did not mark one's trail with scent. The chakeedas seemed to have lost their ability to navigate by scent, making the Misty Forest a particularly hazardous place for them to be and they knew it. The chakeedas had begun to solve their problem by cutting down the trees and building their nests. Needless to say, the chakeedas were no longer welcome by the inhabitants of the forest.

For those who rarely ventured into the Misty Forest, the lack of sunlight gave it a feeling of oppressive gloominess. Except for the occasional fern, the only colors one saw were greys and blacks and browns. Another thing about the Misty Forest that gave it such an eerie feeling were the sounds. Or, actually, the lack of sound. Every sound seemed muffled by the mist that never seemed to leave. The infrequent chatter of squirrels high in the canopy seemed muted. Even the howl of the timber wolves late at night sounded like a distant whisper. Everything seemed too quiet. Though, one redeeming feature was the thick bed of pine needles that covered the forest floor. The accumulation of pine needles was so great in fact that it had broken the fall of more than one youthful squirrel that had miscalculated a jump between branches. Or at least that was the story that certain particularly boastful squirrels had told at a World Council meeting. Whether it was true or not, no one knew.

At ground level, the Misty Forest was home to brown rabbits, grey squirrels, various rodents, a few deer, tortoises, and, of course, the timber wolves. The extremely rare grey forest cougar also lived in the Misty Forest. But the only time that anyone ever saw one was at the meetings of the World Council of Living Things. Considering their husky, muscular build and the size of their fangs, one was well advised to avoid contact with grey cougars on their home range.

The elephant and rhino representatives left the savanna together. The elephant's name was Jabari and the rhino's name was Chaga. As Jake had expected, they arrived at the western edge of the Misty Forest after ten days of travel. Jabari and Chaga walked about 10 body lengths into the forest before they stopped. There they rested and waited. There was no particular place that they were suppose to meet. They knew that no matter where they were in the Misty Forest, the timber wolves would soon be aware of their presence.

It was not too long before they found themselves surrounded by a pack of timber wolves. The leader of the pack stepped forward and demanded, "What is the password?" Buffalo Jake had arranged for a password as an added security precaution.

Jabari stepped forward, "When the earth is black and the sky is brown..."

To this the wolf continued softly, "When the forests are gone and the sun beats down..."

It was now Chaga's turn, "When the rivers are dead and winds carry none of our sounds..."

The wolf concluded, "The chakeedas will learn too late that they cannot live alone."

The wolf leader, Wolf Daniel, thought the password was a bit melodramatic, even if it was true. The expression on his face betrayed his embarrassment. Even so, Daniel went along with it because it made sense as an extra security precaution. One could never be too cautious when dealing with the chakeedas.

Daniel said, "Welcome to the Misty Forest. We will be your escort. Follow us."

With that, Jabari and Chaga followed the timber wolf leader in single file with Chaga right behind Jabari. As they travelled deeper into the forest, the elephant would occasionally look back at the rhino and exchange uneasy glances. Both were feeling uncomfortable because the forest provided them little room to maneuver their massive bodies if they were attacked. The rhino was even more uneasy because he had poor eyesight and the dim light made seeing anything even more difficult. They preferred to charge any potential aggressors. This usually was all that was necessary. But if the chakeedas were to attack here, they would be totally dependent on the timber wolves for protection. The other members of the wolf pack had spread out on their flanks. Occasionally, one of their escorts could be seen as nothing more than a shadow in the darkness of the forest to either side of them. But as they travelled into the deepest, darkest interior of the forest, even these welcome shadows disappeared from view. Daniel sensed their distress. "Don't worry," he said. "There are several wolf packs on all sides of us at this moment. There is no way any chakeeda will be able to penetrate them." The words were reassuring to the rhino and elephant, but both knew they'd be glad to be back on the savanna.

When Jabari and Chaga reached the meeting place the panther and leopard representatives had already arrived. The big cats had been escorted by the rare forest cougar. At the secret meeting place, the mood was appropriately serious. The animals acknowledged each other's presence with their eyes and nods of their heads. But no words were spoken. The only animal that had not arrived yet was Buffalo Jake. The animals sat about in silence waiting for his arrival. The tension hung heavy in the air. It weighed on their chests and made it difficult to breath. Time seemed to be moving very slowly. But no one complained. Everyone knew that they would wait at this very spot in this strange forest until Jake arrived. It never crossed anyone's mind that something could have happened to him. Certainly his escort of timber wolves would protect him.

* * * * *

The chakeedas had suspected that Jake had a plan. What the plan was, the chakeedas did not know. But chakeeda Real was notoriously paranoid and assumed any threats were against him personally. Real was angry with both Ajar and Blueth that they had not yet killed Jake. They were not to return until Jake was dead. Ajar and Blueth understood. They had been keeping the central buffalo herd under surveillance for several days when their break came. They knew something was happening when Buffalo Jake, Nick, and a group of his lieutenants broke off from the herd and started heading in a direction that the buffalo had never gone before. On the third night of this journey, the chakeedas realized Jake's destination.

He was heading on a direct course for the Misty Forest. Killing him out on the prairie was too risky because it was so open. Too easy to be detected. The Misty Forest would be the perfect place to kill him. They could disappear into the darkness before anyone knew what had happened.

But Ajar and Blueth were not stupid. They knew that their life expectancy would be short in the Misty Forest because the animals were so ferocious there. Or so they had always been told. They decided that they needed a plan— some plan that would permit them to avoid the dangers of the forest while taking full advantage of its darkness and mistiness to avoid detection during their escape. They needed to race ahead of Jake so that they could prepare before he made it there.

When Jake stopped to rest on the third night of his journey, the chakeedas continued on and entered the Misty Forest under cover of darkness. They traveled as far as they could and still see the moonlight penetrating the forest's edge. They dared not go any farther. At this point, they looked at each other. Each could see the fear and doubt in the other's eyes. Nervously, they initiated the first phase of their plan. They began to whine as they imagined an injured wolf puppy would sound. At first, their fake whimpers were barely audible and unrealistic. But within a short time, their cries of distress grew louder and more convincing. From a distance, they sounded just like injured puppies.

The closest wolves to the chakeedas were asleep deep in the forest. No timber wolf was awaken by the chakeedas distant cry, except for Rebecca. Rebecca was a magnificent example of a female timber wolf in her prime. She had a strong, sleek body covered in a gorgeous charcoal grey coat. As with every night for the past twelve years, Rebecca was curled up next to her life partner, Daniel. They had raised several puppies together. Survived severe winters together. Nursed each other back to health when the other had been sick. And barely survived a devastating forest fire together. Neither of them could ever imagine what life would be like without the other.

On this particular night, Rebecca was still awake. Daniel had fallen asleep earlier. He was laying on his side next to her and she was laying behind him with her head resting on his shoulder. She sometimes liked to lay next to him like this and simply watch him breathe. Watch the gentle rising and falling of his chest. She also liked to watch his paws kick when he dreamed. These simple things gave her a warm feeling inside that made her feel content and satisfied.

Rebecca was about to dose off when she heard the distress call of puppies in the distance. She immediately looked around for her own two puppies. She breathed easier when she saw that they were still curled up next to each other asleep. She was settling down, when she heard the sound again. It sounded of wolf pups in trouble, but she couldn't be sure. She waited and listened for the sound with her ears straight up at full attention. Again, she heard the cry. The sound was faint, but unmistakable. She thought that their mother or father would soon come to their aide. But even after more time had passed, the cries persisted and even seemed to grow more desperate. The sound gnawed at her motherly instincts. Finally, she could stand it no longer and set out to see what the problem was. What Rebecca did not know was that one of her puppies had woken up and was following her.

When Ajar and Blueth saw a wolf approaching, they began their retreat to the edge of the Misty Forest. Rebecca continued to follow until she detected the scent of chakeeda. She stopped and sniffed the air. The scent was unmistakable. Her muscles became rigid with anger and she let out a low growl. She knew that chakeedas were dangerous creatures. She thought that she should go back and get Daniel and the other members of the pack. But before she could think it through, she heard the sound of the puppies again. This time it sounded like the whimpers were coming from outside the forest. If she went back for help, she was certain it would be too late. She charged ahead to the edge of the forest and listened again. The cries were coming from a gully between the edge of the forest and the river.

She left the safety of the forest and creeped toward the gully prepared to attack. When she got to the edge, she peered into the gully, but could see nothing in the darkness. The chakeedas must have taken the puppies in there, she thought, because the scent of chakeedas was so heavy. In her excitement, she did not stop to think that she did not smell any puppies.

As Rebecca descended into the gully, she heard a soft puppy whimper come from behind a large rock. When she was right in front of the rock, Ajar raised his head and stared right in her face and let out the cry of a wolf puppy. For a brief moment, Rebecca tilted her head in bewilderment at what she was seeing. Ajar made the sound again, but followed it with a hideous chakeeda laugh. An icy chill went through her body before she had a conscious awareness of the chakeeda deception. In the instant of realization, Blueth hit her full force in her back legs with the heaviest rock he could lift. The bone in her left leg snapped and broke through the skin sending Rebecca crumbling to the ground in agony. The chakeedas immediately began beating Rebecca with rocks and large sticks. None of the blows were fatal by themselves even though they broke her ribs and ripped her flesh. She tried to fight back, but moving her body was just as painful as the blows themselves. Rebecca cried out for help, howling as loud as she could. But her voice was soon silenced when she had to focus on clearing the blood from her throat just to breath. The beating continued for sometime before they killed her.

The puppy that had followed Rebecca was shaking uncontrollably. He had witnessed the entire beating. When the chakeedas saw him shaking and whimpering, they immediately went after him with their clubs. But the puppy darted between their legs and sent them on a clumsy chase through the gully. Instinctively, the puppy ran to his mother for protection. As the chakeedas approached, he licked at her face and scratched at her body. He could not understand why his mother would not wake up. But he stayed next to her body certain that she would leap to her feet to protect him. Ajar and Blueth hesitated for a moment, some ancient sense of mercy holding them back from beating the innocent pup. It was an odd feeling. They looked at each other briefly. They knew what they had to do. They dared not leave any proof that this was a chakeeda attack, even the account of a trembling puppy. Chakeeda Real would certainly kill them if they did. The pup tried to huddle closer to Rebecca's body, but it was futile. When they were done, they had not left a single bone unbroken.

* * * * *

At the moment that Rebecca's spirit left her body, Daniel stood straight up out of a sound sleep and let out a howling, uncontrollable scream. Tears flooded his eyes. His howls quivered with a strange eeriness. Daniel knew. He needed no confirmation. Rebecca's spirit told him. She was dead, and one of his puppies was dead. He could feel that it had been a horrible death.

The agonizing howls of pain that followed were heard in every crevice of the forest. Not a single animal remained asleep. Shivers went down the spines of every animal as they listened. Some understood. Some did not. But regardless, they all instinctively knew that this was not any normal pain. This was something much worse, something foreign to them all. They sensed that the rules had been violently broken. It was a feeling of terrible danger. It was close to the feeling they had in the pit of their stomachs when they smelled the first whiff of smoke from a forest fire. But there was no forest fire. There was no physical sign of an approaching enemy. That's what made it so scary. At least they could run from a forest fire. At least they could see or smell their enemy. But they sensed that this was not an enemy that they could run from or fight. The forest was no longer safe. Their home was no longer safe. Howls of sympathy went out from throughout the Misty Forest. The birds squawked and squirrels chattered and leaped from tree to tree. The frantic communications would continue throughout the night. No one would sleep.

* * * * *

In the gully, Ajar and Blueth were staring at Rebecca's brutalized body. Both were grinning with great pride. They congratulated themselves on bringing down such a dangerous, wild beast. They marvelled at the solid muscles and powerful jaws. Nervously, they laughed at the thought that the creature could have killed both of them instantly if it had a chance. But they reassured themselves that it was through their superior intelligence that they had prevailed. Ajar nervously poked at the body to make sure it was dead. They ignored the puppy's body as though it did not exist. The sounds coming from the forest seemed unusually loud, but they made no connection between the sounds and anything they had done.

As they decapitated Rebecca's head, they argued over the bragging rights to the kill. It was agreed that they both would share the credit. They looked about for a safe place to store the head until they could return to the Great Valley with it. They had not hit the beast in the head because they did not want its face damaged. If its face was damaged, it would not be as attractive mounted in their nest.

After they stored the head in a cool spot hidden in the side of the rocky gully, they proceeded to strip the body of its fur. When they were finished, they wrapped themselves in Rebecca's beautiful grey coat. They licked the blood from where it had been splattered from the beating. When they were finished, they complimented each other on how attractive they looked. Their new fur was far more beautiful than their own ugly, wrinkled skin that it now hid. They now believed they could maneuver throughout the forest using the wolf's scent rapped around them to disguise their own.

In the morning when they awoke, Ajar and Blueth realized too late that they should not have slept in the freshly skinned fur because the inside of the skin dried during the night. In the process, the fur had become stuck to parts of their backs and arms. To get it off, they had to yank at it, which painfully ripped off the top layer of their own skin in places. They worried about scars. After they tended to their wounds, they slipped back into the forest to await Jake's arrival. They took Rebecca's head with them since they decided their prize might be stolen if left it in their hiding place.

* * * * *

Buffalo Jake arrived at the edge of the Misty Forest in the late afternoon of the day following Rebecca's death. It had been an overcast day and the evening mist had moved into the forest early. Jake did not need his lieutenants any longer. They doubled back to return to the herd. Within a short time, Jake found himself surrounded by his escort of timber wolves. There was no secret code because it was not necessary. Everyone knew Jake by sight and scent. There was no other.

When Jake arrived at the meeting place deep in the forest, the elephant, rhino and big cats broke into smiles. After friendly greetings, Jake told them about the dream, or rather nightmare, that he had many days earlier. After Jake was finished, he said, "I believe that if we don't do something drastic now, we will wake up someday to find my nightmare has become our reality."

The elephant responded, "Jake, you do not have to convince us. We have no doubt that the chakeedas are a threat to the survival of us all. I'm still at a loss to understand what happened to the chakeedas, but it no longer matters. We will all be extinct within a few generations if something is not done. All you need to do is tell us what we must do and we will do it." The rhino and big cats expressed their wholehearted agreement.

Jake took a deep breath and began, "The plan is simple. We must amass all of the elephants and all of the rhinos from every elephant species and every rhino species from every savanna and every jungle from every corner of the earth. Once they are assembled, when the moment is right, they must all charge into the Great Valley crushing every chakeeda in their path under their great weight. The cheetahs and panthers will ride on the backs of the rhinos and elephants. If any chakeeda is seen escaping, the cats will chase down the escapee."

* * * * *

Ajar and Blueth had managed to dodge from tree to tree and hide within the patches of fog so that they were within ear shot of the meeting. Their gruesome trick to mask their scent had prevented any of the timber wolves from detecting their presence. After they heard Jake describe the basic plan, they decided they should return home before they were discovered. Ajar and Blueth agreed that the information was too important. Real needed to know as soon as possible even if it meant killing Jake another day.

Out of the 200 or so wolf packs that were providing security for the meeting, only those wolves in Daniel's pack were familiar with Rebecca's scent. For that reason, none of the wolves that smelled the retreating chakeedas became suspicious. If the chakeedas had not lost their sense of smell, Ajar and Blueth could have successfully back tracked out of the forest. But such was not the case. Their only method of navigation was by sight. The problem, of course, was that one part of the forest looked just like any other part of the forest. The fog only made things worse. Inevitably, Ajar and Blueth began to argue over the best way out. Each accused the other of getting them lost. After more than half the night, they found themselves still wandering about wondering if they were closer to the edge or only deeper in the forest. Having to constantly hide from patrolling timber wolves and occasional grey forest cougars only made them more confused.

Daniel's wolf pack was not part of Jake's escort on this day. It had remained in its home range mourning the loss of Rebecca. Daniel was looking at his remaining puppy with a worried expression. The puppy had been whining for food, but Daniel had no idea how he was going to feed him. Usually if a mother died, another nursing mother in the pack would take over the care of the surviving puppies. But there were no other nursing mothers in the pack this time, and the puppy was too young to eat regular food.

As Daniel sat staring at his puppy, the little creature stopped whining and began wagging his tail and barking. This behavior puzzled Daniel until he got a whiff of what the puppy had detected. It was the scent of Rebecca. The adult wolves looked about at each other with serious expressions and communicated their concern with tail signals. When the puppy charged in the direction of the scent, one of his uncles intercepted him and picked him up by the scruff of the neck and delivered him to his aunt. Then Daniel and the other members of the pack started toward the scent with Daniel in the lead. They approached the scent cautiously, uncertain of what they would find. Their imaginations ran wild with possibilities. As they came closer, Daniel allowed a glimmer of hope to rise within him that Rebecca might still be alive. He quickened the pace.

None were prepared for what they saw. Before them stood Ajar and Blueth wrapped in Rebecca's fur. At first the pack was puzzled. They did not understand. Not even Daniel could fully comprehend. Then Ajar accidentally dropped Rebecca's head from his shaking hands. For a long moment, the wolves stared at the head, then they looked back at the fur wrapped around the chakeedas and saw the gashes where Rebecca had been beaten to death. They understood. The members of the pack lowered their heads and crept into position around the chakeedas before their prey had a chance to react.

Ajar and Blueth looked about for an escape route, but the wolves were perfectly spaced. They looked about to see which wolf would be easiest to challenge. But they all looked as if they could kill a chakeeda with little effort. While Ajar and Blueth tried to decide whether to attempt to fight or flee, two more packs of wolves arrived on the scene. More were on the way as the grey squirrels spread the news of the intruders throughout the forest.

Ajar and Blueth strained their minds, convinced that they could find a way to out smart the wolves. They threw sticks at them. Shouted at them in an attempt to confuse them. Threw things behind them to try to distract them. Ajar even tried to reason with them. But in the end, Ajar and Blueth died painlessly. The wolves simply snapped their necks. It was over within a single breath. In a short time, there was nothing left of their pathetic bodies. Even their fragile bones had been eaten.

Daniel's surviving puppy died a few days later of starvation.

CHAPTER THIRTEEN

Buffalo Jake Meets the Greatest of All Wolves

By the time the secret meeting was over, it was too late to begin the long trek out of the Misty Forest. It was agreed that the attendees would stay the night. To limit the risk of losing all of the leaders at the same time, each was taken to a different location. Buffalo Jake was taken to the den that belonged to Daniel's wolf pack. The den was part of a natural hollow carved in the side of a large formation of granite, which was mostly covered in lichens and moss. An ancient oak tree grew next to the granite formation. Its roots grew over part of the granite and partially covered the hollow. It was very unusual for the simple reason that very few oak trees grew among the tall pines of the Misty Forest. In front of the den was a small clearing. A brook bordered one side of the clearing. The brook originated from an underground spring that bubbled up on one side of the granite formation creating a small watering hole. Buffalo Jake could probably have emptied the entire watering hole if he had lay down in it.

Buffalo Jake stepped forward into the middle of the small clearing and looked about. He instantly found it to be a calm and relaxing place. The members of his wolf escort began emerging from the shadows and joined him in the clearing. Several trotted over to the watering hole for a drink. Four puppies soon emerged from the den to greet the returning pack with wagging tails and cries of delight. The pups were at first startled by the presence of Buffalo Jake— one even raced back into the den. But Daniel soon explained to them that the large buffalo was a friend of all wolves. He also explained to them that Buffalo Jake was a great buffalo, Leader of the World Council of Living Things, and that they should respect him as much as they respect Samuel, the Greatest of All Wolves. At the mere mention of the name of Samuel, the pups' entire mood changed. They immediately sank to the ground and rolled over in a sign of submission and proper respect in front of Buffalo Jake.

The pups had never met Samuel, but the legendary wisdom and exploits of this great wolf were the first stories told to all pups. The exploits of Samuel's father and his father's father were also told to all pups. But not even Samuel's ancestors were respected, admired, and loved as much as Samuel himself was among wolves. He represented the Magical Age of Wolves.

Samuel was not a timber wolf, he was a white wolf from the arctic north. Even the timber wolves, who were known for their self-pride, admired Samuel more than they admired any of their own. This was because the principles by which Samuel had lived his life transcended all boundaries. The timber wolves were simply honored that they shared a common ancestry with him no matter how long ago timber wolves and white wolves had taken different paths. Physically, Samuel had been among the most agile and most handsome of all white wolves. He had a rich, full mane and his coat glistened in the arctic sun as he chased his prey across the permafrost.[2]

Samuel was no longer the powerful wolf he had once been. But he had aged with great dignity and was still considered extremely handsome. Most wolves never lived as long as Samuel because of the demands of survival. He had lived as long as he had because wolves everywhere had demanded that he be given special treatment. As part of this plan, the arctic wolves had insisted that Samuel move to a warmer climate to help with his stiffening joints. The timber wolves had welcomed him to their forest as a hero. While it did snow in the winter in the forest, the winters were much milder than on the arctic tundra and the summers were much longer.

The timber wolves felt it was their solemn responsibility to protect Samuel and provide for all of his needs, which they did so well that Samuel sometimes found them to be annoying. But he always accepted their assistance graciously as if he were a humble guest rather than the

---

2. Research Note: From the description provided in the Panda record, it is believed that Samuel was a descendant of the present breed of domesticated dog commonly known as Samoyeds. Apparently, before the domestication of this line of wolves, Samoyeds were larger than present day white wolves or else broke off from an ancient line of white wolves creating a separate subspecies. The fact that the modern day descendants of the legendary leader are called Sam-oyeds may be mere coincidence or else may suggest that some form of communication of animal legends occurred between humans and animals as recently as the domestication of wolves. If this is true, then it would be interesting to study the ancient culture of Mongolia from which the Samoyed breed is believed to have originated. Wolf legends contained in Mongolian history may serve as a basis for independently verifying the historical accuracy of the panda record.

undisputed leader of all wolves. Buffalo Jake would soon learn first hand why Samuel was so revered.

* * * * *

Normally, after returning from a trip, the pack would have lazily relaxed in the clearing. Some would have enjoyed a welcome nap while others would have played with the rambunctious pups. But Daniel never forgot the purpose of their assignment. After allowing the visiting wolf packs to quench their thirst, he assigned them to various posts on the perimeter and set up three pairs of roving patrols from his own pack. While it was true that there were three other packs also assigned to protect Buffalo Jake, and they were at this moment positioned on the outer perimeter, Daniel only really trusted his own pack with such an important task as guarding Buffalo Jake's life. After Buffalo Jake had a drink, Daniel offered him a place to lie down in the clearing. Jake offered his heartfelt condolences for the loss of Rebecca and his pup. Daniel remained stoic.

Daniel wanted to know what role the wolves would have in the fight with the chakeedas. He had many reasons for wanting to be a part of the plan. He had seen too many timber wolves lured to their deaths by the fresh meat that the chakeedas place in their hideous traps. He had seen wolves bloody their mouths and break off teeth trying to free themselves. He had even seen wolves bite off their own leg to escape the violent pain. It was so sickening to watch that even some chakeedas found the practice offensive, but in typical chakeeda style they looked away rather than do anything about it.

Daniel had racked his brain trying to think of some rational reason why the chakeedas would want to torture his brothers and sisters. But there was no reason. The wolves had never harmed the chakeedas. Daniel concluded that Buffalo Jake was right. The chakeedas were no longer animals. They couldn't be. They had become incapable of normal animal feelings. But finding an explanation of why the chakeedas had become so deranged was no longer of any interest to Daniel. It was personal now. A seething anger was smoldering within him. The savage death of Rebecca and his pup had changed his world forever. He would avenge their deaths. It was all his mind had left to hold on to.

Daniel asked Buffalo Jake what role the wolves would play in the attack. Jake knew he had no role for them, but seeing the anger in Daniel's eyes made Jake think he should find a place for them in his plan. Jake decided that the wolves could patrol the edges of the Great Valley for any chakeedas that might try to escape the main charge by the elephants and rhinos. Daniel was not happy about it. He wanted to do more to prove his dedication to Rebecca, but he did not complain. He knew it was not a time for the animals to be fighting among themselves.

* * * * *

After resting for awhile in the clearing, Buffalo Jake asked Daniel to take him to see Samuel. It was very late and Samuel would certainly be tired, but there really was no other time. Buffalo Jake would have to leave before sun up. If they were ever going to meet, it would have to be now.

The rapport between the two great animals was instantaneous. They were clearly old friends in spirit. That was good because there was no time for formalities. Buffalo Jake had been privately agonizing over whether he was doing the right thing and expressed his doubts to Samuel about the plan.

Samuel asked, "What happened to the Buffalo Jake that had convinced the World Council of Living Things to accept the fact that there was no compromising with the chakeedas? Have you forgotten your own words already? Have you already forgotten the horrible sight of that bear... what was her name... I can't remember...I was not there to see her. But just the horrible descriptions I heard of her pain was enough that I will never forget her."

"Nicole... Nicole," said Buffalo Jake.

"How many more of us must suffer her fate?" asked Samuel.

"I just don't understand them. One moment I know we must kill them. But then I think maybe if we wait, they'll wake up," said Buffalo Jake.

"Wake up from what?" asked Samuel.

"I don't know," said Jake.

"They are not going to wake up because they're not asleep. They know what they're doing and they're doing it because they want to," said Samuel.

"But I really don't understand. Why are they so evil? Don't they realize that if they continue doing what they're doing, there won't be anything left for even them?" asked Jake.

"If we had more than one planet... If we had an extra planet, then I might be curious to find out where this destructive experiment will end. But we don't have an extra planet, Jake, do you see an extra planet hidden around here?"

Samuel turned to the ever present ring of wolves that were his bodyguards and asked, "Do any of you have an extra planet buried around here somewhere?" The timber wolves were so well trained to serve Samuel that they reflexively began to sniff the ground before they realized what they were doing. There was general amusement. Even Buffalo Jake grinned.

Samuel continued, "Usually evolution is self-correcting. But in the case of the chakeedas, something went terribly wrong. Time has run out for it to correct itself."

[Research Note: At this point in the story, the panda record was destroyed by erosion apparently resulting from a shift in the seasonal flow of an underground stream in the cave. Approximately four meters of the record were worn smooth by the seasonal flooding. It is amazing that more of the record has not been damaged by erosion. The story appears to continue with the same conversation between Buffalo Jake and Samuel.]

"...but... did... he choose me?" asked Jake. "And why me? Why not some predator who would seem more suited to the task of killing?"

"If we could live for a thousand seasons, then we'd have the time to contemplate such things. But for better or worse, our lives are short. There simply is no time to find the answers to all questions," said Samuel.

Buffalo Jake did not reply. He stared off watching the currents of the ground fog around them.

"This is your destiny," Samuel repeated. "But how you fulfill that destiny—whether you do it heroically or as a coward— whether you succeed or fail— is controlled by you alone. You have been chosen. Accept that as a fact. But it is up to you to decide whether you will love or hate yourself for what you do to fulfill your destiny."

"How can you be so certain that I have been chosen?" asked Jake.

Samuel paused and sighed. "You had a dream, didn't you?"

"Of course, I have dreams," muttered Buffalo Jake evasively.

Samuel smiled a tired smile. He did not have enough breath left to engage in drawn out dialogue. But he felt one last lecture welling up inside of himself.

"You know exactly what I'm talking about. It was a vision of the future. It scared you. The earth was stripped bare. The ground was hard and black and burned your hooves. You could see waves of heat rise up from the lifeless earth. Then you heard cries rising up from a crack in the hardened ground. They were crying for you to help them. But you were chased by the chakeedas. There was also a large elephant. Isn't that true? Shall I continue?"

"Yes, it is true. But how did you know? How did you know the details?"

"I had the same dream," answered Samuel.

Buffalo Jake thought about this, then asked, "But if you had the dream, then why aren't you the chosen one? Why isn't it your destiny to lead the battle against the chakeedas."

"No, I had the same dream. It was the identical dream in every detail. I was not in it. You were. It was your hooves burning. It was you that heard the voices crying out. It was you that was chased by the chakeedas. It was you that realized the meaning of the elephant. It was a vision of your destiny. Not mine. My life is almost over. Your purpose is just beginning. But remember this, our enemy is strong enough without you fighting yourself. Lead us into this crusade with the certainty that our cause is just. If you do not win, they will kill us all. It may take them many seasons... but they will exterminate the planet. Don't let them do it, Jake. Please don't let them do it."

Samuel rolled onto his side. His tongue hung slightly out of his mouth. His panting was slow and shallow. He closed his eyes and was soon asleep. The conversation had exhausted every bit of strength from his old body.

Buffalo Jake knew it would probably be the last time he would see Samuel. He did not want to leave. But when it was time to return to the hollow, Jake wanted to at least say something to the sleeping wolf. Yet, there were no words that were adequate anymore. There had been enough talk. Buffalo Jake turned and disappeared into the Misty Forest with Daniel's wolf pack scrambling into formation around him. It was time to take the fight to the chakeedas.

CHAPTER FOURTEEN

Return to the Savanna

It took eight days before Rhino Chaga and Elephant Jabari reached the northern edge of the savanna. Both were glad to be out of the misty forest and in familiar territory. But it would still be another two to three days of travel before they reached their home ranges in the central savanna. They had not talked much during most of their journey. Their minds focused more on their fear of a surprise attack by the chakeedas. The unfamiliar landscape with all its unusual sounds and scents only added to their fear. But now that they were back on the savanna, they were able to relax and talk.

Jabari, the elephant, was 68 seasons old and had been the undisputed leader of his herd for over thirty seasons. His enormous size and massive tusks had assured him of this position. In fact, it had been eleven seasons since the last time that a younger bull had dared to challenge his role as leader of the herd. Now that he was older, Jabari doubted that he could defend his position if he were ever challenged by some younger, stronger bull again. But because of Jabari's legendary reputation among all the elephants, not just his own herd, there were no challengers. The fights, when they occurred, were for the number two and number three positions in the herd. The number one position was Jabari's alone.

The respect that Jabari had earned came from more than just his size and fighting ability. He had also managed the herd well. His instincts were very good and the herds had prospered under his control. Because of his leadership, Jabari's herd had become the central herd among the elephants. The central herd was the herd around which all other herds established their grazing patterns. It was also responsible for directing the various herds to watering holes so that no one hole became overly crowded during any part of the day.

The elephants communicated by using very low, but extremely powerful, sounds that could travel over great distances. Only other elephants were able to hear the message from far away. The sounds were made with their trunks and were used to communicate with the other herds. By repeating the messages sent out by the central herd, the elephants in even more distant herds were able to receive their instructions. By using this complex web of communication, the elephants were able to best manage the resources of the savanna.

As Jabari and Chaga continued on their journey to the central savanna, Jabari began talking about his doubts concerning his role as leader of the herd.

"I'm getting old, you know, Chaga," Jabari said.

"So are we all," said Chaga.

"But I've been thinking... this chakeeda thing... I've been leading the herd for a long time, you know, and I've been looking forward to the day when I wouldn't have to worry about so many things. But now I find that Jake wants me to lead the largest herd of elephants ever assembled on a mission that could decide the fate of our species. It could decide the fate of all species everywhere! I don't want to let anyone down, but I'm tired, Chaga, I'm not as young as Buffalo Jake. I don't know if I can do it. I think that maybe a younger bull would be better suited for the task," said Jabari.

"You can't be serious. You're the only elephant alive that could unite all the elephant herds. You're it whether you want to be or not. You have a responsibility to everyone to see this thing through. And you promised Jake that you would do it."

"I didn't promise Jake that *I* would do it. I promised him that it would be done", said Jabari.

"It's the same thing because you're the only one that *can* do it," said Chaga.

"I don't think so. I have faith in the younger bulls. I've been watching them. At some point, we have to give them the opportunity to lead. They'll make mistakes, but they'll learn," said Jabari.

"I would normally agree with you, but this is no time for mistakes. We can't afford mistakes. We need experience. There's no other elephant that can unite the herds as you can," said Chaga.

"One should never overestimate one's own self-importance," said Jabari.

"Maybe so, but one should never underestimate one's own importance either. Someday there will be another elephant as strong as you. But not now. We need leadership now," said Chaga.

Jabari did not respond. Instead, he reached up into the branches of a tree they were passing and snatched some fresh vegetation. He offered some to Chaga, but Chaga politely declined. They continued on their journey as Jabari ate his snack.

Chaga was getting seriously worried because if the elephants were not united, then the primary responsibility for the mission would fall on the rhinos. Chaga knew that the mission would not succeed if that happened. It wasn't because the rhinos were less capable than the elephants. Personally, Chaga felt rhinos were even more physically and emotionally suited for the task. On this point, Chaga felt the elephants were too patient and peaceful. The notoriously shorter temper and hot headedness of rhinos made them far more suited to aggressive combat on the massive scale that Buffalo Jake was proposing, thought Chaga.

The problem was in the numbers. There simply were not enough rhinos in the whole world to carry out the mission alone. The plan would only work if the rhinos and elephants combined their forces. Jake had known this. That is why he had called them both to the Misty Forest. Chaga knew it too. Therefore, the thought of disorganized herds of elephants charging randomly into the Great Valley conjured up images of a terrible slaughter. There was no question that Jabari had to be convinced that he must lead the elephants.

Chaga tried a different approach, "I think the real reason that you don't want to lead the herd is because your scared. Jabari, the great leader of the elephants, has gone so long without being challenged that he has become too comfortable, he's become lazy and soft in his old age."

Chaga continued trying his best to provoke Jabari, but it was hard to say such mean things about his old friend even if it was for his own good. When Chaga looked over at Jabari to see if his strategy was working, he discovered that his friend had not heard a word he had said. Chaga was relieved. The words had sounded embarrassingly foolish once they were said. But what else could he say?

Jabari's attention was directed to something else. His massive ears were spread wide listening for the standard chatter between elephant herds. Chaga stood silently waiting for Jabari's assessment of the distant conversations. Jabari trumpeted a general greeting to any herd within listening range. He waited and listened for a reply. After a while he repeated his greeting and waited and listened again. The animals that lived in this part of the savanna knew who Jabari was and soon realized he was having difficulty hearing. The birds in the lowland trees nearby stopped singing, and the monkeys stopped their chatter. All fell silent. The silence went on for a long time as Jabari listened. The animals tried to be perfectly still so as not to make any noise. The silence was almost painful to maintain. It seemed at any moment there would be an explosion of built up animal noises. But the explosion never happened. Everyone knew the importance of Jabari's mission even if they did not know what it was.

Finally, Chaga softly whispered, "I don't think we travelled as fast coming back. We probably still have a ways to go before you're within range."

Jabari stared off across the savanna. The air was still and cooling off. It was late in the afternoon. They would soon have to rest for the night. Jabari nervously swung his trunk back and forth, "Maybe so. Let's hope you're right."

The elephant and the rhino continued on their journey. After they moved on, the savanna remained strangely quiet.

* * * * *

The next day, the rhino and elephant got an early start. Chaga could tell that Jabari was deep in thought. They did not speak. Occasionally, Jabari would stop to listen. But after only a few moments, he would fold back his massive ears and continue on without saying a word. At midday, Jabari announced, "I'm turning the herd over to my son, Akin, and the third in command will be Kafa. Together, they will lead the herd." He said it as a matter of fact. Chaga was stunned and had no idea what he should say. It was clear that Jabari had made up his mind.

Jabari continued, "I have been thinking about what you said. I understand your concerns. But I want you to know why I think this is best. Normally, a younger bull would have challenged me by now. But I have been blessed with a special reputation. With such a reputation comes responsibility. As part of that responsibility, I must know when it is time for me to step aside and I have decided that it is now. When I was a young bull, the elder bulls were consulted for their wisdom and experience. But the younger bulls were the ones that lead the herd. That is the way it should be again. But you are right, this is a time in which we need leadership to unite all the elephant herds. I will stand behind Akin and Kafa to see that their orders are followed.

"Another reason I must step aside is because it's dangerous for so much power to be concentrated in one elephant. If I should die of old age or be killed by the chakeedas, who would continue the battle? Instinctively, there would be a fight for control between all the herds. That would be disastrous. I also know my own limits. At my age, I doubt I have the strength to execute Jake's plan alone. I know what I am doing. This is for the best."

Chaga thought to himself that Jabari was leading the elephant herds even in his final act of stepping aside. Only Jabari could do that, he thought. Chaga nodded his head in a sign of acceptance of Jabari's decision.

By mid-afternoon, the pair were very close to the central savanna. Jabari stopped to listen. This time he listened for a long time. He trumpeted his greeting to any herds within range. He listened again. He heard nothing. Chaga had never seen Jabari so agitated. He was now stomping the ground and swinging his trunk wildly throwing dirt and grass high in the air. Jabari exploded, "There's something wrong! There's something terribly wrong! I should be hearing herds talking to each other from all directions by now! But I don't hear anything! Not a single voice from any direction!"

Chaga looked at Jabari with a puzzled, worried expression on his rhino face. Jabari reacted, "You don't understand because you can't hear all the chatter between elephant herds. But for me, the silence is unnerving. All those familiar voices are gone. It's as though I am alone. It's as though I'm the only elephant alive!"

Jabari charged ahead at full speed. Chaga followed as best he could. In spite of the midday heat, Jabari ran as fast as he could to reach the grazing grounds where he expected to find his herd. To his great dismay, his body could not continue the grueling pace he wanted to maintain. But even so, they arrived in the central savanna by mid-afternoon. Jabari announced his arrival. He spread his ear flaps wide and listened. There was no response. It was too unreal.

Then there was the smell. He charged through a stand of lowland trees and burst into a clearing. The sight before him was so unthinkably terrifying that his mind tried to block it out with a sudden flash of white light. His front legs gave out from under him forcing him to his knees. His head became too heavy to hold up. It rolled to one side as he fought to keep from falling over.

Chaga came up even with Jabari. Chaga's breathing became fast and heavy with anger. Rage coursed through his body as he surveyed the slaughter. There were hundreds, maybe even thousands, of magnificent elephants before them. Several herds had been wiped out. Their bodies mostly untouched except for their horribly bloodied faces where their tusks had been savagely hacked from them.

Their expressions of terror frozen in death told the story that many had witnessed the hacking of their sons, daughters, brothers, sisters, mothers, fathers, and friends before they themselves were killed. Later Chaga would learn that the horrified expressions of some of the elephants was because their own tusks had been chopped from their faces before they were dead. Flies buzzed about the bloodied cavities where their tusks had been. No scavengers were anywhere to be seen. The smell of chakeedas still hung too heavy in the air.

Chaga wanted to scream out some word or phrase that would rob the breath from the lungs of every chakeeda on the planet. But no matter how hard he willed it, he knew that no such word or phrase existed. It disgusted him that he was forced to share the same air with the chakeedas. And when no words could come to mind to do justice to his intense anger, the tears began to stream down his face. He looked over at his friend, Jabari, who was now lying on his side sobbing, his eyes staring off blankly at what was once his mighty herd. Chaga knew that he could say nothing to console his friend. He chose to leave him alone.

Chaga walked among the bodies trying to figure out how this could have happened. The chakeedas had such weak, little, ugly bodies. It was hard to understand how they had survived as a species at all. So how could they have done this? The question of how concerned Chaga far more than the question of why. There was no way to understand why chakeedas had such sick minds. But how the ugly little creatures could kill hundreds, maybe thousands, of elephants scared Chaga.

As he walked among the corpses, he soon found the bodies of many chakeedas that had been gored by the elephants. He also found a few bodies of other animals such as zebras, water buffalo, and hyenas. It soon became apparent that there had indeed been a great battle. But it was also clear that the fight had been quite lopsided. There were far more elephant corpses than bodies of chakeedas. From the number of elephants, Chaga surmised that other elephant herds had come in response to distress calls only to be slaughtered themselves. It all seemed so unreal. That so many elephants could be so senselessly slaughtered seemed beyond comprehension to Chaga. He kept expecting them to all get up and give some explanation that would make sense out of the senseless. He blinked repeatedly to clear the tears from his eyes.

When he reached the other side of the clearing, he saw an elephant among a clump of lowland trees. He thought he saw the glimmer of white tusks. He walked into the brush toward the elephant. When Chaga was next to the mighty beast, he recognized him as Jabari's son, Akin. His eyes were closed. He was dead. But he still had his tusks. He had speared two chakeedas, one on each tusk. Akin had then rammed his tusks into the largest tree trunk he could find. The bodies of other chakeedas lay wasted between Akin and the clearing. He had put up a great fight. Chaga realized that Jabari had been right, Akin would have been a great leader to execute Jake's plan. But with Akin dead and Jabari emotionally paralyzed, Chaga feared that Jake's plan was now no more than a distant dream.

Chaga wanted to go get Jabari and show him Akin's body—show him the heroic way in which his son had died fighting for the herd. But Chaga decided against it. Maybe later. Asking Jabari to view his son's corpse at this moment was cruel regardless of the purpose. Nevertheless, Chaga vowed to himself that he would never let anyone forget for as long as he lived what the chakeedas had done here and what Akin had done to try to stop them.

When Chaga walked out of the clearing, he saw several herds of zebra, gazelles, and water buffalo approaching. The leader of the zebras was the first to speak. Her name was Maki. Maki said softly, "We're sorry, Chaga, there was nothing we could do. We tried. But there were so many. Not even the elephants had a chance."

Chaga glanced over at the corpses of zebras and other animals that had tried to help as if to acknowledge the truth in what Maki had just said to him. Chaga asked, "How did it happen?"

This simple question caused quite a stir among the assembled herds. After a few moments, the murmurs subsided. Chaga looked at Maki for an explanation. Tears were streaming down her cheeks. Maki regained her composure and began, "We don't know. The chakeedas seemed to be able to kill them without ever touching them. The only reason any chakeedas died at all was because I don't think they were prepared for the number of herds of elephants that came racing to help."

At this point, Jabari came up and stood absently next to Chaga, lost in an emotional haze.

"Go on," said Chaga.

Maki continued, "It took a long time for them to kill some of the elephants. They were very strong. Akin directed the counterattack. No matter how badly they hurt him, he would not go down. But when the end was near for him, I think he realized that they couldn't win. He ordered everyone that could, to run south. I have received reports that the other elephant herds that were on their way to help changed direction and headed south. That's where most of the remaining elephant herds are now, I suppose. It was too late for the elephants that had already arrived. The chakeedas had them surrounded."

"There were no survivors?" ask Chaga. Chaga thought he knew the answer, but it was so incredible to believe that he had to hear Maki say it. But to Chaga's surprise, Maki said, "Not exactly."

Maki then gave the order and the herds parted exposing their interior. Several baby elephants came into view. "We were able to hide these young ones within our herds," said Maki.

When Jabari saw the little elephants, the emotional fog seemed to clear from his eyes. When the little ones saw him, they ran directly to him. Jabari hugged them all with his trunk. There were only four of them, but they were still members of Jabari's herd. In fact, they were all that was left of his herd. He would take care of them. He would teach them. And he would protect them. Through tear filled eyes, Jabari thanked the zebras, water buffalo, and other animals for what they had done. They apologized for not being able to do more and promised their complete allegiance to Jabari in their fight against the chakeedas.

There was so much to teach them, too. Elephants were considered among the most intelligent animals on the planet. Very little of elephant culture was instinctive. Most everything was learned and passed on from generation to generation. Jabari knew that in a single day, the chakeedas had wiped out hundreds of seasons of elephant knowledge and wisdom. There was certainly much that other members of the herd could have taught these little ones that Jabari did not know. But he also knew that he must do his best to teach them what he did know. He would not fail them.

In the tradition of elephants, the dead were usually covered with branches and vegetation. This would be the first lesson that the young elephants would learn. It took most of the next three days to complete the task. Chaga wanted to have his rhino herd help, but Jabari politely declined the offer. Chaga understood.

Jabari was very proud of his son when the animals told him of his bravery. Chaga wanted to at least help with Akin's body. At first Jabari refused, but the difficulty of removing his son's tusks from the tree while keeping his body balanced was too difficult, and Jabari graciously accepted Chaga's renewed offer to help. Jabari had summoned the strength to be as stoic as he could while covering his son's body, but he broke down when he covered his life partner, Asha.

As he stroked her back with his trunk, he said, "I'm sorry, Asha. I'm so sorry I wasn't here to protect you."

He sat next to her body for a long time, crying quietly. His memories made him smile. She was still so real to him that he could not accept that she was really gone. He spoke to her, and he heard her voice answer him. The sound of her voice was comforting until he stroked her body with his trunk. Her body was cold. It was a harsh, ugly coldness that did not belong. The warmth of life was gone.

It was time to lead the young ones to the local watering hole. He left her body reluctantly. It was common among some elephants to deal with their grief by returning much later to the place of death to hold the dried boned with their trunks. Jabari could not imagine himself doing that with Asha's bones. He placed extra branches over her body. His eyes were so full of tears that the pile of branches was just a watery blur of green, brown and grey. When he covered the last grey spot in the blur, he turned to the young ones and did not look back. He knew he could not return.

CHAPTER FIFTEEN

Prisoner of the Chakeedas

When Pei Woo began to come around, she had a feeling that she was in a strange place before she even opened her eyes. The smells were very different from those of the bamboo forest. The sounds were different, too. Even the ground felt different. Pei Woo opened her eyes and rubbed the blurriness from them with her paws. She found herself not only in a strange place, but also inside a very strange thing. It looked like she was surrounded by bamboo stocks. But the stocks were not made of bamboo. When she touched them, they were cold. They seemed to be made of the same kind of hard stuff from which the chakeedas made their traps.

On the other side of the hard stocks, it looked like she was inside a chakeeda nest. She had a vague memory of what the insides of a chakeeda nest looked like from when she lived with the chakeedas as a cub. There were many changes and many new things that she did not recognize, but there was no doubt in her mind that she was inside of a chakeeda nest. It was apparent from the size of the place that it was the nest of a very important chakeeda. She looked toward what appeared to be the entrance of the nest, but she still could not see outside. The entrance seemed to open up into another nest instead. In another part of the nest she saw a different entrance that she had not noticed before, but it too seemed to lead into another nest.

She wanted to get up and see if she could get passed the hard stocks, but she was still feeling very groggy so she saw no point in moving around just yet. As Pei Woo lay their trying to figure out where she was and what she should do next, she heard the sound of chakeedas approaching. She quickly closed her eyes, deciding that it would be better to pretend she was still asleep. The chakeedas came up to the hard stocks and began speaking to each other. Pei Woo recognized their voices. It was Betty, John, and Real.

"So this is one of Jake's inner circle. She looks pathetic. Why is she so thin?" asked Real.

"We needed the land where their bamboo grows for other purposes, so there's not enough bamboo left to keep them alive," said John.

"Don't they eat anything other than bamboo?" asked Real.

"Well, yes, but bamboo leaves and bark are the major part of their diet," said John.

"What a stupid species. How can any animal expect to survive if they depend upon only one plant for most of their food?" asked Real.

"They've been doing it for thousands of seasons, maybe longer," said Betty softly.

Real gave Betty an icy stare. She had obviously given Real the wrong answer. John tried to cover for her, "Well, yes, but things change. Animals must learn to adapt to a changing world or perish."

"Exactly, we chakeedas cannot stand around and wait for the animals to catch up with us. They'll just have to learn to evolve more quickly. If they can't, it certainly is not our fault," said Real, once again smiling broadly, showing his stained and jagged teeth.

Real looked back at Pei Woo and asked, "So what exactly did this miserable creature tell you?"

"She said the attack would happen during the next full moon. I think she was going to tell us more, but she somehow figured out we didn't really know anything about the attack. That's when she started to panic and run away. We took her down at that point," said John.

"Did she say anything about the size of the attack or where it would be or which animals would attack?" asked Real.

"No. She didn't say anything else. It was difficult enough getting her to say what she did. All we could find out was that it would be during the next full moon," repeated John.

Real looked at Betty suspiciously. "Are you sure you did all you could to get her to talk?" asked Real.

"I was there," said John. "We did our best."

Real called toward one of the entrances to the nest. Two chakeedas came in. "I want all chakeedas to be on alert. We are expecting an attack from the animals during the next full moon. Every chakeeda should be prepared. I want reinforcements sent to all portions of the rim of the Great Valley, but especially along the border with the Great Plain. I suspect Jake's buffalo herds will lead any attack. Also I want a meeting of the Ruling Board immediately," said Real. The two chakeedas left quickly to distribute Real's orders.

Real continued, "When Pei Woo comes around, get what information you can out of her. Ajar and Blueth will be returning soon. They may have more information. But do what you can to get this panda to talk. I'll be in a meeting in the next nest if there's any news."

* * * * *

When Real arrived at the meeting, everyone was already present and assembled around the eating platform in the center of the nest. The chakeedas stopped grazing on the food before them when Real walked in.

Real began, "Our intelligence sources have discovered that Buffalo Jake is preparing to launch an attack against us during the next full moon. I have already ordered reinforcements to the perimeter of the Valley. I want to hear reports on our supplies and any suggestions on protecting ourselves against the attack."

The Board members each gave their reports in turn. Real listened patiently taking in all the information. When everyone was done, it was clear the situation was not good. There simply was not enough time to prepare. Even under the best scenario, there would be a heavy loss of chakeeda life and severe damage to the nesting areas. One commander asked if there was any way to delay the attack to give themselves more time to prepare. No one had any suggestion. It was at that point Real disclosed the true mission of Ajar and Blueth.

"Ajar and Blueth are not just spies. They have been sent to kill Buffalo Jake," announced Real. The Ruling Board did not take this news well. Everyone began talking at once and they seemed to be saying it was a very dangerous move. Killing Jake could easily turn the tide of emotion of the animals permanently against them. It seemed very, very dangerous indeed. The chakeedas began wringing their hands and wiping their oily little faces. Real motioned for silence.

"While this may evoke a response among the animals, it will also cause enough disorder among them to give us more time to prepare," said Real. His words did nothing to reassure the Ruling Board.

"This is exactly why I didn't tell you before. None of you have the stomach for what must be done," scolded Real.

"Exactly what is that?" asked Betty. Betty had just walked in. Real did not believe he should dignify Betty's question by giving her an answer. But all eyes of the Ruling Board were looking at her and they were clearly expecting a reply. Real knew he needed to come up with an answer that would decisively put Betty in her place once and for all. But with everyone staring at him, he was drawing a complete blank. The silence was growing awkward. He needed to say something, anything fast to give himself time to think.

"Jake must be killed. And all of the other leaders of the World Council of Living Things must be killed as well. The animals must be brought into line. Unless you have forgotten, we are the supreme species on this planet. It is absurd for us to even discuss placing our needs beneath those of the animals. Where there is not a conflict, then the animals will be permitted to survive, but we have the superior claim to the soil, the water, the air, the trees... the oceans. They're our's. Buffalo Jake and his kind have no right to steal these things from us. They have been given to us by a much greater power," said Real indignantly.

Real's argument had natural appeal to the chakeeda mind. Chakeedas were fundamentally insecure about their place in the world. One of the reasons Real had managed to stay in power for so long was because he constantly reassured the chakeedas of their self-importance. The Ruling Board especially liked being told it governed the most supreme species on the planet. It came as no surprise that they were satisfied with Real's response to Betty's question. Betty was not so easily persuaded. She summoned the courage to challenge Real once again.

"But we had an agreement. We would stay in the Great Valley and respect the rights of the animals. We gave our word. Doesn't that mean anything?" asked Betty. This was another one of many difficult questions that the chakeedas preferred not to be asked. It made them feel uneasy and queazy inside. Betty looked around at the board members, trying to make eye contact with each one. Some cast their eyes downward, seemingly afraid of her stare. Others glared back with contempt. She could hear their murmurs—"trouble maker"... "animal freak". But no one had the guts to say it directly to her face. Real felt himself gaining the advantage and went in for the kill.

Real continued, "My dear Betty... you have such a simplistic view of the world. We all would like to see our furry little friends protected. And I promise you we will provide some areas for them to live. But times have changed. We cannot be bound to an agreement that is outdated. We have needs. Those needs must be met. It is our duty to our fellow chakeedas to see that those needs are satisfied. It is a solemn duty, which every one of us must view as our highest priority. The day we forget that will be the day our chakeeda brothers and sisters will remove us from power and replace us with chakeedas that do understand."

The Board was once again very pleased with Real's response. Even though Betty was afraid to challenge Real again, she remained undaunted. She believed too much in the importance of what she had to say.

"Not all chakeedas feel that way. Some do care and do believe we should honor our agreement with the animals," said Betty.

Real immediately snapped back, "All chakeedas are sympathetic to the plight of the animals in principle. But do you know what it really means to carry it out in practice? It means much more than just giving up a few luxuries. It means there must be fewer chakeeda nests and the nests that we do build must be smaller. It means that we can't eat what we want to eat and we can't live where we want to live. It means we must agree to have fewer little chakeedas. And who should decide how many little chakeedas each of us has? And who of us should decide any of these things for our fellow chakeedas?"

Real walked around the feeding platform to where Betty was sitting. He leaned over her shoulder placing his oily face right against her cheek. Real continued with his stinky breath blowing under her nose. Betty tried to move away, but Real grabbed her shoulders to hold her still and leaned even closer.

"So you see, my dear Betty, what chakeedas support in principle and what they do in practice is very different. They want peace with the animals just so long as it does not compromise their life style. Or just as long as it's another chakeeda that has to sacrifice. Just like you, I am just a humble servant and must obey the wishes of my fellow chakeedas. I personally would like to see Jake live, but I have no choice and neither do you."

Betty was finally able to twist free of Real's sweaty grip. She stood up, ignoring Real, and pleading with the Ruling Board, "There must be a better way. I have been talking with some other chakeedas. We have some new ideas. We think we could find a way for us to live in peace with the animals. It's certainly worth a try. It's certainly better than going to war at a time when we're not prepared."

Betty paused a moment, then lowered her voice to a whisper, "We might lose."

The board members began to murmur among themselves. What Betty said made sense to them.

Real, the opportunist, jumped in, "I've changed my mind. I think Betty is absolutely right. There must be a better away. I move that we appoint Betty to head a special inquiry into the matter. Who agrees with me?"

Every chakeeda liked the idea and indicated their approval.

Real turned to Betty and continued, "I hope you were not offended if I seemed hard on you, but this is how we find the truth—the violent clash of ideas is the only way for the real truth to emerge." Betty seemed suspicious of how quickly Real had changed his mind, but said nothing.

Real continued smiling, "We will give you all the resources you need to find a better way."

Betty murmured an obligatory, "Thank you."

The meeting was adjourned.

* * * * *

The next day, Betty was summoned to the place where important announcements were made to the chakeeda masses. The place was located in the center of the largest chakeeda nesting area in the Great Valley. It gently rose up to a flat mound where the announcements were made. Betty was not told why she was needed. But as soon as she arrived, she was ushered up onto the top of the mound. Real was already there. Many thousands of chakeedas had gathered to hear their leader.

Real began, "Thank you for coming today. As you are now aware, Buffalo Jake has decided to launch a massive, unprovoked attack against us. It is very sad that Jake has been able to take control of the World Council of Living Things. Even so, I cannot stand by and allow one buffalo to bring so much pain and suffering into the world. We must protect ourselves and, as the superior species, we must protect the animals from themselves. I have been very troubled by the rift that has developed between ourselves and the animals. It has caused me great personal pain. I have thought long and hard about the problem and I believe I have come up with some new ideas that will allow chakeedas to live in peace together. Betty is going to help me turn these ideas into reality."

Betty was well known among the chakeedas as an animal lover and her work with animals was much admired. Real motioned for Betty to come closer to him, which she reluctantly did. She was annoyed that Real was taking all of the credit, but told herself it was the ideas, not the credit, that really counted. Real put his arm around her and smiled. The crowd approved. Their leader was in control. He would find a guilt free solution to the animal problem.

Betty was not ready for what Real did next. John had a vine tightly wrapped around Pei Woo's neck and was leading her up to the mound. Real started to approach her, but Pei Woo began to bare her teeth.

Real quickly whispered, "You better cooperate or else I'll have you killed." Pei Woo pretended she did not understand.

Real continued, "I know you understand chakeeda. Don't play stupid with me. Quit growling or else."

Pei Woo saw no point in fighting Real any further. She hung her head down and let Real stroke her hair in front of the crowd. It was humiliating. The chakeeda crowd ooed and aawed because it was so cute to them. Real said some final words that made the chakeedas feel warm and fuzzy inside, then concluded the assembly. Betty was amazed at how swiftly nothing had been done while giving the appearance that much had been accomplished.

After the assembly, Betty asked Real if they could talk about some of her ideas. Something about sustainable growth but through closed cycles. Real said it sounded great, but he really didn't have time right at the moment. But he promised to get back with her as quickly as possible and waddled back toward the Ruling Board nesting area, surrounded by his body guards. The crowd was soon gone. When Betty turned around, Pei Woo was gone too. She intended to have a word with John.

* * * * *

John tried to coax Pei Woo into giving more details about the attack, but Pei Woo was not talking. John tried to convince Pei Woo that it was much better for her to talk now rather than have Real's body guards try to get the information out of her, but it was no use. Pei Woo simply did not care anymore what happened to her. She had stopped eating and was drinking very little. Most of the time she just slept. It was her favorite activity. In her dreams she could escape.

She dreamed of late summer days, wandering through the bamboo forest... drinking cool water from the stream... laying on her back eating bamboo leaves and watching the birds flying from tree to tree. Birds had always fascinated her. She often tried to imagine what it must be like to glide on the winds. She had asked several birds to describe it for her, but each had said they could not put the feeling into words. It was something which you had to experience before you could understand it. Pei Woo knew she could never really fly, but in her dreams she set herself free.

In her dreams, Pei Woo soared over the entire bamboo forest. She would fly higher and higher until she could not hear any of the sounds of the forest, just the whistle of the wind in her ears and the feeling of the late afternoon sun warming her fur. It was so relaxing to close her eyes and glide free... rising and falling... banking one way, then the other... no resistance of any kind. Occasionally she would sail through a wispy white cloud. A fine, cool mist would dampen her face. At those moments, she tingled with contentment.

When she would wake up, she felt so relaxed that she sometimes wondered if she really was able to fly in her sleep. She knew the idea of a flying panda sounded silly, but she was never quite able to convince herself that it was completely impossible. After all, she could never truly be sure she wasn't flying when she was asleep because if she was awake to see it happen, she wouldn't be asleep. It was this kind of irrefutable logic which allowed Pei Woo to keep a small glimmer of hope alive that someday she might be able to fly. But until then, she was satisfied gliding through the sky on the winds of her dreams.

Since being captured by the chakeedas, a new reoccurring scene had invaded Pei Woo's dreams. She would be flying above the bamboo forest and see her sister, Kim Ha, below her. Pei Woo would swoop down and shout to her to join her. Kim Ha would say that she could not fly and that she shouldn't either. Pei Woo would climb higher again and swoop back down, trying to show her sister how much fun it was to fly. Kim Ha was not impressed. Each time Pie Woo passed by her, she would scold her and tell her there was work to be done. But that's not what most bothered Pei Woo about this new addition to her dream. What troubled her most was that each time she was at the top of her flying loop, Pei Woo would look back down to earth and the bamboo forest would be smaller than it was before. After about ten loops, there was only a small patch of bamboo encircling Kim Ha. The rest of the forest was gone. On her final pass, she would swoop down and Kim Ha would be holding up a single bamboo branch in her paw. She would say, "Take it, eat it, there's still work to be done." When she would reach for it, she would abruptly wake up. The chakeedas had even ruined her favorite dream.

* * * * *

A few days after Pei Woo's capture, she woke up to find herself laying among a clump of bamboo. She could hear the sound of a creek nearby. She could not remember how she got there, but was certainly happy to be out of the cage and out of the chakeeda nest. She looked around to get her bearings. She seemed to be in some kind of narrow ravine with a small stream running down the center. Pei Woo wondered why the chakeedas had released her. She could not remember anything. She wondered if maybe she escaped and just didn't remember it. At the moment, it did not seem important. There were shear rock cliffs on two sides of her. She looked up to see how high the cliff went on the other side of the stream. She thought she could see the top, but the sun was directly in her eyes. When she looked down stream, she could not see very far because the ravine made a sharp turn. She could not see very far upstream either because the water disappeared into a dense growth of bamboo. It was a nice place, but she certainly would not want to live here. She looked forward to returning to her home range. But first, the most important thing was for Pei Woo to find Buffalo Jake and warn him that the chakeedas knew about the plan. But which way to go? Upstream or downstream?

She decided to go downstream. The stone walls of the ravine quickly closed in and the sandy bank of the stream became smaller until it disappeared altogether. Pei Woo had no choice but to wade down the center of the stream. The water was becoming deeper and was flowing faster. Before she realized it, the water was up to her chin. She lifted her paws off the stream bed and let the current carry her. As she glided along, she had the strange feeling she was being watched. She glanced behind her. There was nothing. She travelled for a little while floating in the water until the stream became wider and shallower again and disappeared into a thicket of bamboo. Pei Woo thought it was best to continue to follow the stream. She climbed through the thicket and emerged with the stream on the other side. She thought she should get as far away from the chakeedas as she could before she stopped. She wanted to go on, but was feeling dizzy from not eating for so long.

On the side of the bamboo thicket where she had just come out, there was a sandy bank along the stream. She decide this would be good place to rest and eat something to gain strength for her journey. As she sat enjoying some delicious bamboo leaves, she noticed something in the sand a little ways further down stream. There were paw prints. They weren't just any paw prints, either. They looked like panda paw prints and they looked fresh. She hurried over to investigate. She smelled the trail. She was puzzled and confused. It did not make any sense. The scent was her own. There was something else strange that just hit her. There were no other animals. She had not seen a single other animal the entire time. There weren't even any fish in the water. She walked up the little beach to a stand of bamboo where she thought she saw some fur. She sniffed it. It was her own. It was only then that she realized she must have travelled in a circle. But how could that be, she thought. No stream goes in a circle. They all travel down hill.

A voice echoed in the ravine, "I see that you have explored your new home. How do you like it, Pei Woo?" Pei Woo's heart sunk. The voice was unmistakable. It was Real's. Pei Woo looked up. The sun had gone down farther and she could now see the top of the ravine. Small tree trunks lined the edge. Real and several of his troop stood on the other side of the tree trunks looking down at Pei Woo.

Real continued, "It has everything a panda could ever want. Plenty of tender bamboo and fresh water. Lots of places to sleep. And its very safe. No tigers to worry about. We take care of all your needs. See, we chakeedas are not so bad. What more could you ask for?"

"My freedom. Let me go home," replied Pei Woo.

"You don't have a home anymore. This is your new home. We went to a lot of trouble to build this for you. You should be grateful," retorted Real, clearly angered that Pei Woo was not excited about her new habitat.

"It really wasn't necessary. My home was just fine. I shared it with many friends and we were happy," said Pei Woo.

Real did not know what else to say. He had thought Pei Woo would be so excited and grateful, she would be willing to answer questions about the attack. But Pei Woo's attitude was a true surprise. She obviously did not know what was good for her. No wonder there were so few of them left, thought Real.

Real turned to his lieutenants, "Let's give it some time. Maybe in a couple of days, she'll come around. Let me know if she starts to talk."

"And if she doesn't talk, are you going to kill her?" asked a lieutenant.

"No, she speaks both chakeeda and the animal language. We may still need her," said Real as he walked away.

Pei Woo could not imagine living in this place for the rest of her life. She rather die than live here with chakeedas staring down at her every day. She stood there on the bank of the stream swaying back and forth. Most animals swayed back and forth when something was very wrong like when a life partner died. That's how she felt now. She stayed on the bank swaying and pacing back and forth long after the sun set. She felt very weak, but did not want to eat. She wanted to die. She began to cry. It was only then that she heard her sister's voice saying, "Take it, eat it, there's still work to be done." The words repeated in her head. She calmed down. She did not know exactly what the words meant, but she decided to obey them. She went to the thicket of bamboo and began to eat. In the darkness, she smiled. It tasted good. She listened to Kim Ha's voice replay in her head again. She did not understand it. But she felt there must be a reason for Kim Ha to say such a thing. Maybe there was a reason for her being here. After she ate, she promised herself that she would begin her search for that reason.

CHAPTER SIXTEEN

A Thunderstorm of Birds

The day for the attack on the chakeedas in the Great Valley had finally come. The biggest challenge for Buffalo Jake was how to invade the Great Valley with tens of thousands of elephants and rhinos and with thousands of predators riding on their backs, without being detected by the chakeedas. The geography of the Great Valley was the key to the plan. The terrain on each side of the Valley was dramatically different. To the south was a dense jungle. At one time, the jungle had continued into the Great Valley and had covered over half of the Valley floor. In fact, the valley had been named the Great Valley in part for the exact reason that it contained some of the most beautiful rain forests on the planet. Some of the plants and animals that lived there were found nowhere else.

On Buffalo Jake's order, Falcon Trevor had arranged for reconnaissance flights over the Great Valley. Trevor reported that most of the rain forest no longer existed. What was left of the rain forest extended down the southern slope of the valley, but the chakeedas had begun to burn down even this last remaining area. The rest of the rain forest was simply gone. The report was so hard to believe that Buffalo Jake questioned Trevor in detail, and also sought confirmation from other sources. But all of the reports were the same. There wasn't even the slightest sign that a magnificent jungle had ever been there. All that one could see now was miles of hard, packed red clay on which nothing could grow. It was hard for any of the animals to understand how a single species could be so destructive. The news pained Buffalo Jake, but he tried to comfort himself with the knowledge that he would soon put an end to this insanity. The northern part of the valley was mostly a dry savanna that gently slopped up to the northern rim.

Beyond the borders of the Great Valley to the west was a swamp. The swamp stopped where the terrain began to slope up toward the rim. The trees in the swamp were magnificent and made up one of the most ancient of all forests. The swamp was home mostly to alligators, crawdads, bob cats, turtles, raccoons, and other such swamp animals. The opposite east end of the valley was open to the sea. The terrain at the east end flattened out into a lush delta. The Central River flowed from west to east into the sea.

The challenge now was to assemble the elephants and rhinos and other animals close to the Great Valley in preparation for the attack without being detected by the chakeedas. This was a particularly serious problem because the elephants and rhinos had no reason to be anywhere near the Great Valley. If the chakeedas saw even one elephant or rhino, it would certainly look suspicious. Hence, the task of assembling thousands of rhinos and elephants near the Great Valley was a tactical nightmare for Buffalo Jake.

After consulting with Elephant Jabari and Rhino Chaga, the decision was made that the elephants and rhinos would assemble in the swamp to the west of the Great Valley. Originally, Buffalo Jake's plan had called for attacking from all sides, but because so many elephants and rhinos had been slaughtered by the chakeedas, there were not enough to surround the entire valley. The revised plan called for the elephants and rhinos to charge from the swamp across the valley floor until they reached the sea. Buffalo Nick advised Jake that it would take roughly a day to reach the sea. Sharks would arrive in the coastal waters at the time the elephants and rhinos reached the ocean to patrol for any chakeedas that might try to escape by sea. The buffalo, wolves, elk, antelope, and zebras would assemble in the savanna to the north. They would not charge into the Great Valley to avoid getting in the way of the advancing elephants and rhinos. However, they would parallel the elephants and rhinos to make sure that no chakeedas tried to escape across the savanna. The water buffalo and wildebeests were assigned the same role, but to the south of the valley where the remaining remnants of the rain forest still stood. Various species of birds were responsible for spotting escaping chakeedas. Any other animals that could be of help without getting in the way of the charging herds were also welcome to participate.

The elephants and rhinos began arriving in the swamp in small groups. Every animal was under strict orders to maintain complete silence. It was the responsibility of the alligators to guide the arrivals to various strategic positions in the swamp to wait for further orders. At first, Buffalo Jake was not sure whether he should trust the alligators with this important task. His distrust of them was more than the ordinary distrust that he had for carnivores. As leader of the World Council of Living Things, Jake knew he must represent all animals. Therefore, he felt obligated to suppress his personal prejudice against certain species. This was particularly difficult to do with respect to the carnivores, which had every right to eat him anywhere outside the safe zone of the Meeting Place of the World Council.

Even though Buffalo Jake was usually very good at not showing his personal feelings with respect to the feeding habits of certain species, the alligators were an exception. Buffalo Jake heard stories of animals coming to the water's edge to drink and being attacked by alligators that seemed to come from nowhere. You could not smell them under the water, so there was no way to know they were approaching. Jake much preferred to die by an attack by a fellow mammal such as a cougar or by a pack of wolves than be dragged under the murky waters by a slimy reptile. Also, one had more of a fighting chance with a cougar or with wolves. There was no way to fight off an alligator attack.

Buffalo Jake's distrust of alligators was caused by more than just their reputation as frighteningly efficient hunters. His fear of them also arose out of the fact that he knew very little about them. Alligators rarely, if ever, attended the meetings of the World Council of Living Things. Hence, no one knew their views and opinions on the important issues of the day. Buffalo Jake worried that the alligators might not be on the side of the World Council. Were they even capable of understanding what the World Council was trying to do? Did they understand the threat of the chakeedas? Would they cooperate? Buffalo Jake even worried that the alligators might be in league with the chakeedas.

Buffalo Jake need not have worried. As it turned out, the alligators harbored a primal hatred for the chakeedas. The only reason that the alligators did not attend the meetings of the World Council was because they had difficulty understanding the Universal Language used at the meetings. Alligators were the oldest living species on the planet. The ancient Universal Language that the alligators instinctively knew was only remotely similar to the present version used at the World Council meetings. This made the alligators feel particularly lonely and isolated because they realized that they were one of the last animals to still speak the ancient version of the Universal Language. Most all of the other animals that had spoken the ancient version had become extinct eons ago as a result of natural causes, except for maybe the crocodiles, the iguanas, and a turtle or two. This depressing thought was a major reason why the alligators did not like to go to the meetings. Considering that the mammals had come to dominate the Council, the alligators knew the chance of one of their own assuming the leadership position was very unlikely.

Even though the alligators did not know the modern version of the Universal Language, communication was still possible. Other animals that lived in the swamp had found it necessary to developed a hybrid language that their alligator neighbors could understand. It was nothing sophisticated, but basic ideas could be communicated. When Buffalo Jake's plan was explained to the alligators using this hybrid language, they virtually demanded that they be given a role. The chakeedas had been launching massive attacks on the alligators for some time. They would kill the alligators by the hundreds in the middle of the night, strip them of their skins, and throw the stripped bodies back in the water. The chakeedas did this on such a massive scale that the bodies would begin to rot and poison the water before scavengers had a chance to consume them all. There were large sections of the swamp in which the alligator population had been completely decimated. Considering the hatred the alligators had for the chakeedas, it would have been dangerous if Buffalo Jake had denied them a role in returning the fight to the chakeedas.

As the elephants and rhinos were led to their assigned locations by the alligators, they were amazed by the mysterious beauty of the swamp. A humid mist hung over the surface of the still waters. Thousand year old trees rose out of the fog creating a canopy over the entire swamp. Here and there, streaks of sunlight broke through the heavy branches, but mostly the swamp was dimly lit. As the few rays of sun disappeared in late afternoon, fire flies began to roam about performing their curious light show. The dancing lights held the fascination of the elephants and rhinos late into the evening.

It took three days for the thousands of elephants and rhinos to fully assemble in the swamp with the leopards, cheetahs, and other fast attack cats riding on their backs. Their massive legs glided through the water without making a single splash. The gentle lapping of swells against the trees was the only sound the massive beasts made. Once in position, the big cats dismounted and sat in the trees waiting for their orders. On the third day when everyone was in position, Buffalo Jake arrived in the late afternoon to give Chaga and Jabari their final instructions. Panda Kim Ha was riding on Jake's back and Trevor, the falcon, was riding on his crooked horn. Trevor reported on what had happened to the rain forests and also reported on the locations of the chakeedas' nests and other geographic information of importance.

After Trevor was finished, Buffalo Jake gave the final orders, "We will attack at nightfall. There will be a full moon tonight. This will help us spot chakeedas..."

Jabari started to interrupted, but Buffalo Jake stopped him with a shake of his head.

"I know what you're thinking," continued Buffalo Jake, "the chakeedas will be able to see you leaving the swamp with a full moon. That is a real danger. The element of surprise is critical. Fortunately, Trevor has thought of a solution. He has arranged for a massive overflight of the Great Valley. He has already pre-positioned a very, very large number of birds in the area for this purpose. There are enough birds that they will be able to block out most of the moonlight. They will also fly high enough so that they'll look like nothing more than a dark cloud from the ground."

Chaga and Jabari looked at Buffalo Jake with disbelief.

Buffalo Jake continued, "At this moment, there are representatives from hundreds of bird species positioned throughout the canopy of the swamp. When I give the order, Trevor will fly up to meet them. At that point, each representative will signal to the members of their species that it is time. When the cloud of birds has completely blocked out the moonlight, you will begin your attack."

Both Jabari and Chaga looked up through the canopy of branches at the moon. It was so bright that it was hard to imagine the birds being able to block out the entire moon. Trevor looked at the elephant and rhino staring up at the full moon. Jabari raised his trunk up to the sky as if to touch the moon. Trevor could see the doubt on their faces.

"Don't worry," said Trevor, "In a short time, it will be as though we plucked the moon from the sky. Starlight will be your only guide."

Trevor jumped from Buffalo Jake's back to a branch and spread his massive falcon wings, casting a shadow over both of their faces. Chaga and Jabari found Trevor's demonstration reassuring. Jabari said, "We are ready."

Buffalo Jake looked up at Trevor perched on the branch and then back at the rhino and elephant before him. He realized that all of these animals were here because of him. Now he was about to give the order that would surely send many of them to their deaths and maybe all of them. He heard an unwelcome voice in his head that asked him whether he was overreacting. Maybe the animals could coexist with the chakeedas if only he tried harder to explain to them what they were doing to the earth and the other animals. Maybe they just did not understand, and if they could be made to understand, they would change their ways.

After years of making difficult decisions leading the elephant herds, Jabari was far too familiar with the voice of self-doubt haunting Buffalo Jake's mind at this moment. In a steady voice, Jabari said, "Buffalo Jake, we have no choice. Too many species have been driven into extinction by the chakeedas, including two species of elephants. More disappear every day. They killed my herd. They killed my family for no reason. Asha and my son are dead. They are literally destroying the planet. There is no time for any other solution. This is it. The chakeedas have made this choice. Not us."

Jabari's words mingled with Buffalo Jake's memory of his conversation with Samuel. One thing that Samuel said kept coming back to him, "They won't wake up because they're not asleep." Jabari and Samuel were both right. Buffalo Jake looked up at Trevor perched on the tree branch and said, "It is time."

* * * * *

Trevor spread his wings and took off on his mission. Three alligators at Jake's feet guided him to the edge of the swamp that bordered nearest the savanna. From there, Jake headed off to join his herd for the attack. Trevor rose above the canopy of the ancient trees of the swamp. As he gained altitude, he could feel a surge of excitement (Or was it fear? He could not tell.) rising up in his gullet. Each of his senses felt super-alive.

There wasn't a cloud in the sky. A gentle breeze was blowing above the humid stillness of the forest swamp. It was a warm, moist breeze that sprayed Trevor's face with silky droplets of water. When Trevor reached the proper altitude, he looked down on the forest below illuminated by the full moon. It was beautiful. The twisted branches of thousand season old trees reached skyward casting strangely beautiful shadows in random patterns. Trevor imagined that each branch had a story to tell of how it came to grow into such a crooked pattern, shaped by tales of surviving violent storms and lighting strikes and other such adventures. But right now the ancient forest was so quiet that it was hard to believe that those branches were filled with millions of birds waiting in silence for his order to rise up into the sky.

Each species was pre-positioned in a different part of the forest canopy. There were tens of thousands of flocks assembled in the tree tops. The birds had rehearsed the way they would fly together to form what would appear from the earth to be an approaching storm front. The rehearsal had gone well. But it had been on a small scale involving no more than one or two flocks from each species. So no one was absolutely certain that it was even possible to perform the task on such a large scale so as to block out the moon from shining on the entire valley.

If there were doubters, Trevor was not among them. Trevor was not like Buffalo Jake— he did not suffer from bouts of self-condemnation and he did not engage in endless mind games of self-analysis searching for some meaning to his existence. Trevor had the classic spirit of a bird of prey. He was supremely confident in everything he did. In his mind, he had a perfect image of how he would assemble the birds into a storm front. Whether the invasion would be a success or not, he did not know. But he was sure that it would not fail because of any moonlight exposing the attack.

Trevor banked to his right to bring the spot at which Buffalo Jake should have emerged from the swamp into view. With his incredible vision, Trevor easily saw Buffalo Jake trotting through the tall grasses that bordered the swamp with Panda Kim Ha on his back. When Buffalo Jake reached the grasslands and joined his herd, Trevor knew it was time to begin.

Trevor swooped down to just above the treetops where the ravens were assembled and screeched his orders. The leader of the ravens cawed back and instantly a great mass of blackness began rising up from the canopy. The blackness twisted higher and higher in a long spiral formation on its way to its assigned altitude. Trevor flew on to the next location without looking back. He trusted the leader of the ravens to carry out his orders with absolute precision.

147

Trevor sailed over the canopy, swooping down to screech out special orders to each species. Soon there were birds of every description climbing skyward. Masses of crows and magpies converged at preassigned locations in the night sky. Swallows, geese, and ducks were ordered to the highest elevations because they were most experienced with the tricky winds at those heights from their long, annual migrations.

Smaller birds such as sparrows, finches, and wrens were assigned to what Trevor considered to be the lower altitudes. While these so-called lower altitudes might have been low for Trevor and other larger birds, they were a challenge for the smaller birds to reach. Yet, they valiantly beat their small wings as hard as they could, determined to fulfill the role Trevor had assigned them. Herons, cormorants, sandpipers, sea gulls, and blue jays rose up from the canopy to their preassigned positions in the middle of the storm front.

The Falcons, osprey, eagles, condors and hawks had a special role. The chakeedas had so decimated these species that there were not enough of them left to contribute significantly to the storm front. So they were assigned positions on the perimeter from which they could monitor the shape of the formation. It was their duty to keep the storm front from falling apart at the edges. Their superior speed was best suited to this task of racing to trouble spots to warn a species if it was drifting too much.

Once each species reached its preassigned location, it began circling as a single massive flock. This was particularly difficult for the geese and ducks because they instinctively flew in a "V" formation in which the spacing was predetermined. To break this pattern took a concentrated effort on the part of all of them. Once everyone was in position, the falcons, osprey, eagles, condors and hawks began their task of moving each mass of swirling feathers and flesh toward each other to form the black clouds that would make up the storm front. When the task was completed, Trevor flew out in front to take in the view. He was pleased. His storm front looked exactly as he imaged it would. Now all he had to do was keep it from breaking apart as it moved toward the Great Valley.

Immediately it became clear that the smaller birds at the bottom of the cloud formations were having a hard time keeping up with the larger birds at the top of the cloud formations. This was causing the clouds to spread out and lose their thickness. There was simply no way to leave the smaller birds behind. Because there were so many of them, they were critical to

148

the mission. Trevor ordered that the smaller birds must keep up the pace. He assigned several falcons and osprey to the task.

In the meantime, Trevor flew to the top of the cloud formations with a contingent of hawks to try to slow the larger birds down. It would not be easy because the strong up drafts at the higher altitudes were already giving the larger birds an advantage that the smaller birds did not have. Trevor thought that what was needed was a strong head wind, but except for the up drafts, the night air was too calm. For the first time, a tinge of doubt crept into Trevor's mind. "No, I can't let this fall apart," Trevor muttered to himself. He dived to the lower elevations to see how the smaller birds were doing. It was not good. The smaller birds had a natural fear of the birds of prey, so the screeches of the falcons and eagles as they raced along the sides of the flocks was enough to keep the smaller birds pumping their wings as fast as they possibly could. Trevor could see the fear in the eyes of the birds that he flew by. He did not like it. He was not the kind of animal to lead by fear. Trevor also worried that if the birds of prey put any more pressure on the small birds, they might panic and break from formation. There had to be a better way. Trevor found the leader of the sparrows and signaled him to break with the flock.

"How are we doing?" asked Trevor.

The little sparrow flew along with Trevor trying to catch his breath. "I'm sorry, Trevor, but we simply can't keep up this pace for much longer. The air is too still... we have no currents to ride on... I've already lost a few members of my flock... Our hearts are in it, but our wings can only take so much... Please do something...".

"Don't worry, just do the best you can," said Trevor. "I'll be back."

Trevor needed to think. He flew out in front of his thunder storm away from the sound of millions of beating wings. He looked ahead to the Great Valley. He could see the edge far in the distance. For the first time, he had to admit to himself that the small birds would not make it. He should have anticipated this problem, he thought. How stupid could he be. He had been too confident. He realized now that when the clouds reached the edge of the Great Valley, all the animals would begin their charge not knowing that the plan was not going to work. He had no choice. He had to call it off. He closed his eyes hoping that some perfect solution would come to him before he had to turn back. But his mind was blank. No thought came to him. The only thing that he could think of was how he was going to explain his failure to Buffalo Jake.

As Trevor turned back, he heard the sound of a lone wolf baying to the north. As he came closer to the storm cloud, which was now beginning to lose its form, the sound of that lone wolf became louder even though Trevor seemed to be flying away from it. The cry was familiar, but he could not place it. The closer Trevor came to his storm of birds, the more he was drawn to the sound of that lone wolf in the distance. The howling seemed to grow louder. It filled his mind pushing out his own thoughts. He seemed somehow connected to the voice. He tried to fight his attraction to the cries. But there was an urgency in the voice that was hard to resist. Trevor knew there was no time to investigate. He still had to break up the cloud and warn Buffalo Jake and the others.

Just as he reached his birds, his resistance failed him. He could not fight the strange attraction any longer. Trevor banked to the north and took off in the direction of the voice. It was a completely insane thing to do at this critical moment. It was though he had no control over his own wings. His body was no longer his. He did not fight it because he could not. When Trevor reached the area from where the howls were coming, he looked down and found nothing. His perfect vision scanned the ground below. In the moonlight, Trevor could see the smallest mouse scampering among the grasses collecting seeds. But there was no wolf anywhere.

Suddenly, a shadow was cast across the area that Trevor was searching. Trevor looked behind him and found his storm of birds approaching. When he had taken off to the north so suddenly, the birds had thought they were suppose to follow. When Trevor looked over the cloud formations, he realized that they were re-gaining their shape. He heard excited chirping from the smaller birds and saw them coasting on a new wind. He flew to the higher elevations where the air currents had changed. Now there was a head wind that was slowing the larger birds. The conditions were perfect. The cloud would hold its shape. Trevor turned toward the Great Valley for their final approach.

As they approached the Great Valley, Trevor once again heard the singular howl of a wolf. The voice had lost its urgency. The tone seemed pleased. He turned to a falcon and an eagle flying next to him and asked, "Did you hear that?"

"Hear what?" was their mutual answer.

"A Wolf."

The two birds of prey looked at each other with puzzled expressions. Trevor did not pursue it. He understood. He whispered his thanks to the Greatest of All Wolves.

CHAPTER SEVENTEEN

The Attack on the Great Valley

The moon vanished and the Great Valley fell dark. Chaga and Jabari gave the order to move out. The first wave of two thousand elephants and rhinos reached the western rim of the Great Valley. There were chakeedas waiting for them. The chakeedas had built an elaborate barricade along the entire western rim. Some of the first elephants and rhinos collapsed to their knees before they even reached the barricade. Some cried out in confusion and agony unable to understand their fate. Others simply fell to the ground forever silent.

Chaga and Jabari knew what was happening immediately. They had both seen the slaughter of Jabari's elephant herd when they had returned to the savanna from their secret meeting with Buffalo Jake. This is what they both had most feared. They had been told that the chakeedas could slaughter dozens at a time without touching their victims. Even though they had seen the result, it still had been too incredible to believe. But now they were seeing it with their own eyes. It was happening at this very moment.

Jabari had dreamed every night of getting his revenge for what the chakeedas had done to his species, to his herd, to his life partner and to his son. But now his dream of revenge was turning into another real life nightmare. At this rate, all of the elephants and rhinos would be slaughtered without a single chakeeda being touched. Chaga and Jabari looked at each other, their minds racing, searching for some solution. But their heads filled with questions without answers. How could they engage an enemy that they could not reach? The whole concept was too foreign to them. They needed a new way of thinking— some radical mental break through. But what they would soon discover is that they would not *think* of the solution, they would *feel* it. It would be a feeling that would travel throughout the ranks of the elephants and rhinos.

As the feeling spread among the animals, the entire first wave of elephants and rhinos stopped their attack on the barricade. They did not stop out of fear or to retreat. They stood quietly and sniffed the night air. It was the smell of the blood of their own. It was the smell of fresh tears of those that had fallen in pain. Elephants paired off and wrapped their trunks around the legs of their fallen friends. With great effort, they dragged the bodies down the slope of the western rim. They did not distinguish between rhinos and elephants. They were treated all the same. The rhinos could not help move the bodies because they did not have trunks. But they did help shield the elephants from the continuing chakeeda attack at loss of life to their own. The great beasts that were assembled behind the first wave covered the bodies with branches in ceremonial fashion in accordance with age old elephant traditions of mourning.

After the bodies were brought down the slope, what remained of the first wave began their climb back up the western rim. The soil was soaked with blood and the smell of tears still hung heavy in the air. As they approached the rim, their breathing grew heavier and heavier. The nostrils of the rhinos flared wide. The eyes of the elephants narrowed in rage. The muscles in their powerful legs surged with new energy, carrying them faster and faster. The pain inflicted by the chakeeda's unknown weapons was absorbed by the rage and anger of the attacking beasts. Their bodies were now being propelled by the spirits of all of the animals that had been tormented by the chakeedas. By the time they reached the rim, they were at a full charge.

This time the barricade snapped like little twigs as the giant beasts blazed their way through. The brave elephants and rhinos that had broken over the top of the rim collapsed from their wounds and slid down the other side. But they must have known that they had done their job well because they must have seen before they died that the chakeedas were panicking and deserting their posts in mass all along the entire rim. With the barricades down, wave after wave of the giant beasts joined the charge. They broke the rim and raced down the interior slope. Soon there was a solid wall of elephant and rhino flesh extending across the entire floor of the valley. The wall was over one hundred animals deep at the ends and almost two hundred and fifty animals deep in the center. The chakeedas that had been at the barricades were pulverized into the earth.

With their superior night vision, they could see the occasional stray chakeeda trying to climb the north or south sides of the Great Valley. The cat would paw at the back of the beast he or she was riding to signal to move to the edge of the stampede. Then the cat would leap to the earth and race toward the chakeeda. There was no need for stalking the chakeedas. They had no sense of smell and very poor night vision. The neck of the escaping chakeeda was painlessly snapped. Before returning to the waiting elephant or rhino, the cat would try to find a hiding place for the kill for later consumption. It was an instinct that could not be suppressed even at this critical time. To hurry things along, some of the elephants picked up the kill themselves with their trunks and flung it into the bushes or placed it in the branches of a tree. The cat would mark the spot with his or her scent and they would rejoin the charge.

The marathon charge to the sea continued throughout the night. The collective sound of thousands of elephant and rhino feet slamming into the earth resembled the roar of a million beating hearts. It contained a deep, powerful rhythm that had a hypnotic effect on the animals. The cadence of so many hooves penetrated into every corner of their minds, merging the animals into a single being for the long run.

* * * * *

Several days before the invasion, the message had been secretly passed to the few animals that still lived in the Great Valley that they should evacuate as soon as possible. There were very few animals that still made their home there, but most of those remaining left as soon as they heard the news. They knew that they would be returning to a much better life without the chakeedas.

But not everyone was willing to leave. The rabbears felt most secure deep within their burrows. They felt that the trip out of the Great Valley would be more dangerous than the risk of a cave-in from a stampede. The mere thought of travelling over millions of body lengths of open land with no burrows to dive into if a hawk should pass over was literally so scary that the thought temporarily paralyzed their legs. So they stayed.

When Buffalo Jake heard that they had refused to evacuate, he was furious. He spat out his cud and began screaming at the messenger, who in this case was a pronghorn deer. Buffalo Jake demanded to know if anyone had explained that this was not just a typical buffalo stampede—it was a stampede that would include every elephant and rhino left on the planet! It would shake and pound their burrows with such great force that they would think the earth was falling apart! Buffalo Jake drove his hooves into the ground and stuck his face right into that of the pronghorn's. Jake demanded to know if anyone had explained the situation to the rabbears in such apocalyptic terms. By this point, the messenger was shaking with fear. The pronghorn did not answer.

"Well?" said Buffalo Jake gruffly.

"You want an answer?" asked the pronghorn in a barely audible voice.

"Yes I want an answer," said Jake.

"I thought it was a rhetorical question," said the pronghorn.

Every buffalo within hearing range practically choked on their cuds when they heard this answer. They expected to see the poor pronghorn sailing through the air at any moment. At a time like this, it was best to blend in with the herd. Everyone stepped back trying to become inconspicuous. When the pronghorn realized her mistake, she closed her eyes and prepared for the worst. She wanted to run, but her legs were shaking so badly that she could not move. Buffalo Jake's face was so close to her own she could feel the buffalo's heavy breath blasting her. Then it happened. The poor pronghorn began to urinate right where she stood. The sound of that single stream of urine hitting the earth sounded as loud as a river. The pronghorn tried to stop herself, but she could not. It went on for what seemed to be an unbearably long time. The herd struggled to suppress their amusement.

When the pronghorn was done, Buffalo Jake asked, "Are you finished?"

"Yes," said the pronghorn.

Jake looked around at his herd. They had turned their backs on him, but he could see that they were shaking uncontrollably trying to contain themselves. Jake shook his head and smiled. He knew that he had been bested by this little creature.

"Let's go for a walk, my friend," Jake said to the pronghorn. Buffalo Jake and the pronghorn walked by themselves.

"I do not lose my temper very often," began Jake, "But when I give orders as leader of the World Council of Living Things, the well being of every animal is my responsibility. It was part of the promise I made that I would never place the lives of one species above that of another. It is an oath that I take very seriously. That's why it is important that the gravity of the situation be explained to the rabbears. I cannot order them to leave, but they need to know that it is too dangerous to stay."

"I don't think that they will cooperate," said the pronghorn. "They have great faith in the strength of their tunnels and underground homes. They take any suggestion that their tunnels will collapse as a personal insult to their engineering skills."

"That's just ridiculous," snorted Jake. "It's hardly an insult. No one could possibly know if their tunnels can survive a stampede of this magnitude. Why risk their families when the tunnels might collapse?"

"Well, even if you could convince them that their tunnels might collapse, they still fear that they would be attacked by predators on their journey to another location. This is a fear that is far more real to them," said the pronghorn.

"Tell them that I grant them immunity from predation on their journey to and from the Great Valley," said Jake.

"But I thought that an animal had to be bathed in the Special Waters before the immunity would be effective?" asked the pronghorn.

Buffalo Jake frowned. This was true. Or at least an animal had to rub up against another animal that had bathed in the Special Water. Any animal that had the scent was protected. Unfortunately, there was no time to send anyone for the scent. The invasion was already under way. Jake had no way to know that the stampede had already reached the valley floor. Buffalo Jake resigned himself to the fact that there was no easy answer.

"Go back and do the best you can. But be careful. And tell them to dig in deep if they're going to stay," said Jake. There was nothing more he could do.

* * * * *

A family of rabbears huddled together in the living room of their burrow several body lengths below the charging stampede. Rabbear Tom snuggled up to Sue, his life partner, and their three beautiful pups, Cynthia, Heather, and little Sam. They lived in a burrow that was connected to the living spaces of their numerous relatives. The burrow included twelve large living quarters for about sixty-five animals and five storage compartments for food. Numerous tunnels connected the rooms together. There were also main access tunnels that provided the primary access to the world above, and there were auxiliary tunnels that had specific functions such as for emergency escapes, for ventilation, and for drainage during heavy rains.

Tom and Joe were the senior tunnel engineers. Contrary to what other animals thought, not all rabbears were good at tunnelling. In each rabbear generation, there were a few animals that had a natural gift for it. The other animals tended to rely upon these individuals to dig the burrows. Both Tom and Joe had shown a knack for burrowing at an early age and had become very close friends over the years. Most of the burrow had been built by earlier generations. But Tom and Joe were responsible for maintaining the structural integrity of the burrow. They had also made modifications and additions that were stylistically identifiable as their work. After all these years, they considered the burrow to be their creation. They were not about to leave it now for a mere stampede.

When the elephants and rhinos broke through the barricades of the western rim and began their stampede in mass, the rabbears could feel the distant vibrations of the earth. Tom and Joe knew from the time the vibrations first started, it would still be a considerable time before the stampede was directly over their burrow. They reasoned that there was still time for one last inspection.

Tom and Joe travelled through the maze of familiar tunnels looking for anything unusual. A small cave-in here or there was nothing to worry about. Their greatest fear was that a small cave-in would spread down a corridor causing the collapse of an entire tunnel. Each living room had two exit tunnels for this very reason. But if both collapsed, it might trap an entire family in one of the living quarters. They both knew that it was very difficult to re-dig a collapsed tunnel because the earth above tended to continue to fall down. The only real hope would be to dig a new tunnel. But they also knew that a family could suffocate by the time they broke through.

On their final inspection, Tom and Joe visited each living quarter. Their confidence in the structural soundness of the burrow was reassuring to the other rabbears. But in the case of living quarter Number 7, Tom and Joe were not as sure of their assessment. They had trouble with the tunnels exiting Number 7 before during a big earthquake, and had considered abandoning it at that time instead of repairing the tunnels. There were no signs of weakness now. But as they felt the building vibrations of the approaching stampede, they now wished they had followed their instincts.

When they entered No. 7, they tried not to show their concern. There was no reason to worry anyone because all things considered, this was still the safest place they could be. Half of all the rabbears still alive that had not been killed by the chakeedas lived there. None of the other quarters had room for so many rabbears. There were no other choices. But before leaving Number 7, Tom and Joe asked the oldest rabbear to step outside into the tunnel. His name was Tony. He was a good friend and somehow related to Tom. But by looking at them, you would never have guessed they came from the same family.

"So what's up?" asked Tony, trying to act calm even though everyone could feel the growing vibrations of the earth.

"We don't want to worry anyone, but just in case we have trouble, we want you to know the alternative plan," said Joe.

"Is there a problem?" Tony asked, trying to make eye contact with Joe or Tom. Both were averting their eyes.

"No, no, there's no problem. We're making alternative plans with everyone," said Tom. Joe smirked at Tom. Joe did not believe in censoring reality, no matter how harsh, whereas Tom was not loyal to any particular reality. At the moment, though, Joe did not feel there was time to argue the point.

Tom continued, "The plan is this. If the worst should happen and there's a double cave-in... which is a very remote possibility... or if there is any problem in Number 7, we don't want you to panic."

Joe added, "Tunnel No. 14 passes almost level with your living quarters. It is about ten body lengths behind your rear wall. If anything happens, we want you to start digging a tunnel in the center of the rear wall. Be sure to dig in a straight line. We will dig from Tunnel No. 14 to meet you. OK?"

"O.K. No problem," said Tony.

Tony looked at both of them, but they still would not make eye contact. Tony began to realize that this was not just a remote possibility. He began to get angry that he had not been told sooner. He was going to say something, but realized that it would not have mattered. This was their home. Everyone who lived in No. 7 would have stayed anyway regardless of the danger.

"I'll see ya soon," said Tom. Tony said nothing and went back inside.

Before returning to their own living quarters, Joe and Tom took a detour to inspect Tunnel No. 14 one last time. It looked good. They pinpointed the spot where they would begin digging if Room No. 7 was cut off. Tom marked the spot with a shot of urine. They were satisfied that they had done all they could do for now.

As they left Tunnel No. 14, they passed Ventilation Shaft No. 3. Or at least where No. 3 had once been. They paused briefly. One of their best friends, Nena, had died trying to seal off No. 3. Her body was sealed inside. It happened several seasons ago. The chakeedas had started jamming strange sticks in the burrows of rabbears, prairie dogs, and of other burrowing animals. The sticks had a deadly smell that travelled throughout the burrow, and the chakeedas would cover the hole so that none of the smell could escape. The sticks caused a animal's eyes to bleed and mouth to go dry. With every breath, you could feel your insides burning. If you were lucky, you died immediately. But many animals suffered blindness and simply lost the will to live. Others died slowly because they could no longer breath normally. It was extremely painful.

Tom and Joe had heard horror stories about the chakeeda sticks, but their burrow had been spared until the day that the chakeedas finally discovered them. Nena had been in Tunnel 14 when the chakeedas shoved the stick into Ventilation Shaft No. 3. Nena immediately realized what was happening and pushed it as far back as she could. Tom and Joe heard her yelping. They rushed to help her and pleaded for her to come out of the tunnel, but she said that the stick would slide back down into Tunnel 14 if she let go. She pleaded with them to seal the tunnel. As the smell began to enter Tunnel 14, Tom and Joe had no choice but to bury her alive. The sound of her gasping for breath still haunted their minds every time they passed No. 3. Joe stopped and whispered to her, "Don't be afraid when you hear the earth rumble above you. It's the sound of our friends coming to help us."

"You loved her, didn't you?" asked Tom.

Joe did not answer. The vibrations were getting much stronger now. It was time to go. If they had stayed just a little longer, they might have noticed the small crack developing in the earthen seal to No. 3.

When Joe and Tom reached their own living quarters, the earth was shaking so badly that it was difficult to walk. At this rate, Joe calculated that the shaking would soon be reaching earthquake level and the elephants and rhinos were still some distance away. When they entered their living quarters, their life mates rushed to greet them. They touched noises.

In the darkness, they huddled together with their families. Their bodies were packed together so tightly that Tom could feel Sue's racing heart beat next to him. He tried to think of something to say to reassure her. He wanted to say that he loved her. Even though he felt it with all his spirit, the words did not come to him easily. Instead, he reached over and licked her face. She returned the lick.

When the stampede was directly overhead, pieces of dirt began to fall from the ceiling. Each elephant and rhino hoof that slammed into the earth above seemed like it was going to break right through into their living quarters. Joe and Tom had only seen elephants and rhinos at a great distance at animal celebrations. They knew that elephants and rhinos were larger than buffalo, but whatever creatures were now stampeding above them had to be so enormous that it was completely meaningless to even compare them to buffalo. Creatures this large had not been part of their calculations. No burrow could survive this kind of pounding. Maybe it would have been better to take their chances with the hawks.

If this kept up, Joe and Tom had no doubt that they would all be buried alive. They could feel a coat of dirt growing heavier on their backs as more of the ceiling collapsed. It would not be long before the entire ceiling caved in. Tom felt ashamed. Tom knew the elephants and rhinos would soon be compressing the earth against their backs. It would be impossible to move. He shuddered at the thought of what it would feel like if the heart beat of Sue should stop and he was unable to move to help her. The only consolation was the thought that no matter how bad this was, the chakeedas were also in the path of these enormous creatures with nowhere to hide.

The pounding above died down to a rumble. The rumble faded into a gentle vibration. The stampede was over. Tom could still feel the heart beat next to him. They were still alive. Joe and Tom looked around. Everyone was moving. They looked at the ceiling. It was not safe. There was no time to waste. The entire burrow had to be evacuated. They raced to the main entrance, climbing over fallen rocks and burrowing through small cave-ins. The main entrance had collapsed. But within a short time, they managed to push the dirt out. The cold night air rushed into greet them. Joe and Tom took deep breaths and raced back down into the burrow to begin the evacuation.

Except for a few cuts and bruises, everyone seemed to have survived the stampede well. As rabbears became backed up trying to get to the main entrance, Tom and Joe were trying to squeeze by everyone to get back into the depths of the burrow to see about Living Quarter No. 7. When they reached the primary access tunnel to No. 7, there was a solid wall of dirt where the access tunnel should have been. Tom said that maybe it was just a small cave-in. They tried to dig into it to see if they could break through. But it soon became apparent that the entire tunnel had collapsed. They ran to the backup tunnel. It had collapsed as well. Hopefully, Tony had already begun digging according to their instructions. A cloud of dust still hung heavy in the tunnels. Tunnel No. 14 was no exception. Maybe if it had not been for the dust, they would have seen the damage to the seal to Tunnel No. 3 when they passed by.

Tom and Joe pin pointed the spot that they had marked and frantically began their rescue effort to break through to No. 7. From years of experience, the two of them worked together as though they were one animal. Not a single movement was wasted. The digging went on at a feverish pace until Tunnel 14 had filled up with too much dirt. At that point, Tom told Joe that he was going to move some of the dirt into the next tunnel. Joe said he would continue to work to connect with Tony. This system worked well until the dirt began to pile up again. Joe called down the tunnel to Tom. There was no answer. Joe tried to think of what Tom could be doing. There was no time to go find him. Joe was sure he would return soon and kept on digging. Finally, there was no more room for any more dirt. Joe called down the tunnel to Tom again. There still was no answer. Joe sniffed the air for Tom's scent. He caught a whiff of something familiar, but it was not a smell he liked.

The smell burned his nostrils and his eyes began to water. It couldn't be, he thought. He ran down Tunnel 14 over the piles of dirt that Tom had been moving. He found Tom's body laying in front of Tunnel No. 3. The seal had broken and the chakeeda stick had fallen through. Tom's body was lying on top of it. Joe could see Tom's fresh teeth marks on the stick. Somehow the stick had been reactivated by the air in Tunnel 14. The horrible smell was building. Joe could feel it burning his insides. His vision was become blurred. Joe closed his eyes and tried to move Tom's body off the stick so that he could shove it back into Tunnel No. 3. He did not know that Tom had fallen on the stick to prevent the smell from escaping. As soon as Tom's body fell to one side, the tunnel filled with the horrible smell. Joe began to vomit. He tried to run back down the tunnel to somehow warn Tony to dig in a different direction. But his sight was gone now, and he crashed into the piles of rock and dirt along the way. It was too late. Tony had broken through. Joe slammed right into him. Tony saw the blood oozing from Joe's blinded eyes. The lethal smell filled Living Room No. 7. In the next few moments, half of all rabbears left on the earth died a death too sickening to describe.

* * * * *

As the herd settled into a steady pace, Chaga and Jabari were relieved to see that there were no more barricades. In fact, there was no organized resistance of any kind. Occasionally, the stampede would charge right through a chakeeda nesting area. As the stampede continued toward the sea shore, more and more of these nesting areas were encountered. But because of the darkness, the elephants and rhinos were practically on top of the nests before they saw them. The herd never broke its stride. The nests were trampled into bits and pieces before the chakeedas could react.

Chaga and Jabari were at first pleased with the apparent success of the attack. But something seemed not right. It was too easy. When Chaga and Jabari came upon the next nesting area, they started looking for chakeedas. None came out of the nests that they could see.

Over the roar of the charge, Chaga shouted, "Maybe we caught them hibernating."

"Do they hibernate?" Jabari shouted back.

"I don't really know," said Chaga.

"Well, even if they do hibernate, I don't think they'd do it this early in the season," said Jabari.

They came upon another nesting area and looked down as they raced over it. There did not appear to be any bodies among the crushed debris. This was not good. Something was wrong. To add to the problem, a ground fog was coming in from the ocean. It hovered close to the earth and swirled about their feet. The stampede looked as if it were racing across a layer of clouds. Chaga and Jabari could only wonder and worry about what the chakeedas might hide under the mist.

Jabari turned to his lieutenant and shouted, "I want attack cats along the entire front of the charge. I want them searching ahead for chakeedas. I want reports on how many they see and I want it done now!" Jabari's orders were passed on through the herd. Leopards, jaguars, and cheetahs were soon leaping from back to back of the racing animals to reach the front of the herd. They took up positions along the entire front and began their search. Their superior night vision would certainly spot any chakeedas in the path of the stampede.

The charge was over two-thirds of the way to the ocean. Everyone along the front line expected to encounter substantial resistance at any moment. No one seriously doubted that the chakeedas would have received warning of the stampede by this point and would launch some sort of counterattack. Yet, the big cats saw no sign of any sort of chakeeda response. This was dutifully reported to Jabari and Chaga, which only made them feel more uneasy.

Jabari shouted over the roar of the charge, "How could they not be aware of us by now?"

"I really don't think that they could see us in this darkness," yelled Chaga.

"But they should be able to hear us and feel us by now," shouted Jabari.

"Maybe they don't believe their own reports. Maybe they don't believe we'd ever challenge them on this scale," shouted Chaga.

"I guess it's possible that they've underestimated us. Or maybe we've underestimated them. We could be racing full speed right into a trap," yelled Jabari.

"Where's Buffalo Jake when you need him," muttered Chaga. Jabari did not hear these words, but he knew what Chaga had said because Jabari was thinking the same thing.

"So what do you think we should do?" asked Chaga. Jabari did not answer immediately. While he was thinking, the memory of burying his entire herd came back to him. The rage returned of seeing his life partner's tusks gored from her face. The memory of his eldest son with dead chakeedas strewn about him brought back his resolve.

"We have our orders. We charge on," said the great elephant. The rhino had no objection. Chaga thought that if extinction was to come for his species, he preferred to meet it on his own terms— he had no desire to wait for the chakeedas to pick the time and place. Let them do it now or forever leave rhinos alone. Even so, the pace of the charge was beginning to take its toll. Chaga and Jabari agreed to slow the stampede down. The animals settled into a gentler rhythm that was more comfortable for everyone.

* * * * *

The first dim light of dawn began to ease its lazy tentacles across the sky. The darkness of night fought back, surrendering its grip reluctantly. The ground fog began a slow retreat, trying to act unintimidated by the warming rays of the sun. In the hazy shadows of the early morning, strange shapes began to emerge in the distance. The shapes seemed very odd, they had sharp edges and jutted up from the earth in unnatural, awkward patterns. These were not organic shapes. As the stampede came closer, Chaga and Jabari were awed by the size of these strange structures. Some of them were maybe three or even four times as tall as an elephant. The herd began to slow down. There was no way they could stampede over what they saw before them. They stopped at the edge. The largest group of the chakeeda nests began where they now stood and extended all of the way to the ocean and to each edge of the Great Valley. The tall structures were in the middle of the largest nesting area. So many chakeeda nests, but not a single chakeeda in sight.

To the north of where Chaga and Jabari stood, the rim of the Great Valley was defined by a sharp cliff. At the top of the cliff were flat grasslands. Chaga and Jabari looked up to be greeted by the sight of thousands of buffalo. Even among so many animals, Buffalo Jake's powerful form stood out from the herd. Nick was standing next to him. Buffalo Jake stared down at the unfriendly shapes. Jabari waived to Buffalo Jake with his trunk. Buffalo Jake nodded his head to acknowledge the gesture. Jabari pointed with his trunk to a place closer to the ocean where the grassland slopped down to meet the valley floor. Jake understood to lead his herd in the direction that Jabari had indicated as the best way to descend the northern rim.

When Buffalo Jake and Nick reached Chaga and Jabari some time later, they stood together for a long while just staring at the strange structures. A steady breeze was kicking up off of the ocean. The wind whipped and whistled through the thousands of chakeeda nests surrounding the tall structures. Not a single chakeeda was in sight.

Buffalo Jake asked, "How many did you loose?"

Jabari answered, "Maybe 800 to 1200. They were ready for us when we first crested the western rim. After that, there was no substantial resistance."

"My deepest sympathies for your loses. But at least now we will be free of the chakeedas," said Buffalo Jake.

Jabari said, "We need to speak to you privately."

After they walked away from their herds, Jabari continued, "After we got over the western rim, there were no more chakeedas. None."

Jabari could see the disbelief in Buffalo Jake's eyes.

"O.K., maybe there were a few chakeedas here and there. But there certainly were not hundreds and there certainly were not thousands."

Chaga vigorously demonstrated his agreement by scratching the earth with his left hoof and by kicking dirt in the air with his horn.

"Hardly none," said Chaga. "Hardly none."

"Are you absolutely sure? It was dark... and you were going pretty fast," questioned Buffalo Jake.

"That's why we had the big cats scan ahead for us. They didn't see anything either and they have excellent night vision," said Jabari.

Buffalo Jake seemed baffled, "Where could they hide? Are you absolutely positive?"

Jabari signaled to one of his lieutenants, Gamba, to bring the leaders of the big cats over. The leopards, cheetahs and others were already napping. Gamba gently tapped the leopard with his trunk. Even though they had been living and working together for sometime now in preparation for the invasion, the leopard was quite startled and reached for Gamba's trunk with claws open. Gamba yanked her trunk out of harm's way just in time.

Gamba said, "Excuse me, but Buffalo Jake would like to speak to you."

The leopard stared at Gamba for a few seconds, said "fine", and then rolled over to go back to sleep. Gamba nudged the leopard with her foot, rolling him over. The big cat hissed and took another swipe at Gamba's trunk, which was safely out of reach this time.

The elephant said, "Now."

The cat looked around at the crowd of elephants and understood. The other cats that had been awakened from their naps by the disturbance began walking toward Buffalo Jake without being asked.

The big cats confirmed what Jabari and Chaga had been telling Buffalo Jake: The chakeedas were missing. But where could they be? As the animals pondered this question, the birds that had formed the storm front began arriving. They landed everywhere; on the backs of the rhinos, elephants, and buffalo, on the ground, and on top of the chakeeda nests. The only place they did not land was on the unfriendly shapes in the center of the field of nests. Trevor soon arrived and landed on Buffalo Jake's crooked horn. Buffalo Jake tilted his head to try to see who just landed on him and Trevor almost fell off.

"It's me!" said Trevor.

"Good. I have a question for you. When was the last time that anyone flew over the Great Valley?" asked Buffalo Jake.

"It was before the rhinos and elephants began positioning themselves in the swamp," answered Trevor.

"That was about six days ago," said Jabari.

"Did you see any chakeedas when you flew over?" asked Buffalo Jake.

"I didn't personally fly over. But the report that I received was that there were hundreds of thousands of chakeedas all over the place," said Trevor.

Two of Trevor's lieutenants that were picking at insects on Buffalo Jake's back squawked at Trevor in their species' language.

Trevor continued, "That's right. I did send two eagles over the valley about three days ago, but I don't remember them coming back. So much was happening with organizing the storm front that I guess I forgot to tell you. Is it important?"

"The chakeedas are missing," said Buffalo Jake. The words were painful to hear. The implication was immediately understood. They had all hoped that the battle would have been over by now, but it had not even begun. Buffalo Jake felt particularly responsible since it was his plan.

"Where could they be? There's no way so many of them could all have left the valley. Someone would have seen them," said Trevor. The animals looked at the strange structures in the distance.

Chaga had been quiet up until this point, he was an animal of few words, but now the great rhino launched into one of his rare speeches, "Jake, I know what you're thinking—it may indeed be a trap—but we have not come this far not to find out. If the entire earth is to be their exclusive domain, then let them begin their lonely reign over a barren planet right here today. Don't be afraid to shed our blood. Even if we don't succeed, you'll have let us die with our dignity."

The animals indicated their agreement with mannerisms unique to each species.

"Have the herds reassemble and surround the nesting area," ordered Buffalo Jake. "We're going in."

The animals moved in from every direction except the ocean side. There was no stampede this time. The pace was slow and steady. They looked inside every chakeeda nest. All were empty. The nests were fragile structures that simply could not withstand the weight of buffalos, rhinos, and elephants banging into them and looking inside. There were so many large animals converging on the center that they destroyed the thousands of surrounding nests without even meaning to do so. Once a nest began to collapse, it was hard for the elephants and rhinos to avoid walking over it because the area was so crowded with animals. The area was soon strewn with nothing more than broken sticks where thousands of nests once stood.

They arrived at the first of the strange looking structures in the center of the nesting area. Buffalo Jake requested that Panda Kim Ha be brought to him. Kim Ha had been riding on the back of Buffalo Nick. When she arrived, she hopped over onto Buffalo Jake's back.

"Ask them to come out," said Buffalo Jake. Kim Ha called in the chakeeda language to anyone inside. There was no answer. She repeated her request. Still no answer. Then a soft cry came from inside. Buffalo Jake tilted his head in puzzlement and strained to listen more closely. The sound came again. It sounded like a small animal crying. The sound seemed familiar to Buffalo Jake, but something was different about it. He listened again. He could not place it. But whatever the type of animal, it sounded as if it were in pain. Buffalo Jake nodded to Jabari. Jabari ordered two of his strongest elephant bulls to break in. They rammed the entrance with their tusks, breaking through on the third blow. As they withdrew their tusks, they twisted their heads back and forth causing the wood to splinter into pieces. With the weight of their bodies, they broke the rest of the entrance down.

Buffalo Jake was the first to step inside. Kim Ha was riding on his back. Buffalo Nick followed. Jabari and Chaga remained at the entrance with only their large heads inside. The space inside was maybe five to six buffalos high, twenty buffalos long, and six buffalos wide. It smelled very badly of manure and urine. The sound of flies buzzing about was the only sign of life. Along the walls were small enclosures of some kind. They were way too small for Buffalo Jake to fit inside.

Kim Ha asked in a whisper, "Is this where the chakeedas live?"

Buffalo Jake did not answer. He cautiously stepped further into the interior. The small enclosures appeared to be empty. It was hard to tell because their view was blocked by some kind of strange tree branches that were flat. Buffalo Jake had never seen trees or branches grow flat like that. He was about to look closer at them when he heard the animal cry again. This time he recognized it. It was the cry of a buffalo calf.

He rushed to where the cry came from and found a baby buffalo trapped in one of the enclosures. The space was so small that the calf could not turn himself around. He could take maybe one step forward and one step back, but that was it. Because the calf was facing the wall, he could not see buffalo Jake. Buffalo Jake called to him in the buffalo language for him to step forward so that he could break down the flat branches, but the calf did not respond. Buffalo Jake called to him again in the Universal Language, but the calf still ignored him. Kim Ha gave the same instructions in the chakeeda language. The calf immediately took a step forward as ordered. This was not acceptable. Buffalo Jake's nostrils flared. He rose up on his hind legs and came crashing down on the flat strips of branches with his front hooves. He repeated the process until nothing stood in his way.

The little buffalo did not move. The calf seemed unaware that it was now free. Buffalo Jake wanted to call to him in the buffalo language again, but hesitated because he was afraid that the calf would still not understand. Unanswered questions raced through Buffalo Jake's mind. What terrible thing could the chakeedas have done to this young buffalo to strip him of his understanding of his natural language? And why could he understand chakeeda?! It was sickening. Slowly in a low, calm voice Buffalo Jake said, "Back up, little one. You're free. Come out of there." The calf did not move. Buffalo Jake gently nudged the back of the animal with his broad forehead. The calf stumbled and leaned against the side of the enclosure to regain his balance, but made no attempt to leave. Reluctantly, Buffalo Jake asked Kim Ha to tell the calf to come out, which she did in the chakeeda language. The little buffalo obeyed. Jake cringed.

When the calf saw Jake, he seemed frightened and tried to go back into the enclosure. Buffalo Nick blocked his way. After the calf decided that no one was going to harm him, they were able to lead the little buffalo outside. The distance to the entrance where Jabari and Chaga were waiting was only about ten buffalo lengths from where they found the calf. But it took the little buffalo a long time to reach the entrance. He was not able to walk normally and had to stop frequently to regain his balance. With each troubled step of the young animal, Buffalo Jake's emotions shifted from confusion and pity to anger and rage. At first, Jake had thought the young animal had been trapped by accident in the enclosure. But now as he looked around at the rows of enclosures on both sides of him, he realized that there was some design to this madness. This was no accident. But what possibly could be the purpose? Why do this to young buffalos? Was this just another example of the sickness of chakeedas or did they have some reason?

When the young Buffalo stepped outside, the brightness of the morning sun was too great. The calf shut his eyes tightly to block out the light. He tried to turn around to go back inside, but ended up falling down. He struggled to get back on his feet, but simply lacked the strength to lift his own meager body weight. He lay there with his eyes shut panting heavily from the effort.

The attention of the animals surrounding the calf was diverted by a large commotion some distance away near one of the other large structures. From the hostile tone of the trumpeting elephants, it appeared that a chakeeda had been found. Several wolf packs had also arrived. A fight broke out among three of the wolves over who would have the honor of snapping the chakeeda's neck. But regardless of who performed the execution, it was apparent from the angry mob of animals that had gathered that the chakeeda did not have long to live. Buffalo Jake had too many questions to allow the chakeeda to die so easily. He asked Jabari to go pluck the chakeeda from the crowd. Jabari easily waded into the crowd and wrapped his trunk around the chakeeda, who was trembling badly. When Jabari set the chakeeda down in front of Buffalo Jake, one would have thought the chakeeda would have been grateful for being saved. But the ugly little creature quickly regained his composure and acted as if Jabari should have been honored to do him the favor. When the chakeeda looked up at the buffalo before him and saw the one crooked horn, the chakeeda said, "Buffalo Jake, I take it?"

Kim Ha translated this into the Universal Language. Buffalo Jake did not answer. He stared at the chakeeda for a few long moments. Slowly, deliberately, Buffalo Jake closed the distance between him and the chakeeda until his massive head was directly over the pathetically ugly thing. Kim Ha climbed off of Buffalo Jake's back so that she could translate. In a low deep whisper, Buffalo Jake said, "I just want to know one thing, so pay very close attention. Do you see that calf laying there? I want to know what you did to him." While Kim Ha translated the words, the danger suggested by the forced restraint of Buffalo Jake's voice was something that the chakeeda understood without a translation.

"I guess she was left behind. I thought all of the live stock had been taken," said the chakeeda.

"Live stock?"

"Well, you know, animals we raise for food. We have a right to eat meat. We are carnivores," said the chakeeda.

No one fully understood this answer, but Buffalo Jake was not particularly interested in pursuing it. He wanted to know about the calf. He ordered the chakeeda to go inside the structure where the calf had been found. Other animals followed until the structure was completely full.

Standing before the enclosure in which the calf had been found, Buffalo Jake asked, "How did the calf get trapped in there?"

"Trapped? He wasn't trapped. We simply forgot to bring him. I'm sorry about that," said the chakeeda.

Buffalo Jake was getting angry. "What do you mean, he wasn't trapped? I saw it with my own eyes!"

"He was not trapped because that's where he lives... in that space... that was his stall... what's there to understand?" asked the chakeeda.

Buffalo Jake still did not want to understand. The horrible truth was too inconceivable. He kept hoping that the chakeeda would provide some explanation that would soothe him.

"Let me get this straight. The calf lived in that small enclosure? Is that right?" asked Buffalo Jake.

"Right," answered the chakeeda.

"Did he get out during the day?" ask Buffalo Jake.

"No. That would have defeated the purpose," answered the chakeeda. A roar of hostile animal noises rose up from the gathered crowd.

"So he lived in there all of the time, day and night and was never let out?" asked Buffalo Jake.

"Yes, that's right," answered the chakeeda.

"And all of these other enclosures, they had calves in them too?" asked Buffalo Jake in a voice too stunned to show anger.

"Yes," answered the chakeeda. One could barely hear Kim Ha's translation over the angry hissing, growling, and snorting. Buffalo Jake asked for quiet. The crowd reluctantly settled down.

The chakeeda was truly puzzled by the reaction he was getting. "We are carnivores. Some of you here are carnivores. Why are you so shocked? We have a right to eat, don't we? We have a right to do what we have to do to survive," said the chakeeda.

"But why this?" asked Buffalo Jake, motioning with his head to the enclosures.

"Well, because the calves taste better. If they were allowed to roam freely, their meat would become tough. We kill them when their about a half a season to a season old. We call it veal. It's very good," answered the chakeeda.

Buffalo Jake looked down the row of enclosures imagining the horrible sight of them all filled with buffalo calves. It made him so sad that he had no room for anger. He felt very numb, and hoped when he closed his eyes and reopened them again, all of this would be gone. It did not disappear. It was too real.

"How long has this been going on?" asked Buffalo Nick.

"I don't know. For as long as I can remember," answered the chakeeda.

Buffalo Jake had nothing more to say. He walked out of the structure with his head hanging low. The animals parted to give him a clear path.

He wanted to be with the young calf outside. But before he left, Jabari asked, "Jake, what should we do with the chakeeda?"

Buffalo Jake looked back at the row of chambers and said, "Put him into one of those and don't let him out."

Jabari wrapped his trunk around the chakeeda and tossed him into a fly infested chamber. Buffalo Nick slammed the gate shut. Kim Ha placed a flat branch across it. The chakeeda was trapped.

When the chakeeda realized what they were doing, he began screaming frantically, "You can't do this to me! This is cruel! Let me out of here right now. This is sick! Don't you understand?! You can't do this to me! I'm not an animal. I'm a chakeeda! I'm a chakeeda!"

CHAPTER EIGHTEEN

The Lagoon

Jake stood on the beach flanked by Elephant Jabari and Rhino Chaga. They were all looking out at the sea. From this strip of beach, one could just make out a distant formation of land on the horizon. Today was hazy so it was difficult to see. But on a clear day, the island could be seen relatively easily.

Seeing Chakeeda Island was not the problem. In fact, it would have suited the animals just fine if they were never able to see the island. But that was not the case. The chakeedas were far enough away to prevent the animals from launching an attack, but were close enough that the chakeedas themselves mysteriously had no problem continuing their destructive activities on the mainland while retreating back to the island when the animals tried to stop them. Jake had tried to ignore the chakeedas for many seasons since their retreat to the island, but the problem was once again becoming too severe.

The difficulty that Jake, Jabari, and Chaga were now puzzling over was how to transport thousands of elephants and rhinos to the island for a surprise attack on the chakeedas. This was a problem. The three had been struggling with the issue for the past four seasons. As they stood at the edge of the surf, they had to keep repositioning themselves because their feet kept sinking into the wet sand. Finally, they left the surf and returned to the dry beach.

"Jake, it's time to face reality," said Jabari. "There is no solution. Real simply beat us on this one. There is no way that we're going to get on that island. Maybe we can find some way to keep them off of the mainland, but there is no way we're going to be able to bring the fight to them."

Chaga nodded slowly in reluctant agreement.

Buffalo Jake stared out at Chakeeda Island with intense determination. It had to be possible to transport themselves to the island. Buffalo Jake closed his eyes and tried to wish them there. When he opened his eyes, the three of them were still there on the beach. It had been worth a try, he thought.

"You're right," Buffalo Jake finally said. "It does seem impossible."

Chaga and Jabari were relieved to see that Buffalo Jake was finally coming to terms with the reality of the situation.

Jabari said, "It's alright, Jake. It's not your fault. Some things are just not possible."

"I said that it seemed impossible. I did not say that it was impossible," retorted Jake. "At the end of the season, I want you to assemble your herds at the point." Jake motioned with his head down the coast where the land shot out toward the Island. Chaga and Jabari looked in the direction that Buffalo Jake was pointing. It was true that the point was the closest part of the mainland to the island. But it would still take an entire morning at a full charge to reach the island even if there was not all that water in the way.

Chaga began to protest, "You have to be joking. There is no way..." Jake interrupted Chaga, "I know it seems impossible. But you're going to have to trust me. I'll send a messenger to let you know when the attack will be. Have your herds there when I say and I'll take care of the rest."

Jabari was suspicious. "Why can't you tell us the plan?"

"I just can't. At least not yet. You're going to have to trust me," said Jake.

Jabari and Chaga looked at each other. They did not like it.

"I need you," said Jake. "Don't let me down."

Chaga and Jabari knew that they could not refuse Buffalo Jake and reluctantly agreed. They would leave in the morning to prepare their herds.

After Chaga and Jabari walked off to prepare for their return to the savanna, Buffalos Nick and Anthony approached him. They had overheard the conversation that Jake had just had with Chaga and Jabari. They seemed upset.

"What's the matter?" asked Jake.

"We want to know why you did not tell Chaga and Jabari the truth?" asked Anthony.

"And risk a repeat of the Great Valley invasion? I don't think so. The fewer animals that know the real plan the better. Chaga and Jabari will understand," answered Buffalo Jake.

"But it's not fair. They should be told that they are not a part of the invasion," said Anthony.

"They are a part of the invasion," Buffalo Jake shot back. "They will serve as a diversion. The chakeedas will think we're planning a repeat of the Great Valley invasion. It'll keep them off track. That's an important part of the over-all plan."

"Why can't Chaga and Jabari know that's the plan?" asked Anthony.

"They can't know because too many animals knew the last plan. Somehow the chakeedas found out. Why is that so difficult for you to understand?" asked Buffalo Jake, visibly irritated.

There was an uneasy silence. Anthony was not the only one of Buffalo Jake's lieutenants to be disturbed by his tactics lately. Buffalo Nick was also feeling increasingly uncomfortable. Jake had experienced the same feeling of uneasiness himself. But he had been able to suppress it by justifying his conduct as necessary to the success of the fight against the chakeedas. As he looked at the unsettled expressions of concern on the faces of his lieutenants now, the feeling was coming back to him. He tried to dismissed it again. He had difficult decisions to make. Some were not perfect. But they were necessary if the planet was to be saved.

Buffalo Jake was about to explain his thinking when he looked over the back of Buffalo Anthony and saw something familiar down the beach. A smile came to his face when he saw his good friend, Samuel, The Greatest of All Wolves. Samuel motioned with his snout for Buffalo Jake to follow him down the beach. Jake excused himself from the presence of Nick and Anthony, "I believe we have a special visitor."

Nick and Anthony looked down the beach in the direction that Buffalo Jake was heading. They saw nothing, but assumed that Buffalo Jake was blocking their view.

"What a nice surprise," said Buffalo Jake when he caught up with Samuel. "You must be exhausted. It's a long trip from the Misty Forest."

"It's closer than you might think. It all depends upon which path you take," said Samuel.

Jake was not entirely sure what this meant, but continued, "Well, thank you for coming. Just seeing you lifts a great weight off of my back."

"And what weight is that?" asked Samuel.

"The weight of making the right decisions," said Jake.

"I can't make your decisions for you," said Samuel.

"What do you mean?! You should be making all of these decisions. You would do a far better job than I can," said Jake.

175

The buffalo and the wolf stopped on the beach. It was late afternoon and the sun was almost touching the horizon. The wolf lay down facing the sunset and tucked one of his front paws under him for balance. The buffalo lay down next to him.

"So what is bothering you, Jake?" asked Samuel.

Jake answered, "The decisions are becoming more complicated. The right answers are becoming harder to find."

"What answer are you looking for?" asked Samuel.

Buffalo Jake explained the situation with Jabari and Chaga, then asked, "You told me that the fight against the chakeedas was the right thing to do. Not telling Chaga and Jabari is for the greater good. What is wrong with that?"

Samuel looked at Buffalo Jake as if he was a young pup that was having trouble catching a simple field mouse.

Samuel began, "If all you were doing was keeping Chaga and Jabari in the dark, there would not be a problem. But that's only part of what you're doing. You're also misleading them."

Samuel paused. He panted a bit to catch his breath. His body was failing him more with each day. But he hung on because he knew his mission was not yet complete. Buffalo Jake was not yet ready to lead without him.

Samuel continued, "It is a small thing now, but you are treading on quicksand. With each step, you sink deeper in the sand until it is too late to turn back. The only way to avoid the danger of quicksand is to never trend out onto it in the first place. Going around it may take longer, and you may encounter other dangers on the way, but you really have no choice."

Once again, Samuel had to stop to catch his breath. Buffalo Jake waited for Samuel to continue, thirsty for each word that his wise friend spoke.

"Your lieutenants can sense the danger. They don't know how to express it, but they feel it. Where does deception stop once it has begun? How can you be trusted? I know you can sense the danger—the uneasiness—as well. Do not ignore it. Let it be your internal guide." Samuel stopped again, panting lightly, then continued. "Do not let the chakeedas force you to compromise your internal guide. Don't give them that victory."

Samuel fell gently to his side and lay his head on the beach. A few grains stuck to his damp nose. It was bothersome, but he did not have the strength to lick them off. He closed his eyes to rest.

"Thank you," said Buffalo Jake. "You always bring me back to where I should be." Jake did not know if Samuel could hear him, but he continued, "I could not get through this without you, my friend."

Buffalo Jake leaned over and gently pressed his face against Samuel's body to check that he was OK. He could feel Samuel breathing. His breath was shallow, but steady.

"Hang on," said Jake. "Hang on."

The sun was sinking below the horizon and the beach was getting windy and cold. Jake stayed next to Samuel to give the venerable wolf warmth as he slept.

The tide was completely out now. Jake could see his hoof prints in the sand where he and Samuel had walked. There was something odd about them. He stared at the prints until it finally hit him. Samuel's paw prints were missing. Jake had been on the surf side as they walked. The tide would have washed his hoof prints clean before reaching Samuel's paw prints. At least, he was pretty sure that's how they were walking. He squinted in search of any trace of Samuel's path. There was none. He turned to look at Samuel next to him. The Greatest of All Wolves was gone.

* * * * *

In the morning, Buffalo Jake sent Anthony to find Chaga and Jabari before they left for the savanna. Within a short time, Anthony returned with them along with several other elephants and rhinos that now served as body guards for the two leaders.

"Good morning," said Jake. Chaga and Jabari were not in a particularly good mood. Jabari returned the greeting for both of them with a feeble blow of his trunk. Jake tried to ignore their poor attitude.

"Before you leave, I have something I want to show you," said Jake.

Several words were exchanged between Chaga and his body guards in the rhinoceros language, then Chaga said, "We have a long journey ahead of us. Will this take long?"

"It's close by. I promise I won't keep you any longer than is necessary," said Jake.

"Fine," said Chaga.

"It's this way... just a bit up the coast," said Jake.

It was immediately obvious to Buffalo Jake from Chaga and Jabari's cool attitude that the relationship with the elephants and rhinos had been damaged by excluding them from the preparation of the new plan. The problem was made more obvious when Chaga and Jabari did not walk next to Buffalo Jake, but stayed with their own instead. Anthony could not resist pointing this fact out to Buffalo Jake as if he had foreseen such a result (which he had not). He tried to be discreet by making his comment in the buffalo language. Jake was annoyed by the comment because Anthony was always second guessing his decisions and seemed to find particular delight when one of his decisions proved wrong. Jake was more angry at Anthony for speaking to him in the buffalo language than for what he actually had said. At a time like this, it was critical that he not give the impression that he was hiding something from Chaga and Jabari. So Jake said quite loudly for all to hear, "Use the Universal Language. Anything you have to say to me can be said in front of my friends."

Anthony was surprised by this sudden reaction. He did not know that the words were not actually meant for his ears. He mumbled an acknowledgment and slipped to the rear of the group.

As they moved further up the coast, the beach became narrower as the jungle crept over the sand dunes and squeezed the beach into the ocean. Within a short time, the beach was so narrow that the buffalos and rhinos had to walk single file. Buffalo Jake stopped and looked up and down the beach. He looked out to sea and even up into the trees overhanging the beach. When he was satisfied that no chakeedas were watching, he cut sharply into the thick jungle and called back behind him for everyone to move quickly. After travelling a short distance, they came across a narrow path that paralleled the beach. They travelled down the path until they came to a lagoon. The contingent spread out along the shore of the lagoon on one side. The surprising sight before them brought smiles to the faces of Chaga and Jabari and all of their body guards. They were not sure what exactly they were looking at, but they could sense that it was a very good thing.

There were animals everywhere moving quickly about the lagoon. The animals were from all over the world. There were orangutans, monkeys, pandas, wolves, badgers, bears, wild boars, jaguars, sea turtles and many others. In the middle of the lagoon, there were two gray whales. A few dolphins and porpoises were swimming around the whales.

There was so much to see that Chaga and Jabari did not know where to look first. Directly across the lagoon, a badger was trying to balance himself on the back of a sea turtle that was on the beach while other animals stood about making helpful suggestions. When the sea turtle moved into the water, the badger couldn't keep his balance and was soon splashing back toward the shore. A wolf tried crouching on the back of another sea turtle to see if that would work, but suffered the same fate when the shelled creature entered the water. Sea turtles as a means of transportation did not appear promising. But it had definite possibilities as a form of entertainment.

The whales sprayed water from their blow holes to signal that it was time for them to leave. The lagoon was connected to the ocean by a channel that weaved through the jungle. The whales could only enter and leave the lagoon at high tide. The lagoon itself was too shallow at low tide for the whales to survive. As they turned their massive bodies around to leave, a wave of water splashed up onto the shore where Chaga and Jabari stood. Within a few moments, the whales were down the channel and out to sea until the next high tide.

Buffalo Jake led the contingent over to the animal in charge. Jake knew that no one was really in charge. But there at least had to be someone to whom he could pass on instructions. Orangutan Valin was that animal.

"Good morning," said Buffalo Jake. "I would like for you to meet Elephant Jabari, Great Leader of the Central Elephant Herd of the Savanna and Designated Leader of all Jungle Elephants."

Orangutan Valin set down the durian fruit that he was snacking on and struck his chest once with his left fist and held his hand above his head, which was a traditional orangutan greeting and sign of respect. Jabari trumpeted a traditional elephant greeting in return.

"I would also like for you to meet Rhinoceros Chaga, The Great Leader of the Savanna Rhinos and Designated Leader of the Forest

179

Rhinos," said Jake. The orangutan and rhino exchanged traditional greetings and signs of respect.

After the rest of the contingent was introduced and everyone had become comfortable with all of the new scents, Buffalo Jake said, "I have not told Elephant Jabari and Rhino Chaga about the new plan. It would be appreciated if you could explain it and bring us all up to date."

Orangutan Valin, like most orangutans, was shy by nature. They were good problem solvers, but preferred to operate alone. Suddenly being the focus of so much attention made him uncomfortable. He covered his face with his arms, then turned away from the contingent and asked them to follow him. They walked a short distance into the jungle where they came to a clearing. It was not large. The trees on the edges of the clearing still hung over the clearing at the top of the canopy. In the center of the clearing was a bunch of bamboo lying flat on the ground. Each piece of bamboo was directly next to another piece. Surrounding the flat expanse of bamboo was a group of chimpanzees, lowland gorillas, and orangutans. There were also piles of bamboo on one side and vines next to the pile. The animals raised their heads to see who had arrived, but returned to work when they saw Orangutan Valin and Buffalo Jake.

Orangutan Valin felt safer and was more at ease in the jungle than he had been on the shore of the lagoon. He began to explain his mission, "Buffalo Jake asked me if I had any ideas. He wanted to move big animals—elephants and rhinos—from here to over there." Valin pointed into the jungle. Everyone understood that he was actually pointing in the direction of Chakeeda Island.

Valin continued, "I thought about it. But it wasn't possible to think about it for too long because it can't be done. Not elephants and rhinos. Won't work. Small animals. That's your answer. That's what I told Buffalo Jake."

"But what good would that do?" asked Chaga. "Small animals could never overrun the chakeedas like we did in the attack on the Great Valley. Smaller animals would be massacred."

"They're being killed off like the rest of us already," interjected Buffalo Jake. "I went and asked the attack cats, the wolves, the badgers, the boars, and others if they would be willing to take on the chakeedas if we could get them to the island. Things have gotten so bad that they said they would without a doubt."

"They're good animals," said Chaga. All agreed.

Orangutan Valin continued, "There is a need here. A need to move lots of animals. Move them very quickly. All that water in the way. Surprise attack is important. We found the lagoon. Experimenting with different ideas here. We tried attack animals riding on the backs of dolphins, porpoises, sea lions, and whales. When you arrived, we were trying sea turtles. Doesn't look good. Using the other sea animals wasn't working either. The claws of the animals dig into their backs. Turtles have shells. That might have worked. But it didn't. Too slippery.

"This here is our latest attempt. We use bamboo wrapped together with vines. Makes a good surface animals can stand on. Called a claw protector. Should attach it to the backs of whales. The problem of the claws digging into their backs should be solved."

"Shouldn't it be called a 'back protector'? It protects the backs of whales from claws, right? It doesn't protect claws from whale backs," said Jabari.

The orangutans spoke among themselves for a moment in their species language.

"You're right, it should have been called a 'back protector'. But it's too late to change the name now. It's already built," said orangutan Valin.

Jabari stared at Valin trying to find some indication in his expression that he was joking. Jabari was not familiar enough with orangutan facial expressions to figure Valin out, and considering how private orangutans usually were, no one else was familiar enough with the creatures to figure out if Valin was joking.

Valin turned to Buffalo Jake and said, "There is one problem remaining. We haven't figured out how to attach the claw protectors to the whales yet."

Jake frowned.

"But we're working on it," added the orangutan. "One thing at a time."

Jake said, "The end of the season will be here sooner than you think."

"I know. I know. We're working fast. Fast as possible," said the orangutan. Everyone knew that the only time that it was practical to attack was at the end of the season. This was the only time that everyone was not concerned with raising young, storing food, and preparing for the winter. It should have been a time to rest, reflect, play and enjoy life. But instead, the chakeedas had turned it into a time for counting the number of species that had not survived another season and for wondering who would be next.

One of the lowland gorillas informed Orangutan Valin that the claw protector was complete.

"How are you going to get it to the lagoon?" asked Jabari.

"You're here. Can't you do it?" asked Valin.

"Well, yes... but you didn't know that we would be here when you started the project," said Jabari.

"But you're here now," replied Valin.

"But we might not have been here. I mean, you didn't know we would be here. We might not of been here," said the elephant leader.

"So what's your point?" asked the orangutan.

"My point is that if we had not come along, you would have a back protector for whales—or a claw protector if you insist—in the middle of a jungle where there are no whales."

The orangutan just stared at Jabari blankly, so Jabari continued his thought, "...and so you would have this thing made for whales in the middle of the jungle without any way of getting it to the lagoon where the whales are suppose to be."

"Yea, you're right. So what's your point?" asked Valin.

Jabari looked around at the other animals for help, but no one else seemed interested in joining in.

Finally, Jabari said, "Where do you want it?"

"Anywhere on the shore of the lagoon is fine," said Valin.

As the elephants lifted the whale protector onto the back of one the rhino body guards, Jabari whispered to Buffalo Jake, "I can't believe that you left an orangutan in charge of this project. The way they think—or should I say—the way they don't think, I'm surprised that they haven't driven themselves into extinction."

"Don't be so sure that you know how all species should think," whispered Buffalo Jake.

"But, Jake, some things are just common sense," pleaded Jabari.

"To an elephant mind maybe. To a buffalo mind maybe. But to a orangutan mind, who's to know?" said Jake.

Jabari was too flustered to respond, so Jake continued, "Diversity is the one thing that we have more of than the chakeedas. If we're to win this crusade, we have to turn diversity into strength. So give the orangutans a chance."

When they got the claw protector to the water, they hid it in the middle of some tall sea grass located in the far corner of the lagoon. It would be early evening before the whales came back with the tide, so the animals divided up to go foraging. High in the jungle canopy, a troop of chimpanzees and several toucans continued to maintain a vigil for any chakeedas that might, by chance, travel through. It would be very difficult to explain the presence of buffalos, wolves, bears and other non-jungle animals so far from their home ranges. The chimps and toucans provided an early warning system so that the non-jungle animals could hide if any chakeedas were spotted.

It was early evening when the whales returned. The animals came out of the jungle down to the shore to greet them. Orangutan Valin explained the claw protector to the whales. The whales immediately expressed concern that the claw protector might slip over their blow holes. Orangutan Valin assured the whales that the claw protector would be placed behind their blow holes. But the whales were so afraid of drowning if anything covered their blow holes that not even Buffalo Jake could convince the whales to try the idea. But finally, after much discussion, the whales' concerns were overcome when it was agreed that a special slit would be cut in the claw protector just in case it slipped forward. At least for the moment, this was acceptable to the whales.

The claw protector was brought out of its hiding place and set down in the water at the edge of the shore. Several badgers and wolves, including Daniel, boarded the claw protector and three dolphins pushed it out into the lagoon over the back of one of the whales, carefully avoiding the whale's blow hole. The solution to the problem of how to attach the claw protector to the whale seemed obvious to the three dolphins. They swam away and in a short time came back with long strands of sea weed. With one end of the sea weed in her mouth, the lead dolphin, Donna, dove right over the top of the whale, reentered the water on the other side, and looped back under the belly of the whale to where she started. She repeated this process two more times. It worked. The claw protector was ready for its first sea trial.

A half moon was just beginning to rise over the jungle when the whale circled the lagoon once and headed down the channel to the ocean. The other whale and the dolphins followed to observe and to help if needed. Buffalo Jake and the other animals on the shore watched the strange, moonlit silhouette of several wolves and badgers gliding along the surface of the water until the image disappeared into the darkness.

"All we can do now is wait," said Buffalo Jake.

"What if it doesn't work?" asked Anthony.

No one answered. The animals were too tired to think about it.

"What will we do?" asked Anthony again. The animals moaned and hissed in annoyance at what they considered a stupid question. It was clear in everyone's mind what they would do. They would simply try again and again and again until they found something that did work.

"What do you think we'll do, Buffalo Jake?" asked Anthony.

"Ask the orangutan," said Buffalo Jake as he settled down for a nap.

When Anthony asked Valin, he said, "Simple, we'll take Elephant Jabari's suggestion. We'll build a new one and call it a 'back protector', then it should work perfectly."

All the animals laughed except Anthony. He walked away certain that he was being left out of some sort of inside joke.

The moon was high over the lagoon, when splashing noises woke up the animals. The whale had returned. The wolves and badgers were splashing ashore.

"How did it go?" asked Buffalo Jake excitedly.

"It went great," said Daniel. "Except that we lost one of the badgers. But that was close to shore when we came back in. I saw him swim to the beach. He's O.K.."

Another wolf added, "It's getting past the surf that's the worst part. But once you're out there, it's actually kind of fun."

"Super!" exclaimed Buffalo Jake.

Jake asked dolphin Donna to ask the whale how it went for him. The whale knew how to speak the Universal Language, but Buffalo Jake could understand a dolphin's accent better than a whale's. Donna reported that the whale had no problems. In fact, he thought that he could probably carry twice the number of animals without any problem.

"Thank you all. This is a great night for all living things!" announced Buffalo Jake. All the animals of the jungle erupted into a cacophony of cheers in their respective species languages and the whale splashed water on everybody.

"How many of these can you build?" asked Buffalo Jake.

"As many as you need," said Orangutan Valin. "Every one hundred seasons or so, the bamboo dies off. That happened last season in this area. The pandas have stripped what they need and moved on to another area. So we have plenty of bamboo."

Everyone was so excited that they spent the rest of the night working through logistical problems and planning the attack itself.

Anthony went off by himself again. He had privately hoped the claw protector would not work. He was certain that there still must be some way to reach a compromise with the chakeedas. He went into the jungle to try to think of another solution as he had tried to do so many times before.

* * * * *

Several days after the test of the first claw protector, Buffalo Jake received a message that a problem had developed and that he was needed at the lagoon immediately. When Buffalo Jake arrived in the late evening, Orangutan Valin was pacing about muttering under his breath in his species' language. Buffalo Jake looked out on the lagoon. There were two whales with claw protectors on their backs. They looked perfect to Buffalo Jake.

"What's the matter?" asked Buffalo Jake.

"It's best that I show you," answered Valin.

Orangutan Valin walked to the shore and told Dolphin Donna to send the whales out to sea.

Valin, Jake, and Nick walked along the edge of the channel to the beach. When Jake looked out at the whales, the problem was immediately obvious. The green bamboo had dried out and turned a light tan color and the sea water was turning the bamboo whiter. The claw protectors could easily be seen from shore. They stood out so much on the black ocean water that the chakeedas would certainly see the animals coming long before they reached the island. It would be disastrous.

"We've tried all sorts of things to change the color, but nothing is working," said Orangutan Valin.

Buffalo Jake stood looking out at the bright bamboo claw protectors as the whales swam back and forth on the other side of the break water.

185

"There must be a solution. We've come too far," said Buffalo Jake.

"Actually, there is," said Orangutan Valin. "But the decision to use it is not so easy. It's a big decision. Let's go to the lagoon. There's someone there you need to talk to."

Back at the lagoon, Buffalo Jake was introduced to Panda Nao. Nao looked very sad and averted her eyes from looking directly at Buffalo Jake. Orangutan Valin showed Buffalo Jake some black bamboo that his troop had found.

"This is great," said Buffalo Jake. "Why won't this work?"

"It would be great," said Valin. "But Panda Nao is from a special species. They're the striped pandas. Black and white stripes. All of them. The stripes are on their backs. Big problem. Striped pandas eat black bamboo. Not much else. Not much black bamboo left. Chakeedas, ya' know. If we use up black bamboo for claw protectors, big problem for striped pandas."

Without hesitation, Buffalo Jake said firmly, "That's completely out of the question. I am not going to give the order to drive a species into extinction."

Anthony looked at Buffalo Jake with a surprised expression of hope.

Buffalo Jake restated what he just said for Anthony's benefit with one important addition, "I am not going to give the order to drive an innocent species into extinction that has committed no crimes against animality."

Panda Nao stepped forward. "You don't have to give the order, Buffalo Jake. We're offering the black bamboo freely. There is no other choice," said Panda Nao.

"How can you do that? You'll have nothing to eat. I can't permit it," said Buffalo Jake.

"We're already starving to death. The chakeedas have already destroyed most of our range. It's only a matter of time before they destroy what remains of the black bamboo. There is no hope at all for us if the chakeedas are not stopped. Maybe... maybe if you can stop them, a few of us can survive on insects and such things until the bamboo grows back. At least it will grow back if you cut it down. But the chakeedas... they don't just cut it down. They change the land. It will never grow again where the chakeedas have been," said Panda Nao.

"You know that it won't grow back in time to save you," said Buffalo Jake.

Panda Nao looked down at the ground and replied in a soft voice, "We know."

Buffalo Jake did not know what to say. It was an impossible decision. He looked at Panda Nao and could only manage to whisper a humble, "Thank you." Panda Nao bowed and turned around to go back to the jungle to be with her family and friends before the harvest of the last of the black bamboo.

CHAPTER NINETEEN

Messengers of the Sea

The mountain ridges jutted up sharply from the valley floor before descending on the other side into a deep, ravine that bubbled and boiled with gaseous steam vents. The opposite side of the ravine was a shear cliff that rose up so high that one could not see the top. Of course, no one could actually "see" the mountain ridges or the steam vents or the cliff. Sunlight had not shone on these mountains and valleys for millions of seasons, maybe even longer. Yet, at the moment, it was a very crowded place. One could hear the echoes of thousands of animals.

At this deepest of ocean depths, the water was uniformally cool and calm. The gaseous steam vents caused small ripples of warmth, but did little to interfere with the smooth, caressing sensation that these deep waters provided for the whales as they gently glided passed each other. Occasionally, one would see the flash of a bioluminescent fish, but other than that, the place was pitch black. Even so, it did not seem that way to the whales. There were hundreds of whales gliding through the waters. The squeals, squeaks, whistles and wapping of the various species bounced off the contours of the ocean floor and lit up the area as brightly in the minds of the whales as if they were at the ocean surface at midday.

Erik, the leader of the blue whales, was growing concerned. The messengers should have arrived by now. Dolphins were usually such dependable creatures, especially Donna. He did not think anything would have happened to them. It was the land animals that concerned him. They seemed to think differently in some ways that did not make sense to him. But from what he was able to piece together from the meetings at the World Council, he imagined that life on land must be very difficult. Given the apparent troubles that the land creatures faced with day to day survival, he reasoned that they did not have as much time to devote to thinking as whales did. For this reason, he would have preferred if an ocean animal was in charge of the fight against the chakeedas. But he tried to reassure himself that Buffalo Jake seemed to be one of the more intelligent land creatures he had met. And, maybe more importantly, Buffalo Jake seemed to have developed an understanding of the chakeeda mind. This was something that Erik was not able to do. Erik had concluded that it must be some land animal thing.

It was at that moment that a panicked chill went through Erik's body. It occurred to him in a sudden instant the reason why Donna had not arrived. He scolded himself for being so stupid. She could never dive this deep. It was impossible for a dolphin. Donna and her pod were probably killing themselves at this very moment trying to reach him. The thought made him even more furious with himself for not leaving several whales closer to the surface to relay the message. So much for his superior intellect.

Erik did not wait to see if his theory was correct. If it was, then valuable time was being lost. He immediately began squeaking out orders on a frequency reserved for him to communicate with his lieutenants and the representatives from the other whale species. The whales responded by falling silent and began to organize into formation for the journey to the coast. Only whale leaders continued sound communication, which all the whales used for echo location.

Erik paired off with his second in command. His four lieutenants paired off behind them and to one side. Erik communicated his concern regarding the dolphins. They all agreed that the dolphins would kill themselves trying to reach them before the little creatures would abandon their mission. Erik and his whales raced up the face of the cliff wall listening for the distinctive high pitch of dolphin voices. Erik was hoping that his theory was wrong. But all too soon, he heard the faint clicks of dolphins in distress. It was so far that it was hard to hear, but their voices were unmistakable. He listened again and realized that the dolphins were still descending in spite of the intense pain of diving far below their capability. Erik screamed orders for his pod unit to pick up the pace. At this depth, it was difficult for even whales to fight the weight of an entire ocean pressing down upon them, but they did what they could to increase their speed.

"We hear you! We hear you!" Erik screamed ahead in the Universal Language.

Erik listened again and realized the dolphins were still slowly descending. Erik yelled again, "We hear you! Stop where you are! We're on our way!"

It was useless. Erik was sure that Donna could hear him, but the pressure was effecting her thinking. Erik and his pod were reaching depths that were now more realistic for high speed ascents. Erik ordered his pod unit into emergency formation. This was a formation rarely used by the whales because it had little practical value. It was far too fast to be useful for feeding and it required far too much energy to be useful for migrating. The emergency formation created the equivalent of a single, massive whale out of six to eight whales. This massive body created an enormous wave of water ahead of the formation. The effect was to essentially create a high speed tunnel through the ocean. The whales could travel at literally three times their maximum speed compared with any other formation. The formation was used only rarely to respond to distant distress calls from other whales.

The problem with the formation was its serious danger. At such high speeds, any change in direction had to be timed perfectly. If there was the slightest miscalculation, it could send the whales slamming into each other. The crushing force at these speeds was more than enough to inflict fatal injuries. In fact, a whale spinning sideways out of control at these speeds could have his spine snapped. To avoid tragedy, it was critical that the whales all listen to the lead whale. The water tunnel had the effect of blocking out sound from outside of the tunnel for all of the whales except for the one in the lead position. This meant that only Erik as the lead whale could still hear the dolphins in distress. The other whales were swimming on blind faith in Erik's skill.

Each slight change in frequency of a click in combination with a squeak indicated a one whale unit change in direction. There was a margin of error of only plus or minus one whale unit. If a whale misinterpreted a command by more than that, it could mean disaster. This was a challenge for most pods because the margin of error for a normal formation was more in the range of 3 to 5 whale units. Erik's pod was one of the most experienced at the emergency formation. Erik was not thinking about the danger; all he could think about was getting to the dolphins.

Erik was unaware of the real danger that the pod faced as it raced through the water tunnel. It had to do with Manuel, one of his most trusted lieutenants that was in the number 5 position in the formation. Manuel had become separated from his birth pod many, many seasons ago during a typhoon. Manuel had been no more than a season old when he was found and adopted by Erik's family. This had been unusual because Manuel belonged to a different whale species. But he adapted to the instincts and customs of his adopted family, which was not terribly difficult because they were very similar to those of his own species.

But there was one problem. Whale units were slightly different for each species. For Erik's species, there were 197 whale units in a circle. But this ranged from 193 to 209 for different species. For Manuel's species, there were 200. Manuel had adjusted to this slight difference when he was young and it had not been a major problem because the difference fell within the margin of error for all normal whale formations. But in the emergency formation, it was a critical difference that Manuel had to consciously correct for. Manuel not only had to recalculate Erik's commands, he had to do it instantaneously to keep up with the pod. Manuel had never told Erik about this problem because he was afraid he would be excluded from the pod. The fear of not belonging prevented him from revealing his secret. He knew he was wrong for hiding the information and he kept promising himself that he would tell Erik, but the moment never seemed right. The present moment seemed particularly inappropriate.

Erik raced ahead toward the dolphins. Schools of fish saw the water tunnel blasting toward the surface. The fish knew exactly what it was and tried to get out of the way, but generally found themselves spinning, tumbling, and smashing into each other in the violent wake that the water tunnel created. Erik was growing more concerned. The dolphins cries had grown less frequent. It was more difficult to navigate without a steady signal to home in on. But with each dolphin clicking sound, he adjusted their course until they now seemed on a direct line for the dolphins. They were growing very close now. Erik ordered the whales to slow down and form a normal formation. As they decelerated, the boundaries of the water tunnel became less distinct until finally they vanished altogether. The whales spread out into a search formation. They were still far below the depth at which sun light, or moon light at this time of night, could reach so they still could not see anything. They tried to listen, but the dolphins had fallen silent. Erik was about to send out echo location signals, when they bumped into something above them.

Six dolphin bodies were floating motionless in the water. Erik ran his dorsal fin gently along the top of one of the dolphins. The other whales did the same thing with the other dolphins. The whales were feeling to see if the dolphins' blow holes had opened up yet, which would mean that the dolphins' lungs would have filled with water. None had opened. This was good. There was still a chance. The whales began pushing the dolphins toward the surface. When they reached the air, only one of the dolphins gasped for breath. The others did not respond. The whales nuzzled them with their heads, gently rocking the dolphins back and forth in the water. They did not respond. Their bodies began to sink back below the waves. The whales protested by pushing the bodies back to the surface. Erik ordered the whales to leave the bodies in peace.

Erik swam over to the one dolphin that was breathing as she floated on the back of one of the whales that was right below the surface serving as a resting place for her. Erik floated next to her looking at the dolphin eye to eye. Her eye was very wide and glazey.

"I'm very sorry. It was my fault. I'm so sorry," Erik said softly.

"You heard us?" asked Donna.

"Yes, we heard you," said Erik.

"Are the whales on the way?" she asked.

"Yes, thousands of them... because you delivered the message," said Erik.

The dolphin seemed happy. She now knew she had done her job. She slipped off the back of the whale she was on and began slowly swimming in circles. Erik thought she would be O.K. until he realized that she was swimming in circles because she was paralyzed on one side. The whales watched as she struggled to swim straight. Eric left Manuel behind so she could rest on his back while Eric and the others continued on to begin the attack on Chakeeda Island.

CHAPTER TWENTY

Journey to Chakeeda Island

When Erik and his pod reached the shore, the first group of whales were already being suited up with back protectors. Large groups of orangutans, gorillas and chimpanzees were dragging them out of the jungle onto the beach and floating them into the water. It was an extremely noisy process because the chimps were screaming and screeching at each other. The chimps even began trying to order around the orangutan and gorilla crews that were working together quietly. But the gorillas soon made it clear that it was in the best interest of the chimps to leave the gorillas and orangutans alone.

Buffalo Jake, who was observing the proceedings, repeatedly asked the leader of the chimps if they could not carry out their mission more quietly just in case there were any chakeedas within hearing range. But the chimps did not seem capable of respecting this request for very long, it simply was not in their nature to be quiet. They seemed to derive pleasure from arguing about every little aspect of the project and exploded into screaming matches with the loudest screamer seeming to prevail. In spite of the noisiness, the chimps were able to do their job just as quickly as their distant cousins. In the end, Jake decided that the result was all that really mattered. If the chakeedas had spies in the area, his plan would be uncovered regardless of how noisy the chimps were.

Once the back protectors were floated into the surf, the dolphins and porpoises moved them out into the deeper waters right beyond the surf where the whales were waiting to be fitted with them. At the height of this phase of the operation, the entire stretch of beach as far as one could see was swarming with work crews carrying back protectors from the jungle to the waiting dolphins and porpoises. Each outfitted whale proceeded further down the peninsula to a point where the beach was replaced with rocky cliffs that dropped directly into the sea. This is where the loading of animals occurred.

The cliffs were the only place other than the lagoon where the water was deep enough for whales to come close enough to shore for the loading process to occur. Using the lagoon would have been made the process easier, but only two whales could enter the lagoon at any one time. Buffalo Jake was not sure of how many whales needed to be loaded at one time, but he was sure that it had to be a lot. Two at a time was not a lot. The cliffs had many ledges carved in them that permitted the cougars, wolves, badgers, wolverines and others to climb down to the water. Many of the animals were more than happy to climb down the cliffs. They had travelled far from their homes to reach the jungle and had been waiting in the jungle for many days. At first, it had been new and interesting, but they were now more than ready to leave it behind.

It had been some time now since the sun had set and the operation had begun. Buffalo Jake looked down the beach. The chimps, gorillas and orangutans had slowed down from the effort, but had settled into a steady pace. The chimps had actually quieted down. Enough whales had been fitted with back protectors to form the first wave that would attack Chakeeda Island. But the job of fitting more whales would go on throughout the night as wave after wave of animals were carried to the island to join the fight.

Buffalo Jake and Nick walked from the beach to the cliffs with Trevor riding on Jake's back. The air was very still and muggy. The usual evening ocean breeze had not arrived. There was not even a wisp of the usual fog or clouds that came in from the ocean every evening. The air seemed too still. But the animals boarding the whales did not seem to mind. Without the winds, the water was calmer, which made it easier to jump onto the claw protectors.

Daniel was seeing that the last of his species that would be a part of the first wave were on board. He was about to descend the cliff to board a whale himself when Buffalo Jake approached. Jake stared at the wolf for a moment as though searching for some sign—Jake was not exactly sure what it would be—but some sign that this time the plan would succeed.

Daniel looked up at Jake and said, "Don't worry, we're going to win this time or we're going to all die trying."

There was so much that Jake wanted to tell Daniel about strategies and possibilities and philosophies to make sure that Daniel knew everything he could possibly need that might make the difference in the fight. What Jake really wanted was to lead the fight himself. But in the end, Jake knew he had to trust Daniel. There really was nothing more to say but to wish him well.

"I know you'll win. I'll see you when it's over," Jake said in his most confident voice, digging up a bit of dust with his hoof for emphasis.

Daniel turned and descended the cliff to the whales waiting below. The first wave of whales that would attack the island fell into formation and headed out to sea. Jake watched from the cliff as the whales with their passengers disappeared into the blackness. The animals that would form the second attack wave were already coming out of their hiding places in the jungle and climbing down the cliff. Jake and Nick did not notice them. He just stared out into the darkness.

Trevor asked, "What do you think will happen?" Jake did not respond. Trevor politely repeated the question, but Jake was still lost in his thoughts, wondering if in the act of destroying the chakeedas, he was not becoming one.

"I think everything will go right this time," said Trevor, answering his own question. "So long as the chakeedas are still on the island."

It was a thought that had not even crossed Buffalo Jake's mind. How could the chakeedas escape from the Island without being noticed? It was a possibility that Jake immediately began to examine. Wouldn't someone have reported seeing a mass migration of chakeedas if they had returned to the mainland? Where could they hide this time? They can't hide forever, Jake thought. But then again, Jake reminded himself, they don't have to hide forever. At the rate of destruction of the homelands, the animals would not have the numbers or resources to fight and win if the battle was not fought soon.

It made perfect sense. It seemed so obvious. Of course that was how Real would try to win a battle such as this. He lacked the personal strength and dignity to fight the battle directly, so he would keep slithering away from the fight knowing that time was on his side. Buffalo Jake could only hope that maybe this time he had out smarted Real and would catch him off-guard. They would find out before the sun rose again. The night breeze kicked up and began to blow. The stillness was gone.

* * * * *

Daniel squeezed his way through the wolves to the front of the claw protector to see where they were going. There was a whale on each side and one in front them. The whales were not very close, but he could still make out the shape of the animals riding on the back protectors in the darkness. On one side, a whale was carrying badgers. On the other side, there were wolverines. In front, there appeared to be panthers or jaguars, he was not sure which, maybe both.

He thought back several seasons to the falling out that occurred at the World Council of Living Things between the wolves and the panthers, jaguars, cougars and lions. It had been a bitter dispute, the details of which he could not exactly remember. But the hostility between the species had remained. It was nothing violent, of course. They were not stupid. But every time they were near each other, it tended to degenerate into a hissing and growling contest. Daniel wondered if the rift would ever be repaired. But at least tonight, Daniel knew that they would fight together. There was no question at all about that.

Daniel looked ahead to Chakeeda Island. It was easily visible even on a moonless evening such as this. The island had a sickly yellowish glow that contaminated the beautiful blackness of the night as if it were a puss-filled wound. It was the same yellowish glow that occurred wherever there were large numbers of chakeedas. The source of the light was a topic of great speculation. But the rumors of why the chakeedas felt compelled to violate the night in this way was even more interesting. The chakeedas did not welcome the night as part of the natural rhythm of life as other animals did. Rumor had it that they were afraid. They were afraid of not only the other animals, they were afraid of themselves. Daniel tried to imagine being afraid of his own wolf pack and being afraid of his own thoughts. What a terrible feeling, thought Daniel. It was so sad to imagine.

"If they were not so dangerous, they would be pathetic," said Daniel, not really speaking to anyone in particular.

"You have that right," howled one of Daniel's lieutenants.

The wind had grown strong and the ocean choppy as they travelled farther from the shore. One could hear the clicking and scratching of the nails of the wolves as they tried to keep their balance on the bamboo claw protector. It was becoming difficult, but they hunched down and did their best. Daniel was not sure if these choppy conditions were normal since he had never been this far from shore. The short practice runs had been much closer to the mainland. What concerned Daniel the most was the behavior of the whales. They were using their own species language so he could not understand them. But by the increased level of communication between them, Daniel sensed that something was wrong.

The ocean's mood was changing rapidly. At first, it had seemed only mildly irritated. But now it was rising and falling with much more feeling and determination. The whales were having greater trouble dealing with the ocean's growing hostility. The swells were now large enough to toss even the largest of the whales about. A wall of sea water crashed over the back of Daniel's whale, slamming everyone down onto the claw protector. Daniel struggled to his feet and looked about. There were fewer wolves on board. This can't be, he thought. They were going to all drown before they reached the island. He wrestled with a feeling of panic and focused on the sound of a voice within him demanded that he take charge of the situation. It was not over yet. He was not sure of what he could do, but he shook himself off and stood defiantly before the ocean and howled in disgust and anger. He berated the ocean for helping the chakeedas and demanded that it immediately stop its onslaught. The ocean responded with another wave, even bigger than the first one, crashing over the claw protector. When it receded, Daniel found himself at the rear. Most of the wolves were gone. Daniel tried not to move, trying to dig his claws into the bamboo to hold on the best he could.

The sky exploded with flashes of light that lit up the entire ocean. The night rumbled with thunder so powerful that it caused Daniel's body to vibrate. When the lightening flashed across the sky again, Daniel looked up to see the most incredible sight. There were massive black clouds so large, so enormous, that he thought he must be imagining them. Again lightening crackled across the night sky. There it was again. The dark clouds formed a long line the entire length of the horizon and reached far higher into the sky than any bird could fly. When they had left the cliff, the sky had been perfectly clear. Now there were clouds everywhere. As Daniel continued to be tossed about on the claw protector, it suddenly dawned on him what was so strange about this storm. There was no rain. Just a powerful wind that sprayed him with the ocean. It was very odd.

Daniel hardly had time to think about the lack of rain for very long. As yet another wave crashed over the claw protector, he could feel his strength draining away. He could not hold on for much longer. "I need some help here," said Daniel bitterly to the ocean. "We're suppose to be on the same side." At that moment, Daniel saw the wolves that had been washed overboard scrambling back on to the claw protector. Daniel tilted his head sideways in puzzled amazement. When the returning wolves had trouble getting back on board, they seemed to get a push from behind. Suddenly, a creature leaped from the ocean onto the back protector. It was a sea lion.

"We saw the approaching storm and thought you might need some help," barked the sea lion over the roar of the ocean.

"Thank you very much," said Daniel. "I thought it was all over."

"The chakeedas aren't going to win just because of a little water. We'll escort you the rest of the way," said the sea lion, who then dove off the back protector to make room for the wolves scrambling back on board. The wolves began trying to shake themselves off as the whales continued to rise and fall in the swells. It was no easy task maintaining their balance, but the wolves were quick learners. None of them had any intention of being swept over board again even if the sea lions were there to rescue them. They crouched down as best they could preparing for the worst.

The worst did not come. As quickly as it had begun, the ocean settled down into a bit of choppiness, then became very calm. Yet, Daniel could still make out the long line of tall, black clouds sitting on the horizon. The clouds did not seem to be moving. It was as though they had come to watch the attack on the chakeedas and no more. Daniel just hoped that the whales could make it to the island before the clouds changed their mind.

The whales picked up their speed considerably in the calm waters and resumed their orderly formation. The sea lions continued to serve as escorts just in case the weather changed dramatically. Daniel looked about at the other whales. The sea lions had apparently saved the other animals because all the whales still had a full load. The situation appearing to be under control, the wolves laid down on the claw protectors to rest. Daniel spoke with a sea lion about the weather situation.

"If those storm clouds move in, we're going to have to postpone the attack," said Daniel. "We can't attack if the weather conditions are too bad. It would delay our reinforcements and I am not sure if we could hold up."

The sea lion said, "I understand. But it is an important decision. Don't you think you should think about it a little more?"

"Well, I just don't know what would happen. It's too risky to fight both the chakeedas and the weather on their own island. Please ask the others and let me know if they agree," said Daniel.

"I'll see what they have to say," said the sea lion.

A little while later, the sea lion returned and said, "They agree. If we can turn back before we're spotted, we can fight another day."

"O.K.," said Daniel. "Let's keep an eye on the weather."

The fight with the sea had made the wolves quite tired and hungry. Their hunger was compounded by the fact that none of them had eaten for almost four days. This had been intentional so that their aggressive instincts would be keenly on edge when they fought the chakeedas. The tactic had been successful because the combination of nearly drowning and going hungry had placed everyone in a very bad mood. This was good. The chakeedas didn't know what they were in for, thought Daniel. But from the growling that Daniel could hear in the darkness, he thought that they better get to the island soon or else his wolf pack was going to start fighting among themselves.

Finally, the shore came into view. This was what they had been waiting for. Daniel tried to remain calm. At first, he wagged his tail only a little bit. But soon everyone, including Daniel, were wagging their tails fast and furiously. They were ready. The whales broke formation and began spreading out into a line heading straight for the shore. Behind the first line was a second line of whales and a third line was behind the second. The initial assault would be comprised of these three waves. More were on their way from the mainland.

The beach was not very wide. A line of palm trees signaled where the beach ended and the interior of the island began. They were getting very close now. Close enough to hear the surf. Daniel looked up into the sky beyond the palm trees. For a moment he thought he saw the massive storm clouds moving toward them from the opposite side of the island. But as they rapidly grew closer to the shore, the palm trees obscured his view. He tried to convince himself that he had only imagined it. The clouds had still been motionless on the distant horizon only a short time ago when he last checked. There was no way the clouds could have moved in so rapidly. Daniel frantically asked himself whether what he saw was real or just his fears playing tricks on him. His mind had no answer. It did not matter. It was too late to call off the attack. They were only moments away from reaching the shore.

The first whale to reach the shore purposely beached himself. The next whale immediately slammed into the shore a short distance from the first one, then another and another. Within moments, the entire length of beach was lined with whales laying in the shallow surf. It was the largest mass beaching of whales that anyone could remember. The beaching had not been part of Buffalo Jake's plan. It was a selfless decision that the whales had made on their own to make sure that they brought the attack animals as close as possible to the shore to prevent drowning of their precious cargo.

In the star light, the animals leaped from the backs of the whales into the shallow water and raced up the beach. Within moments, the sand was swarming with badgers, wolverines, cougars, leopards, wolves and other attack animals. They fell into formations that best suited their particular attack capabilities. Daniel sniffed the air for chakeedas. He could not immediately identify the smell that he was detecting. The other animals also found the smell curious. They discussed it briefly and decided that it reminded them of the smell of a place they called the dark water pond. This was actually not a very good name because the pond did not really have water in it. It had black gooey stuff that was similar to water, but was thicker than water and very sticky and smelly. No one knew what it was and tried to avoid going near the pond. It did not surprise the animals that Chakeeda Island would smell like that.

As the animals began advancing up the beach, they saw chakeedas lurking behind the line of palm trees. That was fine with them. This is what they had come for. They were ready to do battle face to face. The chakeedas had a different plan. The flames started at the base of each palm tree and quickly raced up to the top, exploding in a ball of fire. Within moments the entire line of palm trees was blazing away creating a solid wall of fire. The intensity of the heat drove the animals back. But before they could reach the water, the palm trees began falling toward them.

Above the roar of the fire, Daniel could hear the hideous screams of animals trapped in the flames. Flaming palm trees had fallen on both sides of him. The fire began leaping from one tree to the other leaving Daniel no place to go. Daniel could smell his fur burning as he tried to find his way through the flames back to the water. He did not know what to do. Every direction he turned, he was driven back by the intensity of the flames. He fell to the sand and covered his face with his paws as he felt the flames sweeping over him. The sound of the screaming animals filled his senses. The whales did their best to try to get turned around in an attempt to splash water on the fire storm with their tails. But the water was just too shallow to permit them to maneuver. It would not have mattered. The beach became an impossible wall of flames that not even the whales could have extinguished. They continued to try to get repositioned, but soon fiery embers landed on the claw protectors. The heat was so intense that the claw protectors were quickly drying out and beginning to smolder.

Over the blasting sounds of the fire, an angry sky cracked open and roared even louder. The ominous line of black thunder clouds that Daniel had so feared had moved in right over the shore. Torrents of rain pounded the beach. Solid walls of flame were replaced with solid walls of rain. The down pour was so intense, Daniel could not even see the palm trees that he knew were right next to him. His senses were overwhelmed by the feeling of water pounding his body and the sound of rushing water all around him. There was so much water that the sand could not absorb it all. Daniel could feel it forming little streams that were rushing under his body toward the ocean.

It did not last for long. It did not have to. The angry clouds had made short work of the chakeeda fire storm. The palm trees were soaked. The sky cleared. The air smelled fresh. Daniel looked back toward the whales. Such enormous amounts of water had fallen in such a short time that it had given the whales just enough extra water to maneuver themselves out of the shallow surf. The whales were free.

After the rain stopped, Daniel was at first reluctant to open his eyes. He was most certain that when he looked around, he would find himself to be the only survivor. But such was not the case. Up and down the beach, large numbers of animals were shaking themselves dry. Their fur had been burned, but the rain had come in time to save them from any real injury. Except of course for those animals that had been crushed by the falling palm trees. They were the ones that Daniel had heard screaming. Daniel saw one of his own that had been trapped under the flames. The sight was gruesome. Daniel looked away. But the vast majority of animals were not really hurt. With everyone's fur badly singed, it just looked a lot worse than it actually was. The animals soon came to the collective realization that they were for the most part not any worse off than when they first landed on the beach. They looked back up the beach to where they had last seen the chakeedas. With the palm trees gone, the chakeedas were now standing in full view.

The chakeedas did not move at first. They could not believe what they were seeing. It was not possible. They had just witnessed these same animals consumed by raging fires. How could they be snatched from such a certain death? Then it began to dawn on them that there was a more immediate problem. There was no longer anything standing between them and a very large group of angry animals that they had just tried to burn alive. The animals charged toward the chakeedas. The chakeedas did what all chakeedas do when trickery fails. They ran. The animals were close behind. In typical fashion, some chakeedas pushed their fellow chakeedas down in an attempt to buy themselves more time. But it made little difference. The leopards and wolves quickly overtook the retreating chakeedas. The chakeedas were no match for the animals in one on one combat. In fairness to the chakeedas, they fought as viciously as they could and inflicted heavy casualties. But by late evening, the first battle was over. The beach was now secure for the waves of additional animals that would join the drive into the heart of Chakeeda Island.

CHAPTER TWENTY-ONE

The Aerial Attack

The invasion was going well. The birds were helping as best as they could by dropping rocks on the chakeedas. On Trevor's return from his second bombing run over the island, he landed on the wrong whale by mistake. The whale he landed on was assigned to the condors. The rocks that the condors were using were much heavier than those used by the falcons. Even though Trevor knew better, he hopped onto one of the bigger rocks intended for the condors and tried to get a good grip. At that moment, two condors came in for a landing. As they selected rocks and prepared to take off again, they realized what Trevor was trying to doing. As both condors lifted off again, they shouted to Trevor that he was wasting valuable time. Even so, Trevor wanted to give it one more try. So what if the condors had a wing span that was three times larger than his own. Trevor rationalized that it was all just a matter of technique anyway. After several false starts he managed to get off the deck, but quickly found himself at sea level barely high enough to avoid the ocean swells. With great effort, Trevor was finally able to get himself turned into the wind, which gave him enough lift to bring him to what he thought was an acceptable altitude. As he approached the island, he realized that he still needed about seven falcon lengths to clear the palm trees further inland. He flapped his wings as hard as he could. As he slowly gained altitude, he could feel the burn in his wing muscles. Fortunately, he thought, he would be able to glide back to his whale on the return trip. As he reached the trees beyond the beach, he was quite pleased with himself when he cleared the tops of the palms with a little bit to spare.

Trevor's pleasure with himself quickly vanished as he looked down on the battle below. The chakeedas had managed to encircle a group of about 200 timber wolves that had come in on the first wave. The bodies of another 300 dying and dead wolves were scattered about the gruesome scene. A new wave of reinforcements, made up mostly of ferocious badgers, were battling from the beach toward them. Fortunately, the first arriving badgers were able to divert the attention of at least some of the chakeedas that were trying to slaughter the timber wolves, As more badgers engaged the chakeedas, it looked as if the remaining timber wolves might be rescued. But what worried Trevor from his aerial view was the sight of a large assault force of chakeedas quickly approaching from the center of the island. If they reached the wolves before the badgers were able to punch through to join the wolves, then he knew his wolf friends would be overwhelmed by the sheer number of chakeeda reinforcements. If that happened, the animals might be pushed back to the original beach positions. To have to regain the same territory all over again would be both costly and demoralizing. Whether it could be done at all was not a question that Trevor wanted to have to ever answer.

The only thing separating the approaching chakeeda assault force from the weary wolves was a deep trench. It was about eight wolf lengths deep and fifteen wolf lengths wide. The only way across it was by a bridge made up of bamboo reeds that was less than one wolf length wide. As the first chakeedas reached the crossing, a new determination surged through Trevor's body. There was no way the chakeedas were going to massacre his friends if he could help it. With renewed energy, he flapped his wings as fast and as hard as he possibly could. But not even sheer determination could change the fact that his muscles were fatigued from the weight of the rock. With every passing moment, the rock seemed to grow heavier and heavier. The pain was so great that he was sure that his wings were going to separate from his body. His legs didn't feel much better. They felt as if they were being yanked from their sockets from the weight. Most of all, it was the muscles in his claws that he feared would give out first as he strained to hold onto the heavy load. He could feel his grip slipping. He knew that he needed to get a new grip on the rock or else he would certainly loose it soon. But how?! He thought that if he let go with one claw, he could hold on to it with the other while he got a new grip on it with the first claw. But that meant holding the rock with just one claw for a moment or two when he could barely hold on to the rock with two claws as it was!

As he was thinking, he could feel the rock slipping further and further from his grip. Its scraped across the inside of his claws literally ripping into his callused skin with its jagged edges. The hard rock ground against exposed flesh. The searing pain was just too great for even a seasoned falcon like himself. He lost his grip. In the same moment, he realized what had happened and screamed out in agony, "Nnnooooo!!!!". His whole body surged with power as his claws reached out clasping at thin air. He folded his wings and lunged downward with his body. He got it! His new grip was solid. It was still painful. But it was now tolerable, and the slipping feeling was gone. Now to change the momentum of the rock again. It had only fallen a very short distance. But getting it to change direction took extraordinary effort.

A numbness to the pain had settled over him. He closed his eyes and concentrated on climbing higher and higher. He imagined himself high above the earth; high above all the meaningless death and destruction that the chakeedas had caused. He imagined that the chakeedas did not exist. He liked that thought. It was a peaceful thought. Distant howls from below brought him back to reality. He had thought he had been ascending for only a few moments. But that was not possible because he was now high above the fight below, probably more than 2500 falcon body lengths from the ground. With his falcon's vision, he had no trouble seeing the bamboo crossing even though it looked like a stick from this height.

He knew if he released his rock from this height, it was doubtful it would be a direct hit. So he swooped back his wings and assumed the diving position. In this position, his beak rested on the edge of the rock. The free fall began. 2,200, 2000, 1800, 1600, 1400, 1200 falcon lengths. At one thousand falcon lengths, he was going extremely fast. Approaching the earth, Trevor guided the rock toward its target by shifting his body. The rock obeyed his every gesture.

About 30 chakeedas had already made it across the bridge. Another 20 were on the bamboo crossing and far more waiting their turn to begin crossing when Trevor reached 500 body lengths. Trevor wondered what would happen if the rock hit a chakeeda on the crossing instead of the bridge itself. There was no time to figure that one out now. He aimed for the dead center of the crossing. He was at 200 lengths and falling so fast that he had to squint to see. At 150 lengths he made what he hoped would be the final adjustment in trajectory, but hung on just in case. 100... 75... 50... 25...15! Release! Trevor spread his wings and tail feathers as wide as he could, pull his head up out of the dive, and swooped to the side of the bridge. Fortunately, he had extra room to maneuver because of the depth of the ravine.

The rock was a direct hit! The bamboo splintered into pieces at the point of impact sending bamboo flying everywhere. The weight of the chakeedas on the crossing assured that the entire bridge collapsed. The chakeedas let out hideous screams as they hit the bottom of the rocky ravine. Trevor swooped up and landed safely on the side of the ravine on which the timber wolves and badgers were battling the chakeedas. He looked across at what he had done and was quite please with himself. Maybe the chakeedas could build another crossing, but by that time the badgers and other reinforcements will have arrived, he thought.

The impact of the rock on the bridge had been so sudden and loud that the battle had momentarily stopped because all the animals had been so startled by it. The timber wolves were the first to realize what had happened when they saw Trevor swoop out of the ravine and land. The wolves howled joyfully because they now knew they had a fighting chance of winning the battle. Then the badgers realized what had happened and let out a loud badger cheer. The chakeedas were so stunned and disbelieving that it took them longer to realize that within the space of just a few moments, they had lost their only advantage. The timber wolves ferociously resumed the attack. The badgers followed their lead.

Trevor watched in amusement as the chakeedas on the other side scrambled to find bamboo poles long enough to reach across the ravine. What Trevor had forgotten about were the chakeedas that had fallen into the ravine. Not all of them had been killed by the fall. When a survivor came up behind Trevor, he never heard him, and when he finally saw a chakeeda in his peripheral vision, it was too late. The chakeeda's fist had already smashed the back of his head, sending Trevor somersaulting forward to the edge of the ravine. Trevor lay there motionless in a daze from the blow. When he opened his eyes, he saw the bottom of the chakeeda's foot coming directly for his body. He tried to scramble out of the way, but the chakeeda smashed Trevor's left wing. He could hear the bone crack. This time he knew it was over. He looked up at the chakeeda dazed and numbed from the horrible pain. The chakeeda's face was contorted into an expression of pleasure as it prepared to stomp the life out of Trevor. Trevor closed his eyes preparing himself for death when he heard the chakeeda's sick laughter turn into a gurgling gasp. Trevor opened his eyes and saw the chakeeda's limp body with its neck held firmly within the jaws of a timber wolf.

Trevor squawked at the timber wolf to look behind him. Three chakeedas were charging toward them. The timber wolf turned and took them all on at once. Trevor wanted to help, but his wing was in too much pain. He watched the fight in front of him, yelling warnings to the timber wolf and words of encouragement. But when a fourth chakeeda arrived, it was apparent that the timber wolf would not be able to hold out much longer. Tears streamed down Trevor's cheek feathers as he helplessly watched the animal that had saved his own life being torn apart by the chakeedas.

No, he decided, he was not ready to simply lie there and wait for death. It would not be fair to the wolf that had saved his life because he would have died for no reason. He would not give up while he could still move. He stood up and started hopping parallel to the ravine as best he could. He flapped his wings and found he still had some control over his bad wing. It was painful, but he might just get airborne. He heard the chakeedas behind him. When it sounded as if they were right behind him, he flapped as hard as he dared, but he was still on the ground. At the last moment, he spread his wings and dove into the ravine. He banked upward, found a strong up draft, and skillfully rode up out of the ravine. Within a few more moments, he found himself above the palm trees with the frustrated chakeedas yelling at him from below.

If he could only get high enough so that he could glide out to the whales he knew he would be O.K.. When he flapped his wings, he realized that his bad wing must not be broken. Something was obviously seriously wrong with it. But if it was completely broken, he would not be able to flap it at all. Trevor looked out over the darkened horizon, but he could not see the whales. He would have to climb high enough for him to see them for him to glide in. He flapped as hard as he could to gain altitude. The pain was the kind of white, blinding pain that brought tears to the eyes of even the bravest of animals. But his desire to live was stronger than the pain. He had to get back home, he thought, or else his life partner, Heather, would never forgive him.

Trevor started thinking that he was hunting for Heather and their young falcons. He had to bring back food for them. He had been gone too long. Where are all the field mice today, he thought. He wondered why he could not see any field mice. Trevor began talking out loud to himself. He said, "Maybe I should go lower. If I was lower I bet I could see where they are. It really is too dark today to be hunting for field mice. What color are field mice? How funny. I'm sure I would remember their color if I saw one. I better find some mice soon. I must be too high to see field mice."

As he prepared to dive, he thought not mice. No mice. Must go higher. Hunt whales.

"I have to bring back a whale. I have to go higher to hunt whales. Do falcon's eat whales?" Trevor asked himself. He couldn't remember.

"No, I need to focus. I need to land on a whale. Yes, land on whale," Trevor said.

He forced himself to concentrate on that thought. At this height, he was certain he should be able to see the whales. Why had they gone out so far? He was sure they had been much closer to the island earlier. Maybe the chakeedas attacked them. It occurred to him suddenly. He was on the wrong side of the island!

No! Please! NO! This isn't happening. He looked ahead of him. There was no mainland, just the vast open sea. To get back would mean flying into the wind. He cursed himself for not noticing that when he left the island. From the winds, he should have known he was flying in the wrong direction. He circled around and flapped his good wing as best he could. The head wind was so strong that for every three falcon body lengths that he flew forward, he drifted back two. It would be difficult, but he would not give up.

After a while, the pain slipped away. He felt much better. In fact, he was flying much faster than he ever had before. He would be home very soon, he thought. He started trying to think of a story to tell Heather for why he didn't have any mice. She would be very mad at him for not bringing any food home. He better find some food or else think of a pretty good story to tell her. When he looked down, he saw golden waves of prairie grass blowing in the wind. His skilled eyes pin pointed a prairie mouse scampering from its hole. He banked left to chase the illusion. The move caused the fractured bone in his bad wing to break completely. The broken wing began flapping uncontrollably in the ocean wind. The blinding pain was too much. Trevor blacked out and began his free fall into the whaleless sea.

CHAPTER TWENTY-TWO

The Ruling Chamber

The chakeeda commanders had not been telling Real the truth about the progress of the invasion. At the end of the first day, Real was told the animals had been successfully repelled back into the sea. By the end of the second day, the commanders conceded that some of the animals had broken through the beach defenses, but it was nothing to worry about because they were quickly neutralized by chakeeda patrols. They also reported that the animals had attempted a second wave of landings, but were still pinned down on the beach. Real never doubted the truth of these reports. It was perfectly consistent with his unwavering belief in chakeeda superiority.

On the evening of the third day, Real was enjoying a celebratory meal with the members of the Ruling Board when they began to hear the sounds of fighting. At first the sounds were barely audible. Real and the members of the Ruling Board stopped to listen, but the sounds faded and they resumed their meal and conversation. But as the evening progressed, the distant sounds of large numbers of animals growling, barking, squawking, and howling grew closer and closer. Real's advisors dismissed the sounds as of little significance. One said, "I'm sure it is nothing more than one of our patrols cornering some animals that got through. They'll make quick work of them." The other advisors indicated their agreement with this theory. Another advisor added, "Too bad we can't be there to see it. It must be quite entertaining." Others laughed at each other's descriptions of how Buffalo Jake must feel right now knowing his animals were being slaughtered. They wondered if his lieutenants were telling him the truth about the animal defeat. They doubted it, but Buffalo Jake would find out soon enough when they returned the battle to the mainland.

* * * * *

Daniel and his contingent had returned to the beach. They did not wander out onto the open sand for fear of being spotted. They stayed close to the fallen palm trees and waited for high tide. A single right whale was scheduled to arrive with a special cargo. In time, the whale came into sight and swam as close to the breaking surf as it could. Daniel could see numerous small shadows leaping from the whale's back into the surf. The wolves charged down the beach and leaped into the waves. The wolves grabbed the small creatures by the scruff of the neck with their mouths and swam back ashore. The right whale, seeing his unusual cargo was safely ashore, disappeared into the depths of the ocean. Once back in the bush, the wolves dropped the little creatures to the ground. Their first order of business appeared to be to groom themselves to remove the salt water from their fur. The wolves just shook themselves off and patiently waited for the little creatures to finish their task.

When they were completed, Daniel introduced himself, "I am the leader of the invasion force. I sent for you. Who is your leader?"

Several moments passed before one of the dwarf lemurs stepped forward, "We have no leader."

The small creature paused and look about at his new surroundings slowly, very slowly, then concluded, "No need for a leader. We don't do much together. Don't require one."

These words were spoken in a very calm, soft voice. This was not the voice of an animal prepared to engage in a life and death struggle, Daniel thought. Bringing them here was looking more and more like it might be a mistake. Daniel looked about at the rest of the dwarf lemurs. Their eyes were so large for such small faces that they bulged out from their heads. Many of the small lemurs had already found a tree and had climbed up into its branches where they felt much safer. The lemurs stared back down at Daniel with a fixed gaze. They had never seen a wolf before and were amazed at how small Daniel's eyes were. They wondered how he could see at all.

"So they have no leader," said Daniel, letting the thought sink in as the lemurs slowly dispersed into the branches above him.

"It's a matter of definition," said another lemur. "We are all leaders. We each lead ourselves."

Daniel had become adept at communicating with different species, but these little creatures were clearly a challenge for him. Daniel tried his best to address all of them at once, which was difficult because they were beginning to spread out further as they naturally would have done if they were back on their home ranges.

Daniel began, "I sent for you because we have located the largest nest where we think the leaders of the chakeedas are hiding. It's located on a hill overlooking where the main chakeeda nesting area is located. The problem is that the nest on the hill looks like it's very well defended. Our best chance is to attack at night. We need for you to ride on our backs and be our eyes. What do you think?"

None of the lemurs responded. Daniel did not know what to make of it. Some of the little creatures were peeling back pieces of bark looking for insects. Others seemed to just stare off into the darkness. He heard one whisper something about the beautiful view. Daniel looked in the direction in which the lemur was looking. All Daniel could see was darkness. Daniel was consulting with his lieutenants, trying to decide if they should just send the lemurs back and ask for some other night animal with more of a predatory spirit. Maybe some owls or someone like that. The wolves were in the middle of this conversation when one of the Lemurs pulled on Daniel's tail. The lemur asked, "We were wondering when we were suppose to begin?" Daniel had not heard any of them talking to each other, so he was quite surprised.

"Well, as soon as you can... we wanted to spend some time tonight training and attack tomorrow night," said Daniel.

"Your wolves need training?" whispered the lemur.

"Well, no... we thought you might want to grow accustomed to the Island for one night," responded Daniel.

"Darkness is the same everywhere. Let's not keep the chakeedas waiting," said the lemur softly.

Daniel decided these dwarf lemurs might not be so bad after all.

The lemurs did not say a word. They simply began climbing down from the trees and selecting a wolf as a partner. Soon each wolf had a lemur on his or her back. The wolves stole into the darkness with their new night vision capability firmly gripping the thick fur around their necks. They headed toward the center of the island where the main chakeeda nesting area was located.

The badgers, warthogs, and boars had already taken up positions around the edge of the main nesting area and were moving in. None of these species preyed upon anything as large as a chakeeda, which were easily twice as big as a wild boar. But in spite of the size difference, the animals knew they were stronger than the chakeedas. It was the chakeedas mysterious ability to kill at a distance that was the main threat. The badgers, warthogs, and boars knew the only way to win would be to attack as fast as possible to overrun the chakeedas. The final battle got underway when a swarm of condors flew overhead and released their rocks onto the front line where the chakeedas had dug in. The first wave of animals charged forward at full speed in a suicidal frontal assault. They ran so fast that even those that were fatally wounded were carried forward by their own momentum, crashing directly into the lines of chakeedas. When the animals broke through the outer defenses, the chakeedas set fire to their nests as they retreated. No torrential rain came to the rescue this time. But it did not stop the assault. The battle hardened badgers, warthogs, and boars charged through the flames in pursuit of their enemy. The flames turned out to serve to illuminate the main nesting area for the attacking animals, which deprived the chakeedas of their one real advantage of knowing the lay of the land. It did not take long for the chakeedas to figure out that their burn and retreat strategy of attrition was not a good idea under the circumstances and they soon stopped. The nests that had been set on fire were very dry and burned quickly. Soon the darkness returned to the night, punctuated only by the glow of a few orange embers.

* * * * *

When Daniel's wolves heard the first sounds of the battle, they began their move around the main nesting area to the hill behind it where they suspected the chakeeda leadership was hiding. They stopped briefly when they came closer to allow the light from distant fires on the front line to die down. When the hill was once again shrouded in darkness, the wolves spread out and began their advance. The lemurs could see where each chakeeda was dug in. The wolves quietly leaped over or dug under barriers in their way, and the lemurs warned them in advance as they approached the numerous lethal jaw traps set out all over the hill. If even one wolf were to step in one of the traps, the chakeedas would hear the howl of pain and unleash a devastating counterattack. The lemurs knew this and did not miss spotting a single one.

* * * * *

Inside of the Ruling Chamber, Real and his cohorts were consuming several portions of specially prepared buffalo and boar veal. They savored the delicate flavors. It was so tender, it melted in their mouths. One of Real's advisors exclaimed, as he slid another tender morsel into his mouth, "Our ability to create such sensual pleasures as these separates us from the wild beasts."

As always, there was loud and unanimous agreement concerning any claims of chakeeda superiority. But Real suddenly spat his veal out onto the ground.

"What's this?" Real yelled. The chakeeda who had prepared the veal raced to his side and picked up what Real had spat out to examine it closely.

"I am so sorry. I do not know how this piece got here. It should have been thrown out. It's where one of the calf's sores was located. We usually slice those parts away. I'm so sorry," said the chakeeda.

"Why are you serving me veal from a calf that had any sores? That's outrageous!" yelled Real.

"All veal calves have sores. No matter what we do, the sores develop from being unable to move until they are big enough to slaughter. But I will certainly make sure we are more diligent in cutting away the bad pieces," said the chakeeda.

"Be sure to see to it," demanded Real. Real shoved the next piece into his mouth and smiled in approval. One of his advisors gave a toast to the right of all chakeedas to have sore-free veal. The other chakeedas cheered. The feast continued.

The celebration was interrupted once again by the sounds of battle in the distance. The sound seemed to be drawing closer. Real stopped eating and continued to listen, trying to figure out for himself what the sounds really meant. It was not until he could hear the faint sounds of chakeeda's screaming in pain that Real rose to his feet and demanded to see his commanders. Normally, they would have appeared within just moments of being summoned. This time they did not come at all. The sounds of the battle outside grew louder and louder. This was indeed strange. Maybe there had been a small set back. The commanders were probably occupied bringing things back under control. Real and the members of the Ruling Board went to the entrance of the Ruling Chamber and looked down on the main nesting area.

It was a very dark and overcast night so at best all they could see was an occasional shadow darting from behind one nest to another. It was just too dark to tell what the shapes were. At the very edge of the main nesting area, they could see embers glowing on the ground. Real checked with his personal security forces outside. They had not yet determined what was going on below. Scouts had been sent to get a closer look. No reports had come back yet. But they assured Real that the Ruling Chamber had so many layers of defenses around the perimeter of the hill that it would be suicidal for any animal to try to attack it. Real gave orders to be kept apprised of the situation and returned inside with the members of the Ruling Board.

* * * * *

By gently tugging at the hair of the wolves, the lemurs were able guide the wolves in behind each chakeeda. The wolves attacked silently, grabbing the chakeedas by the throat and cutting off their air before they could yell. The wolf and lemur teams advanced up the hill quickly using these tactics. They were helped by the fact that the chakeedas were preoccupied with listening and preparing for the battle approaching from the main nesting area. It never even occurred to the chakeedas that the animals would think to attack the Ruling Chamber at the same time. But before the night was half way over, the chakeedas' most formidable defenses had been completely decimated without putting up a fight.

Daniel and his contingent lay low in the darkness a short distance from the entrance to the Ruling Chamber itself. This was it. This is what they had been waiting for. Chakeeda Real himself was surely inside with all the other leaders of the chakeedas. At this moment, Daniel thought back to the sight of seeing Ajar and Blueth wearing Rebecca's fur. He thought back to having to watch his young pup die of starvation without his mother's milk. A low growl was welling up within him. He would take great pleasure in avenging the brutal death of his life partner.

* * * * *

Real and the members of the Ruling Board could no longer ignore the sounds they had been hearing. They listened as hard as they could. A twig broke. They listened again. Real thought he heard another twig break. It was hard to tell. It might be the memory of the sound of the first twig still echoing in his head. Reality and memory were hard to keep separate at moments like these. Real looked about the room. Everyone was absorbed in the act of listening. Real felt a primitive sense of foreboding. Some premonition of something about to happen. He did not like the feeling. He did not trust it. He preferred chakeeda logic to instinct. Chakeeda reasoning to gut reaction. He tried to think instead of feel. Yet, the premonition that something was seriously wrong grew stronger with every passing moment.

* * * * *

Daniel's wolves charged the opening to the Ruling Chamber, lunging at the chakeeda security forces outside. Other wolves had climbed onto the top of the Ruling Chamber. They ripped open the roof with their teeth and leaped inside. The chakeedas scattered in all directions. The wolves lunged at whichever chakeeda was closest. They sunk their teeth into whatever part of the chakeeda they could grab and held on. The chakeedas grabbed fat, heavy sticks and began clubbing the wolves. But the wolves would not let go. Even as they felt the blood running down the back of their throats and with deafness setting in from the blows to their head, the wolves still would not let go. Even after fading into unconsciousness, their jaws remained locked in place, remaining forever loyal to the cause.

The frontal assault did not go well. The chakeedas that were guarding the Ruling Chamber were able to kill at a distance. The animals had still not figured out how to distinguish chakeedas that could kill without touching from those that could not. The only thing that was noticeably different was a frightening loud sound. But by the time that the animals heard the sound, it was usually too late. Fortunately, not all chakeedas had this capability. But, naturally, the elite guarding Real and his Ruling Chamber had the capability.

Daniel's heart sank as he saw his wolves falling dead in front of the chakeedas. He had a feeling the assault on the hill up to this point had been too easy. He should have known the chakeedas would put up the greatest resistance at the Ruling Chamber itself. But the sight of the falling wolves did not stop the attack. Instinct took over. The wolves were now protecting their own. They leaped over the bodies of their fallen brothers and sisters and ripped at the flesh of the chakeeda enemy. Once the wolves were able to reach the chakeedas, even the most elite among them was no match for an organized assault by a wolf pack. The chakeedas began to retreat inside the Ruling Chamber and the wolves followed. Once inside, the battle disintegrated into complete chaos.

In all of the confusion, Betty had avoided being attacked and chose not to attack the animals. She still believed that a compromise might be reached. As she crouched down trying not to be noticed, she felt something grab her from behind. Instantly, she knew it was not a wolf. She recognized the hot, sweaty grip on her shoulders. She knew she had felt that grip before. She tried to break free so she could confirm her suspicion, but the paws slid toward her neck and around her throat too quickly for her to react effectively. She tried to cry out the name of her attacker, but his grip was far too tight now. She could feel the soft bones in her throat bending inward in ways they were never intended. She gasped again for a breath, but nothing came. She reached around and tried to grab at her attacker and she felt her claws raking across flesh. It was no use. She slumped into unconsciousness before she could inflict any damage.

The fighting inside the Ruling Chamber went on from compartment to compartment. This was the kind of fight best suited for chakeeda tactics and most alien to the wolves. To make matters worse, when Daniel looked about the Ruling Chamber, the bodies of the entire chakeeda leadership were scattered about all over. Daniel began searching for Real's body to confirm for himself that the demented little coward was dead. He had been given instructions from Buffalo Jake to bring Real back alive if at all possible. But considering the circumstances, Daniel knew he would have no trouble reporting to Buffalo Jake that it had not been possible, which pleased Daniel to no end.

As they cautiously made there way through the passageways of the Ruling Chamber, the walls seemed to be on fire. As their eyes adjusted to the flickering light, it appeared that there were flames at the ends of sticks jutting out of the walls. It made the wolves nervous because it brought back bad memories for all of them of forest fires in the misty forest. But the fire did not spread. It stayed at the ends of the sticks. It was very strange. The wolves began to explore the Ruling Chamber while keeping a suspicious eye on the flames just in case it was some kind of trick.

Daniel and his wolf pack advanced hesitantly through the maze of compartments of the Ruling Chamber. As they made their way deeper and deeper into the maze, the fear of ambush was growing ever stronger. As they entered one of the larger compartments, there were all sorts of animals standing along the edge of the walls. At first, the wolves were startled to see other animals, but quickly surmised that Buffalo Jake must have had another plan of attack in case one failed. The wolves started howling their greetings, happy to see friendly faces. Yet, the other animals did not respond. They just stared straight ahead, not even blinking, keeping some kind of solemn vigil. It was as though if they looked away even for a moment, they might miss the thing for which they were waiting. As Daniel came closer, the animals appeared to be a part of the walls with only their heads sticking out. There were elephants, rhinos, bucks, lions, leopards, boars and even a wolf. There were the fire sticks in between each one. Shadows of their heads flickered on the floor. Daniel stared at their faces and called to them again. But nothing that Daniel said would make them break their silent vigil. Daniel and his pack began slowly backing out, fearing they might suffer the same fate if they stayed.

The wolves were about to leave altogether when they heard a noise. They stopped and tried to focus their eyes in the direction from which the sound came. There appeared to be a chakeeda huddled in a corner. The wolves approached. They had never seen a chakeeda that looked so old. The creature was unable to look up at the wolves. His back would only permit him to look down. To see the faces of the wolves, he had to look to one side and bend his whole body. The chakeeda's ancient face was weathered with wrinkles so deep that Daniel was sure they were going to crack open and bleed if the chakeeda moved too much.

"Who are you?" asked Daniel, not really expecting an answer since the chakeedas no longer spoke the Universal Language.

"My name is Martin," said the chakeeda.

Daniel's ears went up and he tilted his head to one side in puzzlement.

"You speak the Universal Language?" asked Daniel.

"Yes," said Martin.

"How did you learn it?" asked Daniel.

"I do not speak it very well anymore. I remember bits and pieces from ages ago. Before chakeedas lost the ability to speak it," said Martin.

"What happened to these animals?" asked Daniel, looking around the walls again.

"These belong to Real. These are his... his... How should I say... I do not think there is a word for it in the Universal Language. These are his proof of his skill... his strength... his power... his courage... maybe his superiority. He keeps these heads as proof of these things to show off to other chakeedas," said Martin.

"How do these animals prove that?" asked Daniel.

"Because he killed them," answered Martin. The wolves reacted with various exclamations of disbelief.

Daniel expressed their sentiment when he said, "Real couldn't kill any of them. Each one of these animals could have taken on Real with no trouble at all. That's ridiculous. What really happened?"

"What I say is true. Real did kill them. He did not kill them in battle. He killed them at a distance. With the things that make the loud sound," said Martin. Daniel thought about this for a moment before responding.

"Do you mean that Real thought that killing these animals like that would prove his strength? That's absurd. If he wanted to prove his strength, then why didn't he fight them directly? Any one of them could have crushed him. It would have been no contest at all. Killing these animals at a distance did not prove his courage. It proved the exact opposite. It proved he was a coward!" shouted Daniel.

"I do not disagree," said Martin. Daniel was a little surprised by this answer. It made him curious to know more about this chakeeda.

"Who are you?" asked Daniel.

"I am Real's grandfather," said Martin.

Daniel looked at Martin's broken body and exclaimed, "This is how Real treats his grandfather?!" But before Martin could answer, one of Daniel's lieutenants came racing in to report that all of the chakeeda bodies had been examined. None of them was Real. Daniel started howling orders for all ways out of the Ruling Chamber to be sealed off and for an immediate search to begin. Daniel remembered seeing Real in the middle of the fighting. He could not believe Real could have escaped. He should have made Real a priority. But everything had been so confusing. He thought it probably would not have mattered anyway.

After giving his orders, Daniel personally looked at the face of each dead chakeeda. Real was not one of them. A member of Daniel's pack began howling. One of the search teams found Real's trail scent. It led down the back of the hill. The wolves that had found the scent and Daniel's pack joined the search team. They located a few of the dwarf lemurs and prepared to give chase. Martin came out to bid them farewell. Martin was the first chakeeda that Daniel had ever liked. He felt a glimmer of uneasiness that he was about to hunt down Martin's grandson.

"We have no choice but to track him down," said Daniel.

"I understand," said Martin. "In fact, I know better than you how dangerous Real and the chakeedas have become. They have brought this on themselves. They were foolish to believe that they could upset the natural balance so violently without there being terrible consequences. Now they must pay the price. I would join you in your hunt if my body would permit it. Now go! You're wasting precious time."

The wolf pack put their noises to the ground and were soon off on Real's trail.

* * * * *

Pei Woo had been listening to strange sounds for the past three days. They were too far off for her to identify. She was not sure what it meant. But any sign of change gave her hope. She kept looking up at the top of the cliff surrounding her enclosure for any indication of what might be going on up there. Normally, she would see chakeedas peering down at her several times each day. But the last time was three days ago when the strange sounds had started. On this particular night, the sounds had grown much closer and louder—she had thought she could almost make out the voices of other animals. But in the middle of the night, the noises abruptly stopped. Pei Woo continued to listen for a long time, but she was growing tired. Listening so carefully to silence was hard work.

Pei Woo was about to fall asleep when she heard the grunting sounds of a chakeeda. She looked up toward the sound and saw a dark silhouette. Pei Woo could not immediately identify it. Its shape was too amorphous to give any clue as to what it could be. The thing stopped at the edge of the cliff behind the railing to catch its breath. While the shape was difficult to identify, the pathetic whining and wheezing sound the thing made was unmistakable- it had to be a chakeeda. Only a chakeeda's body would complain so much and find so little joy in physical exertion. The chakeeda tried several times to lift himself over the railing, but failed each time. Finally, he rested his pudgy stomach on the edge of the rail and, after much grunting, groaning, and straining, was able to roll its body over the top and land on its back with a thud. The chakeeda lay there trying to catch his breath.

After some time, Pei Woo saw a long vine fall over the edge of the cliff to the bottom of the enclosure. It was not a graceful sight. The chakeeda would slide a short distance, then yelp in pain and grip the vine tightly in panic. The entire time the vine was twirling in circles and banging the chakeeda against the cliff. As the chakeeda reached the bottom, Pei Woo hid herself behind some rocks. In the darkness, the chakeeda walked right past the rocks without seeing Pei Woo, but Pei Woo saw the chakeeda. It was Real.

Real scurried to the back of the enclosure where he began running his paws along the back wall. Pei Woo was surprised to see deep scratches on the backs of Real's paws. She watched him feel along the wall in one direction, then he did the same thing in the opposite direction. Real repeated the procedure farther down the wall and apparently found what he was looking for because he let out with a cry of excitement and immediately began moving the rocks on the ground about in a deliberate manner. A portion of the back wall began to move creating a crack. Real tried to squeeze through, but his body would not fit. Real knew he had to work fast. The sun would soon rise. He looked up at the rim of the enclosure behind him. The overcast sky was growing lighter in the early twilight of morning. Real looked behind him and could see where he had thrown the vine over the edge. That meant that any wolves on his trail that looked down into the enclosure would also be able to see him. He tried to squeeze through the crack again. It was no use. It was just too narrow. He needed to either get through the crack now or go back up the vine and find another route of escape before it was day light. He went through the procedure with moving the rocks again. The wall opened just a little bit further. It was enough. He was in. As Real raced down the tunnel, Pei

Woo approached the crack in the wall. Pei Woo stared at the pattern of the rocks that Real had moved around.

In the tunnel, Real could not see anything. He could only feel the cold surface of the floor of the tunnel as he ran blindly up the path as fast as he could. He knew that there was only one turn in the tunnel, otherwise it was fairly straight and rose steadily uphill. As he approached the point where he thought the turn was, he began to slow down because he did not want to run into the wall. He could smell the salt air now so he knew he was close. He felt his way along the wall. There were several large rocks at the turn that he had to climb over on his stomach, but he was soon past the turn and felt the ocean breeze drafting in to meet him. From here the tunnel was straight down to the sea. He could see the first signs of morning light at the end.

When he reached the end, he looked out at the jagged rocks. There was no beach on this side of the island. The mouth of the cave was flooded part of the day, but right now it was just right. It was lapping at the floor of the cave. There was no time to waste. There was an alcove a little ways up the tunnel where he had everything he needed for his escape. He entered the alcove where his bamboo raft was waiting for him. He froze. It was not there. Or at least not all of it. There were bits and pieces strewn about everywhere. Real grabbed at the pieces thinking he could put it back together. But when he had all the pieces together, there simply wasn't enough to make anything that would carry him beyond the dangerous rocks outside. He crawled around on the floor searching for any pieces he might have missed. There was nothing.

Real left the alcove and looked out at the ocean again. The top edge of the sun was resting on the horizon. He had to think. He could stay here until it got dark again, then try to find another way off the island. But if he waited here all day, the animals might find the tunnel and he would be trapped. He tried to calm himself down. Maybe things were not as bad as they seemed. Maybe the attack on the Ruling Chamber was just an isolated incident. His commanders might be searching for him right now. If that was the case, then he would have to explain why he ran away when the attack began, leaving his advisors to fight for themselves. That was easy. He would tell them that he was captured during the battle. Through his superior power and skill, he was finally able to fight off his captors and escape. He liked that. He could even convince himself in time that it was true. He smiled. He felt better again.

But for the time being, Real thought it best to assume that the animals had overrun the entire island and that he should get out of the cave as fast as he could to find a better hiding place that would afford him more escape routes if he were found. He looked down at the remnants of his escape raft one last time. He still could not understand what happened to it. There was no indication that the ocean had risen this high into the cave. He smelled the bamboo. It did not smell like sea water. It smelled fresh. He suspected that one of his advisors must be a traitor. Only a chakeeda could have gotten into the cave and only a chakeeda could have known the significance of the raft to want to destroy it so completely. He suspected it must have been Betty.

When Real came to the entrance to the tunnel, he did not have to squeeze through the crack this time because it was fully open. Pei Woo was patiently waiting for him. Real looked at the panda. He knew the panda did not have the ability with her paws to move the rocks in the pattern required to open the entrance. Nor did the panda have the intelligence to do it even if she did have the physical ability. Only a chakeeda could have figured out why the entrance was stuck and could have opened it. Now things made more sense. The animals must have succeeded in attacking because there was a traitor among the chakeedas helping them. Real's eyes darted around, expecting to be confronted by the responsible chakeeda. He saw none.

Real demanded, "Have you seen any chakeedas around here?"

"No," answered Pei Woo.

"Are you sure? You must have," said Real.

"The only chakeeda I have seen is you going into the tunnel," said Pei Woo.

"Then how did the entrance open up all of the way? There must be another chakeeda," insisted Real.

"I opened it," said Pei Woo.

"That's impossible! Your paws aren't capable of moving the rocks in the right combination at the same time. Only chakeeda paws are capable of grasping the rocks in the right way," said Real.

"Chakeedas greatly over estimate the alleged superior advantages of their paws. We can do many of the same things, just in our own way," said Pei Woo.

"Nonsense," said Real.

"The entrance is open, isn't it?" retorted Pei Woo. "You couldn't do it."

Real stared at the entrance again with a puzzled look.

Pei Woo continued, "I've been going in there for a long time. The view of the ocean is quite nice."

"You've been in there?" asked Real, still not believing that it could be possible.

"Yes," said Pei Woo.

"Well, then tell me what you saw? Did you see anything special?" asked Real.

"Do you mean the bamboo?" asked Pei Woo.

"Do you know what happened to it?" asked Real.

"I ate it," said Pei Woo.

"You ate it!? I can't believe it! Why!?" exclaimed Real.

"Maybe you haven't heard. That's what pandas do. We eat bamboo. It was green bamboo. So being a panda and knowing that pandas eat bamboo, I thought it might be a good idea if I ate it. So I ate it. I sat and watched the waves and ate the whole thing. It was a very pleasing experience. Thank you," said Pei Woo.

"You idiot! That wasn't food! That was my escape raft!" yelled Real completely red faced.

"Whether it was food is a matter of opinion. As far as it being your means of escape... Well, I admit that I suspected it was some chakeeda's means of escape. It only made the bamboo that much tastier," said Pei Woo.

The sun was rising into the sky now. Real knew he had wasted valuable time arguing with the panda. He ran over to the cliff prepared to climb back up the vine, but the vine was gone. He turned around as Pei Woo strolled up behind him.

"Looking for something?" asked Pei Woo.

"Don't tell me. You ate the vine," said Real.

"Don't be silly. Panda's don't eat vines," said Pei Woo.

"Then what happened to it?" asked Real.

Pei Woo called up to the top of the cliff in the Universal Language. Before Real could ask Pei Woo what she said, Daniel and his wolf pack came to the edge of the cliff and looked down. Daniel had the end of the vine in his mouth and asked through clinched teeth, "Is this what you're looking for?" Pei Woo interpreted for Real. All Real could do was hang his head.

Daniel dropped the vine back down into the enclosure. Both Real and Pei Woo climbed out. Real looked about and found himself surrounded by ferocious looking animals of several species. They looked tired from their long battle. Blood was splattered all over their fur, their hair was singed from the fires, and many had open wounds where they had been attacked. Their heads were slung down low. Their breathing was heavy, kicking up the dusty earth in front of them. Their muscles tensed. Their tails lowered, preparing to strike. Even Real, the powerful leader of the most superior species on the planet, felt small and weak in the face of such awesome animal power.

Real was not prepared to die. He saw no connection between his reign of terror over the planet and the hatred burning in the eyes of the animals surrounding him. He did not deserve to die for leading his species to success. He was a great leader who was terribly misunderstood by the animals. Their misplaced vengeance was only the final proof of their blind jealousy of his success and his superiority. But there was nothing he could do now to save himself. He closed his eyes and prepared himself for the primitive onslaught. He would die proudly, knowing he had always been right. He only hoped his death would be quick—painlessly quick. The hissing and growling of the animals grew more and more intense. He could feel their angry breath drawing closer. He squeezed his eyes tighter. Tears began to stream down his cheeks, mourning his own death. He wondered how the chakeedas would be able to continue without him. He cried for their loss.

"What are you doing?" asked Daniel in a disgusted tone. Pei Woo served as interpreter again.

Real opened his eyes. "Aren't you going to kill me?" asked Real.

"Well, that's not a bad idea. But we really have no intention of giving you the satisfaction of dying here and now," said Daniel.

"What are you going to do with me?" asked Real.

Daniel knew what was planned, but wanted to get the words right so he consulted with his lieutenants in the wolf language.

"You are charged with Crimes Against Animality. You will be tried before the World Council of Living Things. You will be required to explain the atrocities perpetrated by the chakeedas against all of animality," said Daniel. Daniel looked at Real expecting some kind of reaction. Real said nothing. He was already planning how he would escape.

At the beach, whales were riding the surf taking on board the animals that had survived the attack on the island for the trip back to the mainland. On the way to the beach, Real was amazed at what he saw. The sophistication of the animal operations on the island were far beyond anything that Real ever imagined the animals were capable of implementing. This only further convinced Real of the correctness of his theory that a group of traitor chakeedas must have conspired with the animals to overthrow him.

Before the day was over, Real was back on the mainland being escorted to meet with Buffalo Jake.

CHAPTER TWENTY-THREE

The Trial

The trial was held in the Meeting Place of the World Council of Living Things. Every leader of every species was present, but the cavern was still not full. There were many spaces that were left vacant. These were the spaces once used by those species that the chakeedas had driven into extinction. Even though there were many animals that had asked for permission to attend the trial, it was decided that it was especially important that the extinct species be represented even if it were only by their noticeable absence.

When Real arrived, it was not peacefully. In spite of an escort of several bears and even more wolves, Real was constantly trying to escape. Needless to say, his flabby little pale body, mounted on spindly white stick legs, was no match for either the wolves or bears. He was yelling and screaming about something as he was pushed and prodded into the cavern by the swipes of the bears. Finally, Real settled down and looked about the cavern. Kim Ha followed behind to serve as interpreter. It had been a long time since he had been here. He remembered it as being much more crowded. He was about to comment on the apparent lack of interest in the proceedings as a dig at Buffalo Jake, but caught himself when he realized the true reason that the cavern was not filled.

"Oh, I see," said Real. He then turned to Kim Ha and said, "What a pathetic emotional play for the jury's sympathy."

Buffalo Jake was on the platform when Real was brought into the cavern. Real immediately went into a tirade upon seeing Buffalo Jake.

"You miserable, stupid buffalo, what do you think you're doing? What's gotten into you? Don't you know who I am? I'm Real. Or is your tiny little buffalo brain too small to remember that far back? You hurt me and my chakeedas will have no choice but to kill you and your herd. We can't be having wild animals engaging in this kind of nonsense."

Buffalo Jake said nothing.

Real turned to the other animals that had come to watch the trial. "I don't know what this lunatic told you, but you better go back to your home ranges right now and be good little animals or else you're going to be in big trouble."

No one moved.

"If you leave right now, I might forgive you for your role in this madness. So I strongly suggest that if you value the survival of your species that you leave now. There is no reason for you to perish just because Buffalo Jake is leading his species down a suicide path. Is that what you want for your species?"

No one moved.

Real turned to Kim Ha who was translating. "Are you sure that you're interpreting everything I say correctly?"

"Every word," said Kim Ha, which was true.

Real looked back at the animals. "Fine. You want to commit mass suicide, then that's just fine. My chakeedas will get things back under control. So don't be surprised when we're hanging your little fury skins out to dry in few days."

Real's last comment went too far. A low, group growl reverberated throughout cavern.

Big Al said, "That's enough. Shut up and sit down."

When Real failed to obey, one of Big Al's massive bear paws shoved him to the ground. Real looked up at Big Al defiantly and said, "I have special plans for you."

Big Al raised himself up to his full height and leaned over the smart-mouthed leader of the chakeedas. The shadow that Al's body cast over Real could have covered ten chakeedas. Real strained his neck trying to look up to see Big Al's face.

"Why don't you tell me about the special plans that you have for me?" asked Big Al. Black Bear Ron stepped up next to Big Al on one side. A polar bear stepped forward next to Big Al on his other side. For the first time, Real's defiant mood began to change. These animals were not responding as they should. They should be bowing down and grovelling for his forgiveness, Real thought. They should be fearing his power. They should be listening to his every word as though their lives depended on it. This is what Real was used to and what he had come to expect and demand. Yet, these animals somehow did not understand his importance. Real stared up as treacherously sharp claws reached down toward him. The claws cut through the air in front of him. Real sucked in his flabby gut just in time to avoid being slashed. Big Al repeated his demand to know what special plans Real had in store for him. Real was now lying flat on his back with the huge bears hovering over him. Real thought he should say something, but he could feel his throat constricting with fear. He tried to speak.

"No plans," whispered Real. "No plans," he repeated in a quivering voice.

"Good," said Big Al. The bears returned to their positions by the entrance to the cavern.

Buffalo Nick had been observing Real's rantings and ravings with mild amusement. Buffalo Nick had been chosen as the prosecutor. His wildness had faded over time. He had grown up to be the most intelligent buffalo in the central herd. Buffalo Jake entered the cavern and climbed up onto the rock platform.

"Let's get this meeting... um... proceeding underway," said Buffalo Jake. Everyone was staring at Buffalo Jake and Jake was staring back. It was clear that everyone was waiting for something to happen.

Buffalo Nick approached the platform and whispered to Jake, "I think that you're suppose to announce the charges against Real first."

"I thought you were suppose to do that," said Buffalo Jake.

"I don't think so. But if you want me to announce them, I guess it doesn't really matter if I do it," said Nick.

"No. No. I can do it," said Jake.

"Is everyone ready?" asked Jake.

"Hold on. Are you the judge?" asked Real.

Buffalo Jake looked to Nick for the answer. Nick nodded.

"Yes," said Buffalo Jake.

"You can't be the judge. You've been trying to kill me! The judge is suppose to be impartial," protested Real.

"Who here do you feel would be impartial?" asked Buffalo Jake.

Real looked around the cavern. When his eyes came to the bears, Big Al said, "I'll volunteer." The animals snorted and chortled.

"It is obvious that there is no animal here with sufficient experience, education, and training, let alone who is impartial, that would be able to give me a fair trial. Any trial here would be inherently unfair. I move for dismissal of all charges or at least a postponement until one of you evolves sufficiently to acquire the capability to give me a fair trial."

Buffalo Jake was not sure that he understood everything that Real was ranting about because the trial procedures seemed a bit strange to him. But he understood enough to know when he had just been insulted. Nick stepped forward again and whispered, "I think that you're suppose to say that his movement is denied."

"Your movement is denied," announced Buffalo Jake.

"It's not a 'movement', you empty headed cud muncher. It's called a 'motion'," snapped Real.

Big Al did not take kindly to Real's insulting language. The grizzly bear stepped forward again, prepared to put a quick end to the trial before it even began. But Buffalo Jake gave Al a look that said thank you for the concern, but crushing Real's head would not be necessary. The big bear settled back down.

"Whatever you want to call it, I'm not moved by it," said Buffalo Jake. "We are going to announce the charges now."

Real looked about the cavern and toward the entrance. It was as though he was expecting something to happen at any moment and was anxious that it had not already happened.

Buffalo Jake, summoning his deepest voice, began, "You are hereby charged with Crimes Against Animality. Second, you are..."

"Hold on," interrupted Real, "There is no such thing as Crimes Against Animality. It's an absurd notion. This whole thing is a joke. I demand to be immediately released."

This time Big Al was not going to tolerate Real's insolence. Al slammed Real to the ground and told him to shut up and wait for Buffalo Jake to finish.

"Second, you are charged with Tolerance of Crimes Against Animality," said Jake. Jake consulted with Nick again and then asked, "How do you plead?"

"I'm not going to plead. I do not even recognize the authority of this court. You're making charges that have no basis. There is no such crime as Tolerance of Crimes Against Animality or even Crimes Against Animality," said Real.

"So you're not going to plead?" asked Buffalo Jake.

"There's nothing to plead to," said Real.

Jake and Nick consulted again.

"Since you have failed to plead, this Court will enter a plea on your behalf," announced Buffalo Jake. "The Court enters a plea of guilty on all counts. Sentencing will commence...".

"Wait! Wait! You can't do that!" screamed Real. "You're suppose to enter a plea of not guilty! Not guilty! I plead not guilty!"

Kim Ha began to cough, she was still not feeling well. She paused to catch her breath. Real looked at her with pleading eyes waiting for her to translate his words. It was the first time in Real's life that he wished he had learned the Universal Language.

"O.K., the Court accepts your plea," said Buffalo Jake.

"But for the record, I want to make it perfectly clear that I consider this whole proceeding to be a complete sham and it is completely unfair," said Real.

"How can this be a sham? How can it be unfair?" retorted Buffalo Jake. "This style of trial was your idea! We're using your rules. Your procedures. Your methods. This is chakeeda justice."

"Maybe that's the exact reason that it is unfair," interjected Buffalo Nick.

"You can try to imitate our procedures and rules, but you still won't arrive at the correct result. We have special Guardians of Justice that make sure that the system produces the correct results. Without the Guardians, there is no telling what would happen," said Real.

"So who decides what the correct result is?" asked Buffalo Jake.

"The Guardians," said Real.

"But what if the rules say that there should be a different result?" asked Buffalo Nick.

"It does not happen. There is enough flexibility in the system that the Guardians can prevent that from happening. They carefully guide the progress of each case to insure that the correct result is obtained. It is all very logical," said Real.

"Who are these Guardians?" asked Buffalo Jake.

"They are very special individuals who are in constant contact with chakeeda leaders such as myself. They also have special training and skills that give them special insight into the meaning of justice. As a result, they are very sensitive to what is in the best interests of our species as a whole," said Real.

"So these Guardians, they're partly responsible for what the chakeedas species has become, is that correct?" asked Jake.

"Most certainly," said Real. "So now that you see what the qualifications are, it should be obvious to you that there is no animal here that is even remotely capable of understanding the real meaning of justice."

"I do see," said Buffalo Jake. "You're right. There is no way that we could give you a fair chakeeda trial, so we're not. We're going to give you an animal trial."

"I am not an animal!" screamed Real.

"I am not sure that we would disagree with you. That seems to be the exact problem," said Buffalo Nick. The animals murmured in agreement.

"There is going to be a trial," said Buffalo Jake.

"Well, at least you have to tell me the rules for this so-called animal trial," said Real.

"What are the rules?" repeated Buffalo Jake. He did not have an immediate answer. But he could feel the answer somewhere within him. He did not need a guardian to tell him what justice was. He had an internal sense of what it was. It was this sense that had always been his guide. But he had never before tried to formulate that guiding feeling into a set of rules. He retreated into the swirling thoughts and images in his head to try to find the right words."

Choosing his words carefully, Buffalo Jake began to speak in a slow, deliberate voice, "The rules are those of natural balance... ebb and flow... life rising and falling... stopping and starting... around a solid core... a constant point... but in motion... struggling and competing... trusting instincts and feelings... respecting life... and respecting death... a balance among species... we did not evolve here alone... or in isolation... we are dependent on each other... in what ways... in what manner... The Map can help us... but it is not important... we know the truth... we are all connected in a web of life... destroy the web and you destroy us all... this is the one ultimate truth and it cannot be violated... It is according to these guiding principles that you will be tried for Crimes Against Animality."

Real began to object again. Buffalo Jake slammed his front hooves down and shouted, "No! There will be no further delays. Let the trial begin."

Real frantically looked toward the entrance to the cavern, but there was no one there except for the bears standing guard.

"Buffalo Nick, call your first witness," said Buffalo Jake.

The trial went on for several days. The stories all followed the same ruthless theme. There were ugly tales of the massive slaughter of entire herds of animals. The skin ripped from their bodies. Their stripped corpses left to rot in the sun. Others told of chakeedas setting fire to entire jungles and rain forests from the mountains all the way to the ocean. The shallow jungle soil soon washing away, clogging the rivers with silt and killing the fish. The remaining clay too hard for anything to grow on. No animal could explain why the chakeedas would want to do this. It was as if all of the chakeedas had become rabid.

Wherever the chakeedas settled, the forests were the first to go. When Real was permitted to question the witnesses, some admitted that there were parts of some forests left and that some forests had begun to grow back. Real gloated over these admissions. But when Buffalo Nick continued his questioning, the witnesses all said that the remaining forests were not large enough to support many species whose numbers dwindled until there were not enough left for them to survive at all. When the forests began to grow back in some places, it was too late. Many animals were gone forever.

If all of the animals that wanted to testify had been permitted to do so, the trial would have lasted many seasons. But after so many days, it was apparent to Buffalo Jake that the task of interpreting was draining Kim Ha of what little energy she had left. The gruesome testimony was painful enough to hear once. Kim Ha had to repeat it word for word. Her eyes drooped down with sadness. Her coughing was coming deeper from her chest. Pei Woo had come to help her sister do the interpreting, but Pei Woo's health was not much better. Buffalo Jake announced that the jury had heard sufficient testimony and asked for the parties to make their closing arguments.

Buffalo Nick was highly respected among the herd for his intelligence. This was his strength. It was because of his quick, analytical mind that he had been selected as the prosecutor. He was the best that the animals had to offer. He was the only animal with enough raw intelligence to go against Real's brilliantly warped mind. Buffalo Nick had done his job well over the past twenty days. But so had Real.

Real had been able to twist the testimony of even the most damaging witness. No one actually believed that the chakeedas were good, but Real had somehow deprived the animals of their sense of outrage. Real had questioned each witness about every aspect of every gruesome detail of their testimony. He had gone on and on for so long with each witness that it no longer seemed shocking; it almost seemed ordinary. What had seemed so blatantly outrageous and deserving of death at the start of the trial, now seemed only bad. Now was the time for the closing argument to the jury. If Buffalo Nick had a weakness, communicating with other species was it.

The jury was composed of thirteen animals: a squirrel, a mountain zebra, a rhinoceros, a timber wolf, a gorilla, a gazelle, a tiger, an iguana, a condor, a yak, a sea turtle, a monk seal, and a whale. Communicating with the animals on the jury was not Nick's strength. Communicating with the multitude of animals had always been left to Buffalo Jake. Nick was certainly capable of the most intense feelings, but he had difficulty expressing his passion for life with groups of other animals. Or maybe he never felt it was necessary. But whatever the reason, he was not particularly suited for this final task.

On the last day of testimony, Buffalo Jake adjourned the trial early to allow Buffalo Nick extra time to prepare for his closing argument. Buffalo Jake wanted desperately to help Buffalo Nick. It was very difficult staying away. He had not spoken to Buffalo Nick outside of the trial since it began. He wished there was some way to know what he was thinking after twenty days. This was such a critical moment in the history of all living things that Jake was very tempted to go see Buffalo Nick. But Jake knew it would be viewed as improper, even under natural rules, if he were to communicate with the prosecutor outside of the trial.

The next day, the cavern was packed with animals that had come to see the closing arguments. Buffalo Jake had decided to allow the empty spaces of the extinct species to be occupied to allow more animals to attend the closing arguments. The jury was escorted in by the bears. It was time to see what Buffalo Nick was really made of. Buffalo Jake looked down at Buffalo Nick from the stone ledge, searching for some indication in Buffalo Nick's face that he understood the critical importance of his task. Some sign that Nick understood he had to arouse the most basic survival instincts in the hearts of the jury. He had to bring the horror of the chakeeda atrocities to life. He had to be passionate, even fanatical, about the rights of all living things to live in peace. But if Buffalo Nick understood his mission, it was not showing in his face. He seemed absorbed in thought. Jake discerned little else from his expression.

Buffalo Jake stated, "Good morning, animals. If the prosecutor is ready, you may begin your closing argument."

And so Buffalo Nick began. His closing argument went on throughout the morning and into the early afternoon. It was logical. It was precise. It was accurate. It was articulate. But it was not inspired. When he was done, no one doubted that Nick had done his very best. Yet, he had failed to grasp the real spirit of his mission. Buffalo Jake tried to hide his sadness and disappointment, but he was pained by the terrible feeling that this critical moment in animal history was slipping away and there was nothing he could do to save it.

Buffalo Jake stared at Chakeeda Real and the chakeeda just smiled back, proudly showing his ugly stained and crooked teeth.

"The chakeeda defense may present its closing argument," said Buffalo Jake, reluctantly.

Real stayed with his basic strategy of pouring over the details of the atrocities until they seemed commonplace. Real argued that the chakeedas were not doing anything any more offensive than any other animal, which was to survive. Other animals might be jealous of their success, but that was no reason to wipe out the chakeedas. He patiently explained to the jury in great detail the process of attacking and killing an animal. He made it sound gruesome. But then he asked the jury what the difference was between a chakeeda doing the killing for its own survival and some other predator killing its prey? The fact that chakeedas might require more resources than other animals did not change the analysis. All animals have special needs, explained Real. Chakeedas were no different and should not be punished for it. And where does this process end? Who gave Buffalo Jake, or any animal, the power to decide the course of evolution, asked Real. Will your species be next, asked Real. It should be left to survival of the fittest; not the Council of All Living Things. The Council is unnatural, Real argued. It should be disbanded. Your vote against these charges will signal an end to the Council's attempts to control our lives.

It was late afternoon before Real was done. By the end of his closing argument, he had managed not only to argue to save his own life, but had actually placed Buffalo Jake on trial for abusing his authority. Buffalo Jake did not know what to do or say. He needed time to collect his thoughts and regroup. But there was no time left. It would soon be in the hands of the jury. He looked down at Buffalo Nick and asked, "Does the prosecution have any rebuttal?"

Buffalo Nick was finally beginning to understand that he had failed. He looked at Buffalo Jake and saw the pain and disappointment in his broad buffalo face. He looked at Real, who was grinning broadly now at what appeared to be his impending victory. Nick looked into Real's blood shot eyes. He searched hard for some sign of animality, but he saw nothing. Real's eyes seemed vacant as though the animal behind the eyes had left Real's body a long time ago. He was drawn into the emptiness of Real's stare. He wanted to find some sign of animality. The harder he searched, the more he felt his thoughts becoming muddled.

Buffalo Jake repeated his question, "Does the prosecution have any rebuttal?"

Buffalo Nick could hear Jake's voice. He tried to respond, but his mouth would not move. The only body movement Nick could make was to close his eyes. A howl of a solitary wolf filled and reverberated throughout the cavern. The howl grew louder and louder. It went on and on for sometime as though searching and hoping for a reply. Nick wished it would stop. And it did. The wolf's echo faded in the large cavern. It continued in his head for a few moments longer, then there was silence. The air was quiet. Too still. He preferred the howl of the wolf to the silence, but the howl did not return.

He opened his eyes to see how the other animals in the cavern were reacting. He looked where the jury was suppose to be. They were gone. He looked where the animals who had come to see the trial had been. They were gone. Even Buffalo Jake was gone. The only creature left was Real, who was still standing in front of him. Nick looked about at the emptiness of the cavern. The late afternoon wind whistled lightly and stirred a bit of fur in a circular pattern on the floor.

"Can anyone hear me?" Nick cried out in the Universal Language. His voice echoed through the cavern. But there was no reply. He tried again in his native buffalo dialect. Only silence. He smelled the air. There were no scents other than that of Real and his own.

Real said, "Get out of here. Go enjoy your life. What's left of it. There's no more you can do here." Real spoke these words in the buffalo language. He had no right. Nick's breathing grew heavy and labored. He wanted to gore Real with his horns and trample his fat little body.

Real continued, "Calm down, my friend, we'll make a place for you if you're a good buffalo. For a little while at least, until we need the land."

Nick stared back at Real's vacant eyes and realized that the chakeedas could consume the entire world and it would never be enough. Nick closed his eyes and when he reopened them, the cavern was once again filled with the animals. He looked at Real again and was determined to wipe his hideous smile from his face forever.

Nick charged toward the jury! It startled them all. His voice blasted them as if they were being interrogated, "So you think we're being too hard on the chakeedas? You think maybe they're just trying to survive like the rest of us? Are you forgetting what happened to the elephants and rhinos? The chakeedas slaughtered entire herds! Herd after herd! Every herd they could find! And for what!? For food? NO! To protect themselves? NO! Why did they do it? I'll tell you why they did it. They did it for sex!! They did it because chakeedas get off by eating pulverized elephant and rhino horns! We're all going to die just so the chakeedas can get hard ons! That isn't survival of the fittest. That's survival of the sickest!"

Buffalo Nick turned his head in the direction of Elephant Jabari and Chaga, the Rhino.

"And what about them? What will you say to Chaga and Jabari if you allow Real to walk free?"

The jury looked at them both. They were not the same animals they had once known. Jabari looked tired and beaten. His days as the undisputed leader of the elephants of the savanna were gone. It used to be that one could feel a sense of strength and confidence just by being in his presence. But now when you tried to look Jabari in the eyes, he would look away and down at the ground as though he were ashamed. He felt responsible for what had happened to the elephant herds. He would never stop blaming himself. Chaga was the same way. Buffalo Nick let the jury absorb the image of these two broken spirits. There was nothing more Nick could add. He moved on.

Buffalo Nick kicked the trap across the floor of the cavern. It crashed and clanked. None of the animals were use to the hard, cold sound it made. Nick kicked it two more times until it came to rest in front of the jury. The trap still had the broken leg of an animal in it. The flesh was torn, the bone protruding. It was difficult to tell what kind of animal the leg had belonged to. It did not matter.

"This thing is the product of the chakeeda mind. It causes slow, painful, agonizing death. Animals eat off their own legs to try to escape the pain. It does not kill just the weak or the sick. It kills the youngest. The strongest. It kills mothers and leaves their children to die of starvation. The chakeedas have made so many of these things that they have wiped out entire species with them. Think about it. Death by torture on a mass scale."

Nick approached the trap to kick it again, but this time he must of stepped on it the wrong way because the jaws opened releasing the broken leg and violently snapped shut again. Nick jerked his own leg away as fast as he could, but not before the teeth grabbed for his front leg! Buffalo Nick let out a cry! The animals in the cavern shouted in horror! Blood trickled down the front of Nick's leg where he was jabbed, but he had escaped the trap. The animals breathed a collective sigh of relief. The jury stared at the trap as it rocked back and forth on the hard ground. The scent of Nick's fresh blood filled the air. The harsh sound of the trap rocking back and forth faded very slowly. The cavern grew quiet.

When Buffalo Nick continued, he brought to life the destruction of the Great Valley and of entire forests. He described entire jungles stripped and set on fire, the animals either consumed by flames or left to starve to death. He asked the jury to try to remember when the skies were once filled with migrating birds every spring and every fall. They were gone because the wetlands were almost all gone.

The animals were completely absorbed by the images Buffalo Nick was creating with his words. He had their attention for the exact reason that no one ever expected such passion and anger from Buffalo Nick. Just when you would think Buffalo Nick would collapse from exhaustion, he would take a deep breath and his voice would erupt from within his chest and rumble deeply through the Meeting Place. Nick's thick buffalo saliva flew across the cavern with each jerk of his head. It was as if he were possessed by the spirit of all of the animals that had been exterminated by the chakeedas. He found the perfect words and assembled them in the perfect order to explain the real and horrible danger of the chakeedas. How the chakeedas had come to be so destructive, no one knew. But when Buffalo Nick was finally finished at sunset, there was no question of how the jury would vote. The fate of the chakeedas was finally sealed.

CHAPTER TWENTY-FOUR

Real's Escape

Real had been watching the bears very closely each night as they stood guard over him. He observed that the long trial had exhausted all of the animals, including the bears. The bears became more sleepy when Real remained motionless for a long time. His rescuers had never arrived as he had expected. If he was going to escape on his own, tonight would have to be the night because he was pretty sure the jury would not deliberate for very long. After lying very still for most of the night, Real decided to make his move. He got up very quietly and began to slowly slip by the grizzlies. Just as he suspected, the bears had fallen asleep. Real moved past them and into the darkness. Stupid animals, Real thought. It was too easy.

* * * * *

Erik's whale pod was on patrol between the mainland and Chakeeda Island, looking for any sign of any chakeedas that might have gone undertected during the battle and might now be trying to rescue Real. Manuel had still not told Erik about the problem with the circle units being different for his species. He had gotten very good at making the conversion quickly in his mind. But he knew he should still tell Erik about it. In an emergency, there was always the chance that he might not do the conversion properly. He did not like to think about the possible consequences if he should accidentally steer into the pod at high speed.

* * * * *

Real had reached the beach without being detected. He was rapidly searching for any piece of wood large enough for him to float on. He found a log resting against some rocks and was able to roll it down the beach to the water. He needed a long branch of some sort with which to use to push off. When he found a suitable branch, he returned to the log, but found that it had already floated out to sea. He cursed his luck. But was pleased when he soon found another log. It was not as large, but it would do. With the branch, Real pushed off the sand to float himself and the log beyond the surf. Once out in the calmer waters, Real started paddling south along the coast. It was difficult because he was paddling against the current. But the prospect of taking the current north with winter coming soon did not appeal to him. He was sure if he went far enough south he could find a nice place to come ashore where he could start over again.

* * * * *

Erik's pod was having fun as they patrolled the coastal waters. Several of them were practicing their breaching in unison. They leaped into air two and three at a time, rolled over, and splashed back into the ocean on their backs. It felt great. They did not like barnacles growing on their backs and it felt especially good when the impact knocked some of them off. After breaching for sometime, Erik realized that the pod had travelled too far south from the area that they were suppose to be patrolling. They were no longer between Chakeeda Island and the mainland. In fact, they could not see the island. Erik gave the order for the pod to fall into high speed formation. They were soon in their own high speed tunnel of water, racing back to their designated patrol area.

* * * * *

Real felt he was making good progress. The coast was lit up nicely by the moonlight. He could still see familiar landmarks so he knew he had not travelled too far yet. He smiled to himself at the thought of what Jake's reaction would be like when Jake found out that he had escaped. Such stupid creatures, he thought.

* * * * *

The high speed pod of whales was closing in on the designated area. Erik wanted to move more toward the island so he gave the order for the pod to turn fifteen clicks to the left. Whether Manuel heard the clicks wrong or miscalculated the conversion may never be known. But

240

Manuel's body crashed out of the water tunnel and started flipping head over tail! As he felt his body whipping through the water completely out of control, all he could do was hope that he had not hurt anyone else in the pod. When his body finally stopped, he looked around to see if the other members of the pod were all right. No one else was around. He listened closely. It was difficult to hear because he was quite dizzy and his back was hurting from spinning around so much. But even so, he could make out in the distance the sound of a whale pod racing through the water in a high speed formation. When he made the wrong turn he had apparently veered away from the pod rather than into it, which was a great relief. The sound of the pod was fading. It was still heading north. Manuel felt out of breath and started to the top for some air before trying to catch up with the pod.

* * * * *

Real could feel the water swelling under him. He was not sure what it was, but thought it was best to keep paddling. He stuck the branch into the water, but this time he hit something solid that stopped him from completing the down stroke. Before he could look down, he felt the log rising up out of the water higher and higher. Water blew out of the whale's blow hole, then the whale dived under again and disappeared.

* * * * *

Manuel could feel he had hit something. But it did not feel significant and he was not curious to find out what it was. He was more interested in rejoining his pod. So after catching one breath, he was on his way again. It had been a close call. This time, Manuel would tell Erik about the conversion problem.

* * * * *

Real was pulled under the water by the whirling currents left by the whale. When he reached the surface again, he thrashed about for his log. He could not see it, but he knew it had to be around somewhere. It couldn't have just disappeared. He tried paddling in one place to see if it would appear when the waters calmed down again. It was difficult because he was beginning to drift with the current. As he drifted and the water calmed, he saw his log again. He began swimming toward it when he felt something grab one of his feet. He tried to twist free, but the more he twisted, the better the thing seemed to hold on to his foot. He looked at the log again. He was so close. He jerked his foot hard, but this time the thing pulled him under. He kicked hard and was able to bring his head above water for a gasp of breath. Whatever this thing was, he would have to deal with it. He held his breath and reached down toward his foot to fight it off, but it only seemed to wrap around him even more tightly. Other creatures of some sort were now bumping up against him. One kept brushing up against his face. It was strange. They did not seem to be trying to hurt him. This was crazy. He was not going to die like this. He knew he needed to act quickly. He decided to open his eyes to see what he was up against.

Real's mouth reflexively opened in shock at the sight of the creatures surrounding him. Real choked on the sea water that rushed in. He quickly closed his mouth and swallowed what he could. The swollen and bloated face of a pelican was staring at him. Its terrified eyes were wide open. The pelican was staring at Real with one eye. The current shifted, twisting the pelican's head to stare at Real with its other eye before gently brushing against Real's face. Real jerked his head away to avoid the contact and pumped into something on the other side of him. It was the body of a young dolphin caught by the tail. A female dolphin had apparently tried to come to the rescue, but the net had wrapped around her head. Even so, she had not tried to retreat. She was still locked in her eternal struggle to bite through the net to allow the younger dolphin to swim free. The moonlight penetrated the water enough for Real to see the eerie figures of all kinds of creatures drifting in the net, and other sea birds that had dived into the water to grab a fish, only to be caught in the net themselves. As Real struggled to free himself, he kept knocking into the dead bodies around him. The flesh of some of the creatures had begun to rot. Real's thrashing caused the skin and muscle to separate from their bones. A cloud of decomposing flesh whirled about in the murky water.

Real figured out what he was up against. He was caught in a chakeeda drift net. The chakeedas were particularly proud of their drift nets. They were a wonderfully efficient method of harvesting the oceans. Most of the animals killed in the nets were not actually eaten by the chakeedas. The chakeedas were only after two or three species of fish. This was not considered a problem because the trouble of clearing the nets of all the other dead bodies was seen as nothing more than a minor nuisance. But one thing was for sure, drift nets were never intended to drown an innocent chakeeda and Real had no intention of letting that happen now.

Real stopped struggling. Unlike the animals around him, Real knew that struggling would only cause him to become more entangled in the net. He would not be so stupid. But first, he needed more air. He carefully directed all of his motion to swimming toward the surface. The weight of the net laden down with so many dead bodies made it extremely difficult. But Real was able to just get his mouth to the surface. A full, fresh gasp of air filled his lungs. He allowed his body to sink back down with the net and proceeded as quickly as he could to untangle himself. There were so many bits and pieces of dead flesh floating in the water that it looked like a snow storm. The clouds of flesh were beginning to block the moonlight from penetrating the water. It made it difficult to see the tangled net around his feet. Even when debris got in his eyes, it did not matter to Real. He would untangle himself just by feel if necessary. But he wasn't going to die like this. He rather be ripped apart by wolves than drown to death in a net of his own design.

Real could feel he was making progress. The net was losing its grip. But he was also running out of air again. He tried to work more quickly. His face felt red hot. He wanted a breath. Stay calm, he thought. Just a few more twists of the net. A sharp tingling sensation began racing back and forth over his skin. He needed air. He couldn't wait any longer. His instincts took over. He jerked his feet as hard as he could to break the net. Nothing happened. The net was definitely much looser, but it still wasn't loose enough to break free. It did not matter. He would drag the net back up to the surface with him. He had done it once, he could do it again. With all his force, he pushed and pounded and thrashed and fought against the water. The net moved reluctantly upward with him. He kept struggling. He knew he had to be close. The night air teased the top of his head before sinking back just below the surface. He was almost there. He tried to break the surface again. But the weight of the net seemed heavier this time. His muscles felt heavy and numb. He did not care. One last effort was all he needed. One last effort and he knew he could suck in all the air he wanted.

* * * * *

The jurors sent a message to Buffalo Jake in the morning to inform him that they had reached a decision. When the word got out that the jury had decided overnight, animals from all over came to witness the announcement of the verdict. When Buffalo Jake reconvened the proceedings, everyone was present but Chakeeda Real. The animals kept glancing at the entrance to the cavern, anxiously waiting for the bears to escort Real into the meeting place. But as more and more time passed without any sign of Real or the bears, rumors started to spread through the cavern that a group of chakeedas attacked and killed the bears last night and Real had escaped. When Buffalo Jake heard this rumor, he decided not to wait to find out if it was true. He brought the cavern to order and asked the jury to announce its verdict. A silver back highland gorilla had been selected by the jury as their leader. The silver back rose proudly with his knuckles firmly pressed against the ground. He was about to announce the verdict when Big Al, the grizzly bear, came loping into the cavern.

"It was my fault," Big Al stammered. "I don't know how it happened. I'm so sorry. I can't believe it. I'm so sorry."

"Just calm down and tell us what happened," said Jake.

Big Al would not calm down. He was weaving back and forth in terrible distress, frantically trying to tell Buffalo Jake something about Real. But no one could understand exactly what he was saying. He was raving and rambling in a combination of the universal and bear languages, which resulted in a new language that no one in the cavern could understand very well. But between tormented cries, Jake was able to piece together that Real had escaped. Jake ordered all animals to be on the alert and to immediately begin a search. As the animals got up to leave, a black bear came into the cavern and said, "A search won't be necessary. We found him."

The black bear led Buffalo Jake and the other animals down to the beach. The body was lying face down. The waves rolled up to the edge of the body and gently tugged at one arm as the water retreated back into the ocean. The animals watched as the waves repeated the process, trying to pull its prey back out to sea. Daniel had been tricked before and he was not about to be tricked again.

"Are you sure it's Real?" asked Daniel of no one in particular. "Lots of chakeedas look like Real from the back. Shouldn't we check before it floats away."

Buffalo Jake asked the silver back from the jury to turn the chakeeda over. Little sand crabs scurried off the body and burrowed into the sand. The crabs had just started eating at the white belly flesh, but the face was still untouched. The frozen expression of sheer horror made it look as if the chakeeda had died of fear alone. But even so, there was no doubt about the identity. It was Real.

The silver back said, "It's probably just as well. I suspect he would have preferred death to our verdict."

"What was the verdict?" asked Jake.

"He was found guilty of Crimes Against Animality and Tolerance of Crimes Against Animality. No surprise. But it was our sentence that he probably could not have accepted. He would have been sentenced to spending the rest of his life undoing as much of the damage caused by the chakeedas as he could. He would also have to learn the Universal Language and, if there are any surviving chakeedas anywhere, he would have to teach it to them and have them teach it to their offspring. They would have to rejoin the web of life and vow never to destroy the web again."

"If he had failed?" asked Jake.

"He would have to answer to Elephant Jabari," explained the silver back.

* * * * *

The end of the hot season had finally come. The days were become shorter and the late afternoon breezes were growing cooler. It was time to begin the migration. It was the first migration that anyone could remember that was not overshadowed by the fear of the chakeedas. The tension that had gripped the animals for so long faded a little more with each passing day. It was the first season in a long time that the animals resumed their seasonal celebration. They could not convince Buffalo Jake to join in the buffalo tag games. He did not feel right playing the game without his long time partner, Kim Ha. Buffalo Nick tried to convince Jake that Kim Ha would have wanted him to play the game. Buffalo Jake graciously declined. His body was tired and he knew he needed to rest if he was going to make it to the winter range. He found a nice place to lay down from where he could see the festivities. The games no longer extended over the entire prairie because there were so many fewer animals that had survived. Even so, the celebrations were a good thing. It was the beginning of the time to heal the wounds of the earth and to begin to rediscover how to enjoy life again.

It was in late afternoon when Buffalo Jake's instincts told him it was time for the herd to begin the migration. He instructed Buffalo Nick and his lieutenants that they would begin their journey in the morning. Buffalo Jake said his goodbyes to the other animals from the World Council. Everyone lingered longer than usual, finding security in each other's presence even though there was no longer any reason to be afraid. Everyone lingered, except for Jake, who wanted to be alone.

Jake wandered off not really conscious of where his hooves were taking him. After a while, he found himself approaching the place of the rabbear massacre. The feeling was not the same anymore. He use to have to suppress the rising surge of rage every time he came back. But the anger had faded. It was replaced with a feeling of sadness. He wished at least one rabbear had survived to see this day. He thought of all his other friends from the World Council of Living Things who were now the missing pieces in the web of life. It made him sad to know they would never share in the victory over the chakeedas.

Right before reaching the spot where the rabbear massacre had occurred, Buffalo Jake closed his eyes and let the early autumn winds blow across his face. He felt alone. He told himself that the animals had won. He should be happy. But he still felt as if something was missing. It was Kim Ha. Jake would normally give her a ride back to the edge of the forest after the celebrations. He did not realize before how much their small ritual had meant to him. Jake could feel her weight on his back.

Jake said aloud, "We'll rest here for a moment, then I'll take you to the forest."

Buffalo Jake heard her reply, "I'm in no rush. Rest as long as you like."

With his eyes still closed, Jake heard the rustle of falcon wings coming in for a landing. He felt Trevor's familiar talons land on his shoulders. It felt good to have his friends back. He knew it was all just his mind playing tricks on him, but the weight of Kim Ha and the falcon on his back seemed so real. He allowed himself to believe the phantom sensation was indeed his two friends. It made him feel good and secure.

He opened his eyes and his friends were gone. He was once again alone. He stood at the site of the rabbear massacre and looked down at the ground expecting to find the same barren patch of earth on which nothing had grown since the death of the last rabbear. He was not disappointed. The once fertile earth was as hard as stone. But then something caught his eye. There was a small crack in the middle of the barren patch. It had not been there before. Growing from the crack was a single poppy. Jake did not believe what he was seeing at first. He had not seen a poppy since spring. Jake sat down in front of it. The soft autumn winds blew its delicate peddles back and forth. His large nostrils sniffed the purple flower. It was indeed a poppy. He watched its seeds blowing in a little whirlwind on the hardened ground about the flower's stem. Occasionally, a seed or two would drift over the crack in the earth and find a home there. This was good.

Buffalo Jake lay his head down to rest and smiled to himself. Before this moment, he had always had a feeling that he was leaving something undone. That feeling was gone. He felt a sense of completeness. He closed his eyes and breathed a heavy sign. He was not sure how long he lay there sleeping. But when he awoke, he felt the familiar weight of Kim Ha climbing on to his back again. She asked him if he was ready and he said yes. This time, it was no illusion. Jake rose to his feet. Trevor circled overhead.

"Where would you like to go?" asked Jake.

"Anywhere you like. I suspect it really doesn't matter anymore," said Kim Ha.

"Why don't we visit Samuel?" asked Jake.

"That sounds like a wonderful idea," said Kim Ha.

The panda and the buffalo headed north on their eternal journey together.

* * * * *

As the herd began moving south, they kept a respectable distance from Buffalo Jake's resting place. His body appeared as a majestic silhouette in the golden autumn sun. Buffalo Nick stopped for a moment to admire the sight.

A young buffalo named Kellan asked, "What will we do without him?"

Nick paused to think of how Jake might have answered that question. "I don't know," said Nick. "Jake did his part. Let's hope it was not too late for the web of life to heal itself."

"What if some chakeedas survived? What if they return?" asked Kellan, the voice of a new generation.

Nick looked across the herd. Where there had once been a sea of buffalo, now the herd barely filled a small corner of the prairie. Nick looked up into the sky. He remembered when it had once been filled with flock after flock of birds on their migration south. Now he could only hear an occasional flock of geese in the distance. Nick could not imagine how things would ever be the same.

"If the chakeedas return, we won't be able to stop them. There won't be another Buffalo Jake," said Nick.

Daniel had walked up to say goodbye to Buffalo Nick and heard what Nick had said. Daniel agreed.

"Then what should we do?" asked the young buffalo.

Daniel answered, "Pei Woo and the few pandas that have survived are writing down the story of the chakeedas. If the chakeedas return, and if they are as smart as they imagine themselves to be, maybe they can learn from their own story."

"Maybe," said Nick, his voice edged with doubt. "But I would feel better if I knew they would never return."

No one could argue with that.

Daniel said his goodbyes and left for his den. Nick reached down and chomped on some prairie grass to add to his cud. The brown blades were wet from the cold chill in the air. The water brought out the flavor better. Nick looked back one last time at Jake's body. He hoped the pandas did a good job of recording what had happened. If the chakeedas ever did return, they would have to find their place in the web of life because this was the last animal crusade.

Printed in the United States
3873

9 780759 660175